Red Nocturne

Red Nocturne

Bill Mullen

Winchester, UK
Washington, USA

First published by Roundfire Books, 2016
Roundfire Books is an imprint of John Hunt Publishing Ltd., Laurel House, Station Approach,
Alresford, Hants, SO24 9JH, UK
office1@jhpbooks.net
www.johnhuntpublishing.com
www.roundfire-books.com

For distributor details and how to order please visit the 'Ordering' section on our website.

Text copyright: Bill Mullen 2015

ISBN: 978 1 78535 279 9
Library of Congress Control Number: 2015915219

A CIP catalogue record for this book is available from the British Library.

Design: Stuart Davies

Printed and bound by CPI Group (UK) Ltd, Croydon, CR0 4YY

We operate a distinctive and ethical publishing philosophy in all
areas of our business, from our global network of authors to
production and worldwide distribution.

For Molly

Acknowledgements

Thanks to friends, fellow writers, and teachers for your feedback and support: Derek Nikitas, Young Smith, Bob Johnson, Julie Hensley, Russell Helms, Lisa Day, and Kevin Moffett. And thanks to those teachers who got me started: Hal Blythe and Charlie Sweet. Thanks also to my friend MJ Thomas, of the FBI, for her time and expertise—any inaccuracies are my doing. A deep and special thanks to my parents for their unending and unconditional love and support.

"We sometimes encounter people, even perfect strangers, who begin to interest us at first sight, somehow suddenly, all at once, before a word has been spoken."
~Fyodor Dostoevsky, *Crime and Punishment*

Part I

Legato

Chapter 1

1 August 2010. 11:44pm. Downtown Boston.

Anna headed the investigation that led to the arrest of two Arabs plotting to set off a car bomb in Times Square. The third one got away. That was a couple days ago, Providence, Rhode Island. She was back in Boston now, the first night off in two weeks, and she wanted one beer and then sex, but Klein had been gone for nearly a month. Klein—her friend with benefits. And that was it. No phone calls or e-mails asking how she was doing. Nobody making a mess in her apartment while she was at work. And nobody nagging her to open up and talk about her feelings and a relationship and work and the prospect of kids and a house. She didn't have room in her life for that. But, she did need sex once in a while, a warm body, not her own hand.

The Green Dragon Tavern was busy, and Anna ordered Sam Adams Boston Ale and watched the waitress, a blonde college girl who didn't look like she belonged to a sorority, take her time getting to the bar. In the seven minutes it took the girl to give the bartender the order, wait on another table, retrieve Anna's beer, and take her time getting back, two men had approached Anna and asked to buy her a drink. One a fraternity guy that she ignored until he went away, and another, a guy in his thirties wearing a suit he'd probably bought at Kohl's, with a circular indention on his ring finger. She pretended not to notice and told him to sit down. Guys like this didn't ask many questions, didn't stick around long, and they weren't the kind of guys she had to worry about shooting her with her own gun because they found being handcuffed to the bedrail kinky. She needed someone tonight. A stranger. Not often, but tonight was one of those nights.

"So how long have you been—"

"Let's just keep it light on the talk this go 'round. Okay?"

Anna said.

He smiled and sipped his gin and tonic.

The waitress put her ale on a coaster, and Anna said, "His tab," nodding her head once.

Anna picked up the frosted glass and put it to her mouth. The first mouthful was always her favorite because it washed the stress of the day down the drain that was her throat. The creamy foam was thick like meringue, a Czech pour, bubbles sizzling as her upper lip found the coppery ale, and she took in that first mildly bitter mouthful, then pushed out her cheeks, letting the thick ale floss her teeth before swallowing slowly. A citrusy after-taste filled her mouth when she exhaled, clean and clear. Before the glass found the coaster, Anna's Blackberry rang.

"Murphy's fucking law," she whispered.

It was her SSA, of course, his name on the caller ID ensuring that she'd be getting anything but sex tonight. Something had just happened or else he wouldn't have ordered her back to the office. God damn it.

"I have to go," she said, slipping a ten-dollar bill on the table next to her nearly full glass of disappointed beer.

Mouth agape for a moment, the man said, "You don't have to—"

"Maybe some other time," she said on her way out, not looking back to see his reaction.

Keeping with the Blue Line Rule she kept her Bucar at the office a few blocks away, so she jogged down the alley, part red brick, part stone brick, and part concrete slab, to Union Street, the dark deciduous trees and towering glass rectangles of the New England Holocaust Memorial separating the narrow alleys of bars and restaurants from the brutalist city-hall building that seemed to cast its grey eyes over the people just across the avenue. And she kept jogging, through City Hall Plaza to Cambridge Street, where the semi-circular Government Center building followed the curve of Cambridge Street, cupping the

Supreme Court building, the attorney general's office, and the State House, its symbolic golden dome barely visible from street level. At the northern section of Government Center, where the FBI field office was located, Anna stopped and, for the first time tonight, felt the autumn-like chill in the night air, the thin veil of sweat on her skin capturing every shift in the breeze.

"Your stuff's in the SUV," said her partner, Jonathan Meeks.

Other FBI agents were waiting for her, each wearing a bullet-proof vest. Without speaking, they got into three black Chevy Suburbans and headed down Cambridge Street. She sat in the back of the second SUV with Meeks.

"We just got a big tip from one of our CHS's," said Meeks, handing Anna her vest. "Mahmoud Aziz surfaced near Watertown. We have positive ID. We need to take him quickly and quietly."

"You sound like you're on a TV show." She slipped on her vest. "Is Rafferty still watching Aziz's house?" asked Anna.

"Yeah, but we don't think he's going there."

Anna had been working the Aziz case for two months now. Aziz's two partners, the ones she'd helped arrest in Providence, had not given up their partner, the bastard Anna thought was the mastermind behind this small group's plot, so his surfacing in Boston so soon afterwards was a blessing in her eyes. Another case closed after tonight.

"I think DeLaurent has his eyes on you for the supervisor job," said Meeks.

Anna rubbed the back of her teeth with her tongue, staring out the window at her city.

"I overheard him on the STE phone this morning talking about your role in the Russian spy case."

"You had a pretty big role in that case, too," she said, her laconic gaze on him now.

"You didn't write the AAR," he said, then looked down toward the dark floorboard.

"God dammit, Jonathan," she whispered through gritted teeth. *You better not have fucked this up.* "What'd you put in the report?"

"There's a copy on your desk."

"If I'm going to get supervisor," she whispered, "I want it based on the truth. And you did just as much as I did on that case."

"It's the biggest spy case since the end of the Cold War."

"Jonathan—"

"Look, your instincts were right. If you weren't part of that team, they might not have been caught."

She turned her head back to the window. Beyond copious mature trees along the bank, she gazed at lights from MIT campus reflecting off the black Charles River, and it gave her mind ease. She wasn't going to argue with him. She had to focus on Aziz and make sure that he would not escape again.

They sat in silence until the Suburbans stopped one block down from Waverly Street. They got out; the drivers stayed, vehicles running.

SSA Perkins, whose approaching retirement had opened up the supervisor position, said, "Aziz is inside 6695, that blue and white house on the right, just before the Stop sign. Surveillance shows two entry/exit points, front and back. Ariah's team will cover the back. Stern, Meeks, your group the front."

Ariah's team got back in the SUV and drove toward their drop off point. Perkins got in the other SUV.

And so they went. Four FBI agents, guns drawn, approached the blue and white house. What they didn't anticipate was Aziz exiting the house the moment they reached the edge of the front yard. The son of a bitch saw them immediately and dashed back inside and slammed the door behind him.

It was for this reason that Anna felt Meeks should get the promotion to supervisor. Not only was he tall and muscular, but when missions strayed from the plan, he took charge. His deep voice demanded attention and compliance, which it always got. His face, covered in a short and rugged carpet under a bald head, was like iron, a boxer's chin and deep-set eyes. His Glock 23 looked like a child's toy in his hands. Too bad agents weren't authorized to carry a .44 Magnum, it'd certainly be more fitting.

When Anna was in charge, as was the case in Providence, something bad always seemed to happen, which put them in this position tonight. If she had covered all the bases, Aziz would not have gotten away, she would be a beer closer to sex, and the case would be closed. The others, especially Meeks, didn't seem to notice.

One gunshot from inside the house!

"Active shooter," called Anna through the walkie-talkie.

Now two...three!

The four agents scattered, taking cover behind large elm trees nearest them.

Rear team was in front of them a few seconds later, the SUVs bumper to bumper at the edge of the front yard to give them cover; the drivers got out, one with a shotgun and the other an MP5.

"It's all inside," yelled Anna. She and the others took cover behind the SUVs. "We need to make sure there's not an alternative way out of that place. That's how the son of a bitch escaped in Providence." He'd escaped through a tunnel that they had no way of knowing about. She wished arresting Aziz would be as easy as arresting the Russians had been. They hadn't put up a fight. They'd hardly changed facial expressions when she told the 'married' couple to face the wall and that they were under arrest. They hadn't spoken. They hadn't had any weapons. They'd only sent shock through the minds of their neighbors that had "known them for years" and "thought they were great friends."

"Ariah's team is covering the door," said Meeks to Anna. "Blinds are all down in back."

Anna heard Perkins in her earpiece, "Rear team, hold your

position."

Glass breaking. The sound of shards dribbling down the porch roof was like a car driving over gravel.

Gunshots.

The lead Suburban's windshield took the brunt of the damage, its dashboard the rest.

Anna knelt down quickly as Meeks yelled, "Which window is it coming from?"

"Top left," said Anna.

Meeks told the others to stay down as the gunman fired an automatic weapon from the house again. Sledgehammer bullets attacked the SUV like a snare drum.

Anna's earpiece: Perkins was calling in SWAT.

"Fuck, Anna," said Meeks, "you're bleeding. Get against the door."

Anna looked down at her vest, checked her legs. "What?"

Meeks had taken the first-aid kit from his vest, ripped open a gauze packet, and, keeping his eyes forward toward the blue and white house, gun in one hand, covered the seeping wound on Anna's neck.

"Oh, fuck!" Anna flung her free hand up toward her neck, where Meeks was applying pressure with the gauze. She hadn't felt anything until now—a dull ache pulsed in her neck and her heart felt like it was being chiseled out of her chest. She pulled her hand away and let him help her.

"How bad is it?"

"Probably just a graze," said Meeks.

More gunshots.

She nodded. "I'm fine, Johnnie. Thanks. I got it."

Meeks let go of her neck. The cotton stayed in place, soaking up more of his partner's blood. He grabbed two more packs of gauze, tore them open with his teeth, and pushed the cotton squares over the blood-soaked gauze.

She could hear the Glocks and the MP5 returning fire, then

the SUV was hit by four more rounds.

Anna stared up at Meeks, his lips drawn, teeth clenched. She hadn't seen this expression on his face before. She knew that he—

Anna's gaze shifted to the silhouette of a man appearing in the upstairs window of the neighboring house behind Meeks. She saw the gunman take quick aim, yelled, "Get down," as she reached to jerk Meeks to the side, her other hand raising to fire her gun. As she yanked the side of his vest, .357 Magnum shells exploded, three of them. She had gotten off one shot before being blinded by sudden flecks of Meeks' blood stabbing her eyes, and then two thuds to her chest knocked the wind out of her. Her head jerked back and hit the metal door, then she fell forward, her head cradled in a convulsing pillow that was Meeks' hand, most of his body falling on top of her as they fell to the ground. Eyes clasped shut, she tried to gasp for air, but nothing happened. Her body acted as if it was submerged in water and knew better than to inhale. She kept bending her left leg and then straightening it spasmodically, but the pain was still dull. Her left-hand fingers were digging into the thin grass, damp soil packing underneath her unpolished nails as she tried getting out from under Meeks, her Glock still firmly in her right hand.

She felt Meeks' body start to convulse as she continued trying to take in air and yell the word *shooter*, but nothing happened. She and Meeks were going to die because of her inability to react more quickly, she thought; letting Aziz escape in Providence and now not being able to get her breath.

More gunfire from Aziz. Metal deforming and embedding.

On her eighth try, her body finally accepted a lungful of air, and she was able to roll Meeks onto his back. She gasped noisily, yelled, "Second shooter!", and cleared her eyes with her left sleeve while taking aim at the now empty window.

In her periphery, she saw Meeks' convulsions. Trying to move, pain knifed its way from her neck to her ear, and she fell back against the SUV door, mouth gaping, eyes taking in bleary constellations, but she kept her gun raised and ready, even if she couldn't see.

"Sec…" she tried to say again, but coughing filled her throat. She could hear the faint sound of sirens interrupted with more gunfire.

Another thud, this time her left shoulder. She yelped in pain. Another bullet hit her left arm. She knew that she was going to die tonight, on this fucking lawn by this fucking asshole helping a terrorist that she shouldn't have let get away in Providence.

Before her right hand could cover any wound, she felt her body being pulled closer toward the other Suburban, arm burning just above her elbow where the bullet had struck, the sensation like boiling oil on her skin. She willed herself to stay conscious as her warm blood soaked her shirt underneath her vest. To close her eyes would be to give up on Meeks, to give up on capturing or killing Aziz, and, most of all, to give up on life. Closing her eyes would be the last physical movement her living body would make that night. And she couldn't fail at that, too.

Sirens closer.

Gunfire. More gunfire.

The pain in Anna's shoulder and arm grew numb as her eyelids became heavy. She wanted to close her eyes so badly, but knew that she had to stay conscious. That god damn terrorist was not going to win. The Russians had been easy. Aziz's partners had even gone quite easily. But not Aziz. Like a cornered animal, he had something—

"We got 'em," yelled the agent that had pulled her to the SUV.

She tried to focus on the agent's face, but it was blurry. His voice sounded familiar, but she didn't know if he had said 'got them' or 'got him'. All she was certain of was the pungent stink of gunpowder burning in her nostrils, the constant draft of cold, dry air hitting the right side of her face from underneath the Suburban, and her failure tonight.

Wigwags flashed now like an obscene disco ball.

She stared up at her blurry world with a numb body. Her lips were dry.

"You're going to be okay."

"Meeks," she mumbled repeatedly, sounding more like she was repeating "ks" as more figures approached.

"You're going to be okay."

She couldn't move. Could hardly swallow. Is this what it felt like to be paralyzed?

Two figures in white shirts knelt down beside her. She thought they were asking her questions, but their voices sounded more like someone plucking cello strings. And she, "ks, ks, ks…"

As they strapped her to the backboard, she fought to keep her eyes open. As they lifted her up and placed her on the stretcher, she thought about what Meeks had done to the report he'd turned in covering the Russian spy arrests a few months ago. How she knew he loved her. She felt the stretcher rise, the sound of clanking and clasping metal locking into place. The thud of the stretcher as her bleeding, limp body was slid into the ambulance. She wanted to cry. Anna closed her eyes.

Chapter 2

The news about Matthew Rebeck's death hadn't caused a stir in the Boston suburb of Dedham except inside 221 Tremaine, where Kate Rebeck found a blue sedan parked in front of her house and two army officers standing on her doorstep. She'd invited them inside, and one told her that her husband had been killed by an IED. The chaplain was kind enough to define it as a roadside bomb. She had been asked to fly to Dover Air Force Base in Delaware to receive the body. They'd spoken slowly and handed Kate a tissue when it was obvious that she was content to let her mascara and tears fall in black drops to her black skirt.

What Kate hadn't known those two months ago was that her teenage daughter, Lilly, had been standing by the doorway in the other room, listening in on the conversation. When Lilly heard the part about her father being killed in Afghanistan, she retreated to her bedroom. The day had been bright and sunny and cool. There were still no clouds in the sky today, Lilly noticed, gazing out her second-floor window. And her mother hadn't tried talking to her about her father yet—two months, and hardly a word about anything.

Lilly felt obligated to cry today, but her body wouldn't respond. She peered around the room, looking for something sentimental that might jerk a tear from her dry eyes—bare dresser, made bed, a music stand, her violin case, her backpack, her desk, a few Van Gogh and Monet posters on the wall— nothing brought her to mimic her mother's weeping. She loved her father, but it just…just didn't seem real. When he left, he told her that he'd see her next year, and she had prepared herself to be without a father for a full year, and that time was seven months away…nine months when those soldiers had visited to tell her mother that she was a widow. These feelings—or lack of feelings—scared her. Lilly was old enough to know that a child should cry if a parent died. To not cry probably meant that something was wrong with her, like all those sociopaths on her mom's favorite show—*Criminal Minds*. It probably meant that she should see a therapist and start taking one of those pills that filled up the commercial time between scenes of those TV sociopaths killing someone or the theories of how a victimized woman or abused child would cope with their post-traumatic stress. At least that's what her music teacher, Mr. Thompson, would say, she thought. To fill up that commercial time with anything less depressing would be downright criminal. But he was a conspiracy theorist when not at his day job.

Lilly had heard movement downstairs—boots on hardwood. Through her window, she'd watched the men dressed in camouflage walk to the blue sedan, get in, and drive away. Neither stopped to look back at the house or up at her window. Neither noticed her at all. And she didn't care. As the sedan disappeared at the intersection, Lilly remained dry-eyed and confused.

The faint sound of her mother's footsteps coming up the stairs stole Lilly's attention from her memory of that day. Lilly turned around and looked at her bedroom door. Her mother knocked twice, then opened the door. She didn't look as ragged as usual. She mustn't have been crying as much today. Lips were pressed together like she was holding her breath. Mascara had seeped in the crescent grooves around her mouth, making the wrinkles look deeper and more pronounced as if they'd been drawn on with charcoal. It made her look much older than her thirty-five years. Kate stared into Lilly's brown eyes from across the room and put her hands up to her mouth.

Lilly knew her mother's intentions and knew that she wouldn't be able to say it, so she broke the tense silence. "I miss Da..." And there it was—the lump. It came without warning, so fast, and choked her. She clenched her teeth and squeezed her eyelids together. An immense tingling sensation fluttered inside her chest, around her heart, and her stomach tightened as if she were going to vomit. Legs wobbly, she dropped to her knees and felt the first slivers of tears wet her lashes. Her mother's arms were around her now. They were warm, and Lilly defined that warmth as love, a feeling she hadn't gotten from her mother in several months. But her mother was not someone who would be described as affectionate.

It wasn't real until she said it, and she hoped she'd never have to say it again. Her father was dead. It was real now. Eavesdropping hadn't made it real. The funeral was just a lonely blur, standing and watching people cry while staring at a closed wooden coffin with yellow roses covering the lower half. Men in uniforms. Her mother sitting in a chair between the coffin and a metal stand holding a picture of Dad smiling while holding up a catfish he'd just caught at Paragon.

"We're going to be okay," Lilly's mother said, rubbing her daughter's back. She stood and pulled Lilly up with her. "We're going to be alright." She straightened her silky blouse, checked her blonde hair which was in a ponytail, and wiped the narrow pools under her eyes toward her ears. "We're going to get through this."

Lilly, eager to stop her mother from continuing to repeat herself, sniffled, then said, "I know, Mom."

Lilly hadn't cried in four years, and, even under these circumstances, it embarrassed her beyond flushed cheeks—it was more like feathers meandering underneath her skin and filling in her stomach. She wanted her mother to leave, but didn't want to be mean or rude, so she just said, "I think I need to alone," a line from a movie she'd overheard her mother watching a few nights ago.

Her mother took a deep breath and nodded. "Let me know if you," she said, pausing, "need anything, honey. I'll be downstairs in my bedroom." And she left, staggering, and closed the door behind her.

Her mother's leaving didn't make the discomfort go away, but she was able to control her tears. She wiped her face with her shirt and gazed out the window, hearing her mother's shoes on the steps again.

The streetlamps were on now, and what had been a blue sky was now violet. The moon was bulbous and grotesque, an orange blob hanging in the dimming sky behind bare elm-tree branches. And the sight of it demanded her attention; it cleared her thoughts as her pupils dilated and made the image blurry. She stared at it for what felt like minutes, her mind blank, her body calming, until movement on the sidewalk broke her gaze.

It was a woman walking to the side of her house, the tenant who lived in the third-floor apartment. Her parents had bought the house three years ago at her mom's insistence. She wanted the nice Victorian home in the nice part of Boston. And Dedham was nice, but it was very expensive. They converted the triplex into a duplex, keeping the third floor open to rent. Kate went back to work, taking a second shift supervisory position at Walton-Hughes Marketing near downtown. When that wasn't enough money to do all the renovations she had planned, they stuck a For Rent sign in the front yard. It took three days to rent the third-floor apartment. The man, a Finnish immigrant named Lester, stayed there for two and a half years—the perfect tenant—before moving on. He asked Kate if she and her husband would consider renting to a friend, and Kate agreed without consulting Matt. They couldn't have a lapse in rent.

Lilly remembered her father being skeptical about renting to a Russian woman, but Kate reminded him how Lester had paid rent on time each month and hadn't caused any problems. How he'd left the apartment in the same condition as the day he'd moved in. "We should be so lucky to have him recommend someone to take his place. Who cares about nationality? The Cold War's over, Matt!"

Lester reassured him that the woman was quiet and would pay her bills on time. So, Matt, albeit reluctantly, agreed, and the woman moved in a week later. Two weeks later, Matt was aboard a plane headed to the Middle East to fight in a war that the new tenant's countrymen knew well.

Lilly had watched this woman come and go every day, except when she was in school, jotting down notes in one of her journals like a private investigator. The tenant traveled by Metro, the station only a few blocks away, or walked—never took a taxi, never had someone pick her up, and she didn't take the bus anywhere. She paid her mother in cash on the last day of each month when her mom got home from work, sometimes as late as midnight. Her mother never spoke about the woman, as if she was a secret stashed away in the attic as in some Gothic novel. And Lilly never asked. She didn't even know the woman's name. There was just something that intrigued her about the woman upstairs, and, after watching her for several months, realized that it was the woman's loneliness, or what her music teacher might call independence, that made her watch and study the woman's movements. Lilly saw herself being much like the tenant when she reached her adult years, if those years were anything like her current situation at Dedham High School, where Lilly found that her classmates didn't accept her or even give her the chance to be friends. The boy she had a crush on in first period rarely glanced in her direction. The only person that really spoke to her was Mr. Thompson, her music teacher. She had written these things in her journal, too.

The Russian woman was not beautiful. Not terrible to look at either. There were just no distinguishing features about her, at least not from Lilly's second-floor vantage point. She always dressed modestly, whether jeans and a sweater or a knee-length skirt with tights and a plain blouse or shirt to match. Lilly noticed that she usually kept her head down as if not wanting to make eye contact with anyone on the sidewalk, a technique Lilly used in the school hallways when walking from class to class. The woman was pale, had shoulder-length blonde hair, and thin lips above a firm chin. Nose a backwards checkmark. The few wrinkles on her face had Lilly guessing that she was near her mother's age, even somewhat looked like her mother.

But, Lilly was less interested in the woman when she could see her. Watching her comings and goings, while somewhat exciting, did not draw her attention to this woman. It was what the woman did each night that made Lilly feel the strongest connection. And she needed that right now. Music. Though living alone, the woman had her music, the piano, and Lilly had her violin. Music was the important connection they had, Lilly knew. It was through music that they would never be alone.

Lilly heard the woman walking upstairs. Music began playing a minute later. It was muffled, and she could only hear the piano section of the piece. It sounded like Rachmaninov's *Trio élégiaque No. 1 in G minor*, a piece she'd practiced incessantly with Mr. Thompson in September, but she couldn't be sure. She only knew that, as seemed the woman's custom, she was playing a CD of the piece before sitting at her piano and playing it herself.

Not wanting to waste time, Lilly opened her window, hoping the woman's window was open, too, so that she could hear the music clearly. And it was open. The breeze that blew in smelled like a campfire in the rain and was cool enough to make her shiver, carrying with it the somber tones of Rachmaninov. She heard the violin and cello now, which her ceiling had concealed a moment ago.

Lilly retrieved her violin and bow from its black plastic case and stood near the window. When the CD was finished, she waited. Placing her chin on the violin's chin rest, she held the instrument in her left hand. In her right hand, the bow. She closed her eyes. Though she knew the cello and violin were supposed to begin before the piano, she waited for the woman to start playing, then she would sneak into the piece unnoticed.

The sound of a car going by with a loud muffler...and the piano began with its four-note rising motif that spans the fifteen-minute work. Lilly positioned her fingers and readied her bow. And she started playing. Softly at first, to get in rhythm with the woman's piano playing. It took a few starts and stops, but she was in sync with her by the first crescendo one minute into the piece, keeping the volume low so the woman would not hear her.

Eyes tightly shut, her mind filled with colors, dark oranges, maroon, and black, all tightly woven together and dark for miles in every direction like nimbostratus clouds hovering over the prairie. The deeper sound of the cello crept into her mind, grazing the fine hairs on the back of her neck, and she didn't feel the cold anymore. She stayed this way, orange rain pouring out of black clouds and pooling in maroon pits now, losing track of time, but realizing that she had entered the last episode of the elegy where the tempo crawls and the notes are deep and sonorous, slow slides of the bow holding the note for several seconds—the funeral march. And then it was over, seeming to last a few seconds but a quarter of an hour had passed.

Lilly held the bow to her side, pulled the violin away from between her chin and shoulder, and opened her eyes to a dark, deserted street outside her window. She wondered, as she did each night, if the woman upstairs knew that she eavesdropped on her and played along with her when she'd play pieces Lilly was familiar with. And what did it matter if she did? It didn't stop the woman from playing. Maybe the woman knew that Lilly played along and enjoyed it just as much as Lilly did. Or more.

Lilly wanted to meet the woman upstairs, but she didn't know how to approach her. She couldn't even make friends with other girls her own age, let alone a woman her mother's age that probably didn't speak English well. Never mind the fact that her father hadn't completely trusted the woman because she was Russian, regardless of Lester's recommendation.

She placed the violin in its velvet-lined case and locked the bow into the holder. She draped the blanket over the instrument, checked the reading on the hygrometer, and made sure the humidifier did not need water. It didn't, so she gently closed the case and fastened the draw-tight latches before sitting it upright next to her bed.

When Lilly left her bedroom, the feathers came back, just not as intense. It prompted her to go to the kitchen and put some water in a teakettle, light the burner, and have a mug of chamomile tea. Before the kettle whistled, she walked to the other side of the house to her parents' bedroom and knocked on the door.

"I'm making some tea, Mom. Do you want any?"

There was no answer. So, she waited a few seconds before opening the door. The bedroom was dark, but an outline of light emitted from the edges of the bathroom door like in some horror movie, and the sound of water clapped down on a plastic bathtub. She inched the door open and said again, "Mom?"

Her mother's voice was scratchy as if she had laryngitis when she said, "Yeah."

"Do you want some tea?"

"No."

"Okay." And she shut the door.

If she'd tried to say more to her mother, she knew the lump would return and that she'd start crying again, so she was thankful for the short responses. She took in a deep breath and turned around. Lilly was glad the light was off now, knowing that pictures of her father were hiding in the shadows staring at her. That was why her mom had the lights off so often, she thought.

In the kitchen, Lilly took the whistling kettle off the stove, filled a mug with steaming water, and dropped in a teabag. She turned the stove off and replaced the kettle mechanically. She wasn't much of a tea drinker, but a commercial she had seen while her mother was watching television a few nights ago had given her the impression that tea calmed your nerves, and the woman in the ad had a warm fire going in the fireplace, fleece pajamas, a golden retriever laying on a rug in front of the fire, and, most importantly, a relaxing smile. What Lilly wanted was the relaxed smile, the feeling that everything was okay.

When Lilly got to the top of the staircase, she turned to her right, where the staircase would have continued if a locked door wasn't blocking the path. It led to the third floor where the woman lived. A double-key deadbolt kept either side from intruding on the other. She was certain her mother had the key, but had no idea where she kept it. It would be easy to snag it if it was on her key ring, wait for the tenant to leave, then unlock the door and sneak upstairs to find out more about the woman she'd spent so much time watching and listening to. Find out her name and if she had any family. And maybe find out where she went every day and where she worked. If she worked.

In a few seconds, Lilly was back downstairs. Her mother's purse was in a basket next to the front door. She set her tea on the floor, then unzipped the black faux-leather purse. The keys were sitting there like a present she'd just opened. Forgetting her tea, she ran back up the stairs and knelt in front of the door. The first key was silver, and she slid it in slowly and smoothly, a light tick sounding as the key's teeth connected with each pin the key slid under, but it didn't turn. The second, a copper-colored key, went in with some force, grinding metal against metal, and Lilly worried that she was making too much noise. She put her ear to the door, but she didn't hear anything on the other side. So, she pulled the key out and tried the third key. It had *Wal-Mart* branded on the bow, and it went in smoothly. This key turned with ease.

Her heart jack-hammered the back of her chest now, and she quickly relocked the door. Taking in a deep breath, now two and three more deep breaths, Lilly smiled and made her way back down the stairs, slipping off the key before replacing them in her mother's purse and zipping it back up.

She picked up her mug of tea, steam still meandering atop the light brown pond, and went to her freezing room, where she closed her window, sipped the tea, and read a handful of pages in *The Diary of Anne Frank* for her English class before going to sleep, the key she had stolen from her mother sitting atop her nightstand.

Chapter 3

Alexei Volkov felt that he was on the right path, even though he was only twenty-three miles into the United States when pulled over by a Vermont State Police trooper. The package he'd been instructed to pick up in Canada was something he could not let the police or anyone else see. He didn't even know what the item was, as it remained inside a locked briefcase in his trunk.

While the cop did whatever cops do for the five minutes before approaching the vehicle, Alexei stared at the cracked and nearly-deserted I-91 macadam. He had been speeding. Eighty into sixty-five. The trooper had been sitting in a nook just around the curve, hiding behind unkempt bushes like a cat, he thought, hunkered down and ready to lash out and strike the next thing that passed.

As the trooper approached the car, Alexei remembered to switch the radio station to NPR, which was playing *Performance Today*. As instructed, he adjusted the volume so that it would be obvious what he was listening to, but not loud enough to be rude. He rolled down his window. The cool air quickly swirled through his Altima and overpowered the heater, which was set on low.

"Do you know why I pulled you over today, sir?"

The trooper was young but didn't seem nervous. Wasn't cocky either. Just normal, as if they were two guys standing in line at Wal-Mart chatting, he thought. The thick jacket the trooper wore looked inviting to Alexei, who was already starting to get cold.

"Yes, sir," Alexei said, trying to sound as respectful as he could, keeping eye contact. Keeping his hands in plain sight. Not making any sudden movements, even though he wanted to turn the heater on high.

"Where are you coming from and where are you headed?"

"Montreal. Headed home to Boston, sir. Back to my wife and

kids."

"Okay." He asked for and received Alexei's license, registration, and insurance card, then went back to the cruiser.

Alexei stayed calm. He kept the window rolled down, but turned the heat on high and adjusted the vents so that the hot air hit him directly. His jacket was in the trunk, so he knew getting it was out of the question. Each time the arctic air would blow down from Canada and chill him, he thought about his colleagues teasing him, saying that a man from St. Petersburg should be used to the cold, that cold was a Russian's friend. That he had no business complaining unless it was about the summer heat. And he would laugh it off, come up with some retort, and then they'd all get back to work or to watching the game or to eating hamburgers off the grill.

Alexei stared at the pavement again, occupying his mind. He considered the maintenance needed to keep the interstate in like-new condition: the amount of tax dollars spent (millions), the number of construction jobs created (hundreds), the additional safety provided to reduce accidents (much), and even the extended life of commuters' tires (several months to a year). When he had the entire plan mapped out and complete, the trooper was still in his cruiser, so Alexei closed his eyes and turned the radio volume up a few notches, focusing on the distinct timbres of the instruments, trying to relax. He fixated on the string section, predominately the violins, their eerie voices singing high above the staff. There were a few moments when he heard wind instruments, not the big brass, but something small like a clarinet or flute, he didn't know which. And it didn't matter now because the officer was back and had tapped him on the shoulder.

Startled, Alexei opened his eyes and turned the radio down. After one breath, he regained composure and made eye contact with the trooper again. "Sorry."

"You haven't been drinking today, have you, sir?"

"No," replied Alexei with the beginning of a fake laugh. "Sometimes, I get lost in the music."

"Have you gotten enough sleep to be driving safely?"

"Yes, sir."

"I'm going to need you to get out of the vehicle now, sir."

Alexei let out a quiet, deep breath, careful to keep his shoulders up and not let them hunch over—that would be a sign of defeat, of giving up.

If the trooper hadn't taken so long, Alexei would have gotten his speeding ticket and been on his way. How was he supposed to keep his mind occupied when there was nothing around but the cracked and potholed interstate highway? And trees, lots of leafless trees. No animals…a few birds. No other cars. Just him and the state trooper; the flashing lights on the cruiser were reflecting in his rearview mirror and making his eyes throb with pain, the cold air attacking the microscopic holes in his sweater and chilling his skin. Everything would be okay as long as the trooper didn't want to search the vehicle.

Alexei complied. He moved slowly, pulling on the door handle, the trooper opened it all the way after the click, and Alexei stepped out one foot at a time, rising slowly, and kept his hands at his sides.

"You don't have any weapons on your person or in the vehicle, do you, sir?"

"No, sir." *All this for having my eyes closed is ridiculous.*

"Any drugs in the car or on your person?"

"No, sir." This was getting ugly too quickly. What the hell was in that briefcase? He hoped it wasn't a weapon. He'd been assured that it wasn't drugs or money, which was why he'd agreed to do these trips, a personal courier service for a man that called himself Hawthorne. It was Alexei's way of tying up favors owed to old friends.

"Okay, step to the front of the vehicle and place your hands on the hood. I'm just going to give you a quick pat-down."

Alexei did as he was told, by both the trooper and by Hawthorne's instructions—always comply with a cop's command, and don't give them any reason to suspect you of anything.

The trooper produced one wallet, and that was it. "What was the purpose of your visit to Canada, sir?"

"That's none of your business," he whispered.

"What was that, sir?"

He turned his head toward the trooper. "I went on business." He didn't know how much longer he'd be able to comply with this trooper before taking control of the situation. In St. Petersburg, cops knew to leave him alone. They knew his car and knew to ignore it if it happened to be speeding. That perk didn't travel with him to the United States. Here, he was just like everyone else.

"Business?"

"Yes," said Alexei, pointing his right hand at his MIT parking sticker on his windshield, then putting it back on the hood.

"You work at MIT," he said, with a slow nod followed by a "hmmt." The trooper gazed inside the vehicle, looking at anything in plain sight.

"I had a meeting at University of Montreal."

"Care if I take a look inside your vehicle?"

Alexei closed his eyes tightly and realized he was now grinding his teeth. Or maybe his teeth were chattering because he was freezing. He had to keep his wits, but this trooper seemed to have a sixth sense telling him that there was something hidden in this vehicle, that this man he had pulled over was dirty somehow, MIT or not. Alexei wanted to take the trooper's head in his hands and twist until he heard enough tearing and snapping to ensure the man was dead. He would not go to jail under any circumstances. The problem was that the trooper had already put his information in his computer, so there would be no question who killed the son of a bitch. Alexei had no choice. He opened his eyes and said, "Sure," with a forced smile.

The trooper got in the driver's seat and rummaged around the middle console and glove box. Neither contained anything suspicious. He got back out of the car and noticed Alexei shivering.

"Don't you have coat, sir?"

Alexei was silent for several seconds. If he said no, and then the trooper continued to search the vehicle to find Alexei's coat in the trunk, then he would have caught him in a lie and suspicions would arise. Every word Alexei had spoken and every move he'd made would be put in question, more so than it probably already was. However, if the trooper had not planned to continue searching the vehicle, and Alexei replied affirmatively, the sight of the briefcase could raise questions, and the trooper might get curious. He might open the briefcase and find something that could send Alexei to jail or could cost the trooper's life if Alexei killed him in order to protect himself from incarceration. It was a catch-22, and he didn't like it. His only option was to defer, to give a response that didn't answer the initial question.

"I'm okay," he said.

"You can take your hands off the hood now." The trooper handed Alexei his papers and license back.

"Thank you." He took his wallet off the hood and slipped it in his right pants pocket. Alexei got control of his teeth so that they wouldn't chatter.

"We've been cracking down on drug smugglers from Canada and cigarette smugglers from the US, so I appreciate your cooperation. Make sure you stay focused so that you get home safely," the trooper said. "I'm going to let you off with a warning today, sir."

"Thank you, officer. You are very kind." It was nearly impossible to keep his shoulders straight, but he did it. He wanted to slump them, give them a break from staying at attention like a

British grenadier.

"Have a nice day, sir. And drive safely." The trooper walked back to his cruiser, turned off the flashing lights, then drove away.

Alexei got in his car, rolled up the window, and sat there for a few minutes getting warm, then pulled back onto I-91 and set the cruise control at sixty-five miles per hour, then he let out a sigh of relief and let his shoulders slump down in exhaustion. He adjusted the rearview mirror so he could see the trunk was safely closed.

A little over four hours later, Alexei was back in Boston on the MIT campus, McGovern Institute, where he worked as an assistant to the neurotechnology group. He'd been there for three years and had gotten to know the professors and researchers well. Had been to their houses for cookouts, joined them after work for a beer, and was viewed as one of them by now, even though he didn't have a PhD.

His shoulders ached as if he'd been carrying a heavy backpack. He opened the door to his dim office with the leather briefcase in his right hand. Inside, a man was sitting in a chair in front of his desk. The faint light coming in through the window behind the man made him look like a shadow, and it startled him.

"Any problems?" the man asked, his voice like a radio announcer or audio-book narrator.

"I was pulled over in Vermont, but he didn't search the car." Alexei didn't know how deep Hawthorne's hands could get inside state-police records, so he didn't want to take any chances. His role in all of this was almost complete. There was no need to muddy the waters if he didn't have to.

"You followed the rules then. Just like I told you." Hawthorne stood up. "Make them think you're sophisticated, innocent, and they'll let you go, even with your Russian accent." He straightened his sleeves. "Keep your eyes on them, and never look toward what you don't want them to see. Look like you've got something to hide—"

"And they'll find it," Alexei said sardonically, then held the briefcase forward.

As Hawthorne approached him, his shoes sounding like a horse's hooves on the tile floor, light from the hallway erased the shadow, revealing the man's pale, clean-shaven face, his Roman nose sticking as far out as the stingy brim of his grey fedora. He was wearing a dark brown suit with a maroon shirt, no tie. Hawthorne always looked the same, always wore dark clothes. A *GQ* cover imitator, but he didn't have the star look in his face. Rugged, premature wrinkles as if he'd been a druggie not so long ago.

Hawthorne slid his hand into the briefcase handle gently, and Alexei let go. The man's expression did not change.

"Did they give you any trouble in Montreal this time?"

He was referring to Alexei's previous trip to Canada, when the men Alexei met were different than the previous contacts, and they said that they did not trust him, therefore they did not give him the package, therefore forced him to return to Boston empty-handed. They hadn't been rude or violent, just a calm "No." And when he told Hawthorne about it, his expression did not change then either. He just nodded and walked out of Alexei's office.

"No. Whatever your message had been went through loud and clear."

Hawthorne reached in his inside jacket pocket, pulled out an envelope, and handed it to Alexei. "Until next time."

Alexei didn't want there to be a next time. He remained standing, watching as Hawthorne approached the door, opened it, then tilted his head, making sure that his hat obscured his face from the cameras. The echo of his shoes on the tile sounded like a heartbeat slowly fading away. The traveling had gone on for eleven months now, once a month to Montreal to pick up a package and bring it back, each trip worth five thousand dollars and one step closer to paying his debt to Boris for getting him and his sister out of Russia in 1990 when everything fell apart, when their family was taken from them. Alexei had been assured that these packages would not contain drugs, money, or body parts. He was picking up information, and they needed someone who was not involved to ensure the packages would not be opened. But he knew that it couldn't have been legal; otherwise, they would not have taken him through the steps necessary to make himself look innocent if pulled over on his road trips. He knew that it was a form of espionage, and that he was risking everything he'd built in his new life. But debts had to be paid, even twenty-year-old debts. And if this was what Boris wanted, even if he was channeling it all through this Hawthorne fellow, then so be it. Get it paid so he could live out his life with his family, see his children grow up in a world far less bleak and violent than his had been. The only bad his children had witnessed came in the form of vandalism after the arrests earlier that year when ten Russian spies were caught. Those who had heard Alexei speak knew that he had come from that region, and spray cans got emptied on their property, along with a few other small incidences. Kid stuff really. But even the vandalism hadn't been a problem for the past few months. It withered away as the news stopped headlining the case.

It was getting late and colder. Alexei closed his office door and turned on his desk lamp. He took a half-empty bottle of Stolichnaya and a jigger from his top drawer, and filled the jigger to the brim. After sitting the bottle on his clean desk, he downed the double shot and gently put the glass next to the vodka. The burn was welcoming, starting in his throat and seeming to coat his stomach like Pepto-Bismol. It took all of two minutes to relax him and dull the pain in his shoulders.

Before sitting down in his chair, he picked up the 5x7 photograph of his wife Emily and two children, Nina and Victor, which he'd taken at Navy Pier in Chicago three months ago during their summer vacation. The children were a year apart and had started private school in September, the only good use of the money he was getting. Emily still worked part-time at the library. The photo was taken on their last night in Chicago, and the final night of the fireworks. Nina had—

A knock on Alexei's door, and he dropped the picture frame and heard the glass crack when it hit the floor.

"Fuck," he said, and got up. Who would be at his office so late? It wasn't Hawthorne…he would have heard Hawthorne's footsteps. And the door to get inside the building was locked; someone would need the passkey to get inside. Could it be Jenny? She and Jin Won were the only ones that would ever come in after hours, but not on a Saturday. No one showed up on Saturdays, especially after eleven o'clock at night. Besides, they would have announced themselves, not just beat on his door. Unless Hawthorne let someone in on his way out, but that didn't seem like something he would do.

Alexei approached the door slowly. He couldn't remember if he had locked the door or not, and the vodka wasn't serving as liquid courage at the moment. He wanted a weapon. His idea of an unexpected visitor at night meant trouble or the police. And the police didn't knock when they were there to take you to jail.

Another knock.

Whoever was outside knew Alexei was there, so he didn't have a choice but to respond. He'd reached the door and noticed that it was locked.

"Mr. Volkov," came a voice from the other side of the door. "Please open the door so that I may speak with you."

Alexei recognized the accent as Russian, but not Petersburg Russian, southern Russian. He got the bottle of vodka and held it by the neck in his left hand. With his right, he unlocked and opened the door to find a man that looked of Arab descent standing in the dimly lit hallway. He was dressed like an

American businessman, suit grey, hat obscuring.

"How the hell did you get in here?" asked Alexei, keeping the bottle behind his leg and out of the man's sight. He didn't feel more confident. At this point, he just wanted to go home to his family. And the man made him nervous. The Arabs he was familiar with were usually anti-Russian—Chechens—and this man's accent placed him in that region. Furthermore, this man knew his name.

"I just want to talk," the man said. "May I come inside and talk to you?"

"No. You need to leave." He gripped the bottle more tightly. He was taking this man's kindness as completely fake. Who knew what his intentions were?

"I'm not going anywhere until we talk." His voice had dropped a few octaves. "And I don't think Boris would appreciate your turning me away so rudely, Alexei."

The words penetrated his skin, tiny needles at his pores. Alexei stepped aside and let the man enter. They sat across from each other, Alexei in his office chair, the man in the chair Hawthorne had been in a few minutes ago. Alexei put the bottle back on his desk, along with the broken picture frame, face down. The man looked at it for a few seconds, then turned his attention back to Alexei.

"You're Chechen, aren't you?" asked Alexei, already knowing the answer. He had never liked Chechens, especially after a decade of news reports blaming Chechens for several bombings in Russian cities, especially Moscow.

"Yes, and I need some information," the man said, an ugly smile spreading across his dry face. "And you're the person to get it from."

Alexei sat back in his chair, not responding. He knew Chechens were as dangerous to him as Al Qaeda was to Americans. Namedropping Boris or not, Alexei had this strange feeling, that if he had a pistol, he'd shoot the man where he sat, even though he'd never killed a human being. Or even an animal for that matter. Nothing above an insect… And that kindheartedness, he knew, was what drew Emily to him. And what drew her even closer to him was how he was with his children. He knew that most fathers felt something different, an unconditional love, once their children were born, but he never thought he'd be one of them, and this man trying to get him involved in something deeper, and he knew that's what he wanted, bothered him. He didn't want to do it. He didn't even want to continue picking up information in Canada, but it paid his debts to Boris. And it wasn't like Boris to pile on extras like this, if that's what was happening here. He didn't know this man, but more disturbing was that somehow this man knew him and about his secrets, his past. Hawthorne had told him that he was in direct contact with Boris, no middle men, so no one else should know anything. But there had to be a leak somewhere. He couldn't let that leak turn into a flood.

"What's your name?" asked Alexei.

"You can call me Brother."

That wasn't going to happen.

"What is it you think I can help you with? And why the hell are you coming to me?"

"You work here, in neurotechnology. You have access to the labs and information. I need some of this information."

"That's illegal."

"As is transporting certain materials across international borders."

"I don't know what you're talking—"

"I know about Hawthorne, and your dealings with him are over," he said matter-of-factly.

How could he know so much? Had he been watching him? And if so, for how long? For the eleven months? For eleven years? Had he been in Russia so long ago, and was he part of some horror back there? "You need to leave right now," said

Alexei, not meaning to speak those words aloud.

"I'm not asking, Mr. Volkov."

Brother reached inside his pocket, and Alexei thought he was getting a gun. He felt the hairs on his back shift. His armpits moistened and his stomach tingled. Just before he made a move for the bottle, Brother had tossed a folded manila envelope on his desk.

Brother stood, pointing his finger at the envelope as he spoke: "You will have copies of the information that I want by next Monday. What I want is listed on a piece of paper inside that envelope. There are instructions in there, too." He straightened his posture and picked up the photograph of Alexei's family. "Emily, Nina, and Victor. You have a lovely-looking family."

Alexei stood now and took the photo from Brother. Damn him for knowing his family's names. Damn him for making him his pawn.

"I don't ever want to see you again."

"Good night, Mr. Volkov," said Brother, then left Alexei's office.

When the Chechen was out of his office, Alexei sat back down and gazed at the photograph again. The crack in the glass was horizontal and jagged, splitting the photo in half.

He poured another jigger of Stoli and drank it down. That this man, Brother, had gotten into the building was disturbing enough, he thought. He wondered if Hawthorne knew him. If they worked together. And what Brother meant by him not dealing with Hawthorne anymore. And did both of them take orders from Boris, a man that he had no way to contact? If that was so, why hadn't Hawthorne mentioned anything? He'd acted like business as usual, but this Chechen was making a sharp turn.

Alexei put the picture back on his desk, flipping out the stand so that it would stay upright. He collected his things, put the Stoli and jigger back in the desk drawer, and stood, staring at the manila envelope. He frowned, then picked it up. Standing still for what felt like seconds but was actually four full minutes, Alexei crumpled the envelope and threw it in his wastebasket. "Fuck you, Brother."

The night air had gotten much colder or he had just gotten used to the warmth of his office. The Altima started without hesitation, and he began his drive home. The city was busy like a city should be. It wasn't quiet late at night like Chicago or some tiny town without a college. And thirty minutes later, he was a few turns away from his house and family.

Brother's words kept repeating in his mind. That he was not asking... Hawthorne had never threatened him. He'd made him a bit uneasy a few times, but not like the Chechen. He contemplated going back to his office and taking the envelope out of the trash. Getting the god damn information and moving on with his life. If he didn't go back and get it, the janitor would clean out the office trash on Monday morning, envelope with it, and Alexei would be left without a choice but to go against what Brother had demanded if he didn't get to work early enough. And the packages... What were in those packages? Could that be the connection, some sort of surveillance showing him picking up illegal 'stuff' and bringing it into the United States? Turning that information over to the police? It didn't make sense if they were trying to get classified information from him. They had to be involved in something that they would keep as far from police as possible. The University of Montreal did have a substantial neurology lab and highly qualified and successful professors researching the same kinds of things those in his department at MIT were researching. That could be it. But why would they be so adamant to get neuroscience technology? It didn't have the same power as nuclear or weapons technology. It didn't really have political ties. Maybe he should have peeked in one of those packages just to get a glimpse of what he was involved with. And maybe it was the vodka getting to his head, bringing up paranoid thoughts and worries.

He turned on Hempstead Drive and noticed two Boston Police cruisers parked halfway down the block with their blue and red lights flashing. It had to be his house, he thought. He sped up. And when he got closer, he slammed on the brakes and got out of the car. The front door was open, missing one of the four panes of glass.

How could Brother have acted so quickly? How could he have known that Alexei had thrown the manila envelope away?

The image of the photograph taken at Navy Pier filled his mind—his family separated by a long, jagged tear. Muscles in his throat contracted. Teeth clenched, he exhaled slowly, his hot breath like fog seeping through the narrow gaps between his teeth. And as his sight blurred, and a tear fell from each eye, he saw a police officer appear in his doorway. He couldn't tell what kind of expression was on the officer's face, but the officer just stood there, staring at him as if he didn't know what to say, how to console him.

Chapter 4

Clive Thompson's doctor had to speak with him in person, so Clive sped to his office in twenty minutes for the opportunity to sit in the waiting room for an hour and a half before a nurse he'd never seen before opened the "gateway to heaven" and led him to an examination room, where she weighed him, checked his temperature—a new addition to his usual checklist of steps and procedures—checked his blood pressure, noted each result on a sheet of paper clipped inside a manila folder, and then, with a bleached smile, told him that the doctor would be in to see him in a moment. She closed the door normally, but it sounded like a slam because of the tile floor, sparse wall hangings, the most interesting being the biohazard disposal for syringes, and sickly sanitary furniture—the doc's chair, an examination bed with white paper stretched over it, a wastebasket, and a machine in the corner, its name he could not pronounce. He heard the clop of his folder being dropped into the plastic basket attached to the other side of the door.

He crossed his legs, right leg atop the left. After staring at the biohazard symbol on the syringe disposal for twenty minutes and wondering who designed such a symbol, and thinking about the radiation symbol and comparing the two in his mind, Clive then sat for another twenty minutes, switching legs because his right leg was completely asleep, staring at the floor and trying to make out shapes in the tiles, but none emerged like they usually did. They were the black and white tiles he'd always seen in restaurants when he was younger or in a hospital. His right leg was waking up now and feeling like a thousand ants scurrying in every direction underneath his skin.

Doctor Hauzerd opened the door while holding a clipboard, closed it behind him, and sat down, never taking his eyes off the documents. He smelled like latex and cheap shaving cream. He was holding Clive's folder atop his clipboard, but Clive had not heard him take it out of the plastic bin.

"Okay, Mr. Thompson," he said, still eying the paperwork attached to his clipboard. "I've gotten the results back from your x-ray." The doctor stood up now. "Let me just go and get those, and we'll look at them together."

Clive uncrossed his legs, put an elbow on each knee, and buried his face in his hands. He'd been at this man's office for over two hours now, and the son of a bitch leaves again, five seconds after walking in the room. He had a headache, and he had to pee, but he thought going to the bathroom would only prolong his waiting because the doctor would surely not wait on him. And, Murphy's law told him that the moment he went to the bathroom would be the moment the doctor would open the examination-room door to find the room empty, then move on to the next patient. Maybe that was why they called them patients, because a patient had to be so fucking patient. Well, his patience was running thin, regardless of what the x-rays showed. At this point, he didn't care.

But, the doctor was back in less than a minute and pinned up the x-rays and turned on the x-ray reader's backlight. Clive got up and stood next to the doctor, looking at his own bones.

"Do you see this whiteness here in the left lung?" the doctor said, pointing to it with a Bic pen.

Clive nodded.

"It's because of that, that I called you in today."

You didn't call me in; your nurse called me in.

"I don't want to frighten you, but this could be lung cancer."

The words registered immediately, erasing the annoyance of having sat in this man's waiting room and examination room for over two hours. If it was lung cancer, then it was two hours of life that he'd lost, just wasted away doing nothing, and not being happy about it. He had lived seventy-two decent years, he thought, and this was how he was going to go out. Lung cancer.

He imagined how the last months of his life would be—bald from chemotherapy and sick and vomiting from chemotherapy and not being able to continue his work, his passion, because of chemotherapy and finally dying when the chemotherapy didn't work against the cancer filling up his lungs. And then, he thought about his student, who was more like an apprentice, Lilly Rebeck. He'd discovered her four years ago, during her first year of middle school. He had volunteered to help the middle-school music teacher listen to and evaluate the students hoping to be part of the middle-school band. He had been evaluating those interested in strings and drums while the other teacher listened to wind and brass, along with piano and percussion. When Lilly stood in front of him with her violin at the ready, he nodded, and she began to play Mendelssohn. A sixth grader playing Mendelssohn! It wasn't perfect, but it wasn't bad either.

"Where did you learn to play, young lady?" he'd asked.

"I taught myself," she said, lowering the violin. "Watched a lot of performances and lessons online." And she smiled.

He knew talent, and this girl was unique. He could tell that her smile was genuine, that she was truly passionate about music. Though she may not have been a prodigy, she was something special, and he didn't want anything standing in her way. He asked her to come to the hallway with him, that he needed to speak with her.

"I don't want you wasting your time here," Clive said. He could tell that she was nervous because her hands were shaking and her chin slightly quivering, and he realized that she may have taken what he had said the wrong way.

Her shoulders started to slump, and her eyes, which had been gazing up at the man, quickly broke eye contact and focused on the gray carpet at her feet. "What—"

"I mean that you're good," he said quickly, dropping to one knee and putting his index and middle finger under her chin, raising her head so that they were making eye contact again.

Her smile came back, and she started to raise her hands as if to wipe the beginning moisture from her eyes, but one hand gripped the violin, the other the bow, so she relaxed them. "You really think I'm good? You're not just saying that?"

Clive nodded. "I'm not just saying that." He stood up now. "How long have you worked on the piece you played for me?"

"A couple weeks," she said.

"And you don't take lessons?"

"No, just practice by myself."

"And you can read sheet music?"

"Yeah."

"You didn't teach yourself sheet music, too, did you?"

"No, Mrs. Hansen showed me. She was my music teacher at Timberline." She smiled again. "She got mad at me when we were supposed to be singing 'Goober Peas' and I just sat there, wishing to be somewhere else."

"What'd she say?"

"She told me that I had to participate or else my grade would go down. And I told her that I thought it was boring, that I was more interested in the music than the words. She told me that she knew what I was talking about. That was second grade. That's when she taught me notes. In third grade, Dad bought me a violin. Since then, I've been practicing. It's really hard to play something I don't like. But if I like what I'm playing, I don't think I even need sheet music. It just happens."

This made Clive laugh. "Well, you need sheet music to get started, then you memorize it and just know it by heart." Before Lilly could respond, he continued, "How would you like to work with me after school a few days a week? Practicing your violin. I can arrange for us to work together. To perfect your skills."

He could tell that she was getting excited by the way her eyebrows raised and how she took in a deep lungful of air.

"Really?"

"Yes. As I said earlier, you don't need to be wasting your time with a middle-school band."

"I'll have to talk to my dad—"

"Of course," Clive said, laughing again. "Talk to your dad. You've got a lot of potential, and I think you could make one hell of a violinist one day."

"But what about—"

Dr. Hauzerd broke his thought, saying, "So, Mr. Thompson, I propose we move forward with a CT scan and an MRI."

"What will that do that the x-ray won't?" he asked. He felt heavy, as if his head weighed fifty pounds on top of his skinny and old body. The sensation in his shoulders could only be described as exhaustion, he thought, and all he wanted to do was rest.

"It'll give us much more detailed information. We only get a snapshot from an x-ray, a two-dimensional photo. With these two procedures, we'll know the extent of this growth, we'll know many more details, and it will give us a three-dimensional view of what this is in your lungs."

"How sure are you that it's cancer?"

"Well, we'll know more after the CT and MRI. If it still looks like there's a threat, we'll move forward with a biopsy, which is a sample of—"

"I know what a biopsy is." The energy in his body was being fueled by its last resource, anger.

"Well, depending on the results of those two procedures, we may need to do a sputum test and bronchoscopy, in which we'll retrieve the cells for the biopsy."

"Can the scans be done today?"

"Well, if you—"

"It needs to get done today," said Clive, wishing he had said this first instead of asking a question and giving the doctor an opportunity to say no. "Now, if you need to make some phone calls, fine. But, I've been here a long time and you're getting a lot of money for my being here, so you can earn your paycheck and make a few calls to get me in. I don't want to have to keep coming back here," he jabbed his finger toward the floor, "waiting two hours at a time to find out if I'm dying." He clenched his teeth.

"Mr. Thompson, with all due respect, you're not the only one in this world with a possible illness. I have a waiting room full of them. Now, I can see what I can do by making a few phone calls. Now, if you'd care to take a seat," he said, and walked out of the room.

He was right, thought Clive. Those in the waiting room were paying the same fee to see this man, waiting the same chunk of time, and being treated with the same impersonality. Why should he be treated any differently?

His watch read 2:34 and the seconds ticked by, each click forward a second closer to death, he thought. And it depressed him even more.

He remembered that it was Wednesday, one of three days he and Lilly met after school to practice. At the beginning of the school year, he had told her about applying to Juilliard, explaining that, in the music world, it was the difference between a community-college degree and a degree from Harvard. That a professional violinist could make over one hundred thousand dollars a year playing in an orchestra and much more if that violinist was good enough to be a soloist.

"Like Hilary Hahn?" Lilly had asked.

"Yes," Clive said.

"You really think I can get in?"

"I know that you can get in. But it's going to take a lot of work. The audition is at the end of February. By that time, you'll be fifteen years old."

"Audition?" Her eyes were wide open as if in fear.

"It's nothing to worry about, Lilly. We have plenty of time to practice. We'll work on the Paganini étude, a Bach movement, and we have to choose a Romantic piece." He scanned the music room, not focusing on anything, but his way of trying to come up with a piece. "Rachmaninov. He would be perfect, just perfect. And at home, you can practice the easier stuff. The major and minor scales and arpeggios in three octaves."

Lilly was very excited. She wanted to begin right away, so Clive fished out the sheet music from his office and told her to study the notes first, then, at their next meeting, he'd listen to her play and help her get it right.

There were a few things he hadn't told her. Tuition for this pre-college program at Juilliard was over fifteen thousand dollars. Second, she would have to move to New York to attend, which he had a plan for, but it would require her parents' consent. He didn't want to take away any of the joy or excitement he saw in her young face as she scanned the sheet music. He knew the hardest part would be that the two of them could not work together any longer. Juilliard prohibited any outside teaching if enrolled in their program.

He just said to her, "We have other stuff to talk about regarding Juilliard, but we can do that later."

Clive could hear the doctor speaking, figuring that he was on the telephone. What had crept into his mind while thinking about Lilly was what he hadn't told her yet. It had been nearly a year since that conversation, and she had applied for scholarships, so the tuition part would be helped. What she couldn't get, he felt that he could make up the difference. His sister lived in New York and had agreed to let Lilly stay with her while attending, but he hadn't worked that out with Lilly or Lilly's mom yet. It was not the best time to bring it up to Lilly's mother so soon after her husband had been killed. So many kinks to work out...

And now this. His old body was too weak to fight off the big C, he thought. He'd lived alone for so many years, taking care of himself, not having to worry about anyone. And he'd seen what cancer could do. How it could rob you of your independence, humiliate you, and slowly take away every meaningful thing before it takes your life.

Clive knew that he'd kill himself before he got to that point, at least he thought he would.

"Good news," said the doctor, briskly entering the examination room with a small piece of paper in his hand in place of the clipboard he'd had earlier. "Here's the address to O'Conner Laboratories. They can fit you in, but you'll have to go now or else wait until Friday."

The news didn't make him feel better. He'd stood in that examination room letting his mind work to bring up what he called depressing shit. And it had, indeed, depressed him. He took the slip of paper, thanked the doctor, and then left.

On his way to the lab, he phoned the school and had them deliver a message to Lilly, letting her know that he would not be able to make it today. At the lab, the wait was not unbearable, and the scans were performed, and Clive had driven home to his apartment, all the while having the same memories and thoughts play in his mind, rewind, and then play again.

The apartment was small but affordable, and the neighbors were close enough to quiet to be bearable. He rarely spoke with any of them and was glad that none of them had children.

In his closet, he had an unopened bottle of Johnnie Walker blue label, a note still attached: "Here's to another 70, Brother. With all my love, Sis."

Even though Julia was fifteen years his junior, they had always been close. Clive had stayed close to home in Dover, having gone to college at Delaware State University and beginning his teaching at Dover High School. Julia was thirteen when Clive moved to Boston, but he visited every summer, Thanksgiving, and Christmas. Their parents died in a car accident a month after Julia graduated from high school. Clive gave his share of the insurance money to her, and she used it to go to college at NYU. Upon graduating, she decided to stay in New York, where she had been ever since.

He opened the bottle and poured a liberal amount into a tumbler, then replaced the cork. In the corner of his desk was a Bose wave radio, which he powered on. In St. Petersburg a decade ago he watched the Kirov Ballet perform Tchaikovsky's *The Nutcracker* at the Mariinsky Theatre. The men wore tights that were more than a little revealing of their rock-solid legs that had the dexterity and nimbleness of silk shimmering in a breeze. And the women, my god, the women, in puffy lace dresses, their hair all tied back tightly and perfectly in a bun. When they would leap into the air with ease and come down as if they had no weight, as if they were marionettes, they defined the word grace, for Clive had only seen grace in the musical instrument, but that night, he found it in the human body as well, each man lifting a girl in the air, dress flowing, complete ease like choreographed human feathers.

He opened his eyes and finished the Scotch remaining in his glass, then wiped his eyes before tears could snake their way down his wrinkled cheeks. The Scotch was smooth and then smoky, burning its way down near the cancer. He'd not been to a ballet since, knowing that nothing could top those Kirov performers on that freezing December evening.

His phone rang. He turned the music down and got a refill. His answering machine clicked on: "Hello, Mr. Thompson. I just wanted to know if we were going to meet tomorrow after school so I know whether I should bring my violin with me tomorrow. Hope you're okay. Bye."

It was Lilly. Young and talented Lilly. He could always see her being part of the Boston Symphony Orchestra, imagining her on the stage each time he'd watch and listen to a performance. He had even taken her to a few, showing her where all of her hard work and commitment could lead her. And the look in her eyes, that determined and enviable gaze told him that on stage, playing music was where she belonged. Anywhere else, and she'd be out of place, for even though the performers are in a group, they are each in their own, independent world, right where he knew Lilly wanted to be.

She'd made the last four years of his life worthwhile. Meaningful. In fact, he'd have retired had it not been for her. Probably moved to New York near his sister.

He was back in his chair now, taking down his third significant swallow of Johnnie Walker, and he wrote himself a note stating that he had to speak with Lilly's mother tomorrow about her daughter's future. For all he knew, death was just around the corner for him, so he wanted to make sure that Lilly's life would be positioned to head down the right path, the path that would lead to her happiness and fulfillment.

After the note was written, Clive turned the music back on, restarted the CD from the beginning, propped his feet up on his desk, and sipped his drink. He closed his eyes again, marionettes leaping and twirling in his mind until he fell asleep.

Chapter 5

2 December 2010. 8:12am. FBI – Boston Field Office
Special Agent Anna Stern slipped in quietly and sat at her station two weeks before she was scheduled to be back on duty. The other agents saw her, but they did not speak to her or approach her. This seemed odd. Was it because she was back early or because they blamed her for what happened to Meeks? Or did they just not like her, and seeing her again reminded them of that fact?

She logged in to her computer and stared at the screen, waiting for it to load. The chair across from her was usually occupied by Jonathan Meeks, but today it was empty. His desk was messy, as he'd left it, and hers was equally as messy, as she'd left it. She knew there were eyes on her, but she focused on the shimmering Windows icon on her computer, opened her secure database and pulled up the files on Mahmoud Aziz, the son of a bitch that had gotten away, that they had found, and who was responsible for her being shot five times and her partner once. It was the first time she'd gotten the chance to read the official report on the Providence case. Before she was able to get past the first sentence, Special Agent in Charge DeLaurent approached her desk. An older guy, starting his work in Boston PD, then on to the Massachusetts State Police, and shifted to the FBI after heading several big drug cases back in the 1980s. He was Boston through and through. The last person she wanted to talk to right now because there was always tension in the air and sometimes it would ignite.

"Back so soon?"

Fucking prick. "I need to get back into the swing of things, even if it means riding a desk for a few weeks," she said, and she meant it. Anna wasn't ready yet, but there was only so much isolation she could take. She wasn't built to stay cooped up in an apartment watching daytime television and hanging around her neighborhood being friendly. Her father had raised her to live fast, to protect those in the neighborhood, and the protector never slept. The protector had to search out and take down those who tried to harm others.

"If you're back, then you're back, and I need you to come in my office," he said, then turned around and paced back to his desk with jittery energy as if he'd just finished a pot of strong coffee.

She had nothing against her boss and his heavy Boston accent. He was just doing his job, right? Spending tax dollars responsibly as a loyal taxpayer would expect. He hadn't even been at the shooting. Hadn't even ordered them to go after Aziz—that had been Perkins' call after getting the tip. But he had the power to back off a bit and let her ease back into this world rather than firing her out of a cannon.

When she got to his desk, he closed the door and told her to sit down, then pulled out a few files from one of the several file cabinets behind his chair.

"You took the lead on that Russian spy case, Snowstorm, that we made arrests on this past summer."

"What's the problem with it?" she asked, never really knowing whether DeLaurent was pissed off, accusatory, or just conversing. His tone was always the same—intense.

DeLaurent had opened one of the files and looked distracted as he scanned the documents inside.

"No. You did a hell of a job with that case."

"Then—"

"We have to reopen it." He put the file on his desk. "Not your fault."

"What—"

"It looks like we didn't follow through to a deeper source." He read more closely. "You had told *Perkins* that we should be more patient, that the spies *we* arrested would eventually lead us to someone a few more notches up that ladder."

Anna crossed her arms. Perkins was gone now, so any blame immediately shifted to him even though she knew that DeLaurent could have stepped in. SSDD.

"*I* sent it up to Reagan, and *he* said no. Now he says yes. You know how things roll downhill. So, like I said, if you're back, you're back. And you need to start digging deeper into Snowstorm. Overall, we arrested ten of them, and Obama had them deported in some deal with the Russians, trying to keep up the image that we've become friends. But the Cold War will come up again." He shifted in his leather chair and raised his right hand, index finger pointed upwards and pumping it like a politician when he spoke. "Haven't you heard of the thirty-three-year rising?"

Anna shook her head, starting to regret having come back to work earlier than scheduled. DeLaurent could go on and on with his theories, and she couldn't handle it right now. His voice alone was having a nails-on-the-chalkboard effect on her nerves.

"It's some kind of theoretical or philosophical 'saying' that evil will always rise up after a thirty-three-year lull. Don't you see that happening with Russia? You can argue that it's the case with Iraq and Afghanistan, even though it's terrorists in those countries that are the threat rather than the country's government."

"So—"

"Have you been to see Agent Meeks lately?"

It was times like these that Anna wanted to sew DeLaurent's lips together. When he would change subject or topic so suddenly, as if you'd been talking about it the whole time.

"Yeah, I saw him yesterday," Anna said. "He's trying to stay positive, but that's not always the easiest thing to do. He's still not talking much. Just a few words here and there."

"Well—"

It was her turn to interrupt because it was over an issue that really pissed her off. "How about you? When's the last time you drove out to the home to see him? I wouldn't know because I don't ask him about work-related shit."

DeLaurent smirked, making it obvious that he knew she was lying. "I get out there when I can."

Anna stood up, took the files from his desk, and said, "What are you going to give me with this?"

"You have three agents at your disposal. Whatever surveillance equipment you need. We'll have more intel in a few days to help get you moving in the right direction. It looks like the ones that slipped away were a bit further under the radar."

"These three agents...part of the old team that worked on this...for over a year?"

"Sorry. They're all knee deep."

"You want me to dig into this with people who have no experience with it? And you want results quickly? Are you *serious*?"

"I am." He leaned back in his chair.

She wanted to throw the files back at him. "It'll take at least a week to get them up to speed, and that's working overtime."

"I doubt it'll take that long." His hands were behind his head now. "They might be young, might not have much real-time experience, but they're fresh—"

"Jesus fucking Christ, you're giving me rookies." She dropped the files on his desk, knocking over his pen holder. "Three fucking rookies, Derek."

"Hey," he said, standing up now and pointing his finger at her. "You watch yourself, Annie. Your father—"

"Don't—"

"*Your father* had respect in this office. Don't tarnish the family name with a tantrum." He dropped his hand, both now on his desk, holding him up. "So, yes, you have rookies. Three agents out of the academy used to book work, so they'll catch up quickly. Get it!"

"No. I don't get it. What kind of priority does this case have? Put a bunch of fucking kids on the thing."

"You know, lady, getting all shot up and almost dying hasn't changed you a bit. You might want to think about that."

She had thought about it, and it took a conscious effort not to cover the scar on her neck. DeLaurent was wrong. It had changed her. "You might want to—"

"You're getting promoted tomorrow. I need you here at ten a.m."

It shut her up. She let out a loud breath, picked up the files she'd thrown down, and headed for the door.

"Your kids are at your desk," DeLaurent said as she left his office.

So there it was...the first day back, what Meeks had said was true—DeLaurent had her in mind for the position, and tomorrow it would be official. Under the circumstances, even if Meeks had been the top candidate and her the second, she'd still be getting promoted because Meeks had been paralyzed from the bullet that hit his spine. There was a slim chance that he would get better. She couldn't get the image out of her mind of Meeks sitting in a wheelchair and only being able to move by putting a joystick in his mouth.

And now the promotion, the moment she was back. It felt more like a hard slap against her face. She wanted to go back into DeLaurent's office and decline it, but felt that, in some way, it would be betraying Meeks' wishes. Betraying herself. The past few times she'd visited him, he had talked and talked about her getting promoted and that if DeLaurent didn't endorse her, even under the circumstances of her being inactive for several months, that he'd go to the press and tell them... She always cut him off when he started ranting like that.

She was young for a promotion like this, and her father would be proud.

At her desk, three rookies, two males and a female, stood, all looking like high-school graduates, all clean cut, prim and proper. All innocent and young.

"You," she said to the blonde man, "make copies of these files and get them to everyone in this group. You," she said to the woman, "prepare conference-room C. And, you, get coffee ready and take lunch orders. We've got a long day."

After work, she visited Meeks to tell him the news.

"I knew you'd get it," he said. "I'm proud of you."

"Thanks, Johnnie." She called him that now. To call him Jonathan felt too formal. To call him Meeks made him just another agent, a colleague. But to call him Johnnie, that was more intimate. That made him a close friend. And that's what he needed now, a close friend that visited him each day because she wanted to, not out of obligation or guilt, but because she actually gave a damn. And she needed him, too, she realized.

He lay in that bed, covered to the neck in a white blanket with hospital machines that she couldn't name beeping and humming and displaying numbers and shapes that she tried to ignore, that she was in the process of trying to forget.

"I read the report you wrote about the Russians."

"Yeah…"

"DeLaurent's reopened the case."

She saw his lips move, thinking he was about to smile but forcing himself to hold it back.

"It was your idea to keep the case open, so why did you make it seem like it was mine?"

"You know why."

Anna looked from his face to the window, which was facing a lawn, patches of snow still lingering in shady spots.

"I know it never would have worked, but I couldn't help the way I felt about you."

She did know that, but she also tried to convince herself that it was just the way partners were supposed to be, that they shared a certain bond that sometimes overstepped lines set by the

Bureau, lines that paper pushers and lawmakers could never understand.

"And, I had put in for a transfer to the DC office."

"You what?" She didn't know what else to say. It had been obvious that he had a crush on her, but both knew that that line couldn't be crossed, that when it was, people got fired or separated. Anna hadn't known how deeply he felt for her, though. That either way that fateful night went, she'd end up losing him.

He was silent for what felt like minutes, staring up at the white ceiling and wearing a blank expression. "It's not like it matters now, Anna."

It did matter. He cared for her so much that he had to get away from her. Had she led him on somehow? If he hadn't cared so much, would he be in this hospital bed? She felt like it was all her fault. Stupid Anna! Her throat tightened, and she knew what would happen next if she didn't leave.

As she got up, Jonathan said, "Wait. I don't want you to leave like this."

Anna knew that he would have reached out and taken hold of her hand if he could, so she didn't leave; she fought back the tears, swallowing hard and clenching her jaws, tongue pressed firmly to her hard palate. When she turned around, he was looking at her.

"I have to go, Johnnie, but I'll be back to see you real soon."

"I'll be here," he said, seeming to read her expression that was begging him to let her go. He looked toward the ceiling again.

When Anna got to her apartment, it was dark and she didn't want to be alone. She could hear voices on either side of her unit, on the left were a young Irish couple that usually argued each night around dinnertime and on the right a Hispanic couple with a ten-year-old daughter and eleven-year-old son, but she didn't recall their names. They were friendly and generally quiet. If the walls weren't so thin and if they had insulation, she may not have heard them at all.

Anna lived minimally, her apartment looking like a model rather than a lived-in unit. She didn't waste time getting into sweat pants and a t-shirt and sitting up in bed, spreading the Snowstorm files atop her comforter.

Back in June, she and several others on a task force had discovered and arrested ten Russian spies in Boston, Philadelphia, and New York City. It was the largest arrest of spies since the Cold War. If Meeks' suspicions were correct, then the list was just the tip of the iceberg, as he would have said, and could be growing substantially if she was able to get deeper into their circle.

The ten that they'd arrested had been after new nuclear technology, which they'd been infiltrating MIT for; new medicines, which they'd infiltrated Harvard for; and she was reading the other field offices' reports to find out what they had been after in Philadelphia and New York. From what she remembered, the spies had been trying get information technology, computer stuff that she didn't really understand, so they could take it back to Russia and help Russia move a step closer to the United States, getting it back on track to its world-power status in the USSR days.

What they hadn't found were spies looking for military or weapon information, or even politically-motivated information, like details about political figures or trying to get someone close to a political figure. That's not to say that they weren't trying, she thought, but there was no evidence pointing in that direction, which probably meant that it was exactly what they were doing.

The more she looked through the files, the more she felt overwhelmed, felt that she couldn't do this without Meeks' help. And this feeling gave her a sense of loneliness, and she didn't want to be alone.

Anna retrieved her cell phone from the nightstand and scrolled down her list of contacts until Klein's name highlighted.

This would be the first time she called him, or anyone for that matter, to see if he'd just like to spend some time with her. If he would just like to talk to her. If he would just be there.

Chapter 6

Dedham High School still used actual bells to signal the start of the day, class's end, and the beginning of the next period. A little round iron bell, fire-engine red, one hanging in every hall of the building. When the school had been painted two years ago, the painters hadn't touched up the bells, so there were chips in the paint, they were dusty on the outside, and each month, the clanking sound of metal on metal seemed to dull, declining like an unused battery in a cold pantry. For sixty years, they'd been neglected while watching over generations of Boston's youth clambering through the halls, overcoming freshman anxiety, bullies giving everyone a hard time. When its doors opened, guys wore black leather jackets, t-shirts, and jeans, doing their best to impersonate James Dean. They weren't rebels, but they wanted to be. And the girls, poodle skirts for some, others just dressed like their mothers, hoping that they'd get married someday soon, have children, buy that house in the suburbs and be a homemaker, and then get bored and unhappy and realize that the American dream might not be all it's cracked up to be, might not carry those smiles and bliss found on Rockwell's covers of the *Saturday Evening Post*. And from there, it evolved and devolved— dresses declined, hippies and tie-dye grew, big hair came along with brightly colored clothes and plastic, kids' pants started falling off even though they wore belts, clothes became baggy and then tight again, each kid his own personal style. Soon, those rebels went away, and the bullied became the bullies for a day, shooting up schools and killing anyone who happened to be in the way. That was when the metal detectors went up and the budget opened several slots for full-time security officers. And now, at Dedham High School, the students dressed alike—khaki bottoms and white tops, see-through plastic backpacks, and no baggy clothes, no long or oversized coats, and no allowance for individuality. Now, they all looked the same, blended together like apples in a grocery store.

Lilly was okay with that. She wouldn't have fit in anyway even if she could wear what she wanted, how she wanted, and when she wanted. It made being invisible a little easier, just another piece of hay in the haystack, no needles or gemstones. She sat in first period: History. Ms. Knowles had a timeline brought up on the SMARTboard, different moments during the 1300s, focusing on the Bubonic Plague, which wiped out a third of Europe's population. But Lilly hadn't known that it started in Asia. She'd only read about the Plague happening in London and Paris, not that it popped up all over Central Asia and made its way to Europe via trade, the Silk Road where fleas hitched rides on the caravans and the furs and silk and horses that were part of those caravans. How at Kaffa, Genoa's trade hub, Mongols catapulted infected bodies over the city walls, spreading it further as it made its way on the trade ships. On to Messina, Sicily, Venice, and Marseille, and then to Paris and London, Scandinavia, until it reached full circle back to Kaffa. In five years, over twenty million people dead.

Lilly wanted to feel sad, but she didn't. It didn't seem real. It sounded like something in a fiction book, too far removed. She didn't even like a composer from the 1300s. And that's as much attention as she could give to first period. Ms. Knowles hadn't even started speaking yet.

Lilly sat in the middle of the room, and her attention shifted to Kevin Kaiser. She thought it was stupid that his friends called him Keyser Söze. Lilly had watched about a half hour of that movie with her mother before going to her room and practicing her violin. That had been two years ago. Mr. Thompson had given her Handel's *Violin Sonata*, telling her to just keep trying to get it right, even though she never did while practicing on her own. And maybe that was the problem, she thought. She couldn't do anything on her own. She needed guidance and someone to hold her hand. Then why did it feel so good to be alone? In her room with her violin. In the classroom now, alone with her thoughts. Talking to Kevin Kaiser, listening to his adjusting voice, one moment rhythmic and the next a high-pitched, squeaky falsetto like playing the wrong note on the violin, but she thought it was cute even though he'd blush practically every time it happened. Laughing with him and seeing his braced smile reflect light like jewelry does in a store case. Holding hands with him while walking to second period. She loved walking behind him in the hallway after gym class. His shirt would cling to his back, and his hair would be messy—frills mixed with damp and clumpy streaks as if he'd been caught in the rain. But they were months into the school year now, and he hadn't even looked in her direction, hadn't even accidentally made eye contact with her with his nutmeg eyes. Couldn't see the strand of hay for the hay bale.

"Okay, class…"

There she went, starting her lecture on the Black Death. Lilly sighed and tried to pay attention, hoped Ms. Knowles' voice would shift an octave or two to emphasize the moment that she found to be significant, a moment that changed history, or even a moment that just didn't matter. But by the end of class, when the ear-piercing cry of the bell filled the empty halls, Lilly still had an uninspired blank sheet of notebook paper on her desk staring back at her and Ms. Knowles reading off the line that was third from the bottom, about how the Mongols were defeated and the Silk Road was not safe anymore—a century of history told in less than an hour and with the same tone.

Lilly got up and slung her backpack over her shoulder and picked up her violin case. On her way out of class, she found herself shoulder to shoulder with Kevin Kaiser, both approaching the doorway at the same speed. She knew that they couldn't fit through the doorway together and were on their way to what Mr. Thompson would call an awkward moment—should she slow down and let him through or keep going and see if he even noticed her and would be polite enough to let her through first? Of course, they could try to go through together, press themselves against each other. Was that his plan? An excuse to feel her. Was he finally going to reveal that he knew about all of her watching, all of her desire for him, and all of her notes she'd taken in her journal about the way he walked and how she wanted to walk with him, the way he carried on a conversation at the cafeteria table at lunch and how she hoped to be sitting next to him, being part of that discussion. The thought made her cheeks burn as if she'd just stepped a foot too close to a campfire. But another feeling, something in her stomach, tingly. Not like Christmas morning. Not like getting lost in Rachmaninov. This was something different. It, too, felt good. It, too, made her heartbeat thump in her ears. Five paces away stood the open doorway. Now four. Three. Whatever was going to happen would have to happen now. The agonizing months of hope were now going to be rewarded. The majority of the class was behind them. Toby Marcum and Amanda Crane had just gone through the doorway in that order. So they were at the front. Most of the class would see the outcome, the magical moment like a scene from a romance film that her mother liked to watch…or, Jesus Christ, would she be humiliated like a character from one of those 80s high-school films? Molly Ringwald, Patrick Dempsey—who her mother now watched play a doctor, or the redheaded boy from *Weird Science* whose name always escaped her. Where did she fit? Two paces. It was going to be the former, she now knew. They were going to try and go through together. He hadn't sped up or slowed down. She would feel him, and him her. One pace. And that's not what happened.

When Kevin Kaiser hopped forward and slipped out the door in front of her, none of the students behind her snickered. None of them made fun of her. None of them showed any acknowledgement of what had just occurred. Yet, it was an experience that she would never forget. Blatantly rejected in front of a crowd, but the crowd didn't boo. They didn't even see her—the opposite of what Mr. Thompson had told her about performing on stage: "They can see you, but you can't see them. All you see are lights and blackness. You're up there all alone."

If she had been a character in one of those 80s films, she'd be crying, but this was real life. She tightened her grip on the violin case, the plastic handle digging into her palm, the dull pain welcoming like an opening valve spilling the invisible tingly substance that had filled her stomach onto the floor. And by that time she was in the hallway, alone in a crowd, cheeks cool again, heartbeat normal. It seemed to work that way. Quick jolt of something, and then back to normal. Like when her father died. After the funeral, she had gone back to her routine. Music. And trying to figure out the story about the woman upstairs who seemed as invisible as she was.

Lilly's second-period teacher, Mr. Warren, handed her a note when she walked in, instructing her to go to Mr. Thompson's classroom. It was Mr. Thompson's planning period, so there were no students in the room. And it was a strange room meant for classroom instruction, so there was a portion with desks in clumps in front of a blackboard on wheels at the far side of the room; three-tier risers in the middle of the room in the shape of a semi-circle, a grand piano, shiny and black, in the center; and a stage that used to be a place to perform plays and concerts, but now served as only a place for the band to practice or for the drama class to rehearse. The floor was carpeted, hiding where theatre seats were once bolted to the cement floor, three deep levels spanning back to a wall of concrete block, slanted like the side of a triangle, the apex in the corner of the room hidden by a row of glass-front oak cases filled with plaques, pennants, and tall trophies, each bearing the year of success, years that Lilly only knew about through books and movies, as if music at Dedham High School had died after 1978. And covering massive rectangles on that wall were pictures of those boys and girls, forever staring down at the next generation, daring them to be winners. Showing them that they, too, could be immortalized, high up on that concrete wall, each year their images fading from the constant light, their white smiles turning speckled and brown from another layer of dust. How many years would it be before they disappeared completely, blending in with the white, sterile walls?

"Lilly," said Mr. Thompson, sitting at his metal desk next to the blackboard. "Come on over."

"Are we not meeting after school today?" she asked, sitting across from him in an uncomfortable plastic chair. She could hear the strands of static electricity ripping between the chair and her white cotton shirt when she leaned forward to adjust herself. As if afraid, her shirt then gripped her back, swallowing every pocket of air as if vacuum-sealed. And she hated that manacled feeling. She hated the feeling of strands of her long, black hair pulling away from the pack to cling to the back of the chair even more.

"No, we can't meet today." He breathed in as if he'd been under water for a minute and stared down at his bare desk.

"So we're going to practice now instead?" Lilly bent to her right toward her violin case.

"No, no. I..."

Lilly sat upright again. He was acting strange, staring at his desk with his mouth half open. Did she do something wrong? Had she upset him? He'd seemed fine two days ago when they finished practicing. 'Another big step forward today, Lilly,' he'd said. 'The folks at Juilliard will be fools not to accept you.' But he said things like that all the time. 'You're the best student I've ever had, that this school has ever seen,' he'd said. 'One day, you'll make Hahn and Chang jealous,' he'd said, but she didn't believe that. 'One day, I'll see you playing as part of the Boston Symphony Orchestra.' That was more believable. He usually started his compliments with 'one day.' Where did that put her now? What if, every time someone spoke of her, it began with 'one day'? Some year, that would change to 'She could have been...' and Lilly couldn't bear for that to happen.

Mr. Thompson finally looked at her. "How do you feel when you play on your own? At your house, in your room?"

He put his hand to his forehead and massaged his skin, an action she usually associated with someone who had a headache. Is that all it was? A bad headache? Maybe a migraine? She'd never had a migraine, but commercials had taught her that any noise, any light, anything except rest made the pain worse, even adding to its torture nausea.

In almost a whisper, she replied, "I feel okay." She let herself smile. "Pretty good actually. My room's a good place to play, especially at night since Mom doesn't get home until late. I think I'm more inspired at night." She hadn't told Mr. Thompson about the woman upstairs. It was her little secret, not meant to be shared. Didn't everyone have something they didn't want to tell anyone else? Something that belonged to them, and them alone?

"That's good," he said. "The greats always have a way of teaching themselves. Knowing themselves." He stopped massaging his forehead and put his hands together atop his desk.

"What do you mean, 'knowing themselves'?"

"When you know yourself, you'll know what I mean."

He often did that, too. Said things that didn't have much of a foundation. He called it philosophy, and told her to read some of it, and to keep reading and rereading it even when it didn't make sense. That it would enrich her music and enrich her soul. And that an enriched soul would make her unique. Lilly believed him, but she hadn't read any philosophy yet. That could happen tomorrow or the next day. Today was for music. For Kevin Kaiser. For the woman upstairs.

But something else he had just said didn't make sense. The greats teaching themselves...? Who was he talking about? The greats had mentors. Hahn had Jascha Brodsky and Brodsky had Eugene Ysaÿe and Ysaÿe had his father and Massart and Vieuxtemps and on and on... A line of legendary musicians, composers, geniuses. The legends worked with legends. Mr. Thompson never spoke of his mentor, if he had one. He wasn't a legend. So, again, what did that make her? Is that why he was pushing for Juilliard so much? For her to meet her mentor? She thought it would be better not to bring up this inconsistency, but she couldn't help herself. The day had already begun badly, so why not push this more than she usually pushed. Get an answer to one of her many questions rather than just accepting what she was told. No more of living so deeply in her head and letting others just have their way.

"But the greats didn't teach themselves," she said in a voice louder than she'd meant to, in a condescending tone that came out without her brain's permission. But it felt good, this new feeling. It felt liberating.

Mr. Thompson's eyes widened and then turned toward the high ceiling. His chair squeaked as he leaned back, mouth half open again. When he did this, Lilly noticed for the first time in the conversation that he hadn't shaved in what had to be a few days. And that wasn't like him. His skin usually shined, usually glowed a bit, but today it seemed to absorb the light, making his deep wrinkles black and weary.

"Lilly, I didn't mean forever." He straightened himself again. "I just meant..." He sighed and then opened the top desk drawer, withdrew a large manila envelope, and gently laid it on the table.

"What's that?" Lilly realized that her heart was beating in her ear again, that dull thump on either side of her head. She could even feel it in her right temple, like little bubbles growing and then popping underneath her skin.

"I have all of the sheet music that you'll need here. All of the forms and information sheets for Juilliard. Everything you'll need, Lilly." He slid the folder in her direction. "I want you to go over all of it with your mother this weekend."

Why was he doing this now? She already had much of the sheet music in her bedroom. And her mother, god damn it, she was still a basket case. She wouldn't understand any of this stuff. He was supposed to do it. Mr. Thompson said that he would talk to her and convince her how talented she was and how important Juilliard would be to her future. Her mother wouldn't listen to her! Lilly didn't even know what to say. Didn't know the details and plans. Mr. Thompson was taking care of all that. He had everything planned out from transportation to the audition to living and travel arrangements once she was accepted...all the way to the high school she'd attend and the classes she'd take at that high school. He'd made promises. Promises that she would be great and that he would help her every step of the way. And to suddenly push it to her. Suddenly give her all of those responsibilities. Why? It didn't make sense.

"Calm down, Lilly. It'll be okay."

It took her a second to register how Mr. Thompson knew that she was worried. She hadn't spoken those thoughts. It was her forehead, layered with sweat as if she'd just stepped into a sauna. Lilly wiped the sweat away with her sleeve and tried to swallow, but her mouth was too dry and her attempt almost made her start coughing.

"Really, it'll be okay," he said.

He was looking into her eyes now. The Mr. Thompson of two days ago at practice had returned. There was a little life in his cheeks now, though still not their usual, lively hue. It was almost like seeing someone not wear makeup for the first time—a double-look to make sure it was who you thought it was, and then a somewhat frightening feeling that you never verbalized. Another secret that you kept to yourself, but knew you weren't the only one who thought it.

"I have to go away, Lilly. You can do this on your own. I

promise you can."

She had to say something. She couldn't just sit there, sweating, silent, anxious, letting him throw her away like this. There was fear there, too. She couldn't do this without him. But maybe that feeling in her chest wasn't fear. Fear didn't hurt like that. This pain, like a hundred carpenter bees slowly gnawing away at her breastbone, burrowing in her hollowed-out body, this pain was anger. *It* had started when Mr. Thompson lied about the greats teaching themselves, *it* told her that *it* was there when she rebuked him, and now *it* had taken control, and there was nothing she could do about it.

Mr. Thompson was abandoning her. "You motherfucker—"

"Lilly Rebeck," he said as if he was her father. And that was all he said. All he could say.

"I don't need your stupid help," she let out as she got to her feet. Lilly yanked her bag off the carpet and deposited a strap over her left shoulder. "You're cruel." She then yanked her violin case off the carpet with her right hand. "I trusted you." She grabbed the manila envelope with her left hand and realized that she was crying even though there was no lump in her throat. Maybe that was the difference between tears of sadness and tears of anger and abandonment. One choked you while the other occurred without much awareness. Lilly wanted to say more, but just turned and made a slow walk across the room, in front of the stage, under the gaze of the school's past winners, to the thick wooden door. She pushed the door open, and when she was halfway through, looked back at Mr. Thompson's desk at the other end of the room. Mr. Thompson was gone, and the room empty.

"I trusted you," she whispered, then left the room, the heavy door slamming with a metal-on-metal clank, a door she hoped she would never have to go through again.

Chapter 7

Alexei got out of his car and tried to run to his house, where the police officer stood in the open doorway, but his knees felt like they were coming apart, the sinews used up and the bones crumbling under his weight. He managed a few staggering steps before dropping to the frozen grass in his front yard, hunched over. In the background, he heard hard shoe soles on pavement, Hawthorne-like, grinding gravel like sandpaper crawling on wood.

"Sir, are you okay?" came a deep voice.

Alexei didn't look up. He couldn't face the officer. He didn't want to hear the rehearsed lines officers had to give when something like this happened. And everyone else's scripted lines. I'm very sorry for your loss. They're in a better place now. It was quick; at least they didn't suffer. What monster could have done this? We'll find them and bring them to justice if it's the last thing we do.

He knew that the past would catch up to him someday, that his life was cursed the same way his sister's had been back in Russia. Maybe it was still that way. Alexei didn't know because he didn't see or speak to his sister anymore.

Getting out of Petersburg and into America made family an option. And when he'd met Emily, then a graduate student at Queens College, at a café after settling in New York, it took two dates for him to figure out that she was the one. That he wanted to start a life with her, a new life. But he didn't tell her that right away. He wanted her to make some mention of it, and she did three months later.

"Will you move to Boston with me after I graduate next semester?" she asked over dinner at his apartment.

"And what will your parents think of you dating a foreigner and bringing him home?"

64

She laughed at this. "When they see how happy you make me, where you're from won't matter."

They were eating over candlelight, and Alexei knew how light from a flame erased blemishes, how it made flesh look so perfect. And how it would flicker, allowing shadows to hide her for a moment, like a cruel game. She had her black hair down that night, resting on her shoulders, curving its way down her cheeks, one collected strand bending in too far and getting in her line of sight, and she would keep brushing it aside, even when he told her how pretty it was when her hair did that.

And, so, even though he hadn't planned to do it that way, even though he hadn't planned to do it that night, he said to her, without the candle flickering once, "What if you were bringing home a foreigner as your husband instead?"

She didn't respond right away, just sat there, lips parted just enough to take in air, eyes wide open, reflecting the shifting candle flame. "Alexei…"

Before she could get the next word out, he was out of his chair and next to hers, on a knee. Her eyes followed his.

"I want you to be my wife. Marry me, Emily."

And she did. And they moved to Boston. And her family loved him. She loved him. They had their children. They had their home. And with the help of his father-in-law, who got Alexei connected with people at MIT, he had a career. The American dream. And, now, that dream had shifted. The past had caught up with him, crept in, and killed that dream.

"Sir." The officer was kneeling by him now. "Do you live here?"

His weeping was silent. He knew who did this, and he would get revenge, even if he had to call on his sister for help. She knew what it was like to lose loved ones. She knew what it took to take revenge.

"Alexei," came a woman's voice.

It didn't register immediately. But when it came a second

time, he looked up and saw Emily.

"Ma'am, you know—"

"It's my husband." By the time she had said this, she was standing by him, then helping him up. "What's going on, Alexei?"

He looked at her, and she looked as beautiful as she had that night in his apartment. Her skin reflected blue and then red and then blue and red again as if they were at a techno club. Alexei pulled her to him and held her tightly, taking in a deep breath, the scent of her jasmine perfume filling his head and calming him like warm milk to a crying baby.

"The kids…?"

"They're fine, Alexei. In their bedrooms. Just a little scared."

She let him go, then cupped her palms under his chin, pressing lightly on his cheeks with her thin but strong fingers. Her dark eyes met his, and like a therapist might do, she said, "Everything's okay. We're all okay."

He cleared his throat, a quivering smile spreading across his face. "What happened?" He wiped tears from his face with his shirtsleeve after Emily dropped her hands.

"A brick through the door window this time," she whispered, then let out a deep breath, the white fog obscuring her amber eyes for a moment as she looked up at the moon.

"It's probably kids, high-schoolers," the officer said. "In a neighborhood like this, I don't see it escalating to anything more serious—"

"This is the fourth time something's happened." His voice had regained its guttural force and control. "And I don't care what you don't see. It *has* escalated."

"Alexei—"

"It's gone from spray paint to a brick through my fucking door." It felt good letting this out. He'd been constricted too much today, with the Vermont state trooper, Hawthorne, and that son of a bitch Brother.

"Calm down, sir. We're here to help," he said, as if reading lines from a movie script.

Alexei pulled Emily to him gently, his arm around her shoulder and keeping her close. She leaned into him, then turned to slide her arms around his body, hugging him tightly, laying her head on his chest. The coconut scent of her conditioner filling Alexei's nostrils now, but he kept his fierce gaze on the officer.

By now, the other officer had come out of the house and was standing with them. She was a tall woman with her hair up and under her hat. A boxer's face, rough and stony. But there was something feminine there, in the eyes.

"We have a lot of patrols in this neighborhood," the female officer said. "The only recommendation I can give is to put in a more advanced security system. Looks like you have ADT, and, frankly, they suck. Might try Ironclad. Maybe put a fence up in the front yard."

She had a soft voice, not what Alexei had anticipated, and her candor gave him ease because she was right. Why not get a better security system, one with a camera, especially a camera that had nightshot? And a fence? That wasn't too expensive, a few thousand dollars. He realized that they were alike, him and the female officer. She was calm and treated him with the attitude that would settle him, that would appease his hostility the way that he had tried to do with the state trooper earlier in order to prevent suspicion. And they were both successful. So in response, Alexei nodded and unclenched his teeth.

He looked down at Emily now, and she up to him. A glimmer of a smile, and he kissed her lips briefly.

"Anything else happens, you be sure and call us," the female officer said.

"Thank you," said Emily, turning around now, nodding and pressing her lips together.

After Alexei had affixed a piece of thin plywood over the broken pane, and after he had kissed his children goodnight, he asked Emily how she felt about living somewhere else, somewhere far away from Boston. Seattle maybe. Or live in a small town in the Rockies, close to Denver or Salt Lake City.

"This will pass, Alexei. This only seems to happen when stories about those spies come up."

"That was over six months ago when that happened," he said.

"Well, this morning's *Globe* ran a story about Bezrukov getting hired by Rosneft. Pretty high position."

"So every time there's a story about a Russian doing something, we can expect vandals."

"It'll pass, Alexei."

"Emily, we need to move," he said, knowing that it wouldn't happen. That Boston was their home.

"Why were you crying in the front yard?"

He knew this question was coming, and he knew that he could not tell her the truth. She wouldn't understand. She would call the entire marriage one big lie and file for a divorce. She'd never see him again, and he'd never see his children again. She only knew that he was from Russia but an American citizen. His accent gave that away. He'd told her that he was a student back home and came to the States to further his education and make a new life out of Communist Russia. Having told her that his time there was too hard to talk about, she didn't ask questions and he didn't give her any more information. So, Alexei's only option here was to deflect the question, like he'd done with the trooper.

"It's been a really long day, my love. Let's go to bed and talk in the morning."

"Don't do that," she said, tilting her head as if scolding Victor. "We've always been open and honest with each other." She got up from the sofa and looked out the window, into the backyard, or maybe just stared at her reflection in the glass pane.

Dammit. She knew him too well. He couldn't lie to her. He could keep things from her, hide things away, but he couldn't lie. It would show up on his face, in his voice, and she would know.

But maybe he could tell her part of the truth and she wouldn't keep probing. But it was a can of worms he would be opening.

"I just thought something really bad had happened. Listening to the news too much, that's all."

Emily turned around now and sat on his lap. She was still a tiny thing, had worked off both pregnancies a few months after each birth. Hair a few inches shorter these days. A hint or two by her eyes and mouth where wrinkles would set in, in the coming years, but for now her skin was still smooth, still gleamed with life and energy and youth.

She smiled at him, lips only, and then buried her face in his neck, kissing him while working her arms around his back. "We just need you." And she kissed him again, this time his ear. "Nothing bad's going to happen as long as you're here."

He wasn't so sure of that, but her scent, her natural oils mixing with the jasmine perfume, had a way of clearing his mind of worry, of responsibility, of Brother. And he closed his eyes.

When her warm breath met the skin behind his ear, it seemed to travel across every pore, waking tiny hairs on his back, on his groin, on his legs. He kissed her cheek, running his hands up her back and through her straight hair. Grabbing her hair and pulling, exposing her neck, he traced an invisible pattern there with his lips. And when he heard her moan, he traced another pattern and then pulled her closer and kissed her parted lips.

He could feel her hands on him, under his sweater, unbuttoning his pants, taking down his zipper. His hands were under her blouse now, skin feverish.

"Is something wrong?" she whispered, breaking the moment.

Alexei opened his eyes, as if awakened from a dream or snapping out of a trance. There was nothing wrong. The mood was perfect. She was perfect. And then he realized what she meant. He looked down at his shriveled, pathetic member resting in her hand. He'd never had trouble down there before. Jesus Christ, was he impotent now? The image of a smiling old man from the Viagra commercial popped in his head, but he forced it out.

"No, I don't know."

She let him go and stood up, and he put himself back in his pants and zipped up, joining her.

"Emily, I...I don't know. Maybe I'm just tired or stressed out." God damn that Chechen.

"That's never happened before, Alexei." She pulled her lips tight, then started to frown. "You still find me—"

"Yes, of course...Emily. It...it's not you. I've just had a hell-of-a-day." He knew she would be crying in the next few seconds, so he reached out for her just as her chin started to quiver and held her.

"There's something..." she started to say, but her voice cracked.

"It's all right, honey. I'm not going anywhere."

"I'm scared, Alexei." She pulled away from him gently so she could look into his blue eyes as she spoke.

It had been a short cry, the effects still lingering in the smeared mascara under her eyes. There was something so stunning about that look. Only, he imagined that it was caused by the rain, like the night he'd proposed to her, and they'd walked to Athabaska's to celebrate. The rain had fallen halfway back to the apartment, and when they'd gotten inside, her eyes looked just as they did now. And he'd made love to her then. He had been able to then.

"I didn't want to tell you, but I can't keep it from you."

"Emily—"

"There was a rubber band around the brick that broke the window." She was breathing hard now, forehead wrinkled, eyebrows raised. "Holding a piece of paper."

Alexei could see her brown eyes welling up with tears again, and he wanted to comfort her, but he knew he couldn't right now. She had to finish telling him the story. Telling him what was written on that paper, and he knew better than to rush her. If he did that, she'd not be able to get it out.

"So cruel," she said. "Why do they have to be so damn cruel?" She turned away from him and went into the kitchen.

"Emily?" He followed her. When he got to the doorway, she was at the kitchen table opening her purse, a few tears falling on the wood.

She pulled out a piece of wide-ruled notebook paper, folded and crinkled. As she walked back to him, paper held out for him to take, she said, "I can't speak it, I'm sorry. You'll have to read it yourself."

When he took it, her hand went to her mouth, covering her thin lips.

"After the letter, after seeing you on the ground out front and then talking about moving..." She lowered herself to the floor, back against the wall and sliding down, and bowed her head, eyes closed. "It's just too much."

Alexei stepped toward her.

"Please just read it first," she said without looking at him.

So he did. He unfolded the paper, red granules falling to the tiles at his feet as he did so. And when it was open, he knew why Emily was so frightened, so upset. The previous incidents were toward him, calling him a Commie, ordering him to go home to Russia, wordplay and misspelling by calling him KGB—Kunt Grown Bastard, which seemed to point towards middle-school kids or possibly high-school kids as the culprits because it didn't make sense and just didn't sound like something an adult, especially a motivated and risk-taking adult would say. But this was different. This was directed at her, his wife. And more disturbing, it was directed at their children.

In a messy handwriting, black Sharpie marker it seemed, was scrawled *Russian-Loving Bitch Need American Dick. Commie Children Must Die. We're Watching U. Leave or Pay the Price.*

Alexei calmly folded the note and put it in his pocket. He wanted to be angry, but the sight of Emily sitting on the floor, knees up, face buried in her hands took his full attention.

"Sweetheart," he said, by her side in one quick motion, "we're going to be okay. I'm going to make sure that we're okay."

She looked at him, a concerned smile spread across her lips. "I didn't show that to the police. I couldn't bear someone else reading it. It's just kids, like they say. And we're going to be alright."

"Yes, sweetheart," he said, reaching his hands out and helping Emily up. "We're going to be just fine." He held her tight. "It's good that you didn't show this to the police. It's none of their business."

"Maybe we should show it to them. Was it stupid of me to hide it?"

Part of him wanted to laugh at this, hiding something so small when he was hiding information that could get him life in prison, information that could turn his family against him, surprise them, and make them afraid to trust anyone. The thought of his family being killed still haunted him, and he let those emotions flavor his response: "It wasn't stupid at all. You were protecting us."

"We have to protect each other, be there for each other no matter what."

"We can only rely on each other. Trust each other," he said, mimicking her style.

Emily let go of him and sat back down. As she looked up at him, the reflection of the lamplight made her eyes almost sparkle. So beautiful.

"I've always trusted you, Alexei." She took his hand and pulled him down to the couch. "Have you always trusted me?"

"I wouldn't have asked you to be my wife if I didn't trust you."

"You really worried me earlier, in the front yard. I've never seen you like that before."

Her gaze was burning a hole in his eaten-away conscience.

72

"I'm just—"

"Something more is going on, Alexei." She gripped his hand tightly now. "Tell me that you still love me and want to be with us. Tell me there's no one else."

"Emily." He scooted closer to her, noticing her eyes glistening now, slowly pooling at the bottom again. "You, Victor, and Nina are my life." It was his turn to put his hands to her cheeks. "I was overcome earlier." He had to give a partial truth now. "All I saw were police, flashing lights. I thought something had happened to you." He forced his eyes to well up now, something he'd been taught to do in Russia as part of his job—it worked well to ease others and give him credibility, to help lure them to their interrogation or worse. And it worked.

Emily smiled. "I know that you love us. You're our lives, too, you know? We have to take care of you, too."

She kissed him and then got up and headed to the bedroom. And when they were in bed together, he said to her, "I'll get things where they need to be in the morning."

Chapter 8

3 December 2010. 6:11am. Anna Stern's Apartment.

Anna opened her eyes and saw Klein sleeping as the morning sun streamed in through her bedroom window. She realized that it was the first time she had seen him in daylight. They'd met about six months ago at Paddy's, Anna just having closed a year-long case that put ten Russian spies in jail. He'd bought her a drink and hadn't asked her to dance. A quick introduction, a finishing of drinks, and, as if he had access to her mind, an invitation to go for a walk, which took them to her place. He made love to her three times that night, each time a few minutes longer than the previous. And when they were through, an exchange of cellphone numbers and a kiss goodbye. No questions. No expectations. No drama.

The sunlight revealed that his skin wasn't perfect, a few red bumps underneath a close-shaved beard. A scar on his left cheek a few inches long. And she could see a few tiny flakes of dandruff hiding in his chestnut hair. Klein didn't snore. He didn't move about in his sleep. But he did dream, she knew. The hazel orbs under his eyelids had been busy last night, and they were busy right now. She didn't wonder what he was dreaming, just enjoyed that he was still there.

Anna got out of bed without shaking the latex mattress or pulling the goose-down comforter so that she would not wake Klein. The carpet tickled her feet, as it did each time she got out of bed. She never understood how the bed could make her feet so vulnerable, so sensitive. Any other time they were dull, heavy, not renewed as the sheets seemed to make them. And she liked that feeling, the only sensation that made her feel like a child again, even if it only lasted about a minute each morning.

Her bag was on the edge of dresser, and she slowly unzipped it, quietly moved a few files around, until she found her Glock 23, which she took out and carried with her out of the room, along with her jeans that were strewn across the floor. When the coffee was made and the eggs had been fried, she put two pieces of bread into the toaster, and in the toaster's reflection saw Klein walk into the kitchen and sit at a bar stool.

"Good morning," he said.

It took her a moment to respond. She'd felt fine making coffee and cooking, but to see him awake, hear him behind her, it ignited the lining of her stomach, made her relaxed heartbeat slam into the back of her breastbone. Anna turned around—an embarrassed nerdy thirteen-year-old with the school heartthrob. When she heard the sound of her own voice tell him good morning, too, she was brought back to reality. Thank God she hadn't giggled.

"I accidentally knocked over your bag while I was getting dressed," he said. "But I put it back on your dresser."

"Oh, no," she said quickly. "Did it—"

"Nothing fell out." And he laughed, quickly putting his hands out, palms up, saying, "What did I do to get the royal treatment? The only people who've made me breakfast are the ladies at the Waffle House."

"Maybe I'm trying to entice you to stay over more." She smiled at him.

He put his hands down. "What if I can't?"

"Can you?"

"You were pretty specific about our arrangement."

She couldn't argue with that. If ever he started to doze, she would tap his chest and remind him that he needed to leave. There were some nights she wouldn't even say goodbye. And then there were those strange nights when she would lock herself in the bathroom right after sex and, through the door, tell him to be on his way.

"Why are you still here now?"

"I don't know." He swallowed hard, his Adam's apple sliding

up his neck and disappearing for a few seconds, as if he was holding it there the way one might hold one's breath while anticipating the answer to an important question. It dropped again as his lips parted and he said, "I guess I'm still here because you didn't ask me to leave." He stood up now and went to her. "I like being here, Anna."

The morning had been a collection of emotions, the once freshly mown lawn replaced by a field of wild flowers. And now something else. Something that blurred those lines. She had expected Klein to give a simple yes. But he hadn't because she was blurred. She had needed her independence and had kept distance. Now, she needed a companion. It made her think of Johnnie, that she was betraying him somehow. But the man in front of her, hadn't she betrayed him, too? Treated him horribly; yet, he was still here. It had to be something more than a physical relationship through his eyes or else he would have disappeared a long time ago. If it had been only physical, he wouldn't have showed up at the hospital so many nights to bring her flowers or to just slip in and say hello and see how her wounds were healing. Even though he'd only stay for ten minutes at a time, he had been there and would have stayed much longer, she now knew, had she asked him to.

"I don't think I can ask you to leave anymore," she said.

"You might change that tune once you get to know me."

"Do I get the chance to find out?"

Before Klein could answer, the toaster clanked and two black squares jutted out of its slots, a hairline of smoke winding its way up to the window and then disappearing. They both looked at the toaster. And they both laughed.

"Yeah," he said. "I want to find out, too. I want to know all I can about you."

Klein's words made her not want to go into work, but she knew that that wasn't an option. But they ate breakfast together. Showered together. And then left her apartment together.

"Johnnie," said Anna in a low voice, the way she imagined a parent would try to wake a child.

When there was no response, she sat on his bed and put her hand on his cheek, repeating, "Johnnie."

This time, he opened his eyes. "Hey."

Seeing him smile like that at the sight of her made her happy and sad at the same time. His eyes looked dry, and she could see how his pupils seemed to sit atop the whites of his eyes like designer contacts.

"Do you remember what you told me that night we were going after Aziz? We'd just—"

"Congratulations, Anna..."

And Johnnie kept things light that way for another ten minutes, even having Anna show him her new badge, before asking her what baggage came with the promotion.

"He opened up the Russian case again."

"And?"

"My team's reviewing the files. It's going to take some time. They're all rookies. Part of me feels like a rookie getting back into this case. I almost feel like I'm not ready to be back, but the other part of me can't just sit and do nothing. I think we'll start at Harvard—"

"MIT," he said. "The ones that we arrested had already gotten into Harvard, and they were working on several places at MIT. Remember? If I were you, that's where I'd start. They've had seven months of us keeping our eyes off them. There's no telling how many there are now. I had started doing some digging on my own before this," he shook his head, "happened."

She knew that he wanted to point to the gunshot wound that had paralyzed him.

"Why didn't you tell me? I could have helped." A meaningless question right now, and she realized it immediately. "Forget I said that. Over forty thousand Russians in Boston—"

"Don't forget that they don't have to be Russian. With all the heat from the public, they're probably not Russian."

Hearing Johnnie speak about her case was comforting. His instincts were usually solid. She didn't feel like she could do this on her own. She needed him. Needed to know what he had uncovered when he'd gone solo on the case.

"How much do you know, Johnnie? Am I in over my head trying to close this case with three rookies?"

"Way over your head."

"If it's that big, then why didn't you say anything? Why didn't you tell me?"

"Because I didn't have all the facts, Anna. A few leads." He started to cough.

"We don't have to talk about this stuff," she said. They usually talked about other things when she'd visit. The past. How in childhood, Johnnie used to be a bully. How he would have been voted the kid to least likely succeed and most likely to live his adult years in a prison if that had been a yearbook category. They talked about how she had been bred for this line of work, her father a thirty-five-year veteran of the Bureau. How she wished she could have met her mother, who had died eleven minutes after Anna had been born.

And here she sat, working on the same thing her father had worked on for so many years and so many years ago. The only difference was the title. Back then, it was the Cold War. Today...today, she didn't know what to call it.

"I don't mind talking about it," he said. "Makes me feel useful. Gives me something to look forward to."

As much as she wanted to be happy about that, it made her feel like she was standing in a shadow. Talking to him about it took away her leadership and undermined her ability to handle a difficult case, to head a difficult case. The other part of her felt that she owed him this opportunity as a friend. More than a friend, she owed him her life. If she had been paying attention, she would have taken cover, and Meeks wouldn't have been in a position to get shot. And look at him. Paralyzed, just as she felt now. Two paths before her, and she had to take one.

"Well," she said, "at least it doesn't have to take up all of our time."

"That's all I have anymore, Anna." He gazed at the tiles on the ceiling. "Nothing I can do about that."

He was right. He would never not be a cop. Once it got in your blood, it stayed like an incurable disease. Anna had seen it with her father. The Bureau threw him a large retirement party. Open bar with top-shelf liquor, of which her father had none. A final toast at the end of the evening, Dom Pérignon, of which her father had none. An oak plaque with a brass engraved plate with his name on it, giving the dates of his service and excellence, which found a home at the dump next garbage day.

And this disease got worse in civilian life. Going in each day, working the case, following leads, interrogating witnesses and suspects, reading through crime-scene reports, forensic data, even the mundane task of writing a report, it all worked to keep the disease under control, to keep the symptoms at bay. When her father retired, which she later learned was not his choice, his only solace was whiskey or any other caramel-colored drink eighty proof or above, though that solace didn't last long.

Anna had been twenty-five years old when he died, just getting settled in to her Bureau job. He had used a .38 special. She hadn't told anyone, not even Johnnie Meeks, that that same gun was nestled in her ankle holster, one chamber empty.

So when Johnnie said that it was all he had, Anna understood what he meant probably more than Johnnie Meeks himself.

"So how much manpower and surveillance should I devote to MIT?"

He turned his head toward her again, his eyes not looking as dry as before, but healthy and moist. "Half," he said. "Review the security tapes. Find out who has been there at odd hours by checking the logs—everyone has a passkey to get in—and run the names through the database. Set up surveillance of the labs, the entrances, and research facilities. It won't take long to start narrowing that down based on what you see."

"And the other half?" She almost let out a sigh, knowing that when Meeks said half, he meant half the office, not half of her small group. What he was talking about required twenty agents, not two.

"I don't know. Use your best judgment."

He always did that. He tried to make her feel like they were each taking half the responsibility, making half the decisions, but in the end, he'd always be the one that was right. The other half of the decisions being based on his instincts. She wasn't a bad agent, but she knew that Johnnie was better.

"MIT's a big place. Those few facts you said you have…"

"Might be dead ends. But look in the sciences. Not the major, high-profile stuff either like nuclear. The stuff that doesn't seem to be dangerous."

"So look in—"

"I want you to go to my apartment. You know my safe combination. It's a start. I didn't get very far because of our open cases. The Aziz case. I can't remember everything in the files, but they should point you in the right direction and cross a few places off the list."

All she could do was nod. The case itself had gone to the back of her mind rather quickly, and she couldn't help thinking about how things were before the shooting. How Johnnie deserved this promotion so much more.

"Do you really think I'm cut out to be a supervisor?" she asked. It wasn't the direction she really wanted to go with the conversation, but she couldn't keep it bottled up any longer.

"Do you?"

Hesitating, she said, "I don't know."

"You know the case just as well as I do, Anna. If I hadn't mentioned MIT, you would have realized it once you got back into the file. And if I know you like I think I do, you'd have found my personal files on this case at my apartment soon enough without my telling you about them."

"You ever think that you have too much faith in me?"

"Only when you doubt yourself."

"And why do you think I doubt myself, Johnnie?"

He started to answer, but she cut him off.

"You never let me take one step ahead. You're always there, making sure I don't fall. Keeping an eye on me. Giving me credit in the reports that I really don't deserve. Protecting me from all the bad guys out there... If you don't let me do anything on my own, how am I ever going to be able to take care of myself when that time comes? I need to be able to do this on my own. You can't keep holding my hand, guiding me, and protecting me." She didn't mean for it to go that far, but it all just spilled out without her control. She appreciated him and she did love him, but she needed to be on her own. Johnnie's detective work on the side was needed information, but she couldn't keep relying on him, not now. If she couldn't prove to herself that she was worthy of this promotion, then it would show soon and she'd get demoted, embarrassed. It would turn out to be something terrible.

"I didn't protect you very well that night. It was you who saved my life, not the other way around. That was the night you proved that you're the better agent." A jittery smile now. "That you earned your promotion. You're different than you were before that night, too. The first time you came to see me, I saw that you had changed. For the better. Seems like you're not carrying so much anymore. That your father's ghost is off your shoulders. So, do I think you deserve to be supervisor? Definitely. You're gonna be great."

"John—"

"And I need you to leave now, Anna." Lips quivering.

"But—"

"Just go."

She could see the moisture building in his eyes and knew that he didn't want her to see him cry. She got up from the side of the bed and walked toward the door. When she reached the doorway, she heard him say, in a low and broken voice, "Maybe you shouldn't come back for a while." With her head lowered, she kept walking, down the hallway, down the three flights of steps, and out the side door to the parking lot, where the snow had erased the canvas of her world. A blank slate in front of her for which she would be the creator, the artist. It would be her painting now, not her father's image, not with Meeks' guiding hand, but hers alone...to revise and refine that blurriness to a sharper image.

Johnnie Meeks had released her out of love, she knew. And she felt it, as if the manacles had fallen off as she ran down the stairs. There, standing in the light from a lamppost, Anna tilted her head back, closed her eyes, and let the small snowflakes melt against her warm skin.

Chapter 9

Lilly walked the two miles home without taking a break, clenching the violin case so hard that her hand felt numb, as did her face and ears from the cold. Her footsteps were loud as she ran up the staircase. Before she reached the top, she heard her mother's voice.

"Shouldn't you be in school, young lady?"

She stopped and turned around, looking down at what was left of her mother. Not quite a skeleton, but getting dangerously close as her skin had started sagging even more under her eyes, seemingly detaching itself from her forehead and resting atop her eyebrows like a stack of pancakes. And she'd stopped wearing makeup, her skin ashen and jaundiced. Dull blonde hair pulled in a ponytail, creeks of grey now rivers.

Lilly realized that it had been almost a week since she'd seen her mother, and the first time in daylight in over a month. Second shift meant that Lilly was gone to school while her mother slept, and Lilly was usually in bed or getting ready for bed when her mother returned home. And the weekends, her mother stayed in her dark room, coming out sometime after seven at night, as if she was a vampire, except she didn't feed on blood, rather red wine or something stronger. Then, she'd sit like a zombie or more precisely like a lobotomy patient, staring at the television screen, hardly blinking. Sometimes, Lilly didn't know if her mother was even seeing the program on the television. Sometimes, it was as if she was in her own world, her own thoughts, far away from the house, far away from Boston, maybe even far away from the entire planet. And she stayed like that until she went to bed, the alcohol never seeming to change her state of mind.

Before Lilly could respond, her mother said, "Your nose is running."

"I had to leave school today, Mom." She put her things down at the top of the stairs and stepped halfway down the staircase before sitting down. "Mr. Thompson—"

"I'll be stopping at the grocery on my way home, so I'll be a little later than usual." Same dull and dead tone.

"Mom, I need to talk—"

"What, Lilly? What is it?" She was getting her coat now. Picking up her purse.

Lilly had read about coping after her father had died, a book Mr. Thompson had let her read, though she only read the section on grief. Her mother seemed to be going from the depression stage to the anger stage, out of order from how the book described it, but that's what she saw downstairs. Lilly had gone from denial, to crying about it, to acceptance in a relatively short time, but her mother was stuck and she couldn't figure out why. Maybe it was the music that helped Lilly through it all, the desire to keep moving forward to new things and a new life. Her mother was right where she wanted to be, had the house and job and family. Maybe Lilly would understand it all if music was taken away. But hadn't Mr. Thompson done that today?

"I just need to talk to you. It's really important."

"I don't have time, Lilly."

With those words, Kate walked out the front door, leaving her daughter alone on the staircase.

She didn't know how long she'd sat staring at the wooden floor at the foot of the stairs, but it was long enough to make her lower back start to ache. Long enough that she had to use the rails to help her up because her legs had grown stiff. When she walked into her bedroom, she thought that she was doing exactly what her mother was doing, imprisoning herself there, and it made her nauseous. She'd always thought that she'd taken after her father, able to handle the stress and anything that came her way with indifference and ease, but not today. She'd snapped at Mr. Thompson, walked away from him just like her mother had done her, and she let her mother make her feel invisible, worthless. Right now, she could only see her mother in her.

Everything had been so much different when her father was alive. Or maybe it hadn't been. Maybe her father just had a way of hiding that part of her mother from her. It had always been Dad listening to her play, encouraging her. It had always been Dad taking her places and talking to her. Mom was always in the background, doing her own thing. Worrying about herself. Lilly hadn't realized how isolated her mother had been for so many years even when her father had been there. Not that it mattered now. Nothing mattered now...except, of course, the woman upstairs. She was the only part of Lilly's life that hadn't turned against her, that hadn't been taken away. The morning sunlight reflecting off the key, creating a puddle of light on her ceiling. She snatched it off her nightstand and stared at it.

Was the woman home or had she left yet? Had it been the weekend, she'd be gone, but Lilly wasn't usually home at this time on weekdays. How would she find out? She took out her journal and turned to the portion set aside for the woman upstairs. Weekdays...weekdays. She would usually get home after dark, but that didn't help with what time she left on those days. All she had was her Thanksgiving break to go by. But didn't schedules get all messed up during the holidays? But if she was Russian, she wouldn't celebrate Thanksgiving... It didn't matter. She looked up November 24, 25, and 26, the days she had been out of school for the holiday. The woman had left at 10:30 each morning, returned at 7:15 each night. On November 27 and 28, the weekend, she left earlier, 8:45 each morning and returned later, 9:20 each night. And that was the typical weekend, give or take fifteen minutes. Each night, all seven days, around 10:00, she would put in a CD, listen to a track, and then play that track on her piano. That's what Lilly looked forward to each night. That was her regularly scheduled program. She didn't always play her violin, only when she recognized the composition. On those other nights, she just enjoyed listening, being a spectator. Listening to the woman play took her to another place, a place where her classmates didn't ignore her, where her mother was happy and her father alive, and where Lilly could smile. She couldn't remember the last time she'd smiled a real smile when music wasn't involved. So long ago.

And with that thought, she stood up and marched to the locked door that led upstairs. Without hesitating, she put the key in the lock and turned. When she opened the door, she called out, "Hello?" When there was no reply, she yelled, "Hello!" She would have asked if anyone was there, but it was too much like television. Like a cheesy horror movie her mother would have on.

The staircase was dim, bare walls on each side leading up to a sunlit landing, nail holes where Lester, the previous tenant, had hung pictures were scattered and unused, some holes looking as large as a quarter and darker where the plaster had cracked and fallen. Perfect nooks for spiders' homes. Lilly left the key in the door and slowly took one step at a time, the boards creaking beneath her feet. The steps were dusty on the left and right sides, but it looked as though the centers were clean. And that's where she stepped, not wanting to leave her shoeprint in the dust.

At the top of the staircase, Lilly scanned the main room. To the right was the kitchen. To the left, the rest of the apartment. It was much bigger than she remembered. She'd come with her father a few times to see Lester, to collect rent or fix a minor problem with the electric or plumbing. Lester had had a lot of stuff, pictures of him with different people, which Lilly presumed to be family, artwork, furniture, a television, plenty of items to fill the place up comfortably, to make it a home, to make Lilly want to reach out, take a closer look, and ask questions. And when she asked those questions, Lester would oblige with a long, enthralling story about some event in his life, usually something that had happened in his native Finland. Talking to her and her father as if they were in the woods sitting around a campfire. But this woman lived spare. It reminded Lilly of a motel room...no, of a model home. The furniture—a love seat and two chairs with a bare table in front and tall lamp in between—was small and white, and it didn't look very comfortable. No TV. No pictures on the walls or on shelves, only a few books that did not look like they'd been opened once. She knew model homes well. Weeks of walking through them while her mother and father decided whether it would be a place they'd call home, where they'd settle for a while. But they were all so bland, so weak were the walls. "Sterile," her father had called them. "No mature trees in the yard, the grass looks out of place, artificial. Even the god damn floors aren't really wood." It took Lilly a moment to realize what he'd been talking about. She'd knelt down and rubbed her hand over the floor, which looked like hard wood, but it was something else. To walk on it sounded like walking atop something hollow. The sound she might hear if she tapped her chest and there was no heart behind it. "Laminate flooring," the realtor called it. It drove them away from those newer suburbs and into Dedham, where they found an older home, plaster walls, sturdy and settled foundation, real wood, and history. But, somehow, the woman had made all of that go away. There was nothing interesting here, nothing to ask questions about, lifeless like the waiting room of a doctor's office.

As she moved deeper into the room, Lilly could see the piano through a doorway, and she went to it. It was a silver piano, a digital Yamaha with keys that matched a real piano. When Lilly pushed down on a few keys, she noticed that they were weighted, giving it a real piano feel. No noise came, of course, because the power was turned off. This had to be the room above her bedroom. The room where *she* played, the woman upstairs. Lilly sat on the piano bench, imagining herself being the woman, seeing what the woman saw each night when she'd play. Closed sheet music stared at her: *In Stiller Nacht,* a German piece she remembered from seventh grade. The choir had sung it at a school concert, both the German lyrics and the English translation. She didn't speak German, but preferred the German lyrics, preferred to feel the words and the energy and passion rather than be told what was happening, feel the chill from the haunting tones. Mr. Thompson had agreed. On a small table next to the piano was a Bose wave radio, and not three feet away, the window facing the street, the window Lilly knew had been open most nights.

Lilly stood and stared out the window, the parked cars along the street looking just a little bit smaller, the elm trees' branches a little thinner; she could see the top of the bird's nest from here, and more of the city lurking past the rooftops of other houses on the street, an endless black and grey sea of rooftops. Tall apartment buildings jutting up here and there. Downtown still too far away to see, not even a vague outline on the horizon. Lilly wasn't even sure if downtown was in that direction. But she understood why the woman had the piano in this room, situated so she'd sit with her right side facing the window, the way it would have been set up on a performance stage at a music hall. So that when she played with the window open, her audience was the whole world, a sea of listeners, the night shrouding that audience just like a spotlight in the eyes of the entertainer. And that's why she played every night. The world was there, waiting on her, demanding it. And Lilly, she stayed below in the orchestra pit, playing in the background, playing where no one could see her.

"Are you enjoying the view, Lilly?"

The voice came from behind her, stiffening every vein in her body. Her eyes adjusted, blurring the city beyond the window and focusing on the translucent reflection of the woman standing in the doorway to the piano room. And the woman knew her name. How could she know her name? Lilly tried to turn around, but her body didn't budge.

"Why are you in my apartment?"

There didn't seem to be any malice or anger in the woman's voice, which didn't help Lilly's paralysis. However, it was direct and its tone much deeper than her mother's. Lilly realized that this was the first time she'd ever heard the woman speak. If she hadn't known the woman was from Russia, there was nothing that would hide that fact now. Her accent was so thick, Lilly barely understood what the woman was asking.

Lilly slowly turned and faced the woman, whose arms were crossed at her chest, whose jawline pulsed as if she was grinding her teeth. Pale skin. A few more wrinkles that she'd not noticed through her bedroom window those many days and nights of watching the woman come and go. It was the first time she'd seen her eyes up close, blue and penetrating. And she was a foot taller, at least, than Lilly had imagined, towering over her like a double bass to a viola.

She parted her lips to respond, then closed them again. Lilly realized that her arms were pulled in tight against her chest and that her legs were shaky as if she'd had too much sugar. After a few more hour-long seconds, she tried again, and this time her voice worked. "I'm sorry." The words squeaked out; she barely heard them herself. It was another moment when she realized that real life was not like TV. The actors she'd seen her mother watching would start rambling in a situation like this, never seeming to take a breath until the person she was rambling to yelled for her to shut up and that it would be okay. That it was no big deal. She knew that wouldn't be the case this morning.

When the woman did not respond, but just kept staring at her with the same rigid expression, Lilly let out the only question that was on her mind. "How do you know my name?"

"You're the landlady's daughter," she shot back, "of course I know your name." She uncrossed her arms and put her hands on her hips. "Why are you here?"

"I don't know," she said, sounding frustrated, as if she'd answered the same question with the same answer a hundred times and was sick of it. She realized that her mouth was still open, not quite slack, but surprised. What was wrong with her? Where did these emotions come from? Just a few hours ago she'd called Mr. Thompson, her mentor, her teacher, her only real friend, the worst thing. And it came so suddenly. Not so long ago, she couldn't remember how many days, she tried to talk about her father, and a different emotion came charging up through her stomach and catching in her throat like a snare—the more she fought it, the tighter it became. This was different. With her father, she had no control...he was dead. With Mr. Thompson, he'd been the one to push her away. But this, this was all her doing. It was her idea to watch the woman, to write down the woman's movements, to steal the key and trespass into this woman's home. Where did she get the right to snap back at her like that? Lilly brought her lips back together, took in a deep, nasal breath, then said, "Forgive me."

"You need to leave."

So direct. Her legs were still weak and shaky. She hoped it wasn't visible through her khaki pants, but she looked down to be sure. Lilly couldn't tell. She was having a hard time focusing, her eyes seeming to slide back and forth as if she was in REM sleep, but her eyelids open.

"Did you hear what I said?"

She had heard, but it had been too much. If this woman made her leave, it would be the fourth person to dispose of her the way Mr. Thompson had, to see right through her as if she wasn't even there like the boy from class, Kevin Kaiser; her own mother had turned her back on her not more than an hour ago. At least she thought it was less than an hour now, the time on the staircase still not quite clear. She couldn't lose the last bolt holding her together.

"I can't," she said.

"What?"

She met her eyes, and, as if the movement of shifting her head up adjusted her focus, Lilly said, "I can't leave. Please don't make me leave."

The expression on the woman's face changed, as if the rigidness of her jawline had been finely sanded as her lips rose up, resting at the dividing line between a smile and a frown. Her elbows, jutting out like the wings of a bird about to take flight, eased in and relaxed. Even the lines on her forehead smoothed, waxing off a few years of age.

They just looked at each other, neither seeming to know what to say or do next. How do you follow up with a response like that?

It was Lilly who broke the stare and the silence. "Will you tell me your name?" She realized that she had regained control of her voice now. The sound that escaped her lips was her own, spoken how she meant it to be spoken.

Silence. The woman's gaze shifted from Lilly to the window.

Lilly didn't care about the consequence now. She had nothing to lose. If nothing else, she would find out the woman's name and do it on her own. She wouldn't get it from her mother. Wouldn't go snooping in any paperwork to uncover it. It was time to stop imagining what might happen, to stop imagining what she wanted to happen. She should have let Kevin know how she felt or at least put the idea in his head the way the other girls did it. They talked to the other boys. They flirted with them. They made it clear as melted snow what was on their minds. And why shouldn't she do the same? After all, what was the worst that could happen?

The woman pursed her lips the way Lilly's mother used to do right between being just mad and being pissed off. Lilly braced herself, squinting and raising her cheeks the way she'd do on the Fourth of July right when she thought the firecrackers would detonate, as if that expression would filter the report and make her ears ring a little less. It never worked, but that didn't stop her from displaying that hideous expression every single time the wick was lit.

What the woman said surprised her: "My name is Svetlana."

Now, it was Lilly's turn to be silent.

"You still haven't told me what you're doing in my apartment." Svetlana stepped forward and then leaned her back against the wall, leaving the doorway open now, reminding Lilly where the exit was.

"I wasn't going to steal anything or mess anything up."

"I believe that, but you still need to leave. Come on," she said, waving her hand toward her a few times as if Lilly didn't understand English.

The first two steps were the most difficult, but Lilly shot her gaze to the floor then walked briskly past Svetlana and on to the top of the staircase. Only then did she raise her head and look toward the piano room, where the woman was standing in the doorway again, facing her.

Lilly knew that if she didn't say what was on her mind now, she would not get the opportunity to do so again. And she had given a little. She'd done half of what Svetlana had asked by heading back to the staircase, hoping that it would be enough for the woman to take in what she was about to say. To know that it was true and not just something to ease the tension that had built in the apartment.

"I listen to you play at night," Lilly said softly, but with enough volume that made her confident that Svetlana had heard her.

The only part of the woman's body that moved was her eyes. They broke contact and fixed on the bookshelf.

"I really like to hear you play. My room's right underneath yours." She put her hand on the rail and took one step down, everything below her chest hidden from Svetlana now by the short wall separating the living room from the staircase. "I even open my window, no matter how cold it is, so that I can hear it better."

Lilly saw the closest thing to a smile appear on Svetlana's face, her lips spreading horizontal, not really curving up or down. As this happened, the woman crossed her arms again, taking her eyes from something on the bookshelf to meet Lilly's.

"You join in once in a while, too," Svetlana said.

"I guess if you stopped playing, I'd never get to practice with anyone anymore."

Her words were met with a confused expression. And she didn't want to have to explain.

"I hope you don't hate me because of this. I'm really sorry."

The woman nodded, and Lilly stepped down the staircase, closing and locking the door behind her. She heard the woman begin walking after she turned the key. And then the sound of a door closing. Svetlana was leaving again.

Lilly went to her room, catching only a glimpse of the woman as she turned right from the front yard to the sidewalk, heading toward the Metro station a few blocks away. Pulling out her journal, Lilly began writing about her first encounter with the woman upstairs. The woman whose name was Svetlana.

Chapter 10

When Alexei had explained the extent the vandals had gone to, the Ironclad sales rep offered him expedited service, which was a little more expensive, but he'd agreed and an installer was at his home before noon. Six hidden cameras outside, motion lights, interior motion-detectors for the doors and windows, silent alarm, the man even replaced the broken front-door window. It was all finished rather quickly, before Emily got home from the library and the kids from school. And when Alexei shook the man's hand and then pulled out his wallet to pay him, the installer informed him that the bill had already been taken care of.

"By who?" asked Alexei.

"No clue. They just called me about an hour ago telling me that the bill was paid, so you're good to go."

While Alexei stood silently, trying to find a way to explain to the installer that there had to be a mistake, that he was the only one, besides his wife and she didn't have the credit card, who knew that he was getting this system installed, the man had found his way back to the black Ironclad van, gotten inside, and started to drive away. Alexei headed back inside to call the Ironclad rep, but a blaring car horn startled him before he made it to the door. A Lexus sedan. Tinted windows. Three seats taken.

"Alexei," came the familiar voice of Hawthorne from the passenger seat.

He went to the car, seeing Hawthorne in daylight for the first time. So average. So able to blend into a crowd. He was without his fedora, hair white as a crashing wave. Skin not as pale as Alexei had once thought, but blemished. Or maybe those were just healing bruises, he couldn't tell. But American, yes. Like so many businessmen that populated downtown Boston, Hawthorne belonged there and could blend in with the crowd easily.

"Get in," Hawthorne said.

Alexei hesitated. Emily would be home in forty-five minutes, and he promised her he'd be there, waiting on her. And hadn't Brother said that he'd not be dealing with Hawthorne anymore?

"I'm not asking, Alexei."

He heard the click of the automatic door locks and knew that he had no choice. He opened the back door, got in, and there was Brother sitting next to him, holding a manila envelope in his gloved hands.

"Surprised, Alexei?" Brother said.

He wasn't surprised. The rhythm of his heartbeat remained steady, his palms and forehead dry. Part of him knew that Brother and Hawthorne had some sort of partnership. Brother was Hawthorne's boss. Alexei didn't need the Chechen to tell him that much. At least it explained how he got in the institute last night. So why the secrecy? Why hadn't the son of a bitch just told him that he was Hawthorne's boss last night? It didn't make sense.

Brother dropped the manila envelope in Alexei's lap. "You forgot this last night."

Alexei didn't touch it, just looked at it.

"Close the door, Alexei."

He did, and the driver pulled away.

Alexei didn't know what to say. In fact, what was going through his mind, and he didn't know why, was how good the car smelled. It must have been a recent model, still carrying that new-car scent, itself not so appealing, but what it represented, something special. Like a new home. Like taking a step up in life. Leather seats, soft and smooth as a baby's bottom. And they were slightly different, those aromas. A new Altima didn't smell like a new Lexus the same way Tvarscki vodka didn't taste like Stoli.

"I heard about what happened last night," said Brother, "and it made me angry." He was looking forward while talking.

Who would have told him? They didn't put things like petty vandalism on the news or print it in the newspaper—this wasn't Mayberry. That left the police. Had they told him? Or maybe a neighbor? Had Brother had him followed? Watched? The thought of it started to sicken him, his stomach gurgling and begging to empty itself.

"Family is so important, Alexei." Brother said these words slowly, deliberately, and let them hang in the air for a while.

Why would he say that? Did he know? How could he? It was a long time ago. Russia had been a different place then. He had been a different person with a different name. And Hawthorne never gave any signs that he knew of Alexei's past, just that he owed Boris, and that Boris was going through Hawthorne to get that debt repaid. But, now, this Brother. How much did he know? What was he willing to do to get what he wanted? When would the debt be clear? Would it ever be clear or was this just going to be another trap that he couldn't get out of alone? Another prison? And how much had Boris told him? Trustworthy Boris, hand-picked by his sister.

"I took the liberty of paying for that security system for your home," Brother said.

Of course. At least that mystery was solved. "I'll give you the money for it. No more debts. I've already paid my debt to Boris through those trips to Canada."

"Lucrative."

"What?"

"You never did look in the briefcases, did you?" He laughed. "The honest criminal."

"I don't care what was in them. Just that it cleared my family's obligation."

"Yes, well, more than you know."

He did want to know what was in them. If it was just money, then Brother was right. More than repaid his debt. If they'd lied to him and it had really been drugs, even more than repaid his debt. What could be so damn important that they needed more information from MIT's neuroscience researchers? And why the hell were they being so aggressive? If it was weapons, political, or nuclear, sure. But there was nothing pressing here. Medical information and technology wouldn't bring Russia back to the USSR's former status as a superpower, but these assholes were acting like it was the only thing that could. No!

"So I'm done, Brother."

"It's about time you called me that." He smiled. "But, it's not done. You are who you are, Alexei."

So he did know about Russia, the details. Memories that Alexei wanted to box up and throw on a fire. His mother had died of pneumonia a few months after learning that his father's helicopter had been destroyed by the Mujahideen in Afghanistan, leaving Alexei and two of three siblings alone in Petersburg. He had an older sister, Donya, who was married with one child and living in Moscow, and a younger sister and brother, Nina and Victor, whom he had named his children after. In those days, Alexei had been called Lenka. And for years, he had done what he had to do to survive. He'd done what he had to do to protect Nina and Victor.

"I am not that anymore. And I never will be again."

"Well," Brother said, "there is a little more at stake here."

They always came with threats. Alexei knew that there was no use trying to negotiate or refuse. After all, his role in Petersburg was like Brother's role here in Boston—make the demands, make the threats, toy with the prey if necessary, and let the others do the dirty work because he didn't have the stomach or lack of conscience for it. These weren't Americans he was dealing with, at least not behind the curtain. How bad could it really be? Some information from his colleagues' research. They'd never know. Brother would be satisfied. Alexei would have some extra money, too. There was just something nagging at his conscience, something telling him that this had to do with far more than neurotechnology. But whatever that was, Brother was not telling him…at least not yet.

Clouds had crept in from the west, dense and grey, darkening the city and sprinkling snow. It would get a lot worse as the day went on, if the weatherman had been accurate. Petersburg had many days like this. It had been a day like this so many years ago that Alexei's life shifted again when his sister stopped him on his way back from his latest assignment. Dusk had come, and he had been walking along the embankment, just past the lit-up Troitskaya Ploshchad, the bridge's lights reflecting on the dark water of the River Neva. It had been a good day, and his apartment was just around the corner.

"Donya? When did you get to Petersburg?"

"Something's happened, Lenka," said Donya, putting her hand on his shoulder and leaning in close to him.

It was the first time he'd seen his sister cry. She'd even kept it together when their parents had died.

"What is it?" Lenka put his hands to her cheeks, wiping her tears away with his thumbs. She looked so pitiful, so helpless there next to the river, the streetlamps making her tears glisten as they streamed down from her bloodshot eyes. Her whole face was damp and corpse-like pale.

Struggling to get the words out, she said to him, "They're all dead, Lenka." She was shaking her head as she spoke, mouth never closing, but hanging open as if gasping for air. "Fyodor." She took several deep breaths. "Lenka, they killed my Lukerya."

He pulled her to him now, not believing what she was saying, but knowing it was the truth. Her husband and her daughter.

"I've never harmed a child," she said, a bit muffled because the side of her face was buried in his sweater. "They tortured her, Lenka. They tortured my Lukerya."

Lenka held her tighter now, his lips pressed on the top of her head. He could see people walking by, just able to see their knees to their feet, not knowing or caring if they were looking at them.

Wishing this was just a nightmare and that he'd wake up.

It took her several minutes to get control of herself, to release from his hold and look him in the eyes again. And when she did, when she had dried her eyes on her sleeve, she was Donya again. Ice-cold Donya. Her blonde hair short and masculine, military-like. Her mouth closed now, jawline firm.

"Lenka, it's just you and me now."

It didn't immediately register what she meant, but a few seconds later he understood. Nina and Victor had been killed, too. The rest of his family taken from him. He was too shocked to react, just stood there, stoic.

Donya looked past him now, raised her arm as if waving to someone, but Lenka didn't turn to see who.

"You have to come with me. I'm getting us out of Russia. It's not safe here anymore," she said.

When he didn't move, Donya stepped closer to him. "Lenka!" She smacked him, hard. "We don't have time, Lenka. We have to go now. Boris is waiting for us."

The sting of her slap lingered as she practically pulled him toward the street where a car had pulled up. It was Boris waiting in a new red Lady Samara. They both got in the back seat.

Lenka should have seen this coming. So many had died already either by the hands of enemies or from the weather or starvation. There was no way that they could have steered clear of any repercussions when they were so deeply involved.

He was able to find his voice now. "But we did everything they asked."

"You did, Lenka."

"What happened? Why did they do this, Donya?"

"Someone in the KGB leaked information, my files. In less than twenty-four hours, they did this. And they're coming after us now."

"Who did this?"

Boris spoke for the first time now, but kept his eyes forward.

"It looks like Chechen mafia, but could be some other bratva. It's not an inside job from the looks of it."

"Why did they have to kill them, Donya?" The words took much effort to get out. He was okay until he tried to speak; that's when he had to force himself to keep it together as if words were the keys to locked up rooms of emotion.

"You know why." She was sitting with her back to the door, facing Lenka, keeping her hands in her lap, fingers intertwined.

"But I've never killed anyone. I haven't tortured or hurt anyone."

"That's right, Lenka. That wasn't your job," she said, staring at him until his eyes met hers. "It was mine," she said, then faced forward.

Nina and Victor, even Lukerya, just children, helpless kids. They hadn't done anything to deserve torture and death, but maybe death was a blessing. A way out before the Americans dropped nukes on them and the whole country, maybe the entire world, fell apart. What gave him the right to escape it all? What was he going to do? Run forever? There was nowhere in Russia they could go and be safe. They would have to hide, live in the shadows wherever they went, behind fake documents, a new language, a new way of life. They would be on their own.

"Where are we going?" he asked, the River Neva still visible outside the car window.

"Finland," said Boris. "And then we're getting you into Canada and on to America." He looked back at Lenka to say, "New York City. Plenty of Russians to blend with."

Lenka looked to Donya now. "The United States? I don't speak English. Why are we trying to get into one of the hardest countries for a Russian to get into?"

"It's part of the agreement. They'll get us out of Russia, safe from those who are trying to kill us. In return, we'll give them information, whatever they want, when they ask for it, until we're even."

"Spies?"

"Spies." She turned toward him now, her gaze seeming feral. "It is the only way that we can survive, Lenka. It's not like we have anything left here." Her words were spoken with disgust, and her lips finishing with a pronounced frown.

"Are you in agreement, Lenka?" asked Boris.

"Everything's going to go through you?"

"Everything is through me. Yes."

"You're sure this is what you want?" he asked Donya.

"It's our only option, Lenka. This or be tortured and murdered by those animals."

"I'll stand by your decision and do what you tell me."

"We're both in agreement," she said to Boris.

It was completely dark by the time they'd made it to the pier.

Still in the car, Boris said, "You will be in Finland for six months, Canada for two years, then taken to the United States. You'll learn English. You'll blend in. And you'll hear from me when it's time. And it might be a long time from now, so don't forget."

And that began their journey, their new lives.

Alexei remembered the smell of Boris's car, the red Lady Samara. It had smelled like Brother's Lexus. And Brother was right. There was more at stake. His siblings had been innocent, but they'd been born into a world of violence, turmoil. America was not that place. Emily and his children didn't know what violence really was. Paranoia, yes, from a brick through the front-door window. Words from stupid teenagers, yes. But they couldn't understand true violence. True manipulation. Torture. Alexei knew that he had to act much more upset than he truly was when the vandals struck. In truth, the vandalism was a blessing in comparison.

"Besides, Alexei," said Brother, "what we're asking of you is nothing compared with what you did in Petersburg. No one gets hurt here."

"How do I know that?"

"You don't. But you tell me what's worse: giving me names and information or your wife finding out who her husband really is. And what he used to be." He adjusted in his seat. "You may not have used the hammer or pulled the trigger, but you opened the door and let them in. Doesn't that make you equally responsible?"

"I didn't have a choice." God damn it! Why did Boris have to give all the details? Especially to a piece of shit like Brother, a filthy Chechen. And if he gave those details to Brother, who else could know?

"You always have a choice, Alexei. But you have to live with the consequences."

"I did *not* have a choice."

"Alexei, we both know how this is going to end," said Brother. "Wouldn't you rather help those who helped you and your sister escape from Russia? Those who saved your lives."

"You had nothing to do with that."

"Who do you think Boris went to, to get you and Donya to Finland and on to America to start a new life? My people. Me," he said, the words becoming more guttural, almost a growl.

"How do I know that it wasn't your people who killed my brother and sister," Alexei shot back, raising in his seat a few inches as if about to attack. "My niece! I know you're Chechen mafia, Brother. And I know that Chechen mafia is responsible for what happened." He wanted to point out the unlikelihood of someone atop Boris to be in the USA riding around trying to get information from people like him. If he was higher on the chain than Boris, he'd never show his face, and he certainly wouldn't be in America. Not even Boris would come to America. Brother had slipped up here, accidentally shown Alexei one of his cards.

"No, Alexei. Believe it or not, Chechen mafia had nothing to do with it. It was KGB."

"You're lying. Donya *was* KGB."

"Yes, but there are things you don't know, Alexei. Some of which I don't even know. Only your sister has those answers, and we have no idea where she is. Do you realize that she hasn't been in contact with anyone? Has left the burden of this debt on your shoulders. And she could be right here in Boston for all we know. Or Canada. We don't even know what her name is now. Maybe she's going by Donya again."

Alexei knew what Brother was doing, so he kept his mouth shut, making sure he didn't say anything that would give Brother an inkling about Donya's location. It didn't matter what his sister's name was, he would always call her Donya. When they had arrived at JFK and got into a cab together those years ago, Donya told him to keep distance. That she would always watch over him as best she could. And when he stayed in New York, he'd receive letters from her like clockwork—every three months. No geographic specifics, just that she was doing well. That she could see he was doing well. That his girlfriend was beautiful. That she wished she could attend the wedding. Most of all, that she was happy for him. That his lovely daughter reminded her of her own Lukerya. And, when he'd moved to Boston and the letters became more random, the more recent letters urged him to stop with the transports to Canada. That debts were well paid. He hadn't seen her since they met their contact in Brooklyn, a Finnish man whose name Alexei never learned. But he gave them money, driver's license, and other paperwork in order for them to begin afresh—birth certificate, resume, general medical records, city information, a manila envelope full of the stuff. Donya had hugged Alexei tightly that evening, kissed him on the cheek, and told him that she loved him. Then, got into a taxi of her own, and he hadn't seen her since. He only found a small note in his folder: *Emergency— Newspaper Classified: The Moon is Red and the skies in Limbo. I will come.*

"I wouldn't know," said Alexei. "But if we're trusting each

other, why don't you tell me why KGB would have turned against us."

"It's probably best that you don't know."

"Because I couldn't handle it?"

"Because the past should stay in the past." Brother rested his head on the seat, letting out a noisy breath. "Your debts are paid, Alexei. Plenty paid. What happens from now on involves the present and the future." He turned his head to look at Alexei now. "There are worse things than losing a family. For them to be dead, having died loving you, and you visiting their graves and mourning them and remembering them, that's one thing. Wouldn't it be worse for that family to leave you, to leave fearing you, hating you, never wanting to see you again? Still living, but you being dead to them, and them happy about it?"

Alexei could feel his will wavering. He should have known better than to have fallen in love and started a family. Should have known better than to pull anyone close to him. Why would America be so much different than Russia? He knew about demons, how they attach themselves to a person and help him do things, terrible things. And how they manipulate a person, making him believe that they've gone only to find out that they've just been sleeping a while. Waiting. The geography didn't matter. He was stuck on a circle, nearing the part where he would lose his loved ones again, be saved by his sister again, and then be happy, only to lose it all over again. Only the geography would change. Maybe it'd be somewhere in South America, Africa, or Australia.

"Why do you think you're living in Boston?" said Brother. "Do you think it's just luck that you found yourself working at MIT, in the department that's working on science that we want?"

Alexei's stomach lining seemed to shiver at these words.

"We know Emily's father. Where do you think he got the idea to set you up with people at MIT?"

This was getting to be too much, too farfetched. "If you have so many people in high places, why do you need me to get you the information? If you can break into the building and take the information the same way you got into my office and took this folder out of my trashcan, why do you need me?"

"I wish I could say because you're so good, but that's not true."

"Then what is it? If my obligation is over, why won't you people just leave me alone?"

Brother paused a moment, a dramatic pause like a film director might call for before an important line is spoken, one that clears up a character's confusion. And Alexei knew, before the words came out of Brother's mouth, what they would be: "Because you're expendable."

And that was that. A private on the front line, a body to take up space and take as many enemy bullets as possible while the important ones stayed back and watched from a safe distance. Watched from the safety of shadows.

"It's enough talk, Alexei." Brother handed Alexei another manila folder. "Do what I say or a copy of this file will be sent to the FBI field office and another copy will be delivered to your wife."

Alexei didn't have to open the folder. He knew exactly what it contained. It was his file. Detailing his actions in Russia, every single one of them. His role. The son of a bitch probably added photos of his murdered siblings, of Donya's murdered family. He stared at the folders for a long time, at least it felt like a long time, until Brother's voice broke his trance.

"You're home now, Alexei. I'll see you soon."

And he would see him soon, Alexei knew. In all of it, he never had a choice. Why Brother had drawn it out, he did not know. He could have just said these things last night, but he'd waited. None of it made sense. And paying for the security system… Why? And why choose him, a man with a sordid past? He knew that a bit of digging would uncover who he really was, so why was Brother risking his own safety by associating with him so directly? Regardless, Brother was wrong about one thing—Alexei did not know how it would all end. That part remained to be seen.

"That means we're done here for now, Alexei."

He got out of the car and stayed on the sidewalk as it headed to the stop light, made a left turn, and disappeared. Alexei glanced at his watch. It was three o'clock. Emily would be home in fifteen minutes with the children. He got the mail and then went inside. By the time he'd reached his office, the telephone rang. An Ironclad representative asked if everything was okay, if the police were needed. Deactivating the silent alarm would take some getting used to.

Alexei unlocked his bottom desk drawer and put the folders inside, then locked it back. The small stack of mail was mostly computer-generated bills—about as impersonal as it gets. But one envelope had his name and address handwritten in blue ink, no return address, and he did not recognize the handwriting. It was in block capitals, and each letter seeming to have been engraved into the paper as if the writer was angry. A masculine hand. Even more odd was that, while the envelope had a stamp in the top right corner, it did not have a postmark.

The folded parchment inside bore a much different handwriting, an elegant mixture of cursive and print slightly slanted to the right, each letter a consistent size and depth, the ink seeming to rest on the surface with minor indention. A feminine hand. Donya's hand.

My Dear Brother,

I long for the day that we can see each other again. This time of year always makes me think of home, the good memories with Mama and Daddy, and the bad. The winter always has that effect on me, a mixture of happiness and nightmare. It comforts me to know that you are doing well. That Emily and the children are doing well.

I had not planned to write you this letter, but what happened last night made it necessary. The man you spoke with last night after Hawthorne left is dangerous. I do not know what he told you, but he is Chechen. He is the enemy. I remember his face. He was one of three on a hit list back in Moscow. Though I do not have proof, I believe he had something to do with the murder of my husband and daughter. I guess the proof is in him finding you. Only Boris knew we were leaving Russia, and he would not give you up. If he has threatened your life or your family's life, do not go to work tomorrow. If there is some other arrangement, go to work and keep him close and do as he says. Do not give him any reason to suspect that you would go against him. Most important, tell him nothing about me, and do not believe anything he may say about me. I need time to find more information. I am afraid that you may have a history with him, too. Not directly, but you may have been the one responsible for bringing his brother and wife to me in Moscow 1981. If this is so, it's a 30-year grudge, so tread lightly.

I will write again soon. Burn this letter now.

With Love,
Donya

Could Donya have been wrong? Brother knew about Boris, about them escaping to America, and everything about him and his family. What if the hit list was a diversion, a group of people that were to be assassinated like Donya. If Brother wanted to finish the job, kill him and Donya, then why was he still alive? Why were Emily and his children still alive? He had to speak with Donya. She was wrong about this one. She had to be. Brother was just a link in the spy chain like the ten who were arrested several months ago, a spy like he would be soon. Brother was in America to collect information from people like him, those in positions at MIT, Harvard, and any other facility that had cutting-edge technology valuable to a country that was once so powerful, that would do just about anything to get that power back, and he was to pass it on to his superior. And he was the perfect pawn. Not high profile like the professors. Not low profile like a janitor, who had more keys than dollars. He was right in the middle—a happily married man living the American dream and not needing anything, so there was no motive...on the outside. No suspicion would come his way. He was Alexei, the content assistant. Trustworthy and everyone's friend. And he wanted to get more information from Donya. He had been right, too. Alexei had been the only one who had worked to pay off Boris, as far as he knew. He was okay with that, but Brother hadn't lied about that. Alexei had to think this through more. So much of him didn't trust Brother because he was a Chechen. Could he really base it all on that? But Donya's letter, too. What if she was wrong?

It wasn't time to get in touch with Donya directly; he would go to work the following day. He would open the manila envelope Brother had given him and collect the information requested. And he would wait for Brother to contact him. Somehow, he had to get evidence that Brother was not a threat to her. One false move and he could be exposed, lose everything. He felt that he needed to protect Donya, too. If he could prove that Brother was not much higher than a pawn in this chain, that he was just the next step to moving some information, maybe they could both be clean of them all, drop off the radar, and really learn what it meant to live free in the land of the free.

Alexei burned the letter.

Part II

Bariolage

Chapter 11

"Sir, I understand that he's technically not an agent anymore, but he knows more about the original case than anyone," said Anna.

"Shouldn't you know more about the original case than anyone?" DeLaurent replied.

"If you want this case to get closed the right way this time, you'll let me use who I need to use. My team's been looking at recent surveillance videos, reading files, and talking to potential victims; they weren't in the middle of it like Meeks and I were. They don't have experience with these people. They're trying to catch up while the people we're after continue to move forward. I told you that this would happen."

"My hands are tied here, Agent Stern. I'm sorry. Suck it up and find something. You've had almost a month."

Anna closed her cell phone slowly and stared up at her kitchen ceiling. She should have known when he had told her that she could have anything that she needed that he wasn't telling the truth.

"Start of a long day?" asked Klein, coming in as if on cue from the bedroom.

"The case you're sick of hearing me complain about. My boss won't give me the resources I need to close it." She went to him, to his open arms and let him hold her.

"At least your friend can help."

"That's part of what I was talking to him about. He doesn't want Johnnie involved anymore and won't allow me to use the files Johnnie had in his apartment. It's like he just wants to drag this whole thing out and put up roadblocks."

"It's not like TV where everything can be solved in one hour."

"No, it's not unfortunately." She let him go. "But he can't stop me from talking to Johnnie and following the leads from his investigation."

"You're still gonna use them?" he said, seeming almost surprised.

"I would be so far behind if it weren't for Johnnie, Klein. These rookies are really trying, but their lack of experience is something that can't be overcome with a case like this."

"Just don't let your boss find out."

"I don't care if he knows. This case is too big to let it drag out. I think he's so adamant about my keeping Johnnie out of it because of liability."

"Covering his ass," he said, smiling.

"Right."

"Of course, he could have given you this case and put up the roadblocks to keep you busy. Keep you running into dead ends so you'll be away from high-profile cases. After what happened back in the fall, he might be covering his ass in another way. I mean, it's not like Russian spies are really a big deal. Isn't the US allies with the Russian Federation now? It just seems weird. That's all."

It hadn't occurred to her that this could be DeLaurent's motive for assigning her this case. Had he planned this all along? Is that why he barely let her computer load up before getting her neck deep in a case she'd spent so many hours of her life on, telling her that over a year of work was just the tip of the iceberg? Cases like this didn't end; they were like diseases—you can get them under control, cut them down to the point that you think they're cured, but then they come back from seemingly nowhere and rise up again. Hadn't that happened with smallpox just a few years ago? God dammit, Klein was right. He probably backed her promotion to hide this fact, to soften the blow. No one would expect some rookies to be able to do so much. Damn him.

"I wonder what he'd do if I told him that, besides deny it."

"Just don't work so hard," Klein said, sliding his hand around her waist, a few fingers toying with the elastic of her panties.

"Then you can spend more time with me."

Anna smiled at this, and before more words were spoken, they were in the shower together, the water so hot it stung.

Anna loved when the steam would get so dense that she could hardly see her feet. It made her think of her grandmother's house in Newfoundland, where the fog gathered more than half the days of the year. Thick fog that lingered, cushioning them from the outside world like some force field, not letting her father leave when they'd visit, unlike his interrupted time at home. But her father and grandmother were both dead now, her property sold long ago. But she had her memories, and standing so close to Klein, in the building fog, it gave her that same sense of ease, of safety. Nothing could harm them here, in the mist.

As he rubbed soapy hands over her skin, her eyes fixed on the scars on her arm and shoulder. Images of black and purple bruises appeared on her chest.

Fluorescent lights hooked into a dusty ceiling. People around her, mostly women in green tops, masked faces. So much talking, all gibberish. Mouth bitter as if full of liquid metal. "Ks. Ks. Ks." The sound of a rattling shopping cart wheel. Beeps and buzzes at an arcade. Covered in blood. Naked. Helpless. Blackness.

"Hey," said Klein. "Maybe you shouldn't go into work today, honey."

She was sitting in the bathtub, water just dripping on her now as Klein's body acted as an umbrella.

"I didn't pass out."

"Close enough."

She put her fingers to the scar on her neck from Aziz's bullet and rubbed. "I almost died that night. In the hospital. I lost a lot of blood that night." The words came out as if she was under hypnosis—monotone and evenly spaced time between words.

"But you survived." And he kissed her.

"And you came to see me."

"I did."

"Every day."

"I had to be sure you would be all right."

"With flowers."

He didn't respond to this verbally, just wore a tender expression showing her that he adored her and was so glad that she was his.

She let him see her smile, a short one, and then said, "I think I'd like to finish my shower alone. Is that okay?" Anna studied his response, hoping that her words hadn't offended or hurt him. And it didn't appear that they had.

He kissed her again and got out of the shower, the warm water beating down on her skin again. She'd been in long enough so that the heat didn't sting anymore; it almost felt cold. But her palms had whitened and wrinkled, the skin sensitive even to the tug of straightening her fingers.

Klein hadn't wasted any time leaving the bathroom and closing the door behind him. Always considerate and reliable.

She wanted him to move in with her, to have someone waiting on her to get home, even if her hours away were many and often unscheduled. But she knew it wouldn't work, not now. Not while she slept a few hours a night, taking and making calls, sometimes leaving at three in the morning, and still dealing with that violent night on her own, refusing to see a therapist. It wasn't supposed to have gone down that way. Aziz shouldn't have been able to get back inside the house. If she would have run faster from the bar that night, they would have been a few steps closer, able to stop him, arrest him, and Johnnie would still be okay, she'd not have almost died, and Aziz would not be dead either, but alive and able to give intel, to possibly bring more terrorist cells down and save more lives and keep the security of the nation sturdy. That's what a few seconds meant in her profession, small in comparison to the whole like a single key on a grand piano—strike the wrong key once, and the whole performance, the whole design becomes flawed. But those few seconds opened her up to new emotions, to accepting her sweet and loving Klein.

After she got out of surgery and woke up in her hospital room, it was night, and the city beyond the window was lit up, but she didn't see any movement, as if the entire city had evacuated and left all the lights on. An empty place. On her other side was a curtain, separating her from the rest of the room. It was at this moment that she knew being alone was terrible. Even her father had had someone to come home to—her. Someone that loved him. She needed that, something warm in her cold world. Something to care about. Something that would keep her mind on surviving. And that was Klein, the first living thing she saw the following morning, a vase of flowers in hand and a kiss for her cheek. But before he got there, she lay, gazing out the window at an empty city and wondering where all the people were.

She stood in the shower and turned the cold water off, the quick rise in temperature warming her like a bonfire. DeLaurent had to know that she would not follow his orders. That she would show Meeks the files and discuss with him leads and progress. He would have to be naïve to believe otherwise, which he wasn't. He would have to be completely ignorant, too, if he thought she would not realize the game he was playing. Using her like that. Her way at getting back at him would be to get results, and that would require some bold moves. Some risk taking and jumping ahead. It would mean taking Johnnie's files and continuing down that path alone, keeping the rookies on other time-consuming work that would probably lead to more dead ends.

When she got out of the shower, Klein was gone. A note on the kitchen counter read that he had to go to work and that he would call her that evening. The note was unsettling, igniting a pang of anxiety in her empty stomach. What was she thinking by wanting Klein to move in with her? She knew nothing about him. Six months of casual sex and enough dialogue to fill up a page of a novel. And then the past two months, dinner dates, sleepovers, discussions, and emotion to go along with making love...it had all been wonderful, but she had been blinded by that emotion, she now realized. Klein had to go to work, but she didn't know what kind of work he did or even where he did it. How stupid, she didn't even know his last name, had never thought to ask. Or maybe he didn't want her to know. Maybe he had kept the conversations away from his personal life on purpose.

Anna sat, note in hand, trying to figure out what was going on. He knew that she was a federal agent—her firearm, badge, and the FBI seal on her laptop made that clear from day one. So maybe that was it. Because he knew that she couldn't talk much about her work, he usually kept the conversation away from work in general, this morning the exception. Maybe he worked at a job that he wasn't allowed to discuss, too. And maybe because she didn't have family photos displayed in her apartment, he kept the conversation away from getting too personal. Maybe he knew her better than she thought, picking up on all of these little things, keeping the mood pleasant and steering clear of an awkward moment. Or maybe she was giving him too much credit, that he just didn't care about those things and that their relationship was still only about sex, only now it took a little more effort and time to get...on his end. She didn't know. Most of her life had been devoted to keeping distance from others the way her father had taught her to do. She had been the girl that went home after the dance, the one that didn't break curfew. She did her homework and usually ate dinner at home. And she kept secrets. When she was old enough, her father had started telling her about his work, his cases, and making her promise to keep them to herself, that if she spoke of them, terrible things could happen to innocent people, even him. What kind of thing was that to tell a teenage girl, that her father could be killed if she let slip his secrets?

"I need to know that I can trust you," he'd said.

"You can, but I don't understand why you're telling me if it's all such a big secret," Anna had said in her soft fifteen-year-old voice, the one that still had a slight lisp when she tried to make the s sound.

He took his big right hand, which smelled like Irish Spring soap, and brushed her bangs to the side as if to be sure they were making full eye contact. "Because I'm not going to be around forever. And I want you to know who your father is."

It was the only time in her life that she had seen her father come close to tears.

As he was hugging her tightly, he whispered, "I have something else for you." He got up and went into the bedroom for just a few seconds and returned with a thick leather book. "This is your mother's journal, Anna. I know that she would want you to have it."

He placed it in her hands as he sat back down, and she put it on her lap.

"It's up to you whether to read it or not."

Not understanding why he'd just said that, she asked, "Is there stuff in it that you don't want me to know?"

His response began with a rare smile, and then he said, "I haven't read it, Anna."

She didn't ask why because it didn't matter. Anna understood what her father was doing now. Secrets were like invisible weights in an imaginary backpack, and he was trying to let some of his go, to pass them along to her so her featherweight body wouldn't get blown away in a breeze. Because while secrets can be a burden, they are also special and delicate, something to preserve. They can shape a person and give that person meaning, a purpose. So many of her classmates were bubbly, innocent, shallow, and walked around without a care in the world. But not her. She was serious, secrets giving her experience, and growing in depth far beyond those shallow twits roaming in the school hallways.

116

"All I know is that she wrote in that journal before I met her, and she continued to do so until two days before you were born."

And for the next ten years, he had filled her backpack with an almost unbearable weight. But in the hospital, as she stared out that window at the desolate city, not knowing whether it was dream or reality, she let go, keeping only a few morsels tucked tightly away, just enough to keep her feet on the ground. Finally able to stand up straight and realize that she could still be serious, experienced, and have depth without having to lug it around everywhere you went. And at this moment, she understood why her father had carried it around for fifteen long years. His love, her mother, had died, and he withdrew, holding it all in the way Anna had until recently. Part of her knew that he was open with her mother, that he loved her with every ounce of his body. She knew that he told her mother the kinds of things he told her. But the anchor that he didn't know how to break away from was the journal. While he was open with her mother, he couldn't bring himself to find out if her mother was completely open with him. If they were really equal. Maybe it took being in that situation to recognize it, even if it had taken her a decade to understand his handing over the journal. She was in his shoes with Klein now, but it was too early in their relationship to be thinking this way, she knew. So, Anna threw the note away.

If Klein wanted her to know more about him, then he could tell her when he was ready. She wouldn't try and find him in the database or do anything else to get his personal information. While she had very little relationship experience, one thing that she did know was that she would have to trust him if they were to have a good relationship. That it would take patience and understanding, especially considering how their relationship actually began. That if he continued to stay a closed book while she was an open one, it would not work. That they would never be equal. And that it was time to move on. For Anna, she was at a crossroads; she would have to stop blaming herself for what happened the night she and Meeks were shot if she ever wanted to see other parts of her life clearly. To see Klein clearly.

In the corner of her bedroom closet, Anna pressed in the electronic combination to her small safe. There was a small stack of photographs inside, of her and her father, along with older photos of her mother. Underneath sat her mother's journal, the leather strap still tied tightly, keeping the pages hidden. On the front cover, written in black marker, was her mother's name, Annabelle. Her mother hadn't written anything else on the cover, not "The Journal of..." not "The Diary of...," just Annabelle, in an elegant cursive as if her mother had endured training in penmanship, a skill Anna had not mastered. Her writing was usually print written by a rushed hand, but it got the job done. Most of what needed to be written could be done on a computer anyway, so it didn't matter. It occurred to her that her mother knew she would be getting married one day; though Annabelle began writing in the journal before meeting Anna's father, she only wrote her first name, knowing that her last name would change in the future.

If her father had been telling the truth, it meant the journal had not been opened in over thirty years. She'd held it several times, the soft leather cool in her hands. And she'd turned it sideways, noticing a folded piece of paper or an inserted photograph between certain pages, but she never slid them out. She'd kept her mother's thoughts, her mother's secrets tied up in the journal, locked away in a safe, and protected from anyone else's eyes. It was the only item she had that could show her who her mother was. The intimate thoughts and feelings, the experiences and choices, and the truth about life, about how she felt of the coming child, of marriage, of the secrets her husband had to keep and those he shared with her. It was all right there, but she'd kept it closed like her father had, just like she would keep it closed today. She wasn't ready to know yet. But to take it out, to still smell the faint scent of perfume that had soaked into the back cover, darkening the leather a few shades on the bottom half, was all she could handle right now. To see her mother's name and to smell her mother's perfume, but she couldn't get into her mother's head. Not yet. It was almost like knowing a suspect's file, the biographical information, but not *really* knowing that person until he was in the interrogation room, when he spoke what was on his mind...always different than the file. So, like several times before, she put the journal back in the safe and left.

It was time to follow Johnnie's lead and go to MIT. It was busy today. She turned on Amherst Street and then on Ames, where they'd finally finished the media extension building. For months, concrete dividers with FLETT in black letters had separated the sidewalk from the street, a chain-link fence atop the dividers to keep out pedestrians, but it all just made traffic an even larger nightmare. But she was lucky. Her black sedan's license plate signified that it was a federal vehicle, so when she got to Main Street and saw the McGovern Institute entrance to the Brain and Cognitive Sciences Complex and no parking spaces available, she turned around and parallel parked the car half on the sidewalk, where the curb dipped for pedestrians crossing at the crosswalk, and the other half blocking the bicycle lane. Campus and city police never put a ticket on those cars because they knew something important must be happening.

The building was new, which meant there was a lot of wasted space inside, the lobby airy, its only ceiling the glass roof several floors above, letting the sun naturally light the area. While she tried to appreciate the aesthetic quality of this contemporary style, she couldn't help feel manipulated somehow, like opening a giant bag of potato chips and finding two-thirds of it filled with air or biting into a Hostess cherry pie, expecting the filling to ooze out and get all over her face, but only finding a thin layer that looked dried out like maple syrup that's been on a plate too long. Students meandered, iPods blocking out Mozart playing from the lobby speakers hidden somewhere in the walls. Cell-phone keypads clicked and coffee cups emptied. While multi-tasking, the students still carried a determined, mature way about them. Maybe it was the way so many looked groomed with freshly shaved faces, combed hair, and clothes that fit. And the others, they were just plain, as if not fitting into a clique, but independent and comfortable with their awkward, non-matching fashion, like one guy wearing a plain tan sweater that was an inch too short, dark tapered jeans, and bulky white shoes that made his feet look more like a professional basketball player's rather than a six-foot-tall twig of a man. Or the attractive girl, wearing a black blouse, black skirt to her knees, black hose, only to mess it all up with silver and white tennis shoes. Anna didn't sense much apathy or lazy looks of entitlement on their faces, and it was refreshing. At her alma mater, these kinds of kids were in a league of their own, and she had felt like one of them then. Someone with something to prove, something that she would not expect to be handed to her, and she had a fire for it. Even if it had been lit and tended to by her father before she went off to college.

There was a balcony a few floors up, a man in a gray suit looking out over the lobby like a dictator, but she recognized him from his picture on the website as the director of the institute, Charlie Delk. By the time she got to his office, he was wearing a smile and inviting her to have a seat, his soft voice and loose shoulders erasing the image she had of him in the lobby.

After pleasantries, she said, "What kind of research do you do here, and why would someone want to steal that information?" It was direct, but she didn't want to play games right now. If there was something to be said, now was the time. Besides, such directness could bring about a sudden expression telling her if she was on the right track or not.

"Well, this is the largest neuroscience facility in the world. We have state-of-the-art equipment, top researchers in the country...why wouldn't someone want that information." He sipped his coffee from an old mug, dark stains like mildewed mortar from a rock-well wall.

"I noticed that from your website, but what about the technology would someone want? In other words, why would someone risk going to prison to get this information?"

"Thankfully, most of the equipment is large, so they wouldn't be able to take that. Our computers and other smaller machines have GPS devices hidden in them, and I do mean plural. Some are in places that, in order to get to them, you'd have to practically destroy the machine..."

The man kept going on and on discussing the lab equipment, the facilities, and the researchers, never really answering her question, and it almost made Anna angry, but she kept control, trying to think about why he would be diverting the conversation from the research itself.

"And the mainframe requires both fingerprint scan and voice analysis scan..."

She needed something to justify keeping the building under surveillance. A reason to scan the security tapes, put in the hours of researching the staff and doctors working here, and, for DeLaurent, a report explaining why it would be a viable expenditure of the limited budget and resources.

"So the properties of—"

"Thanks for your help, Dr. Delk. I'd like to speak with some others here. Is that okay?"

Dr. Delk's expression was one Anna remembered seeing in school—the slight frown a teacher gives after asking the class a question and receiving a disinterested silence in return.

"Of course." He stood. "There are not many classes right now, and most of the offices and labs are open, so feel free."

And she did. First speaking with Sumitra Sarkar, who was researching how the brain translates intentions into commands, like walking, speaking, or other common actions. Strike one. To Alphonse Toro, explaining how the brain focuses on specific stimuli, filtering out other distractions that are irrelevant to the task at hand, like reading a book and not hearing the traffic outside, the children watching television in the next room, or the clicking sound a dog's nails make on a the hardwood floor as it paces from room to room. There might be something there that a spy could want. So not quite a home run, but she was getting warmer, and when she spoke with Jenny whose last name she could not begin to pronounce, it became clear that neuroscience was a very important division to watch over. Because Jenny dealt with how the brain responds to fear, anxiety, and stress. And while her research was geared to helping those with psychological disorders, Anna was hearing how the science could work in a much more malignant way, using new techniques in interrogation and mental torture rather than physical torture. One method left obvious proof that something had occurred while the other method, barring a recording device, remained intangible like a ghost.

"Jenny, how long have you been researching this at this facility?"

"Two years."

Jenny was young for this facility, based on the others Anna had seen. Probably in her early thirties. She'd recently gotten her doctorate at Duke and had been hired on to continue her research. She did not have to teach any classes, but she had some involvement with students working in psychiatry, she'd told Anna. When they needed an interview with someone for an essay they were writing, she was a common candidate. But none of the students seemed strange or to ask questions out of line with what might be expected from a professor's essay guidelines.

"What about files and other research? Has anything ever turned up missing or misplaced? Or doctored? No pun intended."

"Not in here. Most of us have personal laptops and personal jump drives that we use to keep our research on, so it's always with us. Some of it's on paper and filed, but it would be difficult for someone to decipher that information without the analysis part, which I believe most of us keep on our computers."

"So in order for someone to get all of this information—"

"Why would they want to get all of this information?" She paused, giving the impression that she'd said something out of line. "That's not what I meant. It's just, what we do here…people don't try to steal that kind of stuff. It's never happened. Besides, it would be hard to do without someone noticing."

Jenny's words opened a new can of worms in Anna's mind. For it to happen, there would need to be a hand on the inside. Students would be easy to track, and only certain students were allowed in this part of the facility. Visitors would be watched at all times. There were cameras watching every hallway, security-card readers outside the labs but not the offices, and a seemingly tight-knit group of researchers all working to further the science and help people. There had to be a loose end somewhere, a professor that was unhappy, that didn't have something to lose…or one that had a lot to lose. And the janitors…

"How often do the janitors come through?"

"Once in the morning. We have to be here to let them in."

"So they can't get in the labs or offices on this floor?"

"Only if the fire alarm goes off. That disables the security as per the fire code. At least that's what they told me when I was hired. I've never been here when the alarm has actually gone off."

"Has there been *anything* going on here that's out of the ordinary?" she said, trying to sound desperate in order to pull anything more significant out of this woman, but all she got was "Nothing in my lab…sorry."

Anna gave Jenny her card. She was the only person so far that sounded down to earth, that talked to her like a human being rather than speaking a report into a microphone. The others had been so wrapped up in their research that she felt more like an interloper than an FBI agent. There was something about Jenny, the way she represented herself and carried a conversation, that made Anna want to know her more, to keep her close. Because while she was not socially awkward, Anna could see that Jenny's best friend was her laboratory and the other researchers in the facility just acquaintances, but she wanted more and just couldn't get it. She probably had a cat at home because a dog required more attention and gave more affection. Or maybe just fish, because the lack of a ring on her finger, and any other jewelry for that matter, and the way she dressed—comfortably, wearing her jeans and button-up shirt like someone blended into a crowd, not sticking out and practically unnoticeable—gave several signs of someone living each day with a gaping hole in her life, living a lonely life without even a dog to give affection. And she was attractive, wearing just a touch of makeup, even though she didn't need it. Jenny reminded Anna of herself not so long ago. But Anna had someone now, and it felt so good. Maybe it was time to pass that along, to reach out to someone that was lonely and pull her away from it, to help her feel what life was like.

"We should get coffee sometime," Anna said.

Jenny didn't respond right away, but when she did, she said, "I'd like that."

And with a goodbye, she moved on to dead end after dead end, finally having her curiosity piqued when she entered Dr. Suh's lab. He was sitting on an uncomfortable-looking black stool, the back a weird, modern art-like cross with smoothed edges and minimalist design. He was stooped forward peering into a microscope. There were cages with rats and mice in this room, some active and running around, others looking more paralyzed and staying huddled in the corner.

She looked more closely at some of them. One seemed to be nibbling at a particular spot, the hair gone and the animal bleeding just a little bit. But it persisted as if that spot had a never-ending itch. And another, a raw gash just below its eye to its nose, it, too, hairless around its wound. That they were in cages didn't bother her; she was used to seeing animals confined. But wasn't this borderline abuse? It didn't look like they had ointment on those wounds, but there was water and food. It was comforting that they were only rodents, the kind that broke into your home and stole your food, that spread disease, and used your cupboard as an outhouse. That made them burglars, thieves, terrorists using biological warfare.

"Obsessive compulsive disorder."

Anna quivered, her gaze snapping to her right where the tall Asian man in a white coat stood.

"Excuse me?"

"The rodents." He pointed to the cage holding the rat that wouldn't stop nibbling. "This one has obsessive compulsive disorder. That one," his finger moved to the rodent cowering in the corner, "has paranoia."

There was a rhythm to his soft voice that Anna latched on to. She wanted to hear him speak more, and it didn't matter the subject.

"And what can I help you with, Miss...?"

"Yes, sorry." She reached out her right hand and said, "I'm Anna Stern, FBI."

He shook her hand and wore a confused expression—pursed lips, raised eyebrows, as if to ask her 'What the hell do you want with me?'

"I just stopped by because I had a few questions for you."

"For me?"

"No, I'm sorry," *stop saying that damn word*, "I mean I'm here to speak with the researchers and you're next on the list."

"Why am I on a list?"

That charismatic voice was starting to annoy her now. "Because you work here, Dr. Suh."

"I'm not Dr. Suh."

"Then what's your name?"

"Jin Won. Dr. Suh is for students," he said with an added smile. "Please, come sit down and we can talk."

"Your accent is Korean, right?"

"You're good. Wonju, not too far from Seoul."

"How long have you been here?"

"All due respect, Anna, why are you asking me questions that you already have answers to?"

He was right. Five minutes of browsing his file gave her all those answers. His file also had a brief statement about an incident, but she didn't want to jump directly into that yet.

"Okay, I'll just jump right into the questions that I don't have answers to, like why would someone want to steal your research?"

"That's why you're here?"

"That's why I'm here."

"I don't know why someone would want to steal my research. There's so much documentation and evidence here showing that it's my...our work, that another institution or person wouldn't be able to pass it off as his own. Unless someone just wanted to know the information, but, as you probably know, we don't take many steps to hide what we're doing here. When we get answers, we publish. If the research starts going in a different direction, we're open about it." He smiled. "We're here to help people, so the sooner we get results and get them published, the sooner those people can benefit from the research."

Jin Won's storytelling voice could only take this so far. Anna knew there was something underneath it all that he wasn't telling her, but she didn't know why.

"And the incident that happened recently?"

"Incident?"

"Something happened recently that upset you, that you found out of the ordinary? At least that's what was so briefly mentioned in your file. So tell me about that."

"That was just a student using the lab without my

permission."

"You say that like it's nothing, but you reported it. I guess I'm a little confused."

"It's just a liability. If at some point we find a problem or something missing or damaged, there needs to be documentation about all those who had access to or were present in the lab. That's all."

"Who was the student?"

"Nicholas Grigsby. His girlfriend had let him in. When things like that happen, it's important to show them how serious it is by raising your voice. Then, they and others know not to do it."

"And filing a report?"

"No disciplinary action was taken. Just covering my ass," he said with a grin.

She was getting frustrated because the entire conversation was leading to a dead end...another dead end. But she had to ask all of her questions. If she left a stone unturned, one of her favorite clichés, it would nag at her until she eventually checked it out. In this case, it dealt with the current research, the stuff that hadn't been published yet. And she couldn't take another Delk-like answer.

"The focus right now is on autism. You probably know that it's a genetic disorder that makes it difficult for the person to communicate with others and can often lead to paranoia or OCD, hence our friends over there in the cages. But did you know that autism is also an enhancement? Think about your prodigies in math and music and other areas. It takes us neurotypicals years to understand and master what they seem to be preprogrammed with."

"Neurotypical?"

"It's what they call us, those without autism. We're typical because we don't have a special ability, a genius mutation in our genetic makeup. But we're able to talk, you and I. And go out into the world without much anxiety, visit with friends, talk to strangers in line at the grocery store. The autistic give that up for other gifts. So that's what I'm working on."

"What are you working on? I don't understand."

"OCD right now. I've been researching a synaptic protein gene called Shank3, which is between brain cells and what allows them to communicate. These proteins contribute to brain disorders like autism, especially OCD. At a synapse, a cell sends messages, neurotransmitters, which interact with the postsynaptic cell, the receiving cell, which triggers electrical activity. This causes effects, like turning genes on or off. Shank3 is a scaffold protein, helping organize hundreds of other proteins clustered on the postsynaptic cell membrane, which are required to coordinate the cell's response to synaptic signals. This gene is in the striatum part of the brain, which handles motor activity, decision-making, and emotional aspects of behavior. When things go wrong here, it leads to brain disorders like autism and OCD. My theory is that those disorders are caused by faulty synapses. This also occurred in another postsynaptic protein in the striatum, SAPAP3, which caused the OCD in the rats after I put them through gene mutation."

He was speaking at a normal speed, and Anna tried to keep up. Much of what he was saying made sense to her on an elementary level. Messing with genes in the brain that are to blame for autism and OCD.

"After the mutation, as you can see, there's excess in grooming, paranoia, and a lack of social interaction with the other rats. And rats are social creatures. For instance, look at the rats on the second row. Notice how they're all together, sniffing each other, playing, eating from the same bowl. Those are the control. The ones you were looking at previously are mutated. Don't you see what this means?"

"Tell me." Because she didn't have a clue what it meant.

"It's a breakthrough. It's the first direct evidence that proves that mutations in Shank3 produce autistic-like behavior. Isn't that exciting?"

"So, you caused the mutation?"

"Yes."

"The rats were normal prior?"

"Yes." He had a smile now.

She tensed, and pain, as if she'd just swallowed a needle, scraped the inner lining of her stomach. But she didn't have a concrete reason why. The pain went away after just a second, but the anxious flutter through her veins didn't cease. It was like a moment of epiphany, but she couldn't sharpen the image in her mind enough to see it clearly. Like her subconscious mind was fighting to keep some bit of information from her.

"Jin," came a voice from the doorway.

Anna turned in her chair to see a handsome, middle-aged man with blue eyes holding a file in his left hand.

"Necropsy reports on the two rats from last week," he said, handing Jin Won the file.

His accent was Russian, western region. Anna didn't stare at him, but she noticed that his interest was not in her. While Jin Won seemed to be open about his research, it was always a good idea to get another opinion, especially after having that weird feeling about what he'd said. Johnnie had always told her that she had good intuition, and she hoped he was right. Jin Won didn't seem like one to leak information. He was too passionate about it. But this guy, who was he? It was obvious that he had access to the information. That he was trusted. And he was Russian. But she remembered the last time she'd spoken with Johnnie about the case, about how the ones on this level of the game would probably not be Russian after so many were arrested in the previous case. That it would be too obvious and draw too much attention.

"Is this your assistant?" she asked.

Jin Won had opened the file and was quickly scanning the top page. Looking up, he said, "Yes, this is Alexei. He helps me and several others." He closed the file. "He probably works harder than any of us."

"I doubt that," Alexei said with a laugh, and then turned to leave.

She would have to find him and get more information. From what Jin Won had said, Alexei seemed like someone with a lot of information, and she had the feeling he'd be more informative than Dr. Delk. People like him always had deep-reaching knowledge in a lot of places, like an administrative assistant knows more about the business than the boss himself. She had only looked through the files of researchers so far, so she didn't know anything about this Alexei. Why did he have to be Russian? Maybe it was good that he was Russian. She was thinking about it too much.

"These two died, but it doesn't look like it was my fault."

"What?"

"The rats," he said, tossing the folder on the black table.

"Why OCD?" It just came out of nowhere. One of those moments, and she had had few in her life, when she spoke what was on her mind before realizing that it was on her mind. But, thankfully, Jin Won didn't find it to be as awkward as she did.

"It's more common. Begin with the widespread issue, the one that effects the most people, then work your way down to the more unique variations."

And when he said that, Anna knew why she had felt that pang a few minutes ago. Dr. Suh's research fit exactly what a foreign power like the Russian Federation would want. The USSR had been so powerful, had so many scientists and experts before the fall. They still had many now, but the top researchers, the elite, many had fled. Now, as Russia was making its way back into the category of superpower, it would need technology. Cutting-edge technology. Experts.

"To…"

"Cure autism and other brain disorders. Imagine if there was a cure for bi-polar affective disorder, schizophrenia, OCD, you name it."

"Probably piss off a lot of psychiatrists and psychologists," she replied. But that's not why they would try and steal it, she knew. They weren't interested in the published articles and the cures. Anna gazed at the bleeding and paranoid rats, their black eyes like wet ink. Did they know what was happening to them? Did they know that there was a vast world beyond those cages?

They both laughed at her comment, but Anna's laugh was fake. Only Johnnie or her father would have been able to tell the difference.

"There's a lot of money in the treatment, but not in the cure," she said, keeping her real thoughts to herself.

"That's true. But, realistically, a cure is a long way off. Years of testing, more clinical research, you know how medicine is."

She didn't really.

"To do it right takes decades of research, development, clinicals, testing, more testing, and more testing. Otherwise, you get side effects worse than the condition. And I can't stand by that."

That made more sense. Only, some people didn't care about side effects. If desperate, and to be involved with espionage meant that it was probably so, Anna knew that it wouldn't be rats in the cages. Maybe there was more to this case than she'd thought, that she was stirring up a bee's nest DeLaurent didn't even know existed. Or maybe he did know, and that was why he refused to let Meeks help. So many possibilities.

Jin Won got up and walked to the cages that held the mice and rats. "These little guys are helping us evolve." He looked at Anna. "It's a hell of a lot easier to break something," he said, sticking his finger in the cage and petting a mouse huddled in the corner, "than it is to fix it."

Chapter 12

December 2010 Entry 13

…Her name is Svetlana. She knows who I am. She knows that we play music together. Mom comes home late, like she said she would, with a couple bags of groceries. She goes straight to her bedroom after putting the groceries away. I don't think she believes I'm asleep when she gets home anymore. That doesn't change her routine. She still stays downstairs. She never comes up to say goodnight.

December 2010 Entry 14

Svetlana returned at 1:17 am. She was probably late because I messed up her schedule by breaking into her apartment. She was only inside a few minutes before the CD started. It made me happy that she was not breaking her routine, even if the time was different. I snuck into her apartment again. The CD was Chopin, Nocturne No. 1, *which meant I had just under six minutes before she would finish playing…*

Lilly's shoes thumped and her bare feet made that sticking noise on the hardwood like peeling tape off the back of a poster, so she wore black socks to conceal her approach. Svetlana had been playing just under a minute. Lilly peered over the divider, only able to see the edge of the piano from her position. The lights were off except the lamp in the piano room, the effect like a reverse shadow on the living-room floor, a bright expressionist rectangle surrounded by blackness.

Lilly entered the living room, but there was no place to hide. It was too bare. But she knew about tricks with light and how the eyes were practically blind in a lit room while the person watching from a dark place could see every movement. So, she tiptoed to the bookshelf, where she had a clear view of Svetlana, and watched her. How her fingers glided across the keys with ease, playing at a slower tempo than the CD. There was nothing robotic about her playing, unlike what she had noticed in many pianists. They hit all the right keys, but there was no life in their hands, no expression on their faces, and seemingly nothing going on inside their heads except getting the next note right. But Svetlana was different. She was thinking about something, and it wasn't the music. That was coming too naturally. Her body swayed slightly with the somber rhythm of the nocturne, and Svetlana's moist eyes were closed. Lilly understood what was happening now. She had been wrong before. Svetlana didn't play every night, in front of the window, in front of her audience hidden out there in the blackness of a theatre. She didn't play for herself either. There was someone she was playing to. It was etched in her facial expression, one that Lilly imagined she herself wore when she would play for her father. And the nocturne, such emotional shifts, how it would rise and fall, repeating this cycle over and over, holding the high point for a few seconds, but letting the low points linger. Such repetition. Such melancholy, for the end note was low, held for as long as the chord would hold before slowly fading and falling silent.

December 2010 Entry 14 con'd
…She didn't catch me this time. I was able to sneak back downstairs when she finished.

December 2010 Entry 15
Mr. Thompson was not at school today. The substitute didn't know anything about music. This is Day 1 of practicing on my own. 2 hours of Rachmaninov. The packet Mr. Thompson gave me has a lot of stuff in it that I know Mom won't want to see. He seems to think I can still get into Juilliard, but there's no way. I wish I could talk to him again. I don' t understand why he just left. I wish I wouldn't have cussed at him. I'm sorry. Now if I could only tell him that. Svetlana is back on her usual schedule for a week night, but she

plays Chopin's Nocturne No. 1 again. She usually doesn't play the same piece back to back like that. I don't sneak up there tonight. I just wonder what's going on with her.

December 2010 Entry 18
Christmas break has finally started. Still no Mr. Thompson. I asked the secretary in the main office about him, and she said that she couldn't give me any information. I want to ask Mom to ask the school for me, but I know she won't do it. I don't even know if she's aware that I exist. Spending all that time in her bedroom…

At half past noon, Lilly opened her mother's bedroom door and parted the drapes, letting in light for the first time in a long time. The air in the room was thick with a damp dirty dishrag smell, so Lilly opened the window, letting in freezing air, but it was clean air, and she would suffer through it for now, the breeze making her fingers icy digits that were hard to move…so different than when she was in her room sliding the bow across violin strings. Pictures still hung in their original places, mostly studio-developed with Olan Mills stamped in gold on the bottom right corner. Some of Mom's smiles were genuine, the early ones. The latter seemed forced, lips not quite making the upward arc by the time the camera captured the image—the time when Dad had started to be away at training or the possibility of him having to fly thousands of miles away to the desert to fight another senseless war. That's when her real smiles stopped. But Dad's hadn't. His were always natural, like he had just seen them for the first time after getting back from a lonely trip.

The bed was unmade and dirty clothes were piled on the floor and nightstand mingled with used dishes—some having been there so long they had a layer of sticky dust, looking more like the typical teen's bedroom than a mother's.

Lilly collected the clothes in the hamper and took them to the laundry room, took the dishes to the dishwasher, and pulled the comforter off the bed, revealing several photo albums on her father's side. She knew what was inside. Birthdays, her parents' wedding, Thanksgivings, Christmases, Easters, vacations. A life gone by. A life that would never be again, that couldn't be again. She picked these up, too, refusing to look inside them, and put them back on the small two-shelf bookcase next to the dresser.

When Lilly took the pillowcases off, the sheets off, she realized that they were the same sheets as when her father had been alive. That his scent probably lingered there, which was why her mother probably spent so much time in bed since his death. But if her mother was going to move forward, it had to be done. And she did it. She stuffed load after load into the washer—clothes, towels, bathroom rugs, sheets, all of it. She filled the dishwasher and ran it on hi-temp wash.

She dusted the bedroom, cleaned the filthy bathroom, put new sheets and a clean comforter on the bed, closed the window, and started to vacuum. When the tip of the vacuum went under the bed, Lilly heard a clinking noise. She turned off the machine, frustrated that she hadn't gotten all of the dishes in one load, and bent down to get it. What she saw startled her, sending a paralyzing rift through most of her body. There were bottles there. So many bottles. Wine. Liquor. Beer. *Mom's turned into an alcoholic. Can that happen in just a few months?* Lilly filled six trash bags about halfway each so they wouldn't rip and put them by the curb for the garbage truck.

When she finished vacuuming and straightening up the bedroom, Lilly lit a Yankee jar candle, Sage & Citrus, which refreshed the room after about an hour of burning. But she kept it lit. She tied the drapes back. She tried to show her mother that she cared. And when the laundry was finished drying, she put it away. She put the clean dishes away. She tidied up the rest of the house, which only needed dusting and vacuuming, for neither of them used it much. But she cleaned out the fridge and freezer of expired food, along with the food in the cabinets, and she took all the trash out. And when she was finished, she sat at the dining-room table, proud of herself for finishing everything. Proud of herself because the house looked so clean and perfect. There was no longer spoiled fruit, expired milk, or bread with hints of green mold. The house was cleansed, and Lilly hoped that it would help her mother move on. Stop drinking. That it would help her mother notice her again.

"What gives you the right to go into my room and do what you did?" Kate wailed. "How'd you like it if I took that violin of yours and gave it to the garbage man?"

It was plain to see that Kate Rebeck had come home drunk, but the words still stung Lilly. She didn't know how to respond to her mother's hysteria.

What *had* Lilly done? Why had she shed light into that dark abyss of a room, that prison? It was none of her business. Her mother was now the head of household, and, dammit, Lilly would have to respect that. She would have to go by her mother's rules, even if those rules were to take care of yourself and leave her the hell alone. *Let me die in my own cocoon.*

Lilly turned to walk away and leave her mother alone, and that's when she felt something on her arm, her mother's hand, fingernails digging into Lilly's skin as she gripped it and slung her around.

"Don't you walk away from me, young lady."

The slap landed on Lilly's left cheek and ear, the sound more of a dull thump than a smack. The force didn't knock her down, and the pain didn't seem to register yet. Paralyzed. Her mother had hit her. She'd actually hit her.

They both stood silent, Lilly staring down toward the floor, her mother not moving. But when Lilly looked up at her mother's face, at the way her lips were drawn together as if she was drinking from a straw, she hoped to find a shocked look, a look that said I'm sorry, how could I have done that to you, my sweet daughter? The way it always happened on TV. But that's not what was there. And if it existed, it was well hidden behind her mother's bloodshot eyes, ironclad jaw, and now crossed arms.

"Go to your room."

Lilly had heard what her mother said, but there was something wrong. Her left ear. It was like she was holding a conch shell over it, making her mother's demand muffled like listening to a song with the bass too high. But in her other ear, it was clear and feminine.

"Now, young lady."

She obeyed, but the sound of the dual voices scared her as if her mother was possessed and both the demon's voice and her mother's voice were trying to talk at the same time. Scared that her mother would hit her again, but more scared because her left ear was always just above her violin when she played; it was where the sound was most delicate. Could it be a ruptured eardrum? Could it just be ear wax compacted from the impact? Or was this a permanent thing?

Lilly started up the steps, and the sound frightened her even more, for the sound of her shoes on the wood was different, like that laminate flooring at the model home out in the newer suburbs had been, an artificial, hollow sound that meant there was something missing.

At the top of the staircase, Lilly looked to her right, to the locked door that led to Svetlana, wishing that she could go there. Because though it was a bare apartment, there was something there that didn't seem to exist anymore in her part of the house. She had seen it when watching Svetlana play Chopin, how, though it was a sad moment, it showed that she really cared about someone. Because Lilly's mother didn't care about her anymore. Not only that, but she didn't seem to care about herself either.

December 2010 Entry 21
My hearing is back to normal, finally. Mom is staying home for the

second day in a row. I haven't seen her. She stays in her room. Now Christmas is only three days away, and we haven't put up a tree or any decorations. But I didn't think we would this year anyway. With Daddy gone and Mom being how she is, I feel like an orphan. Why did Mr. Thompson have to leave, too? Maybe if I write that question enough in this stupid journal, an answer will appear. Starting Bach practice today. I really don't know why... Planning on following Svetlana today. I have to know where she goes. Where she works. I just want to know more about her. What does someone so talented do if she doesn't teach music or perform? Maybe if I find that out, I'll have a better idea of what I can do.

December 2010 Entry 22
Well, there's no way I could be a cop. I lost her somewhere between here and the Metro station...2 blocks.

A few minutes after seven o'clock, Lilly saw Svetlana return. She would try a new tactic tonight. Lilly had to break from her old self if she was to make it in this world. No one would hold her hand anymore the way her father used to, when he surprised her with her violin, when he listened to her play and kept a smile on his face even when she missed a note or two. No one was going to lay down a smooth path in front her and help her along the way Mr. Thompson had started to do. And her mother...she was just a batch of negativity. Everything that she did seemed to try and take away Lilly's passion. The isolation, the blank staring at the television screen, and now the violence. She thought her mother had almost impaired her, taken away the sense that gave her the most joy. Her hearing, the place where her passion was strongest. And that was the only way it would be taken away from her, if she couldn't hear anymore. Not Mr. Thompson's abandonment!

Lilly stood over her bed, the open violin case gazing up at her. "We're going to make a new friend," she said, sliding her hand across the smooth, almost glasslike face of the instrument.

She laughed at the absurdity of talking to her violin, imagining herself in a padded room. "Maybe that's where I belong, just you and I." And she giggled again the way one might to make a child feel better after having told a dull joke.

A few minutes later, Lilly was standing outside Svetlana's door, violin case in hand, and knocked. There was a steady breeze, the cold air finding its way between the buttons of Lilly's shirt and making her shiver a little. She couldn't wait for something to happen anymore the way she'd hoped fate would bring her and Kevin Kaiser together in her history-class doorway. She would have to make it happen, to verbalize her wants. And when she did that, it would work. Doors would open. Life would change. That's what happened when people broke out of their shells. They got friends. They found lovers. They excelled. Lilly would be part of that group now, no longer the recluse.

Svetlana's door opened, and now all that separated them was a thin screen door. The Russian woman didn't have an angry expression on her face, didn't look scoldingly at her this time. It was her normal expression, one that Lilly was not familiar with. Lilly had never seen Svetlana like this, only frustrated when Lilly had broken in, determined when she was walking to or from wherever she went, and on the brink of tears, caught in deep emotion, when playing Chopin. It was almost an inviting look, which boosted Lilly's confidence even more.

"Yes?" Svetlana said, not opening the screen door.

"I wanted to apologize for the other day," Lilly said, not being able to help from smiling. "I wanted to come by and ask if I could play music with you tonight." As she finished her sentence, she realized that she'd made an involuntary lift of her feet like a ballerina might do and then plopped back down on her heel like a giddy child right before a room full of presents on Christmas morning.

"No, I don't think that would be a good idea."

And the door closed.

Lilly stood there, that hopeful raise of her eyebrows falling, her lips retreating inward, making the rare smile that had felt so good on her face disappear. She didn't feel the cold air anymore.

Why had it not worked? What was so wrong with her? A knot was tightening in her throat, something much different than what had been there when her mother had talked to her about her father, when she'd cried for him then. This feeling that was intensifying was what she'd feared all along. It was why she never spoke to Kevin Kaiser. Why she didn't think to pursue Juilliard on her own. She was afraid of rejection. Afraid of the way rejection could make her nauseous and messy with tears.

Why couldn't that hit from her mother have made her deaf?

Lilly turned from the door, peering down the steep wooden staircase that led from the side walkway all the way up to the third floor. And with tears coming now, she lifted her violin case and threw it at the stairs, the thump from the black plastic case making a hollow sound on initial impact, then, like sliding a stick back and forth on a snare drum, it skied down to the bottom, landing next to the hedgerow that separated her house from the neighbor's. When she got to the bottom, she kicked the violin case and then continued forward, to the sidewalk, turned to the right, and kept walking and walking and walking through the dark neighborhood, not noticing the houses or stores that she passed. Not even recognizing where she was after what felt like half an hour.

Shivering, eyes still moist and stinging with icy pain each time the wind gusted, she trudged on, not really thinking about anything, just trying to get away from that sickening feeling that had worked its way through her entire bloodstream. She thought that she would exhaust herself and that it would disappear, but that was proving to be false. If anything, it just intensified it, helped it move through her veins even faster the higher her pulse rate got. She wanted to get kidnapped and raped and murdered or beaten and robbed, or at least hit by a car. Surely those things would eliminate that horrible feeling. Or she could just kill herself, throw herself off a bridge or dive into the Charles River and let its frigid water fill her aching lungs. It's not like there was anyone left who would give a damn. *Fuck this world. Fuck it in the mouth and let it drown.*

Looking up and scanning the buildings and houses around her, they didn't look familiar, but it was dark, and the dark had a way of fooling you. And there was no snow on the ground, so the darkness was that much more great.

"You lost?" came a deep voice from behind her.

Lilly turned around to see a man sitting on concrete porch steps that led up to a red-brick apartment building. He was bundled up, looking warm underneath a thick black beard, the red glow of a cigarette end illuminating his eyes as he drew in a deep lungful of smoke, the white cloud hiding his face for a few seconds when he let it out.

He scared her. Why was *this* wish coming true? The kidnapper to take her to some dungeon where she'd be helpless and tortured. Why this instead of something so much more beautiful? Why not her music? He had done one thing, though. The feeling of rejection she'd been carrying around had vanished, replaced with that feathery feeling in the gut, the one that told her to run. And when the man flicked his cigarette to the sidewalk and stood up, that's what she did. She turned immediately without looking and ran into something hard, and it grabbed her arms.

"Whoa, there," said another man, who looked similar to the smoker.

"I think she's lost," the bearded man said.

"Let me go," she said.

And the man did.

"Where do you live?" he asked.

"Lilly," came a woman's voice. "I told you not to wander off."

It was Svetlana. Of all people, the woman upstairs emerged from the darkness and came to her, taking her by the hand, and leading her back the way she'd come.

Lilly was speechless. She hadn't seen the expressions on the men's faces, but they hadn't objected to having her taken away from them.

When they'd gone a few blocks, Lilly recognized a baseball field to her right and trees to the left, a quieter spot. And Svetlana stopped her.

"What are you doing out here, Lilly? You've lived here long enough to know that it's not safe for a young girl to just go walking around at night outside your own neighborhood."

She didn't know how to respond. It was the most Svetlana had spoken to her at once, and she didn't know what to say, but words did come out.

"You followed me?" she said in monotone, not quite believing it until it was spoken aloud.

Svetlana crossed her arms. "I saw what you did with your violin. I saw how you were feeling."

Her voice was not angry, but rather soothing and under-standing.

"Girls can get into a lot of trouble when they feel like that. So, yes, I followed you."

That was more than her mother would have done. Her mother probably would have hit her again and told her how horrible of a person she was to act like that. But not Svetlana.

"I didn't think you cared," Lilly said.

It took Svetlana a moment to respond, but when she did, it was not to what Lilly had said. "Let's get you back home. You'll get pneumonia in this cold, not wearing a jacket."

"You're not wearing a jacket either."

"That's because I'm used to the cold."

When they reached the house, Lilly did not see her violin case in the yard.

"I put it in my apartment. You can come up and get it if you'd like."

She thought it was some kind of test. If she declined, it meant that she was giving up, that maybe Svetlana had wasted her time in watching over her tonight, saving her. If she accepted, it would be an affirmation that she would continue with her music.

"Okay," she said.

It was warm inside. Something about the apartment made it not look as bare this time, but, looking around, Lilly did not notice any changes in décor or arrangement. The only difference was her violin case sitting next to the door, which had nothing to do with this more cozy feeling.

"I'll make us some tea," said Svetlana, heading to the kitchen.

Lilly began to understand what had happened. She had gotten upset and stormed off, another lapse in her being able to control her emotions, and then, when she had yearned for the worst to happen, it almost did. What would those two men have done to her? Raped her? Kept her in a locked room? Sold her? Drugged her? Now that Lilly's mind had thawed, she realized how stupid she'd acted. Her whole life could have changed in those few minutes.

She heard the tap come on and the sound of a filling kettle. Then it was off. And then the clicking noise of the gas-range starter and the whooshing sound fire made when it was brought to life. Lilly went to the kitchen, leaned her right side against the door jamb, and watched the woman get a tin from the cupboard.

"Thank you for saving me tonight."

Svetlana put mugs on the countertop. "Those men weren't going to hurt you." She looked at Lilly now. "They were just trying to help you."

"How do you know that?"

Staring at the kettle atop the blue flame, Svetlana said, "When you get older, when you have a child of our own, you'll understand."

Not knowing what to say, Lilly just nodded. Was Svetlana just trying to make her feel better, not as shaken up about the encounter or had the two men really had good intentions?

"Milk or sugar with your tea?"

"What do you put in yours?"

"Both."

"I'll try it with both."

"Very well. I'll finish the tea. You should check your violin and make sure it's not damaged."

And that's what she did. As she examined the case, it occurred to her that Svetlana was a much better tracker than she was. The time it would have taken to walk down the stairs, get the case, go back up and put it inside, and then back down again…Lilly would have been a few blocks away. Much farther than the time she had followed Svetlana and lost her almost immediately.

The case had protected the violin well, so Lilly sat down in one of the surprisingly comfortable chairs, clicked on the lamp, and waited for Svetlana.

But, again, Lilly felt different being here than the two times before. Maybe it was the perspective of the room, which before was from the staircase side and from the other corner of the room where the bookshelf stood; now it was from the main door and chair. It didn't feel the same as an altered perspective, though. She'd experienced that feeling one day when her family lived in Colorado Springs. They'd lived on a one-way street, but one day, after her father had taken her to Dairy Queen, he turned down the street going the wrong way, and Lilly remembered how her whole world shifted. Shadows were on the wrong side, trees hid different parts of the houses, all of the cars lining the street were facing her, and their house looked strangely foreign. It almost frightened her, a creeping feeling that everything that made her feel safe, everything that made home familiar, could so easily be taken away or guised by a simple shift of perspective. Her dad had called it the *Twilight Zone* effect. But here, that wasn't the feeling at all.

The sound of the whistling kettle filled the warm apartment. And that noise seemed to unlock the mystery dwelling in her mind. It brought back the time she'd made tea, not long after her father had died. Her mother had been in the shower and didn't want any, the early stages of her reclusive behavior and probably the beginning of her alcoholism. But it was also the night when Lilly had gotten into her mother's purse and stolen the key to the stairway door separating Svetlana's apartment from the rest of the house. The difference, she now knew, actually was perspective. Before, she had always viewed the apartment as an interloper, but now she had been invited inside, she was a welcomed guest. And it felt good to see the room with relaxed eyes. It didn't matter how bare a place was because it was the people that made it comfortable, not the furniture or paint color on the walls or even the photos and books.

Svetlana emerged from the kitchen with a mug in each hand, and Lilly got up to take one of them, then they both sat down.

"Thank you."

There were a million questions Lilly wanted to ask her. What part of Russia was she from? Why didn't she have any photos? Where did she work? Where did she go all the time? Who was her favorite composer? What was her favorite musical composition? But what came out was, "Do you celebrate Christmas?"

Svetlana sipped her tea, then said, "Christmas is very different in Russia than here. When I lived there, it was an atheist state, so religious ceremonies were...discouraged. And we don't celebrate it on the twenty-fifth of December."

"When do you celebrate it?"

"January seventh, when we welcome Ded Moroz and Snegurochka...Grandfather Frost and Snow Maiden. But, I don't celebrate anymore."

"Why not?"

"Christmas is different for those who no longer have families, Lilly."

"My mom's not going to celebrate because my father died earlier this year in Afghanistan. She's not handling it too well."

"How long have you played violin?"

"Since I was nine. My dad bought it for me. My teacher, well, my ex-teacher, was trying to get me into Juilliard, but then he just disappeared..." She was about to keep talking, but stopped herself. Lilly didn't know how long this conversation would last, and she wanted to know about Svetlana. She didn't want to regret rambling on and on about herself, probably boring the woman to death, and then leave having learned nothing about her. She wanted Svetlana to ramble on and on about herself, her life, for her to tell stories of Russia the way Lester had told her and her father tales about Finland. She lifted the mug of tea to her mouth and sipped; it was sweet and creamy, leaving a smoky taste on her tongue. It was the best tea she'd ever had, much better than the bland chamomile tea she was used to.

"What kind of tea is this?"

"You like it then?"

"It's like a...a..."

"Campfire."

"Yeah, like a campfire."

"It's Russian Caravan. A blend of several teas, smoked. I like to imagine sitting around a fire in the woods, late autumn or winter. The perfect warm up for cold nights. Like the old merchants used to do on the Silk Road so long ago."

Lilly just smiled and took another sip, so happy that this woman was sharing this moment with her. "I love it."

Svetlana put her mug on the table and glanced toward the bookshelf, and held her gaze there as if she'd seen something before sitting back in the chair and looking at Lilly again.

"Do you like it when I play?" Lilly asked, hoping not to receive the same answer she'd gotten earlier when asking if they could play music together.

"I do." And a momentary smile spread across her face.

"I thought you might not since you've been playing that Chopin nocturne so much."

Svetlana slowly got up and headed for the piano room. "Bring your violin," she said just before reaching the doorway.

And Lilly did.

In the piano room, Svetlana handed Lilly sheet music to Chopin's *Nocturne No. 20 in C-Sharp Minor. Op. post.*

"The nocturnes are not only for piano playing. This sheet music is for piano and violin. Are you familiar with this piece?"

"No," Lilly said.

It would have been one of those nights, like the past few, when Lilly only listened to the music upstairs and could not join in. But Svetlana was bridging that gap now, asking Lilly to participate. And what did that mean? Why was she suddenly being so nice? So open to having her in her apartment in which Lilly had recently been ordered to leave? It couldn't have been only a temper-tantrum response because that wouldn't make sense. Lilly needed to know why Svetlana was being so friendly, why she had followed her, brought her back, introduced her to a unique tea, and was now going to play music with her, in the same room. She hoped it wasn't just a one-time thing, that after tonight, the situation would go back to how it had been. Lilly needed more consistency, more assurance that Svetlana was not acting this way just to appease that initial annoyance of the curious girl downstairs. But, if she mentioned it, it could prevent what was about to happen. And she couldn't allow that. Not now. Not after so much rejection. So, she kept it to herself. Would let the night play out the way it was destined to play out.

"I want you to turn around," said Svetlana, "facing the window and listen to the piano. Then, we will try playing together, the piano and the violin."

Lilly obeyed. Gazing at the opaque reflection in the window

of herself, just a tiny twig of a girl, standing before the woman upstairs as she began playing the somber but beautiful notes, slow tempo, shadowed pits where their eyes should be. For a moment, Lilly felt like Svetlana, listening to the piece before playing it, keeping a tradition alive. That was as far as Lilly allowed her mind to carry because she wanted to stay in the moment and cherish it. Before she knew it, Svetlana had finished, had taken her hands off the keys and leaned back in a relaxed pose.

"Now pick up your violin, open your sheet music, and let's try it. Play through any mistakes and don't stop playing. To stop is to give up. So you must never stop, Lilly."

She felt Svetlana's cool hand on her shoulder.

"Ever."

A few seconds later, Svetlana had removed her hand and had begun playing, and Lilly, making many mistakes but not stopping, played through to the end. And though she couldn't tell by the ghostly reflection, she could feel the burn in her cheeks, imagining that she was radiating an embarrassed red glow.

With the violin at her side now, Lilly said, "That was terrible."

"It was," Svetlana replied. "You have a lot of work to do."

Lilly turned around now, facing Svetlana as she stood up from the piano bench.

"I'm not really a good violin player, am I?"

"Nobody gets it right the first time. And no one is good unless they practice." Svetlana pressed the power button on the piano and then walked into the living room and sat back down.

Svetlana was nothing like Mr. Thompson. If she had been in his classroom and messed up so many times, he would have smiled at her, would have told her that it was okay and that she was getting better, and for them to try it again. And he would continue to say more positive things, slipping in a criticism before they played it the next time. A shower of compliments since that day in middle school when he'd taken her out in the hallway and told her that she was something special. But she would have to prove her worth to Svetlana, would have to work for that approval. Maybe that was a good thing, but it scared her. What if the people at Juilliard were all like her? They wouldn't accept her then. They would say that she needed more practice…or worse, that she didn't belong in music.

Lilly put her violin back in its case and went into the living room, asking, "Was there anything good about it?"

Svetlana picked up her tea and sipped twice. "Do not ask people for compliments. They should come naturally. If they don't, play through. They'll come when they're deserved."

The words stung Lilly's chest even though they were not said in a mean tone, but Svetlana's Russian accent had a built-in gruffness to it that Lilly didn't notice in other accents she'd heard. And having gotten no compliments from Svetlana, Lilly began shifting that sting to another painful place, using it to suppress the aching that Mr. Thompson had put in her. She realized that he'd been lying to her. That she was not Juilliard material. At least not yet. So perhaps Svetlana had saved her again, this time from humiliating herself in front of people who really knew music. It was clear that Mr. Thompson did not. Maybe that was why he disappeared. Maybe he realized what a fraud he was and couldn't stand to keep dragging her down. No wonder the most recent photo in the music room of an award-winning band was 1978.

"You had better go now, Lilly. It's starting to get late."

"It's not like Mom will notice."

Svetlana picked up the mugs and took them to the kitchen, and Lilly took it as a sign that the conversation was over.

With her violin case in hand, Lilly stood at the kitchen entrance and asked, "Can I come back tomorrow?"

Having rinsed out the mugs and placing them on a dish towel, Svetlana said, "If you come back tomorrow, I suggest you borrow the sheet music and practice."

And there it was, an open invitation. It was exactly what Lilly had hoped for. She was going to become friends with the woman upstairs, the pianist whom she had accompanied so many cold autumn nights. Though she was reluctant to do so, Lilly let it come out: "What made you change your mind about me? Is it because I got upset and ran away?"

"No," Svetlana replied. "The reasons don't concern you right now."

After a brief hesitation, Lilly said, "Okay," got the sheet music, and went back to her part of the house. As she lay in bed half an hour later, she could hear music from upstairs. The CD. And a few minutes later, Svetlana playing the piano.

December 2010 Entry 24
Still no compliment today, but we played together for almost a half hour.

Mom left after noon and still hasn't come back. Her bedroom wasn't messed up or anything. No note. I'm a little worried because she didn't have to work today. When I tried her cell, a message from AT&T came on immediately. I guess she hasn't paid the bill.

December 2010 Entry 25
Christmas Eve: Mom is still gone. I try to talk to Svetlana about Mom, but she never responds. She always changes the subject. I guess I understand that. I wouldn't want to get involved either.

No compliment today. But not much else either. She still plays her CD, and then her own personal encore after I've left...all three nights she's done that. Must be come kind of ritual. I need a ritual. I don't do anything that is a must, anything consistently at a consistent time.

December 2010 Entry 26
I heard Mom come in last night...well, this morning around three. I'm glad I'm not young enough to believe that it could have been

Santa...or Grandfather Frost. Or else I would have crept down the stairs, peeked into the living room, and been traumatized to find my mother knocked out cold by Santa...proof that you better put out milk and cookies and keep your butt in bed...or else. I just rolled her on her back, put a pillow under her head, and put the afghan from the couch over her. She didn't smell very good. I could feel her ribs. Her skin looked so loose. She was probably still down there. Merry Christmas morning to me.

At 9:30 am, Lilly knocked on Svetlana's door, hoping that she hadn't left without her realizing it. And she hadn't. Svetlana opened the door wearing a white robe.

"What are you doing here so early?"

Lilly stepped inside and said, "Merry American Christmas, Svetlana." Then, she revealed two packets of Swiss Miss hot cocoa she had gotten from her kitchen. "Every Christmas, Mom would make us all hot cocoa before we opened presents. Even when I was only one, but I only remember that year because of pictures," she said with a smile. "I thought we could have cocoa together—"

Without changing expression, Svetlana replied, "I don't celebrate Christmas, Lilly. I told you that."

When she said those words, Lilly's gaze went to the floor and she wanted to cry. Why did Svetlana's words and actions have such an effect on her? It almost made her angry to be so vulnerable all the time. No, it *did* make her angry. No one else had such a tight grip on her emotions, and so consistently. A few instances with Mr. Thompson, a few with her mother...well, her father came the closest, but he didn't seem to know the power he held over her because it was rare that he would say something or do something that would make her mood shift from content to sad. He would just include her in his life, talk to her without pretending she was too young to understand, and seem to genuinely enjoy the time they spent together, listening to her play violin, laughing with her at one of Lester's stories, or sharing with her his true feelings about whatever topic happened to be on the table, and he did it without that forced feeling that she noticed in so many other adults. How they would stand there, a fake smile spread across their faces, not really knowing how to respond or knowing what to do when a child was in the room. Shifting their gaze as if the child was a different species. Svetlana was different. There were no nervous smiles on her face. No sugarcoating or white lies. She seemed to know she held this power and was testing Lilly, seeing how far she could push before breaking her down. But why? What was the purpose in it all?

Lilly's response came with some difficulty, the words having to fight their way past a tightened throat and Lilly fighting back tears of anger: "Well, we can just have morning cocoa and pretend it's not Christmas. Will that be okay?"

Still without changing expression, Svetlana replied, "That will be fine. I'll put the water on."

December 2010 Entry 27
Mom was in her room all of Christmas day. When I knocked on her bedroom door, she just told me to go away, her voice like gravel. So I left her alone. I just don't know what to do. Would she still be like this if I wasn't here? Am I just a burden to her?

December 2010 Entry 34
New Year's Eve. I've practiced the Chopin piece for exactly 38 hours since Svetlana gave me the sheet music. I have to play it for her and get it right before the ball drops.

Mom has disappeared again. Her bedroom door was open this morning and the car gone. I don't think she's at work...I thought her office was closed on New Year's...

"You're making good progress now, Lilly," Svetlana said.

Lilly put her violin in its case. It was the moment she had been hoping for all week—a compliment from Svetlana. But, surprisingly, she felt next to nothing, like anticipating a huge firework to go off, and once the burning wick had disappeared behind the tissue paper top, a few sparks and then nothing. What did that mean? All week, she'd been imagining the joy and sense of accomplishment that would glide through her veins at positive feedback from the woman upstairs, but not this.

Svetlana didn't seem to notice her indifference, as she simply selected another piece of sheet music and handed it to her.

"You have to keep working on Chopin. Start with it when you practice. Since you're learning it, it can serve as a warm up. And, then, begin practicing this piece."

It was Vivaldi, but she didn't examine it further to get the title. Whatever it was, it would not be easy.

"Do you think these are the best pieces to try playing for the people at Juilliard?"

"Sit down, Lilly."

She took a seat on the floor, Indian-style.

"I don't want you to think about Juilliard."

"Why not?"

"You're not ready for a school like that yet."

"But that's not what Mr. Thompson had—"

"I do not care what Mr. Thompson says."

Lilly didn't know how to respond to that. Because the truth was, she didn't care what Mr. Thompson had said either...not anymore. She was proud of herself, though. Not only had the compliment not shaken her emotions, but Svetlana's directness in practically crushing that lingering dream didn't shake her either. It was another in a series of weird moments. As Svetlana spoke those words to her, Lilly had thought that she should be feeling sad, that she should begin crying. And when that didn't happen on its own, she was glad. She certainly wouldn't force it if she could help it.

"Then I don't either," Lilly said.

The ball would be dropping in Times Square in an hour and a half. If they had begun a normal schedule, it would be time for Lilly to go back downstairs for the night, but New Year's was Lilly's favorite celebration. It was better than birthdays, even at this age when birthdays were nice moments, growing and maturing moments, rather than the latter ones that would become depressing, she'd overheard her mother telling her father one evening, that would change to moments when the person is reminded that she's one step closer to the grave, one more wrinkle to old age. And it was better than Thanksgiving, which was all about food and family; Christmas, which was about gifts; and much better than Easter and the other holidays that just meant a day that she didn't have to go to school. New Year's was a cleansing time. A time to put all the bad stuff behind you and start with a fresh slate. A breath of fresh air. And it was sacred. Lilly could remember spending each New Year's with her parents. Sometimes they'd have company over, but usually not. With her mother usually asleep by the time the ball dropped, she and her father would stay up, and he would always pick her up, kiss her cheek, and give her a grizzly-bear hug, whispering, "Happy New Year, Pumpkin." And they would share their resolutions with each other. Nothing bad ever happened on New Year's...

"Can we spend New Year's together?" Lilly asked. "I can bring my small TV up and we can watch the ball drop."

"Lilly—"

"Please. And don't tell me you don't celebrate New Year's. You can't use that one anymore."

Lilly had made Svetlana start laughing about as much as she imagined the woman could laugh. Fewer than five seconds, but a laugh was a laugh.

"Mom's not home anyway. She probably won't come back tonight."

There was hesitation, but Svetlana responded, "Come back at eleven-thirty. I have to go somewhere."

And that's what she did. The ball started descending, and Svetlana handed her a small glass of champagne.

"Wow."

"It's not enough to do anything, but you drink champagne on New Year's to celebrate."

They clinked glasses, and then sipped the champagne, bitter and bubbly, when the giant lights started flashing 2011 on the television screen.

"So what's your New Year's resolution?" Lilly asked.

Svetlana put her glass on the table and sat back in her chair.

"To close many doors that have been open for too long...open a few that have been shut for a while."

"What's that mean?"

"It's my resolution, Lilly. I'm the only one that has to know what it means."

Again, she didn't feel insulted or feel that pang of embarrassment that she expected. Just indifference, no shift in her current mood as if the cultural barrier between them had started to crumble and was coming down like the Berlin Wall.

"And you?" Svetlana asked.

Lilly smiled. "I have to close some doors, too." She drank the remaining champagne in the glass, just a swallow, and then said, "And open a few." And she giggled.

By the time Lilly had gotten the television hooked back up downstairs and was in her pajamas, she heard the music from above. It was a lengthy piece, and she was asleep before Svetlana had finished playing.

Chapter 13

"Jenny," said Alexei, "who is the woman in Jin's lab?"

"Weren't you just in there?"

"Yes…"

"And you didn't ask?"

"Obviously not, Jenny," he said with a smile.

They usually played around like this, but this morning, Alexei just wanted straight answers. This was a new face, one that was clearly not a student, and he had to be sure that she wasn't a police officer called in to investigate something he had failed to cover up. But, there was something about the woman's face that gave him the feeling of déjà vu. Had he seen her somewhere before?

When Jenny told him that the woman was FBI, it took all his power to cover up the worry that was bound to be etching itself on his face. Alexei's reflection in the glass behind Jenny revealed his shoulders involuntarily sinking, easing down as he realized that his lips were slightly parted, and the coming together of his eyebrows could easily be explained as surprise, as in "What on earth is the FBI doing here?" rather than the worried surprise, "What the fuck did I leave behind for them to have called the FBI?"

Jenny was not as forthcoming as usual, and after she revealed the woman's department, not even giving the woman's name, she started analyzing the top sheet of a stack of papers; she hadn't been focusing on him at all, he finally realized after pulling his gaze away from the glass.

"Okay, I guess I'll see you later."

"She'll probably want to talk to you."

"I'm sure she knows where to find me," he said, but he couldn't read how Jenny meant it. Was it just a nonchalant, worry-free bit of information, a "Hey, by the way…" or was she warning him, telling him that she was his friend and that he needed to run? That this woman was here for him.

He got back to his office without anyone stopping him and asking for something. And not five minutes later, there was a knock at his office door.

"Come in," he said.

The woman walked in. "Hi, Mr. Volkov," she said, closing the door behind her. She approached his desk and reached out her right hand. "I'm Agent Anna Stern with the FBI."

He shook her hand.

"I'd like to ask you some questions if you have the time."

"Of course," he said, letting her hand go. "What can I help you with?"

She sat down in the chair Hawthorne always sat in, and, for a moment, he didn't know which person he dreaded to see more. Hawthorne had not taught him how to deal with an FBI agent, only the state troopers and local police if he got pulled over when he was traveling back and forth to Canada. This was much different. The woman across from him had more training, knew more about interrogation techniques and how to pick up on tiny giveaway gestures or altered inflections when getting a response. He didn't have a radio to play a calming sonata or an open road in front of him to speed down in case things got out of hand; in fact, he would have to get past her to get to the only exit unless he wanted to jump out the window and kill himself. The only option was to see what she wanted and why she was here.

"I think the two of us have a lot to talk about."

Oh, Christ, he had screwed up somewhere. But it had to have been a small screw up or else she'd have cuffs on him and she'd have back up.

"Is that so?" he replied, an almost choking sensation in his throat forcing him to swallow more obviously than he'd liked — cottonmouth.

"You know about everything going on here..." she opened

her notepad and flipped through a few pages, "and I'd appreciate your cooperation."

Was she being vague on purpose? Did she like to see someone in the hot seat? Well, at this point, Alexei didn't feel like he had anything to lose by concealing his frustration and the toxic brew of other emotions blending in his mind. He had to let out a hint of it or he'd explode.

"Come out with it then. What do you want?"

He immediately regretted snapping like this. The look on Agent Stern's face turned from expressionless to serious, her eyes almost glaring at him now.

"I'm sorry. My daughter was up all night, sick. I haven't slept or finished my first cup of coffee this morning."

"We can do this later," she offered.

He liked that idea, until she finished with, "You can come down to the field office after lunch if you'd like."

"I guess it's going to be now then."

"Great. Tell me about what you do here."

"You've talked to some of the others here, and you have access to my job description, so let's not waste each other's time." Alexei put his hands atop his desk, interlocking his fingers and relaxing his shoulders, trying to appear in control the toned-down way rather than the arrogant way Dr. Delk sometimes did, by putting his hands behind his head.

"You all say the same damn thing," she said under her breath, but loud enough for him to hear her.

"My job keeps me very busy."

"Then I'll get right to the point. We have reason to believe that information from this facility is in danger of being stolen or has already been stolen—"

"Are you sure you have the right facility?" he said, trying to appear dumbfounded, but she didn't take the bait.

"Is there a script that everyone here follows? Yes, I'm sure."

"I don't understand. We're doing brain research here, not

developing weapons. I can hardly see a department like this being a target for anything." He felt his left shoulder raise slightly as he spoke and hoped she didn't see it.

"Why would I expect you to say anything different than anyone else?" She sighed. "But I have to ask… So you haven't noticed anything suspicious, nothing missing or out of place, or people that shouldn't be here?"

"Like I said, this is a research facility."

"Instead of deflecting the question, how about a straight answer?"

The tip of Alexei's nose started to tingle, and he rubbed it with his cold hand. "No. Nothing at all." This FBI bitch was trying to get to him, take his family away. She knew what was happening or at least had an idea. And she had to know that he was involved somehow or she wouldn't be so aggressive.

"If there was anything, you'd be the one that would know, right?"

"I—"

"Because you're one of the few people with his hands in everything here, and you're telling me that you haven't seen anything out of the ordinary. Do you even realize how serious this is? How much trouble you can get into if you're lying to me."

"What the hell are you talking about?" he said, hoping that raising his voice would show innocence.

"National security."

"I'm an American citizen, Agent Stern. Don't come in here treating me like some fucking terrorist. Read a little deeper into your files. Do you know the shit my family's been through this past year? We've been threatened, vandalized, made to feel like Nazis living in Jerusalem for God's sake. So instead of coming in here and pointing the finger at me, why don't you put more effort into protecting those who care about this country? They threatened my fucking children. For something I had nothing to do with. My children. Do you have kids? A family?" Alexei didn't notice a change in the woman's expression; he could only hope that he was getting something churning in her mind, something to dismiss him as a potential suspect.

"None of that matters, Mr. Volkov. This is much bigger than that—"

"To you."

"To the country." She stood, letting out a deep breath. When she spoke again, her voice was softer, choosing not to let the conversation escalate. "So if you notice anything suspicious, you call me immediately." She put a business card on the desk, then walked to the door.

"That'll be the fucking day…so you can stick needles in my eyes and drill holes in my teeth. No, thank you."

Agent Stern stopped at the door, stood there for a few seconds in silence, then turned around and was standing in front of Alexei's desk a moment later.

The agent's movements told Alexei that he'd taken it too far. He'd gone from potential suspect to victim and now to suspect in those short minutes.

When Agent Stern spoke, she didn't yell, she didn't show anger or hostility, she just stood there, a smile creeping across her face. "I didn't suspect you, Mr. Volkov. Now, I'm not so sure. You've done something, and it's in your best interest to tell me what it is."

Alexei felt nauseous. He was scared. This was the one consequence he had absolutely no control over. It hadn't been this way in Russia…until the end. Donya had always given them all protection, KGB protection, so he did his job without fear because what he had to lose was protected. But here, there was no protection. The FBI had absolute power in situations like this, and he would lose his family. This bitch was threatening his family. He had to go back on the defensive. That was the only way. If he let up on his innocence now, it would be an obvious tell.

"What kind of FBI agent are you? You come to my workplace and start accusing me of stealing information with no proof, no *nothing*. What's your boss's name? I'm making an official complaint."

"DeLaurent. The number on my card will get you to him, too." She started to leave again. "Have a good day, Mr. Volkov."

Why hadn't Hawthorne shown him how to deal with these people? These were the elite, and simple diversions wouldn't blind them from the truth. The bitch probably had enough evidence against him already and was just enjoying fucking with him, watching him squirm under the heat lamp.

Alexei waited a few minutes, hoping it was enough time for Agent Stern to get out of the building. He downed a shot of Stoli, put on his coat, grabbed his leather messenger bag, and left his office. When he reached the staircase, he heard his name.

"Where are you going?" asked Jenny.

"Victor is sick. I'll be back soon," he said, taking the first steps down.

Jenny shook her head and approached him. "Bullshit, Alexei."

He stopped and turned around. Jenny was at least a full foot taller than him now, and it made him disoriented for a moment, as if his world had shifted. He'd never seen her that way, shadowed and stern, because she always looked up at him, and the lights would always make her face glow like noonday sun, and the way she'd squint to shield the light made her seem innocent and nonthreatening. But not now, not from this perspective.

With one raised eyebrow, she said, "Emily was just here," gritting her teeth now, "so don't lie to me. You're acting weird, and you never just leave work."

"Why was Emily here? Why didn't she stop in?"

"I told her you were in a meeting. She was just dropping off lunch. Said she had a doctor's appointment a few blocks over."

She stepped down to Alexei and almost whispered, "So where are you going?"

Alexei put his hand on Jenny's shoulder, glanced at the floor for effect, and then looked into her eyes. "Jenny, I just have to step out for a little while. Personal matter. I'm sorry for lying to you…it's just an…embarrassing thing that I have to do."

"What is it? I've told you embarrassing things about me. I thought we were friends."

"Why are you pushing so hard?" She was worse than a cop.

Jenny nudged her shoulder, giving Alexei a clear sign that he should remove his hand, and he did. She crossed her arms and turned around, heading back toward the offices.

"Forget it," she said in a low voice. "You want to push me away? Fine. Don't go asking me for any favors," she said, pulling out her cell phone and walking away.

Alexei watched her leave, still not understanding her persistence or why she seemed so hurt by him leaving. Sure, they'd had lunch several times, gotten into deep conversations about the lab, politics, coworkers, and a few slivers of personal life, but it was always platonic. She was his friend, nothing more, and never would be more. Was that it? Did Jenny want more? It didn't make sense, and Alexei didn't have time to figure it out right now. He turned around and left the building.

When he reached level four of the parking garage, he saw Hawthorne standing by his car. They both got in. He started the Altima and turned the heat on high, even though it blew out frigid air.

"You don't handle the FBI so well," said Hawthorne, "like you do regular cops."

"She's working with you?"

"No."

That meant his office was bugged. God damn it.

"What do you want me to do? It's like she knows about everything."

"I don't want you worrying about her. We'll take care of that."

"How?"

"It doesn't matter. Just know that our hands run deep into the FBI."

"Is she one of yours?"

"No."

"Then why is she familiar?"

"She headed the operation that took down ten of your comrades."

Alexei remembered the arrests, that bitch's picture on the second page of the *Boston Globe* standing next to a guy that was probably her boss. He was thankful when they released the names of the Russian spies that his sister was not one of them. He didn't even know what she was involved with, just knew that she was keeping herself hidden, that she didn't trust being in the open like he was. Only changing his name once. Settling down with a family. But her role in Russia had been much more involved. Her job had no boundaries, no ending point, the kind of work that made people want to seek revenge, but his job ended somewhere near the beginning. Donya. Poor Donya. Never knowing innocence. Stripped of everything. How was she still alive? All alone. How had she kept suicide away? Donya. He knew he would have killed himself a long time ago had he been in her shoes. So strong.

Staring at the steering wheel, Alexei replied, "That's right, something I had nothing to do with but am paying for as if I'm an enemy."

Hawthorne smiled. "I guess you are now."

The bastard's words stung Alexei's chest and throat. He *was* the enemy now. The spy. He deserved to be victim to the neighborhood vandals. Thank God he was not in Russia.

"Maybe you want to kill her. Cut her up into tiny pieces and ship her to her family...if she had a family."

"I'm not killing anybody."

"This agent is alone, married to her job. Relentless, yes?"

The only person Alexei wanted to kill was Hawthorne right now…and Brother. They were why he was in this mess. If they would have stopped with Canada, he would be free and clear, no evidence. But, no. They had him stealing from his own facility…breaking the first rule about committing a crime—*never in your own city, dumbass.*

"Why are you asking me? You already know."

Or did he? Maybe his office wasn't bugged after all.

"You're almost done, Alexei."

The air had warmed now, the car's temperature gauge a few notches below the 200-degree mark. Alexei was confused, but he didn't want to keep asking Hawthorne questions. He would find out on his own. His office could be bugged and someone else listening, then calling and telling Hawthorne, prompting Hawthorne to show up out of the blue like this and meet with him. Someone could be on the inside of the McGovern, a human bug, and made the call. So many possibilities.

"I want you out of my life. I want Brother out of my life when this is done."

"I'm sure Brother will have no problem with that once he receives the files and gets reunited with Donya."

"What?" said Alexei, staring daggers into Hawthorne's eyes now. Always something else added to the job, but this he would not do. Donya was not to be part of any of this.

"He wants to see Donya, Alexei."

He was silent for just a moment before letting out a quick but decisive "No."

"And then you will be free."

"I don't know where she is."

"We do know that much. But you can find her. Correspond with her. Set up a meeting."

He couldn't give up his sister, even if it had been over ten years since they'd seen each other. Besides, she was probably listening in on this conversation right now. At least he liked to think she was, always looking in on him and making sure that everything was okay. Like a guardian angel.

"No. You can find her on your own."

"You really don't know what she's involved with, do you?"

Alexei shook his head. "And I don't care."

"What if I told you that she was plotting against you, Alexei? Trying to make you feel comfortable. Trying to get you to keep doing all of this, working with us, so that she can buy her way to freedom. Setting you up."

"I wouldn't believe you."

"Think about it. Has she ever tried to stop you? Warn you? She certainly hasn't done anything to us. To keep us away from you."

"Debts had to be paid."

"And you told me that they were paid, yet here you are."

"You threatened my family."

"And she stands by and lets us." He smiled, letting out a one-breath laugh. "That doesn't sound like the Donya we know. She has been under the radar since you two got the United States. You know there's a reason why, Alexei. She was into a lot more than you knew about. You may have gotten Boris paid off, but she owes a lot of dangerous people, far more dangerous than the those who killed your brother and sister back in Petersburg."

How much did Hawthorne know? If she was listening to this conversation, if she had his car bugged or some hi-tech microphone zoned in on them, did Hawthorne know, and was he baiting her? Had they intercepted his mail and read her letters to him? It was possible. Maybe the altered handwriting on the envelope was not her trying to disguise her style but Hawthorne or Brother's handwriting; after all, it had a masculine form. And would Donya know if that had happened? Did they have someone in the Post Office looking through his mail? If so, then they would know that she told him about Brother being on a hit list. About Alexei possibly taking Brother's family to Donya and her doing God knows what to them before probably killing them or having them sent to a Siberian labor camp or prison. Too many god damn uncertainties.

Alexei had to shift the conversation. He didn't want to imagine Donya betraying him, using him. She wouldn't do that. Not Donya. "Why do you want her so badly?" If they had intercepted the letter, this was the perfect way to try and get them to slip up and mention something that sounded like revenge.

"She has information that we would like."

"That's it?"

"That's it." He let out a long breath. "And we're willing to pay a lot of money for that information…and keep our mouths shut about where she's living these days, or that she's living at all. Not to mention your own personal interest in finding out why she is using you. Like Brother said, we are like family. And we don't want this spat to escalate."

"There is no spat."

"That is your position, Alexei. When you find out otherwise, remember that I tried to tell you."

"What kind of information could she possibly have that you bastards would even know about?"

"That's not your concern."

"It is my fucking concern!"

Hawthorne sat quietly, lips tightening. "You don't want to know, Alexei."

"If you haven't seen her for ten years—"

"Just because we haven't seen her for ten years doesn't mean we don't know the kind of shit she's been into over the past ten years. And her hands are pretty fucking dirty, Alexei. Filthy. And some of that shit's gonna roll on top of you and your family if you let it."

"So you're looking out for me, that's it?"

"I'm gonna level with you, Alexei. We're not looking out for you. Brother told you to your face that you were expendable, and he meant it. But you have access to something that we want. No, we need it. And it just so happens that it can be a win-win. We'll get the information we want, and in doing so, protect you from a serious shitstorm that could land you in jail or the graveyard. No extra sweat off our backs, and then we never have to see each other again." He leaned in. "Ever."

"I'll have the rest of the information for you by the middle of next week. That's the best I can do."

"That's not the best you can do, Alexei. You got the FBI on you, your sister's betraying you and you're too god damn stubborn to see it, and then you have me and Brother—I suggest you help us before we find someone else who will. Because you're all alone, Alexei. Think about that on your way home."

Hawthorne got out of the warm car, and Alexei was accelerating before the passenger door fully closed. He was afraid to speak, afraid who would be listening. Donya, Hawthorne, and the FBI could all have his car, his office, even his house bugged. And that bastard Brother. He probably had access to his new security system. What did it matter? To them, he was an open book and there was nothing he could do about it. He didn't know how to fall below the radar; that was Donya's specialty. He couldn't live in the shadows; it would drive him mad. Alexei wanted life, people who loved him. If he had no one to protect, there was no reason to live. And Donya could take care of herself. Could Emily? She had an education, parents with money; she'd be fine. And the children. Millions of them grew up in single-parent homes and turned out just fine. Surely Brother wouldn't expose his past if Alexei killed himself. And they wouldn't have enough information to complete whatever devious plot they were concocting with the information he was stealing. The FBI wouldn't divulge the information they had to Emily. And Donya could be free from looking after him. If she would ever be found, it would be through him, he knew. He didn't want to keep the performance going any longer. And he didn't want to believe, no, couldn't believe that Donya would ever turn against him, even if she was involved in horrible, unspeakable things and with the most dangerous of people.

Alexei checked his rearview every couple seconds, "you are all alone," looking for any cars that might be following him. He turned down streets that were not on his usual route home to see which cars did the same. He even stopped and parked a few times to see if anyone mirrored his actions. None stood out, but that didn't mean they weren't there. What if they had several vehicles alternating surveillance? When he turned, the second in line followed. When he turned again, a third car, and so on and so on.

He turned on the radio, pushing the volume button up and up until the sound stopped getting louder. If those bastards were listening to him, then he wanted them to suffer. Unless it was Donya...and he contemplated turning it back down or completely off.

Speeding out on the street again, keeping the music up, he passed cars wildly, swerved from lane to lane, blew through a few stop signs and red lights, luckily not causing any accidents. And, still, he couldn't tell who was following him. They were good. Then it hit him. If he was being pursued by the FBI, they wouldn't waste resources on five separate cars following in separate intervals; they'd follow him from above. Alexei stopped the car, horns erupting behind him as he rolled down his window and looked skyward. He didn't hear a helicopter, and how could he: blaring horns behind him, Queen in the middle of "Bohemian Rhapsody" ripping from his speakers, his mind filled with yelling, telling him to hide, telling him to kill himself. The sky was clear of helicopters, but if they were following him, they wouldn't be right overhead. They'd be out of sight so he wouldn't know. He couldn't see much to the right and left because of the buildings, and that's where it would be. But if it was Hawthorne, there'd be a GPS device somewhere in his car or under it. Alexei got out of the car, as did the man in the Nissan behind him. When Alexei got to the trunk, he dropped to his knees to look underneath, and the man grabbed him by his jacket and picked him up.

"What the hell do you think you're doing?" the man said, Southie accent. "You can't just stop in the middle of the street, ya prick."

Alexei couldn't reply. He just shook free of the man and tried to look again.

"I'm talking to you, asshole."

"Fuck you."

Alexei felt the man's shoe connect with the side of his face, and he was on his side in seconds.

"Move your god damn car, you yuppie son of a bitch. Some of us got interviews."

The pain felt good, penance for his sins. It cleared his mind for a moment, and he looked up at the man and said, "Again."

The expression on the man's face before he turned around and got back in his car made Alexei laugh. And Alexei stood and thrust both fists down on the man's hood, yelling "Fuck you" again. "Fuck you all!"

With a smile plastered on his face and taking deep breaths, Alexei got back into his car and drove home calmly, going the speed limit and abiding traffic laws. He held it back physically, but in his mind images of people screaming recurred. Eyes clamped shut, veins bulging from necks, hands clenched into fists and near the temples, and mouths open bellowing out dark cries. But they weren't angry, they weren't in pain, they were shrill cries for help. Before he knew it, the images disappeared, and his hands were gripping the steering wheel so tight his knuckles were white and *he* was screaming, heaving his body forward and then thrusting it back into the seat over and over for what seemed like an hour. Banged his fists against the wheel.

And when his throat was hoarse and the muscles in his cheeks ached, when his knuckles had blood on them, he brought his hands to his face and wept and wept and wept. Not caring who saw him. He did this for a long time.

His legs were weak and barely held his weight when he got out of the car. Dragging himself to the front door, Alexei knew that he could no longer do this on his own. He needed Donya, and he had to contact her without Brother knowing about it. He had to warn her that she was being hunted and that he was the bait. But maybe that was exactly what they wanted him to do.

Standing in the doorway of his home office, Alexei couldn't move. If he spoke, someone would hear him. If he checked the video feeds, he would see that people were following him, watching him. If he tried to contact Donya, they would find her and do God knows what. He was paralyzed, wanting to crawl into the shadowed corner and hide.

"Alexei," he heard, his muscles stiffening with a jolt.

He turned around, and there was nothing there, beams of sunlight speckled with dust in an empty hallway. This felt worse than the USSR. At least there, it all happened suddenly. The murders, the escape. There was no psychological game being played, destroying someone from the inside out, as was happening here. He almost preferred having his fingers snapped and pieces of flesh cut off his body; at least then he'd know what was happening.

Alexei dropped to the floor, resting his back on the door jamb, and he stayed there until Emily walked through the front door with Nina and Victor.

When Emily saw him, she said, "You two go to your rooms," then went to him. "Alexei, I was so worried about you. Jenny called and said that you'd left work suddenly. You didn't answer your cell." She was knelt down beside him now. "What's wrong?" She put her hand on his cheek.

His vision was slightly blurred, eyes dry from staring. "I need help, Emily."

"You're scaring me, Alexei." Both hands were on his face now, as if holding it up. "What's going on?"

"I'm not strong. They know I'm not strong."

"I don't know what you're talking about."

He put his arms around her and pulled her to him. "Just stay here, right here. Don't go anywhere. Don't say anything."

And she didn't say anything.

It was what he needed to get his mind in order. His love. Close to him. They couldn't take her away if she was in his arms. The tightening in his chest eased as he breathed in the scent of her lavender perfume, feeling her heartbeat through her knitted green sweater and her soft black hair against his cheek. He belonged to her. In his heart, he'd known that back in New York, that she was his salvation. And he had to protect her.

"I never want to be away from you, Emily."

She leaned back, looked him in the eyes, and said, "Then don't be."

Emily stood and helped him up with both hands. Though he felt better, his mind and body felt like he hadn't slept in days. A thunderstorm trapped under his skull.

She kissed him deeply like she always did, no loss of passion through ten years and two pregnancies. And there was none now, in the midst of his breakdown. The unbreakable rock that held everything together.

"I might have to be away."

"No," she said as if to a child asking if there were monsters under the bed, her hands always touching him, reassuring him of her love. "You don't."

"Emily..." Tears now. "What if I'm a bad person? Will you still love me? Will you love me if I did have to go away for a short time? Will—"

"Alexei," she said, her right hand going over his mouth to silence him, "stop talking like this. You're my husband, the father of our children. You're a good man." Her hand dropped now. "I don't know what's going on with you right now, but we'll get through it. We'll be okay."

Her face, that lovely face. It gave him so much ease. "I love you."

"Go upstairs and lie down," she said. "I'll bring you up a plate of dinner in a few hours."

"Okay," he said, then started up the staircase.

"And I love you, too. Always."

He hoped so, and before he went to bed, he looked in on Nina and Victor, both happy to see their father and tell him about their day, and he eager to listen.

The days had started getting longer, January sunlight brightening the room at four o'clock, but the cold winter air had not ceased. Alexei could feel slivers of frigid air coming in through tiny holes in the window frame. It made the tip of his nose icy and the want to be under the thick maroon comforter that much stronger. He took off his shoes and slid into bed fully clothed. A few minutes being under the cool sheets, his body heat turned the left side of the bed into a warm cocoon where he felt safe. Where he fell asleep quickly and did not dream.

Chapter 14

"Agent Stern," yelled DeLaurent. "Alert levels have been raised. Inform your team."

"Because there are so many of us and we carry so much experience... What happened?"

"Terrorist attack in Moscow. Domodedovo Airport. Your surveillance and tap requests are all approved. Herrera and Young worked on this case with you before... I'm pulling them off their current case and giving them to you. Hobson and Dobbs are also yours, give you some experience on your team. This incident has given this case top priority. Get busy."

"Has anyone taken responsibility?"

"Not yet, but it's probably Chechnya like the others were, so I'm doubting anything will come of it here in the US—"

"And because this case has direct Russian ties, it'll give me leverage. I'm on it."

"Right. I promoted you for a reason. I expect this case to be closed soon."

Apparently Klein had been wrong. This wasn't a dead-end case, just one that needed a little boost. And that was that. DeLaurent hadn't been punishing her or just covering his own ass; she had been given a case that was on the brink of high priority, and now that line had been crossed because of some angry Chechen in the Russian Federation. She assembled her team in the conference room.

"Agents Herrera and Young, take an hour and get caught up, then you're in charge of Volkov. I want to know where he's at, at all times, who he's talking to, what his emails say. Find out why he enters the building late at night sometimes when only janitors should be there. Flag any janitor on the lab floor; I was told that they should only be there in the morning, when the researchers let them in." Anna handed them the equipment-approval form. "Hobson and Dobbs, you'll keep an eye on Dr. Jin Won Suh. I believe they're after his information. Unless I completely misread him, he doesn't seem involved, so keep an eye on him and his work. Morgan, you'll go with me to watch Jenny Fraustento...however you pronounce her last name... She's hiding something. You two," she said, referring to the two male rookies, Abbott and Blake, "are working surveillance or at the computers finding out who keeps dodging the security camera the nights Volkov is in the institute, monitoring emails and phone calls, finding out all we know about these people, their families, and their friends. You've all read the files. You know names of those connected with this group. I want full reports tomorrow, but call if any red flags go up." Anna picked up her files and headed for the door, saying, "It took us years to build this case and make the arrests last summer, but we were starting from scratch. And we don't have that kind of time."

"Stern," said Herrera, and she stopped and faced him. "What are they looking for? This is a brain-research facility, not the nuclear—"

"It doesn't matter what kind of information they are stealing. It is conspiracy, espionage, treason...take your pick. And it's our job to stop it from happening, Herrera."

"Yes, ma'am. My apologies."

"Morgan, let's go."

It had started snowing, the clouds so thick you couldn't tell where the sky was, like being trapped in dense fog. The black Suburban was the worst undercover vehicle in this weather, but Anna chose it anyway. Traffic was thick, but she wasn't in a hurry yet. Jenny would be at MIT for another two hours.

"Agent Stern," said Morgan, "why did you choose me to work with you? I have the least experience."

"What better way to get experience?" Anna said, turning left.

"Isn't MIT the other way?"

"There's somewhere we need to stop first."

"It's not because I'm a woman, is it?"

"You're an FBI agent, Danielle. I don't care what is or is not between your legs." But part of her did care. She couldn't be in the same position that she had been in with Meeks. That was one bright spot in her promotion, that she would not have a designated partner, but she could choose anyone at any time or even go alone.

She pulled into the clinic parking lot and told Danielle to wait for her.

Jonathan Meeks didn't look any better than he had before Christmas, and he sounded like a sick old man on his deathbed.

"There's fluid in my lungs," he said. "But I'll survive even if I don't sound like it."

She knew pneumonia killed off more people in hospitals than anything else, but that's because they were old and frail. Meeks was young. His body had been healthy.

"I know you will." She stood next to his bed. "I can't stay long. I just wanted to give you an update. Everything you said about MIT seems to be paying off. I picked up where your files left off. The only place that has had suspicious activity is the McGovern Institute, and we're looking at some of the people there. It's hard to tell if there's someone on the inside yet, especially since you said that we need to look at people who aren't Russian."

"I don't understand."

"A Russian man works at the institute, Alexei Volkov. I did mess with him a little bit, but nothing going too far, and he acted defensive and scared. I mean, he didn't react like I thought he would."

"You've spoken with him?" There was a slight alarm in his voice, as much as there could be in his condition.

"Yes, and I already have agents keeping an eye on him in case he tries anything sudden. Like I said, he just acted—"

"You have to do something to calm him down. To make him feel comfortable, but keep close surveillance on him."

"What do you want me to do, bake him a pie? What's done is done. Besides, anything I do will be suspicious."

"I guess just keeping distance then and letting your agents keep an eye on him from afar."

"Then I'll do that."

"You said there were people there…more than just this Russian guy that you suspect?"

"A researcher, Jenny. Last name starts with an F."

"Frautschi. It's German."

"You know of her?"

"She was connected to a few blips on the radar, but I don't remember why. I was getting ready to dig into her files and see what turned up…before Aziz. Did you speak with her, too?"

"Yeah. Something about her just doesn't fit there. It all seems too convenient. She started there a few months after Volkov. I'm not certain that it means anything, but it might. It's something to keep an eye on. She just fits too many of the researcher stereotypes, like overkill. It'll take a little more time to really know for sure."

"Who's keeping an eye on her?"

"I am."

"Good." He closed his eyes for several seconds before opening them again. "Do me a favor and tell me what you uncover with Volkov. I hadn't even gotten as far as him, so I'm curious. Will you do that for me?"

"Sure, Johnnie." She was getting that feeling again, that sadness and regret creeping in, and she tried to keep her closed-mouth smile so he wouldn't see what was going on in her mind because just pushing it out wasn't working.

"And keep your eyes on Jenny Frautschi, every move, Anna."

"Do you think they could be working together?"

"No. There's usually only one. Two raises the possibility for too many leaks. Of course, I can't be one hundred percent sure, but it's so rare that I can't imagine it being the case here. How do you feel about them?"

"I don't know. Volkov sent up some red flags. Jenny...she just...I don't know. The stereotypical lonely researcher, married to her work. There's just something about her telling me that she's into something."

"Your instincts are usually precise, right on the money."

"Key word, usually."

"Nothing's a hundred percent. I just recommend keeping a closer eye on Volkov."

"A few southern-Canadian universities reported minor damage to their facilities, stuff to the doors at Montreal and the windows at a university in Toronto, around similar times that Volkov was in Canada. It's a stretch, but it's something else added to the pile."

"Make sure he's covered."

She didn't want to bring it up, but she had to ask if there had been any progress, if the doctor had given any glimmer of hope that Johnnie would get better, and when he told her no, she kissed his forehead.

"Well, the regular therapy shouldn't take so much longer. You'll be out of this place soon. I'll take you to Manfredi's on the day you get out."

It was his favorite restaurant, owned by his high-school friend, Anthony. The best Italian food in the Northeast in Johnnie's opinion.

"I guess I better get rid of this fluid on my lungs, making me sound like Darth Vader."

"Star Wars, really?" She tried to make him comfortable, putting her hand to his cheek. "I need to tell them to hurry up before you become a Trekkie. Then I'll have to kill you myself."

"Never gonna happen."

She left, telling him that she'd be back soon.

"This came through while you were inside," said Danielle.

"Read it to me. We have to get to MIT." Anna felt good about this. Her instinct had drawn her to this woman, and Meeks had backed her. Maybe the case would get closed sooner than she thought. All she had to do was gather intel, follow her, bug her lab and phones and home, get into her computer, find out who she associated with and who she was selling information to. It could all happen in a matter of days. The computer would be tricky. It was an offline computer, no network ports, designed to be protected from hackers or other outside entities. To get information from the laptops, someone would have to physically have the machine, login, and extract the files manually with a flash drive. One of the techs would be needed to get past the password security, but that was it. And it had to be covert. She couldn't have an agent nab the computer like a purse-snatcher or break into her apartment; if she was a spy, the whole operation would be put in jeopardy if she knew that her cover had been compromised. Well, if she was doing anything wrong, that is.

"Jenny Frautschi, born and raised in Presque Isle, Maine. Undergraduate work at Husson University in Bangor, got a B.S. in psychology. Then she did her graduate work at Duke before joining MIT. She has a clean sheet. No siblings. Parents have clean sheets save a few speeding tickets years ago. No connections, no nothing."

"That would make sense," said Anna. "Nothing that would send up any flags in any system. The perfect child, the perfect family, the perfect everything. Are her parents still alive?"

"Yes, still living in Presque Isle."

"How did she pay for graduate school at Duke?"

"Assistantship. She scored high on everything."

"Of course she did. MIT wouldn't have hired her if she hadn't."

"I was looking through Volkov's and Suh's files."

"And?"

"Suh also went to Duke. He got his doctorate there and eventually made it to MIT."

"Why didn't I see that?" She glanced right. "Nice pickup, Danielle." Maybe her instincts were as good as Meeks had said.

They were four miles from the McGovern Institute now, and they had nothing. Anna's instinct and Meeks' seconding to her instinct. But nothing was ever so perfect. That didn't exist without special favors, people erasing those mistakes along the way. And she was certain that this woman had a few skeletons in her closet.

"Have them do a deeper search. Newspapers, any photos…I want to make sure that Jenny Frautschi was always her name, and have proof of that. If she's part of this, there's nothing saying that she wasn't recruited from high-school age or earlier. We need something. They snag them young. And look deep into the parents. It's possible that they have some connection with someone that was involved with something—"

"I'll have them do a level-five search on them all."

Anna smiled, knowing that she had started rambling and liked how Danielle handled it.

"What do we have on Volkov?"

"Sort of similar. He came to the US in the early nineties, went through the application process for citizenship, everything checked out with immigration, and he lived in New York City for eight years before settling in Boston. He holds two degrees from Moscow University, which met the requirements for his job at MIT. Married to Emily Vandenburgh-Volkov. She works at South Point Library. Her father has wealth, but he's not big time. Two children, Nina Volkov, nine years old. Victor Volkov, five years old. Ah, I think this might be an important piece to Mr. Volkov."

"I don't like suspense, Danielle."

"Since the arrests that started this whole case, the ten from last summer, his home has been vandalized several times. The reports show that it's anti-Russian comments spray-painted and—"

"God dammit! He wasn't lying. That explains why he was so fucking angry and weird when I confronted him. I'm in his office practically interrogating him, and he's an actual victim because of this case. I should have looked at the files of everyone there first."

"But that's not why you were there. I mean, you were giving a general check of all possible target buildings, and you can't review every person working there."

"I don't like brown-nosing either, Danielle."

"I'm not. I'm just saying that you followed protocol for this case, so you shouldn't feel bad."

"He's right, though. I pushed him pretty hard." Anna looked at Danielle for a moment while they were stopped at a red light. "Sometimes you play the wrong card. It's not right to treat a victim that way. God!" She let out a deep and noisy breath. "I wish I could just apologize to him, but I can't yet. You ever do something that just made you feel like total shit?"

"Yes, ma'am."

Part of her was glad that Alexei Volkov was in the clear, at least in her mind. He was a victim, and she wished that she could tell Meeks right now, discuss this with him and see if sentiments changed, but it was impossible. She could only hope that he would feel the same way as she did.

Chapter 15

Svetlana was a woman of little emotion. A few facial expressions. Direct and short with her speech. She only spoke when there was something important to say. If Lilly kept track of her words, it would probably be less than one journal page per day. And she was okay with that. It taught her to choose her words carefully, to live inside her head so others couldn't read her so easily. Opening your mouth turned you into a window, allowing others to peer inside your soul and understand most things about you, and that scared her. The blabbering girls at her school were shallow, and she knew that she wasn't. So when Svetlana didn't speak at all that day, when she barely made eye contact, Lilly didn't pry. Not yet. Getting a nod, she headed toward the piano and the window to the world, took out her instrument, and began playing without accompaniment.

Twenty minutes passed, and nothing. When Lilly leaned toward the doorway to see what Svetlana was doing, the dreadful squeal of playing a wrong chord startled her. Even startled Svetlana, who was just sitting in a chair staring at the bookcase. Lilly put the violin down. She knew Svetlana well enough to pry.

"What's bothering you today?"

She was silent for what felt like a minute, then said, "I don't think it's something you can understand, Lilly."

Lilly had to be direct. Aside from music, Svetlana had taught her that. "Tell me anyway. Stop being so closed off to me."

Lilly felt a pang in her stomach, a jolt that made her want to look away. She spoke what was on her mind. She didn't let herself be silent this time. And it finally worked.

"Something happened in my country. An explosion. Many people are dead."

She sat down after hearing this. She was too young to

remember 9/11 and knew that it was what Svetlana had meant when she said that she wouldn't understand. And she was right. Lilly didn't understand why it would affect her so much unless someone she knew died. So maybe that was it.

"Did something happen to someone you know?"

"I don't think so," she replied quickly. "You just wouldn't understand."

"Stop saying that!" She did look away this time. That force in her again boiling up instantly, her just saying what she felt without a filter. It started to feel liberating, but there had to be some control over it. "I mean—"

"You're right." Svetlana stood now and leaned on the rail next to the stairs. "The answer is no. I did not know anyone that was harmed by this, but you have to understand that it still hurts when something happens to your home. Your home is always part of you. And for me, it runs deeper, Lilly. It makes things complicated. Do you understand? They say here the snowball effect?"

Lilly did know about the snowball effect. She was running from a giant snowball right now, a whole avalanche. And this woman was protecting her from it. There was a silence again, nothing that was abnormal with the two of them, but this time it was Lilly keeping silent. If Svetlana meant so much to her then what did she mean to Svetlana? Was she part of that snowball chasing her down and trying to bury her in an icy grave? She knew that she shouldn't ask, but she had to.

"Am I part of that snowball?" She broke eye contact after asking.

It was so quiet in that apartment. The air so still. There weren't even cars rumbling by outside. Neighbors yelling.

"You are like a summer sun, Lilly."

And that made her smile. Her own mother hadn't said anything like that or made her feel that way in years, possibly half a decade. Lilly hadn't realized that Svetlana had come to her side. She looked up at her as Svetlana was bending down and taking her hands.

"I had a daughter once. Lukerya. She was your age before I came to the United States. She was taken from me, Lilly. Like your father was taken from you. So, see, we share a darkness. Things that we will carry with us forever. And we must find ways to handle life when the darkness feels like it's consuming us."

"Music," said Lilly.

Another rare smile spread across Svetlana's lips. "Music." And she touched Lilly's cheek with her hand and then stood.

Svetlana went to the bookcase, pulled down one of the few books, and took the book jacket off, revealing a single piece of paper, which she brought to Lilly.

It was a photo. Svetlana, a handsome man with dark hair and a mustache, and a teenage girl whose soft features took more after the man than Svetlana.

"That is all I have left of them, Lilly. A single photograph."

"But you have memories."

Svetlana took the photo back and stared at it. "Memories fade. And we fill them in with what we wanted them to be, the happy times happier, the bad times more dire. But a photograph is perfect, capturing that split second of time, and that cannot change."

Lilly knew what she meant, thinking back to the photos of her family hanging in her mother's bedroom.

"And music is like that. Interpretations can change, but the notes are the same, and they have ways to remind us of what we have forgotten. Of what is important."

She got up and started putting the photo back in the book and reapplying the jacket when a knock came at the door.

"Wait in here," she said, then answered the door.

Lilly heard the door close, heard paper ripping and ruffling, and then Svetlana finally returned with an open envelope in her hand. The sentiment and smile had disappeared. It was back to stern Svetlana, emotionless and expressionless Svetlana. The Svetlana that walked with purpose before meeting Lilly.

"I have something that I have to do right now, Lilly. I need you to come back later on tonight," she said, gripping the envelope tightly. "You can go through the house." She pointed to the staircase.

By the time Lilly had gotten to her room and put her violin on her bed, the sound of the apartment door upstairs closing prompted her to run to the window. With a small purse tightly under her right hand, Svetlana was off with purpose, her strides so fluid and smooth, Lilly didn't know if she'd be able to keep up if she even tried to follow her. Not if she was moving like that.

When she was out of sight, Lilly pulled out her journal. It was a rare moment — she had learned about Svetlana's life. No wonder she'd stayed holed up and alone. She had known happiness and love at one time. She knew what it meant to be a mother and have a life. And that life had ended somehow, leaving her alone and away from her home country. Was that what Lilly had to do? Her father gone and her mother absent. Was that what Juilliard was now? Her escape from the pain that was her home. And had it been that all along? Was it some rite of passage that one had to suffer and then flee in order to learn how to grow independent? How to be an adult? Then what of Mr. Thompson? What was he running away from? Abandoning what seemed like a sturdy foundation, a place to call home, at the hint of storm.

Lilly threw the pen down and ran out of the house. She could catch up with Svetlana, follow her like she'd intended.

Svetlana was at the end of the street when Lilly reached the sidewalk, headed left toward the Metro. And she ran, the intersection seeming far, a mirage that kept disappearing and then reappearing farther away, but she made it. The Metro stop wasn't far, just an outdoor train platform with a metal canopy in case of bad weather, one line of parking spaces for commuters, and a concrete sidewalk leading toward the asphalt crossing across the tracks. The Endicott stop. Svetlana was there, taking a seat on the bench under the canopy. Lilly stood by a hedgerow about a half block away and watched. Svetlana just sat there, purse on her lap, while other people smoked or laughed and talked while waiting for the train. But everyone looked like they were smoking, white gusts appearing and then disappearing amongst the crowd, and it made her shiver, look down and realize that she had forgotten her jacket. Furthermore, if she could see their breath, wouldn't Svetlana be able to see hers if she gazed in her direction?

Lilly slid behind the hedge a bit more, spying through the evergreens, the image almost like a cropped photo, the crowd almost non-existent. Then, she disappeared behind a wall of silver and red as the train pulled into the station. Peering around the hedge now, the train had stopped, and Lilly ran toward it. But, when the train pulled away, Svetlana was still on the bench. Lilly's muscles tightened all at once, almost making her topple to the cold asphalt, but she regained her balance and stood like a statue, wanting to turn around and hide, but unable to make the rest of her body respond for several seconds. The nearest cover was a station wagon, so she hid behind it. Peering through windows powdered with dry salt, she noticed a man with his back to Svetlana leaning on the bench, at least Lilly figured he was a man, wearing a baseball cap and heavy tan coat. Her line of sight was so hazy that she couldn't be sure what she was seeing. Was Svetlana talking to him or he speaking to her? It looked like Svetlana was just sitting there, not really moving much, and then the man leaned over and put something under the bench. And she sat there. And the man stood back up. A statue.

Shivering and with a runny nose, Lilly persisted as more people gathered at the platform, some standing in front of Svetlana. She had to get closer and see what was really going on, so out from behind the station wagon and onto the sidewalk, Lilly made her way toward Grant Avenue, which ran parallel to the tracks, and to the row of parked cars to the right. Grant Avenue was like a tunnel to the left, the gigantic trees' branches intertwining twenty feet above the macadam. Should she go left, hide behind a tree, or right and hide behind a car? She chose a car, a Jeep Cherokee whose windows were clean and had a light tint, a large white van with few windows to her back.

She could still see the man standing with his back to Svetlana. Turning his head to the right and speaking to seemingly no one. Svetlana was behind two people, a man and woman dressed as if going to a stuffy office, only Svetlana's blue jeans visible through the sliver of space the couple allowed between them. This went on for ten freezing minutes. Her legs were shaking, and she couldn't keep her chin still, the sound of her chattering teeth like a group of tap dancers in her ear. She heard the train approaching, but she kept her eyes on Svetlana. It looked like she was moving. And now she was standing, walking away from the bench with something under her arm that wasn't her purse. And the train came, this one going in the other direction and not stopping. When it had passed, Svetlana was gone. So quickly. She must have gone the other direction with whatever it was that the man had put under the bench, because there was nothing under the bench now.

What about the man in the trench coat? Footsteps on concrete, and her shivering stopped. He was walking down the path toward the line of cars, her line of cars, face toward the ground for just a moment, walking briskly. That's what Svetlana had done. Met someone at this stop and picked up a package after getting a letter telling her to do so. But what was in it? And would she bring it back to the apartment? Lilly didn't think so because she was gone, heading in a different direction…somewhere.

When the man looked up, Lilly finally saw his face, and her mouth dropped because she knew this man. It was Lester, the man who had lived upstairs and who had told her and her father stories about Finland. The man who had recommended Svetlana be allowed to rent from them when he left.

He didn't see her as he started past the Jeep, but her stunned expression was quickly taken control of, and she called out, "Lester."

He had passed the space between the Jeep and the white van, so she wasn't certain that he'd heard her, but a few seconds later, his kind face peered around the corner of the van and he wore a smile.

"Lilly?"

She ran to him and gave him a big hug, and he gave one right back.

"I can't believe it's you. I thought I'd never see you again," she said, the sound of the train's squeaking brakes behind her. "I thought you'd gone back to Finland."

"My goodness. What are you doing here? No coat? You poor girl."

Behind Lester, a silver car slammed on its brakes.

Lester glanced at the car, then back at Lilly. "Run," he said in a guttural whisper.

"What?" she said.

"Run, Lilly. Hurry."

Lester's back was to her now as a man started getting out of the driver's side of the silver car. She backed away, hiding behind the back of the van as she heard the train moving on from the station. She was shivering again, but this time it wasn't from the cold. She lay on her belly and scooted under the back end of the van, peering up at Lester from behind the back wheel.

"Where the hell's the woman you were meeting here?" said the man, his accent local.

"I don't know what you're talking about," said Lester.

When the man pushed Lester against the Jeep, his back to her, Lilly put her hand over her mouth so that she wouldn't cry out.

"Boris is dead, motherfucker," said the man, pulling out a black pistol and pressing it into Lester's side. "So you're gonna tell me what I wanna know or you're gonna be in the ground, too."

Lester was staring the man in the eyes, not flinching, not looking away. "I'm not telling you anything, motherfucker."

"You sure about that?"

"Rot in hell."

Lester caught Lilly's gaze, and when he did, his eyes grew big and his nostrils flared a bit as if the sight of her frightened him. It looked like he was about to say something to her when the crack of gunshot hit her eardrum like an ice pick. Lilly's body tensed so much, she couldn't get a scream out as Lester fell to the ground, his eyes staying with hers, her ears ringing so loudly that she didn't hear the thud of his body hitting the pavement. Just as quickly, the second shot, Lester's face exploding, sending a spray of what she thought was blood on her face and hands. This time, she let out a wail, Lester's body convulsing as blood poured from the giant hole in his forehead, steam billowing up from the red river flowing toward her. A third shot and a fourth.

She glanced up at the shooter, a white man wearing a fedora and a frown, and in that moment, she saw a blade enter his neck, come out, and enter again and again and again, a wheezing, bubbling gurgle, the dull clunk of the gun dropping down in front of her, and then the shooter fell to the ground, his body squirming as if being electrocuted. She stared at him, the fedora dropping and soaking up what its owner was leaking out, and that's when she realized she was lying in a pooling puddle of blood, her eyes blurry with tears, her mouth open and pushing out sounds that she couldn't hear, that she could only feel vibrating in her throat. Pants warm with urine.

"Lilly?" came a woman's voice. Svetlana's voice.

She heard her name a few more times, but she couldn't move. Frozen. She felt her body being pulled out from underneath the truck and carried to the silver car, the blood multiplying the cold on her skin like water does. Svetlana put her in the back seat, and then drove the car...somewhere. Her eyes could only stay focused on the back of the driver's seat, but she didn't see that black leather headrest, didn't notice the blood she was soaked in coagulating and forming a sticky shell atop her skin. She only saw Lester's eyes, staring at her. What was he going to say to her? In the moment before he died, his words were for her, but they weren't let out soon enough. Would he have told her to run? To close her eyes?

"Lilly."

Her ears weren't ringing anymore, she finally noticed.

"Lilly."

Lilly looked up and saw Svetlana's eyes in the rearview mirror.

"You're going to be okay, Lilly."

She felt the car come to a stop, looked out the windows to see trees, nothing but trees. Svetlana got out of the car, opened the back door, and helped her out, leading her toward the trees as if she was blind.

"You're going to be okay, Lilly. Everything is going to be alright."

A flash: Lilly and her mother standing in the bedroom, finally talking about her father's death. Finally crying. Svetlana's words were almost identical, and Lilly spoke the third line as if under hypnosis, "We're going to get through this."

"That's right, Lilly. You're going to get through this."

That was the difference, she suddenly realized, between her mother and Svetlana. Her mother had said 'we' while Svetlana was only talking about her, only concerned about her, like a mother should be.

"We're here."

Lilly had been watching the ground as Svetlana guided her through the forest. But when she looked up, there was a small cabin built in a nook of trees. It felt like the middle of nowhere, but she noticed an electric line attached to the side, so it wasn't as primitive as she suspected. The door was unlocked, and they went inside, where it felt colder than being out in the wintry forest. Inside was dark, thick drapes over the windows.

"Come on," said Svetlana. "I have to get you cleaned up and into some fresh clothes."

She wasn't frightened being here; she didn't know what to think, just that she had to keep her mind off what had happened. And the only thing that came to mind was Vivaldi, the piece she had been practicing. If she could keep the image of that sheet music and the sound of what her violin should sound like when she played it, she *would* be okay.

"Where are we?"

"A safe place."

In the bathroom there was only a shower stall for bathing, and Svetlana turned the water on and began taking Lilly's clothes off, the sticky sounds the cotton made when being slid off her skin sending chills through her body. Steam quickly bellowed out of the stall, and a few minutes later they were letting the hot water melt off the blood that had soaked their clothes.

Svetlana stood behind Lilly, working shampoo into her hair, a deep red lather forming as she untangled the clumps that had fused together, the lines of bubbles streaming down her arms and stomach.

"Rinse it all out, and I'll do it again."

"Until the bubbles stay white?"

"Until the bubbles stay white, Lilly."

And that's what she did. Stood there while Svetlana washed her hair, massaging the painful memories and helping her relax, for Svetlana's hands were delicate and loving. Lilly let the hot water thaw her frozen body, took a washcloth with a bar of soap and scrubbed every part of her skin twice, making sure she had gotten it all. And when the water began cooling, they got out, cleansed and warmed, and wrapped themselves in thick towels.

"I have clothes in the bedroom that may be a bit big, but they will do for now."

As Lilly walked to the steamed-up mirror, she stubbed her toe on something. Looking at the hardwood floor through the steam, she made out a small piece of metal. Lilly knelt down to inspect it, a metal flap that covered an indention no bigger than a nickel.

"What's this?" she asked Svetlana.

"Push that flap down."

She did. "But what is it?"

"Door to the tunnel. Sneak in, sneak out if need be."

A secret tunnel. She'd never seen one before and wanted to open the door just to see it. "How far does it go?"

"Not far. Now let's get dressed."

The clothes were too big, but it didn't matter. They were comfortable, and she sat on the sofa staring at the fire Svetlana had started in the fireplace while she was getting dressed.

"Why did you follow me today?"

Svetlana was sitting next to Lilly on the couch, one leg bent under her and the other stretched out. Her hair was slicked back, and her skin looked flawless in the firelight. Why did fire do that? Why did something have to be so painful and destructive yet so beautiful and comforting? Itself so harsh, yet its aura so soft?

Lilly said, "Because I was tired of wondering."

"This must remain between the two of us. You don't speak of it. You don't write it down. You pretend like it never happened."

"You killed that man."

"I did," Svetlana said, her tone even and emotionless.

Lilly could feel her emotions writhing at the thought of speaking her next question, but she started asking anyway. "Why did he kill...Lester?" And she was able to hold them back.

"He was a bad man. And I don't know why he killed Lester."

"I think he was asking Lester about you. And he...he..." she let out a deep breath, "refused to say anything, so then the man shot him."

Svetlana just looked at her, her jawline flinching as if she was grinding her teeth.

"Why would a bad man be looking for you? Why would he murder someone to find you?"

Svetlana got up and stood in front of the fire, gazing into the flames, the yellow reflecting in her eyes.

"When you asked me if someone I knew died in the explosion in Moscow, I told you no. I then learned that a good friend of mine, a friend that helped me at a time of direst need, had been killed in that blast. Those responsible for that are looking for me. They're also responsible for killing my family so many years ago."

"Why do they want you?"

"That's as much as I'm going to tell you right now, Lilly." Her gaze went from the fire to Lilly now. "There are some things about me that you do not need to know."

Everyone had things that they didn't want to share with others. Lilly could respect that. She was just glad that Svetlana had finally opened up and told her something that she didn't know. Something that showed her that she mattered, that she could be trusted.

"I'll never tell anyone."

"You really shouldn't have followed me today, Lilly."

"I'm okay. I can be strong." She wanted to say that she could be strong like her.

Svetlana shook her head as she said, "It has nothing to do with being strong, Lilly. What happened today will never leave. Unless you lose your memory, you will think of this every day for the rest of your life."

Something clicked here. Svetlana wasn't talking about her; she was revealing herself, what she thought about every day. Every day...

"Why do you listen to a piece every night, then play it? Every single night that you have lived in our house, you've done this. Why?"

"The music, Lilly. It keeps my daughter's memories alive." She turned back toward the fire. "She and my husband died because of me."

"Did Lester die because of me? Because I distracted him and that man drove up behind him like that?"

"No," she said in a whisper, as if there was someone in the fire, someone she didn't want to disturb.

"You're not just saying that to make me feel better, are you?"

"No. You know me well enough to know that I wouldn't do that."

There was a long silence. Lilly got up to stand by Svetlana, both of them gazing into the fire now. She had one question that she couldn't keep bottled up, not after today.

"Svetlana, how many people have you killed?"

"No more questions, Lilly."

"But—"

"*Net*! No more!"

Lilly took a few steps back thinking Svetlana might slap her, but she didn't even raise her hand. The woman barely moved.

"It is time for us to go back."

Outside, the air had grown colder and clouds had formed thick overhead, so thick that it was impossible to tell where the sky began because it was suffocatingly close, practically atop the trees waiting to dump the day's snow, give Massachusetts a clean canvas. But they walked to the dirt road where the silver car still sat.

"Sit up front with me," Svetlana said.

And she did. When they reached Walpole, Svetlana pulled off I-95 and pulled into Walpole Mall.

"Take this. It is plenty for a cab home. There is a cab right there."

Lilly took the two one-hundred-dollar bills and got out of the car. The sun was starting to go down now, and the clouds were less dense here.

"Are you coming back tonight?" she asked.

"Later. I have a few things that I have to do."

So, Lilly did as she was told, and the cab driver didn't speak the entire way to her house, the silence almost unbearable. But the silence was another piece to the puzzle that she had been working on. Svetlana used music not only to keep memories alive, but to suppress those that she wanted to forget...that she couldn't forget. Lilly realized that she did the same thing. She'd barely thought of her father; yet, he had been the biggest advocate for her violin playing. And there was no way that she was to blame for his death, so there was a big difference there. But death was death. Memories were either haunting, pleasant, or they were suppressed, shooed in a dark room whose door was locked with a key the warden tried to keep hidden.

She was sure that Svetlana had killed others. It was all in her reaction. She had killed that man in the fedora, Lester's murderer, and didn't show one hint of remorse or sign of having a conscience. Not when it came to that. But, she did have one or else she wouldn't have followed Lilly that night when she threw her violin down the stairs, the night she took off and could have been kidnapped, raped, or even killed. It confused Lilly because it didn't make sense. You either had a conscience or not; it wasn't categorical. So if Svetlana did have one, she had a seemingly supernatural power to hide the fact. And Lilly wanted that power, that kind of emotional control. But maybe she had it and didn't know it. She thought of her mother. How could a person completely walk away from her mother, not think about her deceased father, stop caring about her mentor of four years, and put all of her energy, all of herself into a stranger renting a room above her bedroom, music being the only connection? Was music really that important, really that strong? Maybe it was. After all,

they both used it for several purposes. The music was thera-
peutic, it was challenging, it gave life meaning, it shaped the
world they lived in, and it created what Lilly saw as an
unbreakable bond between them. Because Svetlana didn't have
to tell Lilly to keep what had happened between the two of them;
she would have done that anyway.

And before she could think more deeply into it, the cab
stopped, and the driver spoke for the second time, the first time
just to ask her 'where to?'. She paid the man, then walked inside,
back to the empty house. To the violin that would help lift her
out of the pit that was her life here, that would guide her away
from the house that was her mother's prison, the place where her
mother was slowly killing herself, cutting all the ties she had
with those who loved her. Even Lilly. That thread was almost
gone now, a string about to snap and emit music no more. Her
violin was the key, its shape even reminded Lilly of a key.

Her mother's bedroom door was closed, and she opened it
one more time. It was bomb-shelter dark with a more than faint
musty odor. When she turned on the light and saw the mess, she
knew that her mother was gone and that she had no way to
return to her life. That Lilly didn't matter anymore. She might as
well have been in that explosion with her father.

She turned off the light, closed the door, and went to her
bedroom. For three hours, she played. For the next three, she lay
in bed staring at the ceiling. She heard her mother walking
downstairs. She heard the piano playing above. Her window was
dark, with a faint yellow glow from the streetlamp. But dark.
Very dark. A new moon.

Lilly got out of bed and picked up her violin case and sheet
music. She gently took the stairway door key in her other hand
and left her room. At the top of the stairs, she gazed down to try
to catch a glimpse of her mother. It sounded like she was in the
kitchen, the sound of a few glasses clinking. Lilly shook her head
in disgust, then slipped the key into the stairway door and

turned it with ease. Turning the handle, it unlatched and glided open as if on its own. The stairs were still dusty on the sides, but she didn't notice. She simply closed the door behind her and locked it, leaving the key in place. Although making her way up the stairs silently, she knew Svetlana would know that she was there. In the sitting room, she retrieved her violin and started playing along while walking into the piano room where she would perform for the world. Svetlana looked at her and caught her eyes, giving a slight nod before changing expression.

The piano stopped, but Lilly did not stop playing. She stared at Svetlana, continually increasing the tempo. She was no longer getting lost in the piece, closing her eyes while playing the piece, or swaying with the rhythm. Unblinking, she owned the piece. A collection of emotions all wrapped up in one, and it was fierce, and it could only be seen in her eyes. Svetlana had to have seen it because when Lilly finished the piece, she said, "Maybe I was wrong about Julliard."

Lilly almost gasped. It registered immediately that Svetlana had given her a great compliment about her playing. So it was *that* which she had to find in order to master a piece. But what in the hell was *that*? Where did it come from? And since she didn't have the answer to those questions, she also didn't know how to get it back or if she could get it back.

"How do I play like that all the time?"

"You don't, Lilly. No one does."

"I don't understand."

"I don't know who it was for, but you were performing just then. Not practicing, not playing. It's something that just happens, that can't be taught."

Lilly didn't know who it was for either. She hadn't done it for Svetlana, hadn't done it for her father, hadn't done it in memory of Lester, and surely hadn't for her mother. Maybe this was for herself.

"Okay." It had been for herself. She had to know that it could be done, that she had nothing to worry about. It was all in her hands.

She nodded at Svetlana, and Svetlana turned on the bench and began playing. Lilly joined, and they played for almost an hour.

"What time did you get back?"

"Not long before you came up here."

"You had to—"

"Yes. Get rid of the evidence. So no more talk of this, yes?"

"Yes," she said, then finished with "Goodnight."

When Lilly got back downstairs, there was a note taped to her bedroom door: *I didn't want to wake you. I want to apologize for the way I've been since your father died. I've gotten help, and I think it's working. I need to talk to you, Lilly. I need to explain some things. I will see you in the morning. I love you so much. Mom.*

Lilly held the letter while going inside her room. She crumpled it up and threw it in the corner, then went to bed.

Chapter 16

Drapes were drawn and the children off to school. For the second day, Alexei sat in front of the computer staring at the video feeds from his security cameras, analyzing each car that drove by, the faces of men and women, even children, that walked past, keeping notes on a steno pad. He recognized most of the people's faces, most of the cars, but those that he didn't made him nervous. He'd stare, pause the video and print out a photo. But it was doing no good. They could be FBI. They could be working for Brother. They could be people just going for a walk. Boston was a big city, and there was no way he'd be able to know everyone on his street. There was no way to tell if someone was watching his house or not unless they just sat in their car and stared at it.

The doorbell rang, and his gaze shot to the screen. Jenny. It was too early for her lunch break. Dammit, why did she have to be here? Nosy woman. She rang again.

Alexei opened the front door and let her in.

"I'm glad to see that you're still alive," she said. "What the hell's going on? Two days, Alexei. And nothing."

"It's not your concern, Jenny—"

"It is. Now get ready. It's enough of this. And you're staying after to make up the time you've missed."

Alexei hadn't seen her like this before. Taking charge as if she was his boss or something. She was far from his boss. Dr. Delk, that son of a bitch, was the only real person over his head, and she hadn't mentioned his name.

"I can't go in yet."

"Yes you can, Alexei."

"Jenny—"

"Today, you don't have a choice. You're going to work."

"Is that what Delk said?"

"Fuck Delk. You have a lot of important work to do. And I'm not covering for you again."

"What do you mean, covering for me?"

"I told him that you were really upset about what happened in Russia yesterday."

"What did happen in Russia yesterday?"

"What the hell have you been doing? You haven't watched the news? The terrorist attack."

"I don't—"

"In Moscow. A suicide bomber at Domodedovo. They think Chechen terrorists are responsible."

Alexei didn't reply, just let the information sink in.

"Let's go."

"I can drive myself to work, Jenny, for God's sake."

"I don't think so. Not today. You've been acting weird, and I'm making sure that it stops now."

"Why."

"Because I'm your friend." She opened her door. "That's what friends do, idiot."

He got in her car. It was only when they were a bit over halfway there that he realized he'd not been looking around for tails or listening for a helicopter overhead; that he finally felt okay and safe, even if only for a handful of minutes.

Jenny did care about him, and it was more than a friend. That her anger the other day when he was trying to leave work after Anna the FBI agent basically accused him of doing, well, exactly what he was doing, was the kind of anger a sister has toward a brother. Genuine concern. And it made him feel good for the first time in days. More so, it made him think of Donya. Where was she, and should he get in touch with her? Yes, he had to see her. He missed his real sister, even if Jenny was taking over that role right now...and practically had been since she had started working at the institute.

Maybe that was it. If he was being watched so closely by

Brother as they tried to find his sister, he could pass a message along through Jenny because there was no reason why she would be watched by anyone. And shouldn't he mention it right now, here, in her car? It wouldn't be bugged.

"Jenny."

"Yeah," she said, quickly shifting her gaze to him and then back on the road.

"If there was something that I needed you to do for me, something important, could I count on you? No questions?"

Her head tilted back and there was a slight smile emerging from the corner of her mouth. "That depends on what it is."

Alexei saw her reaction clearly and it paralyzed him. *Don't over-think everything! She's happy to be able to help, that's all.* But what if she had been waiting to get in a position to get information? Oh, the paranoia coming back...it had to end somewhere. *Jenny is not working with the FBI or Brother or anyone else. She works for MIT and MIT alone.*

"Just delivering a message."

She laughed now. "Sounds easy enough...unless you mean like a mafia message or something."

Though she was giggling and Alexei usually found her giggling to be contagious, his expression didn't change. Not this time.

"No. Nothing like that."

"And why can't you—"

"No questions, remember?"

"Fine. I guess I should just be happy that I got you to work."

"That's not like you to give in."

"You have to pick your battles," she said without taking her eyes off the road. "And you didn't put up much of a fight this morning, so returning the favor. What do you need me to do?"

He didn't want to tell her yet because he had to be sure that she could be trusted. Too much room for mistakes. The only real safety was in Emily, but that meant keeping everything from her to keep her safe. So repetitive were his thoughts, a maddening circle of worry, paranoia, and anger that he wasn't sure what to do. It seemed as though every path he could travel led to something bad. That he was living a cursed life. He had to do something that would reunite him with Donya, would set up Brother the enemy, and keep the FBI as far from it all as possible.

"I just need to know that you'll be there when I need you."

"I'm here now, Alexei," she said, turning into the parking garage. "Don't you think you should do whatever it is you need to do? Because something's obviously bothering you."

It was too early. He needed time to plan it all out. Alexei didn't respond, just got out of the car after she'd parked and waited for her to collect her bag.

"You're really not going to tell me right now, are you?"

"It'll have to wait, Jen."

"I might not be much help if you wait," she said, then started walking faster, leaving him behind.

It was one of the things women did, he knew, when they were angry. Even women who were experts of the mind. But she had nothing to do with what was bothering him. Shouldn't he be able to solve his problems on his own time? Or maybe she was right. Enough waiting. Just get something in motion. Have her get a message to Donya. Take a fucking step forward to getting a clean break from his former life. To take a giant step out of hell so he could breathe again. At least she wasn't using textbook psychology on him. She was just being human.

"Jen."

She stopped abruptly, her tennis shoe making that basketball court squeak on the smooth concrete. The wind was gusting, blowing her thick brown hair to the right as she just stood there with her back to him, head tilted down a bit. And he approached her.

"I'm sorry."

She raised her head.

"You're right."

"I know I'm right, Alexei."

There wasn't anger in her voice. It sounded more pitiful than anything. Almost helpless, which didn't seem to fit what had led up to this exchange. It didn't fit her personality either.

"Are you okay?" he asked, putting his hand on her shoulder.

Jenny finally turned around. No tears, thank god.

"I'm just worried about you. I mean, you don't really tell me anything. You lied to me the other day. You come in to work really late sometimes. I mean, you're my best friend. And you're acting weird after this FBI lady comes in."

"She practically accused me of stealing information. How do you think I should react?"

"Well, I guess pretty angry, but she doesn't suspect you."

"Bullshit, Jen. She told me to my face that she does."

"She was just under a lot of pressure, and you were pissed off and not being cooperative."

"You weren't there."

"I met with her the day after. She took me to lunch, and we started talking. When you came into the conversation, she acted all uncomfortable. Said she felt bad for treating you that way. So relax, Alexei."

So he didn't need to worry about the FBI. That didn't make sense. Why couldn't she just have told him personally? And would he have believed her? Probably not.

"Why did you all have lunch together? That's…I don't know, strange."

"Because she's nice, Alexei."

"It doesn't strike you as odd that an FBI agent interrogating people just strikes up a friendship with one of the people she's questioning? That doesn't make you wonder?"

Alexei knew that he was verging on crossing a line he didn't want to cross. The fact was, Jenny didn't have many friends; he hadn't known until now that she considered him her best friend.

She never went out to lunch with anyone except the occasional colleague, and he didn't know much about her personal life. Jesus, he felt sorry for her right now. FBI Anna was probably acting like her friend and would drop her once the case ran cold…or once he was caught, which he couldn't let happen. God damn those people who use others. Poor vulnerable souls. In thinking that, he knew that he was even damning himself.

"Don't do that," she said.

"I just don't want to see you get hurt." And after a silent moment, he said, "Maybe she is lonely and the two of you really did just hit it off." And he smiled, hoping it would cut down some of the tension. "So it was a good lunch?"

"It was."

"What else did she say?"

"It was a long lunch."

"That's very rude," he said, getting the desired laugh out of her, hoping it would sway the discussion and the mood.

"She was nice and just talked about how she had been bogged down with work and that she probably took some of her frustration out on you."

"We better start heading inside," he said abruptly. He wanted to end his show of interest in Anna now because he finally realized that her befriending Jenny, whether genuinely or not, was his way to stay close to Anna, to find out what moves she might be making. It was a way to focus on Brother and to keep Brother away from Donya by going through Jenny.

"Why do you feel that you can't talk to me? Like about Anna. I mean, you do trust me, don't you?"

How could a thief really trust anyone?

"Yes, Jen, I do trust you, which is why I want you to deliver a message—"

"That you won't tell me about."

Damn her. Fine. It had to be done anyway. A whole scheme set in motion that would free him and Donya for good.

"I will give it to you at lunchtime today," he said as they reached the front door.

"Good," she said, and opened the door for him.

Alexei hand wrote the letter, and to read it made no sense: *The Moon is Red and the skies in Limbo.* When he handed it to her and told her to deliver it to the *Boston Globe* to be put in the classified section, she tilted her head and crinkled her brow.

"I don't understand."

"It's what I need you to do."

"Why can't you do it?"

"What happened to no questions?"

"Well, I just feel like you're messing with me. Like, you're having me do this instead of the real thing you were talking about before."

Though he had thought about that, it wasn't the case and he told her so, but she didn't seem convinced.

"I don't know how to get you to believe me."

"Tell me what it means."

He paused. "No."

"Then tell me why."

"It's really personal, Jen. Just know that it will mean a lot to me if you do it, and that it's something that I can't do on my own because it could have negative consequences."

"Am I going to have to say 'Don't kill the messenger'?"

"Nothing like that."

He couldn't understand why she was so adamant to know so much. It wasn't like she opened up so much to him. Maybe he should start asking more questions about her. See how she responded. And at that moment, Alexei realized that not only did he know very little about Jen, but practically nothing about her outside of the McGovern. Well, Duke grad and psychologist or psychiatrist...what the hell was the difference?

"Okay, there's a difference."

"What?"

That happened once in a while, thinking so hard about something that it comes out verbally. "Nothing." He let out a deep breath. "If you could just take that, I'd appreciate it."

And she did. He watched her closely as she took the stairs and headed for the exit. She didn't show any signs of, well, anything. An unbroken expression that meant nothing. Until she reached the door. A slight hesitation and a glance back at him watching her. What did it mean? Her movements were slow but fluid as she turned back around and pushed open the door, made her way to the sidewalk, and then sped up as she turned right and disappeared.

It had to be done. Donya had to meet him face to face so they could be free. So she could live again. Too much suspicion would be aroused if he had gone to the *Globe*. They'd know something immediately; they'd watch him even more closely and find Donya.

Alexei went to the break room to watch the news, hoping something about the bombing would be on since they always splattered that kind of news for a few days until the next big event occurred. The television was turned on WCBV, the news anchor talking about a fiery car accident off I-93 near Braintree.

"It appears that the driver was thrown from the vehicle, but a body has not been found. In other news, police have no suspects in the bizarre double homicide yesterday in Dedham. Commissioner Oakes told WCBV that it could be a mugging gone wrong. One man was shot, and the suspected mugger stabbed to death. Police have identified the gunshot victim as Lester Nords, a Scandinavian tourist."

An image of Lester was superimposed on the screen.

"Can't be," said Alexei.

"And suspected mugger Anthony Hawthorne..."

When Anthony Hawthorne's driver's license photo was superimposed on the screen, Alexei stepped back, almost falling over a chair, not hearing what the anchor continued to say.

Hawthorne was dead and had killed Lester, the man that had helped him and Donya get into the United States, that had given them their papers and places to stay. What in the hell was Lester still doing in Boston? Last Alexei had heard, he had planned to live out his days in British Columbia. And Hawthorne? If Hawthorne had killed Lester, did it mean that they were close to Donya and that Brother had been lying to him, as he'd suspected. Or would they use it as a warning? Showing Alexei that if he didn't deliver the information and give them Donya that he'd end up like Lester. Maybe Hawthorne just fucked up, didn't know that Lester had a bodyguard or partner or something. One thing was for certain, Brother had others that could take Hawthorne's place. And if someone seemingly so close to Brother was expendable, then there was no doubt where Alexei stood. Right where Hawthorne had told him. Nowhere. He meant nothing, was nothing except a pawn able to move one small space at a time, in one direction. But Donya was the queen, most powerful and elusive on the board. And certainly the most dangerous. And that's what Brother wanted to do…take down the queen.

Alexei got to his office and closed the door. It was still early, but he didn't care. He retrieved his Stoli and drank a mouthful straight from the bottle, then did it again, sitting the bottle down on the desk with a loud thump. To contact Donya *was* the right decision, especially now. But to involve Jenny, he wasn't so sure anymore. Any link to her whatsoever could make her a potential target, could get the poor woman killed, now that murder was officially on the table.

It occurred to him that Brother was using multiple angles to get to Donya, but was he doing the same to get the information from Suh? The files that he still needed to get were almost a terabyte in size, he estimated, and Suh was sneaky with file security. He kept certain files on his computer, mainly information that he'd already published or more common details about his research, but other files were encrypted. Alexei had gotten into Suh's computer easily and copied all of the information a while ago, had already delivered it to Brother, but the encrypted files remained encrypted. It took several weeks to finally realize what Suh had done. The son of a bitch had a system. He had separate jump drives with specific information on each—to have one meant you had nothing, like one piece of a large puzzle. One of the jump drives was the decryption program. Take all four and plug them into his laptop, and you'd have all of Suh's research, all of what Boris demanded. But Suh never had all of them on him at once unless he was going out of town, and he was scheduled to speak at his alma mater Duke University two nights from now, when Alexei had planned to break into his hotel room and copy all of the files while he gave his speech. Genetic modification, video feeds, all of it, showing how Suh was able to create autism in the rats and mice, and Alexei would have delivered it to Hawthorne. But, if he was able to do it tonight, to get Suh away long enough for him to get the information, he could have one door closed and add leverage, buy himself two days. They wanted this information, and it seemed that it was priority over finding Donya, so he could use that somehow.

Now, he would have to get Suh out of his house, break in, find Suh's safe where he kept his flash drives, break into it, and then retrieve the files that way, a much longer and more difficult task because Suh had a decent security system. But waiting until the speech, two days plus travel, was just too long. He didn't have that long. And with Hawthorne dead, he didn't know what Brother would do and expect. And if Brother had access to Alexei's security system, then he had to get his family away until all of this was over. There was no more time.

Alexei got to street level and waved down a cab, had it take him a block from South Point Library, where he took the long way through the neighborhood, through a tree-thick park, and then through the back entrance of the library in case he was followed. Emily was at the check-out station, the line three deep with people holding several books each.

He bypassed them. He walked up to her, said "emergency," and met her at the door a few seconds later.

"We have to go right now, Emily."

She didn't protest, just got her purse, and they got inside the car, but she didn't start it.

"What is going on?"

"We don't—"

"I wasn't going to cause a scene in there, but you are going to start talking right now."

"You and the children have to go. You have to drive south to your aunt's vacation home in South Carolina."

"This is crazy. Why?" she asked.

"Because I love you and need you to do what I ask."

She glared at him, tight jawed, then said, "I'm not going anywhere unless you tell me why. You haven't been yourself, and I'm not leaving you alone. Period."

Why were people stubborn at the worst times?

"And I don't think you're in your right mind, Alexei. Since the night someone threw that brick through the window, you've changed, and I don't know, I really don't know what I can do to help you."

"I will get help, but I need you and the children to go while I get better." He took her hands in his own. "I promise you. One week. And when you get back, everything will be back to normal."

If she wouldn't listen to him, would he be able to get Suh's information tonight? Meet Donya tomorrow...as long as she did see the morning paper? It wouldn't work if he had to leave and get a motel. Then how would Donya know where to find him? He had to follow a regular schedule tomorrow, and with Emily and the children around...too much could leak out, too much suspicion.

"I don't think it's a good idea. I can take Nina and Victor to my parents' place, but I'm not leaving you. Not when it's so clear that you need me more than ever right now."

Under any other circumstances, he would have been grateful for such a loyal and loving wife, but his secrets, his baggage could be the death of her. Which would be the death of him.

"Emily…" He put his hands to his face, rubbing his closed eyes, wishing one damn thing would go his way. "I need you to go."

She started the car and began driving.

Would she understand if he just told her everything? How many times had he asked himself that question? The answer was always no.

"Just this one time, please do as I ask. And if you do, I will do absolutely anything you want."

"Idiot," she said quietly. "You already do everything I want. Until now, when you want to push me away."

"I just need—"

"Why are you doing this? Why are you keeping me in the dark? I am your wife. No secrets, Alexei. Now, whatever it is that's going on, you need to feel comfortable telling me. Trust that we'll be able to get through anything that it could be, and that we can get through it together. The way it should be."

As much as he wanted to believe that, he knew it was something that people just said, a false sense of security, because when the truth came out, that hope for understanding disappeared. And didn't most feel deep down that it was infidelity? That they could handle a confession like that. What he had to say was far worse, at least he thought it was.

"I'll tell you when I can. That's the best I can do right now."

Her expression told him that she did not fall into the category of 'most'. She knew that he was faithful. And that's what seemed to disturb her the most. He wasn't in a profession where corruption or other common crimes were committed. So it was a complete mystery. That's what probably made her the most angry, that she had no idea what it could be. And the expression, showing more hurt than anger, was unflinching.

They were silent for a long time. Emily pulled the car into Brothers & Sisters Bakery, just a block from the children's school and finally turned and looked at him.

"How long do you want us gone?"

"I don't want you gone. Don't say it like that."

Her soft lips grew firm and her eyebrows raised.

"Five days."

"When we get back, you're going to tell me everything. Swear to me."

What was a lie at this point? Or was it just a test to see if he'd lie and she hoping to pick up on it if it was so?

"Everything. I swear," he said.

He leaned forward to kiss her, but she pulled back.

"Em—"

"Get out of the car, Alexei."

"But—"

Her lips dipped into a frown and her eyebrows quivered and raised, tears forming in her eyes so quickly. "Just go. Get out!" She was completely sobbing now.

Alexei wanted so badly to hold her, his chest tightening and throat constricting. He had caused this pain, and he knew that the quickest way to make it go away was to do as he was told. To get the hell out of the car. And so he did.

She was still crying as she drove away, not looking back at him. And he wanted to die right there, an eerie wave of nausea crashing in his stomach at the thought of never seeing her again. Why did so many entities want to separate them? If he would lose her anyway, why not just tell her the truth to see if she'd still have him rather than pushing her away, or worse, Brother doing some horrible thing to her?

He was able to get a cab quickly, and he knew there was no

way to get Suh out of his house tonight without incriminating himself. It would just be too obvious. So, he made short work of getting liquid tranquilizer from the lab and a small laptop from his office, of getting back to his empty home and changing into dark clothes and putting on a ski mask—folding it up so it looked like a beanie, and of leaving his house at twilight, taking the darkest streets, slipping through parks and reservations, to his colleague's house four miles away.

Jin Won Suh lived with his wife, and they had no pets. He usually left MIT at six o'clock and got home about forty-five minutes later. His wife, Aletta, worked ten-hour shifts four days per week at a twenty-four-hour veterinarian hospital in Somerville, which meant she would get home around eight-thirty. And Alexei agreed with Hannah, a researcher from Georgia, that Aletta was 'the sweetest woman you ever did see.' Having worked with Jin for several years and having watched him far more closely the past month, Alexei knew that the man came home and had his ritual on nights his wife worked: strip down to a t-shirt, black sweat pants, and no socks; drink two ounces of sake while watching *Jeopardy*; and then have a late dinner with Aletta, which she would usually pick up on her way home.

There seemed to be no change in ritual tonight, which would give him just under an hour and a half to get in, get the information, then get back out. Alexei waited in the man's fenced-in backyard for him to get home, disarm the security system, and then head to his bedroom. And when he did, Alexei pulled the mask down, leaving only his eyes and the upper bridge of his nose exposed, put on his gloves, and picked the lock on the back door, which led to the kitchen, slipped inside, and closed it behind him. The house was silent and dark, save the light from the entryway faintly emitting a late dusk-like light in the back room and the upstairs bedroom and the hall light brightening the staircase. On the counter was a knife set in a butcher-block holder, Alexei noted; if it came to that, he knew where to get a weapon.

In the living room was the small bar, a white ceramic set of sake drinking cups and carafe sitting on the marble top and four different brands of sake. God damn it. Which one would he drink tonight? There was not enough tranquilizer to put in all four bottles, especially if they were all close to being full. He inspected them. Two had been opened, one almost full and the other with only a swallow left.

He heard Jin moving around upstairs; a sense of urgency boiled in his veins and he had a sudden extreme urge to urinate, which always happened to him at stressful times, but he controlled it. Alexei opened both bottles, put a few drops of Acepromazine in one and all but a few cc's in another, keeping a little in a syringe that he put in his inside pocket just in case. The only thing to do now was wait, and he slipped into the dark dining room, which was just past the staircase, to wait for Jin to come down, pour his drink, and turn on the television. He knelt down behind the eight-person table in case Jin looked in on his way to the living room. And a few minutes later, he was downstairs and in the kitchen. Alexei took his shoes off so his footsteps would be silent, put them under a chair and out of sight, and he left the dining room and started up the staircase.

The loud ring of the doorbell startled him, almost making him slip on the hardwood and go crashing down the steps. He had to hurry and make it up before Jin walked past and saw him, but he still had to be silent so he wouldn't hear him. Jin's footsteps sounded like a giant's moving in his direction, and Alexei knew he would not make it; he was only halfway up. He flattened himself against the stairway wall, the bright ceiling light shining directly on him. The urge to piss was painful now, throbbing. But he had to hold it.

If Jin saw him, he would have to attack him and make it seem like a regular robbery. But what about the person at the door? Jin had never mentioned doing things with friends after work, just being a homebody with his wife, so maybe it was just a salesman or a neighbor...fuck! Could a neighbor have seen him break in? Seen him doing something to the sake through the windows? And had he already called the police? He pushed the back of his head into the wall in frustration. The only weapon he had was a syringe with animal tranquilizer in it, not even enough to kill himself if it came to that. He needed a gun, but the thought of it almost sickened him. Alexei wasn't a killer, but he didn't know what he'd do if he was cornered.

Jin was close now, and he walked right past the stairway and on to the front door. Alexei didn't wait; he crept up the steps, got to the top, and had three choices. The upstairs bathroom was in front of him with the door wide open, a guest room to his right, and Jin's bedroom, light still on, to the left. His bladder told him to go straight, to just ease some of that pressure so it didn't feel like he'd been kicked in the nuts repeatedly. But logic told him to go left and complete the main objective here, so he went left, the place where he was sure Jin had his safe; besides, there was nowhere to hide in the bathroom with the door open like that, a clear line of sight from the foot of the staircase.

The bedroom was carpeted, and Alexei scanned the room for any sign of the safe. There weren't many places for it. Two dressers, a bed, and a trunk at the foot of the bed, and that was it. He opened the trunk—sets of sheets. Looked in the open closet—everything nice and neat and no safe. Talking downstairs. It was a man at the door, and Jin had let him inside. He stood in the bedroom doorway to listen to their footsteps, to see where they'd go. It sounded like they were going toward the kitchen and living room, the voices getting louder and louder and then softer as they passed the stairwell. Alexei got back to searching. This was not how he had hoped this would go. It would be so much easier if Jin had just had his drink and conked out on the couch...

Where in the hell was that damn safe? It wasn't behind any of the picture frames on the wall. Maybe in the wall behind a dresser? He knelt to his knees and pressed his face against the wall to look in the small crack behind the dresser, and when he did, he noticed something in his periphery. He looked at the bed, and underneath, a flap of carpet was bent up and over. The son of a bitch hid his safe under his bed, built into the floor. And of all things, he had left it open. That would save him ten minutes of work, but it didn't matter under these new circumstances. He had to just work fast to get the information transferred, and that's what he did. On his side, he reached into the safe, and it contained four small jump drives and paperwork, of which Alexei didn't care about. Laptop out and on, he plugged them in and copied the files. The first drive took one minute, the second three minutes. When he got to the third, the popup box gave an estimated twenty minutes to copy the files.

"Jesus Christ," he whispered, watching the green bar just creep along as a folder icon sent a white box to another folder icon over and over again. He could leave the computer here, sneak into the bathroom and relieve himself if the fucking bathroom wasn't at the top of the staircase. The sink was behind the door; maybe he could just do it there.

When the time reached seventeen minutes left, Alexei said, "The hell with it." He stepped lightly, making his way to the door, then eased onto the hardwood of the hallway. Slow baby steps toward the bathroom. Without even making a squeak, he'd made it to the stairway entrance. Now, all he had to do was take two steps and he'd be in the bathroom. He peeked around the corner, down the stairs: nothing. So, he took the first step, and Jin turned the corner and took the first step up the staircase. It startled him so much that he pissed himself for about half a second before clenching and stopping the flow. A deer-in-the-headlights second, and then Alexei was fast to get back to the bedroom, hearing a few squeaks underfoot, but they weren't loud enough to be heard over the clopping coming up the stairs.

Alexei heard the men's voices as he scanned the room again, even though he knew there was no place to hide. Except under the bed, so that's where he went, and he pushed the screen back as far as it would go, making it nearly flat and putting it screen-side down.

Fuck! He was going to get caught. What other reason could Jin have for coming upstairs than to get something from or close up the safe? And he was right next to the fucking thing. Alexei would have to cross the line, he'd have to fight both of them, maybe even kill them in order to escape. But what in the hell could he kill them with other than his bare hands?

They were at the top of the staircase.

Should he slide out and surprise them, run toward them and throw them down the stairs? His whole body was covered in sweat now, his underwear in urine, and he couldn't move. So this was how it was going to end. Him caught stealing research information and too damn afraid to do anything about it. They would either kill him or he'd spend the rest of his life in prison. Oh God, he'd let Emily down, Donya down. Such a fuck up, and all because he locked up when it counted most.

"A little sake…" he heard Jin begin to say, the second part too accented for him to understand.

"Give me that bottle," said the other man.

Alexei recognized the other man's voice now and caught a glimpse of him as they walked into the bedroom. It was Charlie Delk, the director of the institute, taking a significant gulp of sake from the bottle. Alexei didn't get a good look at the bottle, so he didn't know if it had the Acepromazine in it or not.

Alexei tried to get mentally prepared, tried to get his mind to allow his body to move, to stop sweating. His bladder throbbed more now, so much worse than before. He thought about just letting it go. What did it matter now?

Both men walked to the other side of the bed, the side closest to the safe. Both took their shoes off and were still wearing work clothes.

"I've been wanting this all day," Delk said. "It's too bad I wasn't able to free things up to go to North Carolina."

Shit! Of all the days to break in…why choose the day when the boss wants to go over the materials for the Duke trip.

Alexei began sliding his way out from under the bed slowly, hoping to get up and run right when Jin was about to look under the bed and get into his safe. That would give him the best head start. He could get to the kitchen and get a knife. He'd have to. There was no other way. Halfway out now, and he saw Jin drop to his knees, about to bend over and see him. He put his hands on the rail and pulled lightly, and he was out. As he sat up, about to bolt to the door, he heard a loud exhale from one of them, and it made him glance that way.

Jin hadn't been kneeling to get the information from the safe. Charlie Delk had his head back, mouth open, and one hand gripping the sake bottle and the other on Jin's head, pulling it forward toward his groin.

You've got to be fucking kidding me. Jin and Charlie.

Alexei got back on the floor and quietly slid himself back under the bed. He wouldn't have to kill anyone after all. At least he didn't think so.

They left the light on and eventually moved on top of the bed, their clothes in a pile on the floor. He checked the computer. Just one more minute for the copy, and one more jump drive to go. It would take thirty minutes. Alexei didn't know what was worse, his insatiable urge to urinate or the grunting and slapping sounds just a foot away from his face, until they slowed quickly and then stopped.

What the hell had happened? They weren't making any more noise, no movement. Alexei waited a few minutes longer, and when it remained quiet, he chanced a look. Sliding out from under the bed yet again, he saw his partner Jin balls deep in their boss, both men passed out, and he could see them moving slightly as they took in shallow breaths, and a half bottle of sake spilled on the bed. So they had taken the drugged bottle after all.

"So much for stereotypes," he whispered, then took the bottle of sake, went to the bathroom, and pissed for a long time. And when he was finished, he poured the rest of the sake in the toilet, wiped the rim with toilet paper, and flushed it all down.

When the last jump drive finished copying, Alexei closed the laptop, put everything back in the safe, and repositioned the sake bottle on the bed. He didn't worry about being quiet on his way to and down the stairs, clutching the laptop tight with his right hand. But halfway down, "Jin?"

He had forgotten about Aletta. The sound of the front door closing, and Alexei had no choice. He couldn't go back upstairs because she'd see him and have time to run back out of the house and call the police. It wasn't going to be a clean escape. God dammit.

"Jin," she yelled, getting closer.

He knew her well enough that she would probably recognize him if he rushed her and just put his finger to his mouth, showing her to keep quiet because his accent would definitely be recognized. Alexei had come too far now, so he rushed down the remaining stairs, getting to the bottom at the same time Aletta got there. He swung to hit her with his left hand, and she screamed so loud it frightened him and he missed, hitting wall instead. Aletta backed up, picked up a large vase, and threw it at him. Alexei raised his arm to shield his face, and the vase connected, breaking into hundreds of pieces and covering him with fresh flower scum and water. He lunged for her, but the now slick floor underneath his cotton socks sent him crashing to the hardwood, the laptop hitting with a sickening thump. Before he knew it, Aletta was throwing more at him as he tried to get up. The wooden coatrack, which missed. A Yankee jar candle, which hit his forehead and sent him back and against the wall.

And then the dumb bitch threw her large ring of keys at him, and they hit his chest.

She'd realized what she'd done immediately. The front door had a double-key deadbolt, so she was trapped. But she was going to try anyway. And she ran down the hallway to get past him, dodging his outstretched hand a bit too much and finding herself on the floor, too, face down.

Alexei started crawling toward her, hoping that he could reach her before she got up and made it to the kitchen where the knives were. He grabbed her feet, and she rolled over, pulled her right leg back and slammed her tennis shoe right in his face. He felt his head jerk back, his neck shooting with whiplash pain, and then another kick, right to his throat. He rolled toward the wall, hands to his throat coughing, and was finally able to stand, but Aletta was on her feet now, too.

God damn this woman; all he'd wanted to do was leave. Why did she have to get home so soon? And why was she so resourceful. She'd never spoken of self-defense classes, and neither had Jin. This was why he wasn't cut out to do what Donya did. Donya would have put a bullet in the woman's skull and slipped out the back unnoticed.

Making sure his footing was good, Alexei ran after Aletta, but she had already gotten to the kitchen and pulled out the butcher knife and knife sharpener from the set on the counter.

"Why are you in my house? What do you want?"

If he spoke, he would have no choice but to kill her. He reached into his inside pocket to get the syringe. Once he had it and started to pull his hand out, she rushed him, and he quickly started backing away and into the living room. Hand out of his pocket, she would be able to see what he was holding now, and as he backed up, he realized that she probably thought he was reaching for a gun so had nothing to lose. She raised the butcher knife as she closed on him, and he backed into the bar, knocking the bottles to the rug but not breaking them, and then he staggered back more until he lost his balance, hitting the back of the low sofa. She was on him now as he fell backward onto the sofa, throwing both hands up to stop the knife from plowing into his neck, and when he did this, the syringe fell to the floor.

He caught her wrist, and the force knocked the knife out of her hand, the sharpener he saw stuck in a pillow, and the two of them crashed to the floor, knocking over the narrow coffee table in the process. Alexei hit his head hard and was stunned for just a second. He lost hold of her wrist.

She reached for the syringe too quickly for him to do anything about it and jammed it in his neck, injecting the tranquilizer with veterinarian accuracy. He knew that he didn't have long. By his hand, a full bottle of sake. He gripped the neck of the bottle and brought it up as hard as he could, smashing it against Aletta's head, and she fell over and stopped moving.

He pulled the syringe out of his neck and tried to calm himself so that the drug wouldn't spread through his body as quickly, but it was no use. Alexei had to get the hell out of there. He pocketed the syringe and ran to get the laptop that sounded like it had gotten broken in the fall earlier. Slightly dizzying waves altering his vision. When he'd made it to the back door, he realized that he'd forgotten his shoes. In the time it took to get them from the dining room and put them on and get back to the back door, the effect of the drug had doubled. Staggering, he climbed over the fence and made it to the reserve across the street, where there was darkness from the thick trees that went on for a quarter mile. Halfway through the reserve, he fell to the dirt clutching the laptop, unable to keep his eyes open, unable to stay conscious.

Chapter 17

25 January 2011. 12:11pm. *Boston Globe.*

When Klein called, Anna and Danielle had been tailing Jennifer Frautschi in separate vehicles. She had parked, and Anna told Danielle to follow her on foot and she would keep an eye on Jenny's car to make sure it wasn't a switch or drop off or anything else that could open the case up more.

"Are you at your office?" Klein asked.

"No, I'm in the city."

"That's too bad. I was going to stop by and take you out to lunch."

She still wasn't used to this, but it felt good. Having a man thinking about her, wanting to be with her, and treating her well. It just didn't feel real.

"Are you still going to be busy this evening because I could make it a dinner date instead."

"Dinner sounds nice." Nice? Really? That's all she could come up with?

"Seven-thirty."

"Okay."

And when he hung up, she smiled without effort.

It was about fifteen minutes when Danielle returned.

"She went inside the *Boston Globe* and bought a classified, and now she's having lunch across the street," said Danielle.

"Why would she go all the way there rather than just doing it online?" asked Anna, biting her lip. "No trail."

"The moon is red and the skies in limbo."

"That's a code."

"How do you know."

"Because it doesn't make any sense."

"What if she was going in there to meet with somebody, and the classified was just a cover?"

"Good point. Get Herrera here to review video and see who she spoke with."

Anna left Danielle at the *Globe* and followed Jennifer Frautschi back to MIT. Not enough was happening. Her case was moving so slowly, and there were so few leads that she wanted to do something drastic. The report she had been waiting for was still not complete, and what the researchers had was useless, backing up that Jenny had absolutely nothing to do with any illegal activity whatsoever. That she was perfect. However, this message to the *Globe*, Anna suspected could be a break. If it was to someone, that meant something would be happening soon. And if she kept close to Jenny, she'd be there when it happened. Find the missing piece that would make the case make sense again because everything seemed to point towards a dead end. It had to be something. A green light to steal information, a signal to meet, a way to tell someone that she would deliver the information soon. All she had to do was keep watch, and Jenny would lead her to the next person in the chain, and so on, until this case could be closed the right way.

Her cell phone rang as she watched Jenny pull into the parking garage next to the institute. It was DeLaurent, and he ordered her back to the office, his voice not as stern as usual.

"It's not a good time."

"It's an order, Anna."

She had Danielle take over at the institute, but there would be a lapse in surveillance until she got there. It wasn't like DeLaurent to just pull someone off like that.

When she entered the field office, DeLaurent met her in the lobby.

"I'm driving," he said.

She followed him without question, thinking there was something significant happening with her case and that time didn't allow for pauses, that they had to get wherever it was and now. But when they got in the Suburban, DeLaurent didn't put the key in the ignition. He just sat there, staring forward, and let out a deep breath. Then his lips sealed as if he was refusing to let out something that he so badly needed to say.

"Are—"

"Jonathan Meeks is dead."

He didn't say another word. The cold, still air in the truck seemed to thicken, making it hard for Anna to breathe, so she took deeper breaths through her nose, faster breaths. But she kept them quiet while noticing that DeLaurent couldn't look at her, but looked out the window at the concrete wall of the underground parking garage. Her teeth were clenched and she was grinding them. Her eyes, at first open wide, closed halfway but not quite squinting. And in those deep breaths, she could smell the potent, bitter aroma of the Kevlar vests and waterproof jackets in the back. But she did not cry.

Anna whispered, "How?"

It took DeLaurent a moment to respond, as if he hadn't heard what she'd asked, like the word had to travel a while until it reached his ear. "I don't know." He put the key in the ignition and started it, and they pulled into the home about an hour later; neither spoke on the way there.

The doctor said that his heart had given out. "It happens sometimes, sudden like that. It's one of the big dangers at this stage."

Anna wanted to be alone right now. The doctor acted like Anna had to act in tough situations while on the job— emotionless and direct. Without that distance, it would be impossible to cope with just the day-to-day life. But she didn't have that distance. Jonathan Meeks had been her partner. Even more than that on the inside.

"I want to see him," she said.

Like Munch's screamer, his mouth hung open at a slant, but his eyes were closed. His body, the shell of what was once something loving and brilliant, didn't move. Anna had seen corpses before, vacant vessels for something that she tried not to believe in. Animals weren't that way. When Sabaka, her cocker spaniel, died when she was ten, she found him on the back porch, and it seemed like there was still something there in those dark canine eyes. No breath or blinking, but a part of him still lingering until he became part of the earth again. People weren't like that. What remained was nothing. A batch of organic material. When Anna thought of the dead, she remembered a William Faulkner story she'd read in high school. "A Rose for Emily." Sleeping next to a corpse for decades, next to a decaying shell for decades. A woman with nothing. And the subculture of those obsessed with death. To her, it meant being obsessed with nothing, a blank sheet of paper. But, maybe, and this is where she struggled, it wasn't death that was the obsession. Maybe it was something more. A caterpillar life gnawing through the thick and tough leaves and traveling through dirt and bark to a cocoon coffin and on to something grand, to the sky with beautiful wings, with fluttering freedom, and landing and resting in the confines of flower petals, bathing in their natural perfume. Maybe that was life, that hidden gem inside the shell that went on somewhere. To Heaven? Inside a newly created shell? Into the air and then out into space, an unbound wanderer. It was what she thought about. Even at funerals after the mortician had made the corpse look as alive as possible, she felt the same way.

As she pulled the sheet back up to cover his face, part of her felt relieved that he didn't have to live any longer not being able to take care of himself. That his struggle was over. However, the other part of her felt sad and helpless. She was on her own now, had no one to talk things over with or to ask for advice. No one to visit and be waiting for her, hoping that she would come soon. What she had was Klein, but he would only be able to take her places that she didn't think would exist in her life, unlocking the mysteries of people she'd seen in the park holding hands, dating and kissing, making love instead of fucking. But she no longer had her friend. And she could not cry for him right now.

DeLaurent came in the room, but he didn't put his hand on her shoulder for support the way actors always did in movies. He just stood there looking at the white sheet.

"How common is this, Doctor?" he asked.

"Well, it is the chief concern for patients having just had an episode that renders them paralyzed, so not as common for someone several months into therapy, but still generally common for the condition."

She wished he would just say it in a few words. Why did doctors always ramble on with their answers?

"And the signs? Was there a way to prevent this? To see it coming?" asked DeLaurent.

"Um, I'm—"

"I'm not trying to get you to say something that will get you in trouble, but I have to rule out any possibility that this was not a natural death. When an FBI agent dies, it is investigated no matter the circumstances. Understand?"

Anna hadn't thought about that. There was no one from his past that she could think of seeking revenge, but wouldn't a good criminal keep quiet until the right time? The quiet ones that you have to watch...

"I'll have my full report available this evening and will be able to answer your questions then, sir."

"Thank you." He turned to Anna now. "I'll contact his family."

"He doesn't have any," whispered Anna.

There was an almost eerie silence for several seconds.

"Take your time here, Anna. I'll let your team know that they're to report directly to me until tomorrow. I'll be outside when you're ready," he said, then stepped out of the room with the doctor, closing the door behind.

And the silence lingered. What DeLaurent had said was bothering her now. What if he had been murdered? Could it have been her fault? Keeping him in the case, giving his expertise and helping her move in the right direction... If someone on the other side knew about it, knew how much Johnnie was helping her. But who actually knew about his involvement? The answer was nobody. Jesus Christ! If that was the case, it meant that she was being followed, watched. Did that put her sweet Klein in danger? Was every person that she was involved with in need of protection? And what about her? Would they try killing her, too, or were they just keeping an eye on her investigation? If it was nothing, just a death from natural causes, then damn DeLaurent for planting that seed. But she would be careful. She would not allow leaks. She would have to act like one of them, like a spy, both hunter and hunted.

Anna did not tell Klein about Johnnie. She enjoyed dinner and then let him make love to her. He seemed to be especially sweet tonight, taking his time even more than usual. Caressing her more. Kissing her more passionately. And holding her more tightly and for longer periods. How did he know that it was exactly what she needed tonight? Is that what happened when you found the right person? Did the right person just know how to respond with what you needed without even thinking about it, without you having to say anything? Anna hoped that to be true. But if it was just a coincidence, that would be okay also because either way, she needed what he was giving tonight.

And when they were finished and had lain there for a while, he asked, "Are you sure that you're alright? You're very quiet tonight."

"When are we going to your place?"

"When do you want to go to my place?"

"Now."

"It's eleven-thirty."

"Would we wake someone there?"

"No. I just mean it's late and I hadn't planned on getting out of this bed."

But she wasn't tired. How could she be?

"I'm going for a walk."

"Are you upset?"

"No, I just need to clear my head. Long day."

In the living room, her bag sat open. She took out her Glock, cell phone, and ID, then she zipped it up, both zipper handles meeting in the middle, and locked them together with a tiny padlock.

It was so cold outside, but it was refreshing. And it was deserted. The perfect condition to spot anyone following her, watching her. When she made it to the park, overlooking the frigid Atlantic Ocean and the bright skyline of her city, it was here that she wept for Jonathan Meeks, a few streaks down her cheek like drops of melted ice, and then she heard the grinding sound of stepped-on gravel. Her hand instinctively went toward her Glock.

"Is everything alright?" came a deep voice, Midwestern accent.

She turned around to see a shadowed man, probably six and a half feet tall, black trench coat tails flying in the wind, and a hat, a black hat that she'd expect to see a Scotsman wearing.

"I'm fine." Her hand remained near her gun, but it was under her jacket.

If he wanted to attack me, he would have done it already.

"It's late, and this park isn't the safest place."

"Thank you, but I'm fine."

This wouldn't be the person following her either; that person would never show. He'd stay in the dark and watch. Or, maybe he knew that she'd think that and approach her like this to confuse her.

"Very well."

"If it's so dangerous, why are you out here alone?"

She didn't know why she asked him that question. He was probably going to leave, but she kept him there.

"I do well to take care of myself."

He was an imposing figure, like Death, she imagined. But he had kept his distance until now, taking a step forward and reaching his gloved hand out.

"Malcolm Youngblood."

As he leaned forward, she finally saw his face clearly. A black man with a few wrinkles on each side of his mouth. Kind eyes. Like Meeks' had been.

She shook his hand. Firm grip.

"Anna." She let his hand go, and he stepped back to where he had been, back in the shadow cast by the streetlamp behind him. "And you didn't really answer my question."

"Now you sound like the police."

"Not quite," she said, not liking that he'd figured her out, that she was so transparent even to a complete stranger. But maybe he wasn't a stranger.

"I don't know you from anywhere, do I?" she asked.

"It's possible. I meet many people."

She could see his white teeth in the darkness now, smiling. It felt sinister—this smile hovering in the shadow, like it meant more. Like it was saying, 'I killed your friend, and now I'm going to kill you…soon.' Part of her knew that she should feel fear, but anger had crept in. The tears that had fallen were dried now, and her hand back near her Glock. It was stupid to have gone on a walk alone so late at night. This park was not known for its safety. So maybe part of her wanted something bad to happen to her. Like she didn't deserve Klein's warm arms around her making her feel less vulnerable. Like the case she was working on would take so much more from her than she had to give. Her best friend. Her father. And so what if she was able to close the damn thing. There would just be another case waiting for her, demanding all of her time and attention. Leaving her empty again emotionally but even heavier with secrets.

"Are you sure that you're alright?"

"No, but it's no concern of yours."

He raised his hands in mock surrender. "Sorry for bothering you. I'm sure everything will be okay. You have a good night now."

When the man turned around and started walking away, Anna could feel the tension drop in her shoulders slowly like a balloon with a hair-size leak. She just watched him stroll along the asphalt path, and he didn't turn around to look back at her, just disappeared into the night.

Klein was asleep when she got back to the apartment. Again, she didn't know how to feel about that the same way she'd felt about his note a few days ago. If he cared, wouldn't he have stayed awake to be sure that she made it back safely? Did he worry about her at all or was it all in her head? Did she still just want him more but his feelings hadn't really changed?

He lay there breathing lightly, the slight hint of a snore, the kind that usually comes in the first ten minutes of sleep before either growing silent or erupting into some dreadful cacophony. But Klein usually got quiet as if he didn't have a care in the world, as if his dreams were peaceful and happy. That's where she wanted to be, a happy place, and she wanted him to take her there. But seeing him there, able to abandon her like that, she knew that she still led her own way and that it would always be that way. That she controlled where she went, and he or anyone else could either walk alongside her, follow her, or go their own way. No one would lead her. And as she realized this, more tension seemed to ease out of her.

Klein didn't stir as Anna unlocked and opened her bag. On her laptop, she reviewed her case. But that didn't keep her attention for long, as she shifted to older case files, ones that had been typed up by Jonathan Meeks. Was there something out there that he'd left for her, the way it always seemed to work in the movies? If so, where? He seemed to have known so much about these people and she just a fraction. So where did he get it? How did he know it? For just a second, a nasty thought of Meeks working with them popped in her mind. That maybe he had kept certain people safe for as long as he could, and then, when the heat was too much, had pawns, the ten that were arrested, take the fall for the bigger fish. If that was it, then had he been giving her information that would lead her to the big fish? It was preposterous. There was no way he could be involved with them.

Anna kept looking through the files reading Johnnie's notes. So many inconsistencies, but the general information amounted to the same thing—job complete, but who cares how it got that way. There had to be some other record showing what really happened and how much he really knew. A personal computer at his home. A flash drive. Surely he wouldn't just fabricate how some of it happened without having some record of the true steps and what really happened with the people involved. Unless, of course, he had the memory like some genius and could remember everything. That was certainly not how her mind worked. If she didn't write it down, it would be gone in a few days. It was why her reports were so concise and took so long to produce, which was the reason Meeks gave for taking over on writing the reports. It took a quarter of the time, and all she had to do was sign off on what he wrote.

"It's past one," came Klein's voice from behind her. "Aren't you coming to bed?"

Before she could answer, he had entered the room and had his hands on her shoulders, massaging them.

"I'll be in soon."

"You're not going to be worth anything at work tomorrow."

"Insomnia is a side effect of this job."

She wondered how long he had been standing there because she hadn't heard him get up, and her floor wasn't the quietest in the building, but those thoughts were worked out by his hands. Each time he dug his thumbs into her stiff shoulders, a calming tingle would shimmer down her spine and down to her fingertips, up and behind her ears. It felt too good to resist. And after another minute of this bliss, she let herself be led to bed where she lay beside Klein, wrapped in his arms, and fell asleep long enough to realize that she'd fallen asleep when her phone rang.

"Agent Stern, I think we have a serious problem," said Danielle.

"Out with it, Danielle. You know I don't like—"

"They lost Volkov, and something's happened to Jin Won Suh."

"What?"

"I don't know yet. I'm headed to his house right now to find out."

"He's okay, right?"

"I think so. It's not homicide; I know that much."

"So Volkov?"

"Agent Young said that he left around dusk on foot, and he lost him. He hasn't returned to his home yet."

"So something's happened with Suh and Volkov... What about Jenny? Aren't you—"

"DeLaurent pulled me off her to go to Suh's place—"

"So no one's on her?"

"Not right now. From what I could tell, she'd gone to bed before I got DeLaurent's call."

"Hobson and Dobbs were supposed to be on Suh, so why are you getting pulled off?"

"DeLaurent—"

"God dammit. This is one big clusterfuck. Morgan, I need you to go back to Jenny's. I'll get Hobson and Dobbs back on Suh and Herrera and Young on Volkov. I'm going to Suh's now."

"What about DeLaurent? These are all his orders."

"I'll deal with him."

When she ended the call, Klein was sitting up in bed looking at her.

"Bad guys never sleep, do they?"

"Hope not."

She leaned toward him and gave him a kiss.

"I have to go."

"Which means I have to go, too," he said, but not in an annoyed way, just an understanding way.

Before he was able to pull the comforter off him and get out of bed, she put her hand on his and said, "No, you don't."

He responded with a smile. "You mean it?"

She had to try at least once, right? Take a chance on something that felt so good. If she never tried, she'd never know, and that meant being alone. And if it was one thing she knew, it was what loneliness felt like. Those that said the world was a small place were all wrong. It was big, it was dangerous, and it didn't care about you. So you made your own little world and stayed in it. And if you did that, you'd be happy because you played God in your own little world.

"Yeah. I mean it. I want you to stay here. I want you to be here when I get back if you can be." She built up the courage, the feeling like peacock feathers sliding up her torso and neck, all the way to her cheeks. "I'm ready for us to take the next step. And that's just crazy because I don't even know your last name or what you do for a living, but maybe that's what makes it okay." She tried, but she couldn't take away her smile, couldn't hide it.

"Abbott. Klein Abbott. And, embarrassingly enough, I work..." he let out a loud breath, stalling, "as a clerk at a bookstore."

Part of her was relieved. He was a man ashamed of not being anything spectacular, which was perfect reason to keep it from her, especially when she had a demanding career. That much comforted her, reinforcing her decision to let him stay at her place alone, reinforcing her wanting to move forward with him.

"Does that change your mind about me?"

"Not at all."

She kissed him again, the kind of long and emotional kiss that didn't happen often, but when it did, both the kisser and kissee knew exactly what it meant—I love this moment; I love you at this moment; I never want this moment or feeling to end. But it always did; both parties always knew that. But she then said, "I hope you're here when I get back."

"I hope that you're back really soon."

"I won't be. It'll probably be nighttime when I get back."

"It's nighttime right now."

"I mean tomorrow night. I have this feeling that today's going to be…relentless."

"Just promise me that you'll kiss me like that the next time I see you."

"I promise."

Part III

Caccia

Chapter 18

On the ceiling, shadows shimmered, cast from streetlamp light and shaped by bare elm-tree branches and lace curtains. The heater vent was just over the window, and when that warm air blew down on those lace curtains, it made the shadows dance. After an hour, it began to snow, smoothing over the skeletal elm-tree branches and filling the ceiling with shaded confetti. Black snow.

Lilly lay in bed watching it all, unable to close her eyes for longer than a second without seeing Lester staring at her. Without witnessing that man shoot him again and his blood spraying all over her face like warm water. When would that image get out of her head? When would her fatigued body and mind be able to rest?

For the first time in her life, Lilly stayed up all night and barely moved, watching as the dark night transitioned into day, the snow clouds gone toward the ocean now and the blue sky bright outside her window. But it hurt to look at it, her eyes itchy and dry as if sandy air had slipped under her eyelids and kept swirling and swirling.

The doorknob squeaked as it turned, stealing her gaze. What was left of Kate Rebeck entered the room.

"Lilly. You're awake. Good." Kate sat at the foot of Lilly's bed. "I wanted to talk to you last night, but—"

"Why?" said Lilly, sitting up and leaning back against the headboard, tightly crossing her arms. Lilly didn't want to look at the woman, so she focused on the balled-up piece of paper she'd thrown in the corner instead.

"Because I haven't been here for you." She scooted closer, hands together. "Because I've been a bad mother."

Kate's breath smelled of illness, rotting food in a broken fridge, but that's not what made Lilly draw her lips in tighter. Oh, how her eyes itched, how she wanted to rub them. But she didn't want Kate to think that she was brushing aside tears, so it intensified, Lilly enduring its growing irritation.

"I want you to know," she started, reaching her right hand to her daughter and getting no response. She bowed her head, eyeing the carpet while bringing her hands together again. "I want you to know that I've gotten help."

Arms tightening now, Lilly's tired muscles began to ache, but she didn't want to loosen herself. She opened her hands and grabbed a palm full of shirt in each, anchoring her heavy arms in place. Just being in the same room with her mom was sucking what little energy she had away.

"I'm seeing…" Her voice cracked, and she swallowed hard as if she'd been eating a peanut-butter sandwich without a drink. "A therapist, Lilly. I've started a program—"

"Well, you can just skip this step," she said, her fists clenching her shirt even tighter now. Lilly knew about the twelve-step program because Mr. Thompson had discussed the grief process with her after her father had died. It was just too late. Lilly had already made up her mind that she no longer belonged to this abusive, absentee woman that was once deserving of the title Mother, but had since abandoned her post. Besides, she didn't share any real secrets with Kate, no meaningful bonding moments, no nothing. But Svetlana was different. They had shared life and death together, passion together in their instruments, and they understood each other. Svetlana knew how to care for and protect another, but Kate couldn't even care for herself.

"Please, Lilly. I'm trying—"

"You're wicked and cruel!"

Lilly flung her comforter off her legs and jolted out of bed as if it was on fire, fast-paced toward the door.

"Lilly." She stood. "Lilly!"

Glancing back only once, Lilly stormed out of the bedroom

and headed downstairs. When she reached the main hallway, her mother was standing outside Lilly's room holding the violin case at her side.

"Stop, young lady."

And Lilly did.

"You don't walk away from me. I am your mother, and you will treat me with respect."

Lilly's eyes were set on her violin, and only her violin. What was Kate's intention? To take it away? Destroy it? Use it as a means to get what she wanted? This was not a mother. This was a monster that no twelve-step program or therapist could change.

"Do you understand me?"

Silent, Lilly watched as her mother opened the violin case and took the instrument out and held it up over the railing so that Lilly could see it well.

"This is not all there is to life."

"Put that back in its case."

Lilly shuddered as she saw her mother's stern expression smooth and create the first smile she'd seen there in such a long time. But it wasn't a smile of joy or happiness. It was a malignant smile, one that Lilly imagined a dictator might wear. Ugly and transparent. Because all that smile did was highlight the evil brewing inside the woman that was once her mother.

"Is that an order, Daughter?"

"Please put it back in its case." If she had to get on her knees and beg, she would do so. It wasn't the monetary value of the instrument that had her shivering; it wasn't that the violin had great pitch, for it was an average instrument, a print or giclée of an original masterpiece; it was two simple things—her only means to play, and that it had been given to her by her father, the only item she owned that held such sentimental value, the only item that had kept them close without having to speak. She could play, and he would listen, the smile on his face genuine and full of pride. And she had to keep those memories strong because after the events that occurred yesterday, the idea of an afterlife, of a spiritual realm continued to fade. Her father's spirit hadn't saved her. No angels had protected her. It had been Svetlana, flesh and blood, a woman with secrets.

"Are you going to stop this nonsense and talk to me? Stop playing the victim?"

The nerve of this woman to say such things. How do you appease the lunatic? Give her what she wants so that she is occupied, then turn and run and don't look back because lunacy is contagious. So when she said, "Yes, Mother," Lilly knew that she had to devise a plan to escape. But in the meantime, she would have to play the robot.

"Good." Kate put the violin back in its case and snapped the locks in place.

This was all too strange. For months, Kate had practically ignored her, then trying to act sorry, which obviously didn't last long. There had to be something that she wanted or else why would she even bother? Lilly even doubted that Kate had begun a twelve-step program, that it was a lie.

Kate was carrying the violin case on her way downstairs. Lilly's eyes remained fixed on it.

"May I have my violin, Mother?"

"No. I'm going to hold on to it for a few days. Punishment for your actions this morning." Kate sauntered to her bedroom and, without speaking another word, closed the door.

All she could do was stand and stare at Kate's door. The woman being in such a malnourished and haggard state, Lilly would have no trouble physically overpowering her and taking her property back by force, but she did owe her enough respect not to go that far yet; after all, she had carried her for nine months, brought her into the world, and tried to mimic her father's enthusiasm at birthdays, holidays, and other events. Her father would always whisper to her that "Mommy just has the baby blues," but there was always a certain distance between them that Lilly never understood, and her father's death only multiplied that exponentially. Besides, she'd read that postpartum depression usually ended within a year, so it remained a mystery. All Lilly knew was that Kate didn't have a model to imitate anymore. Or maybe that was exactly what she had now, bringing this stern side out, this mean side. Had Kate found someone? Is that where she went so many hours of the day?

When the hall and bedroom door completely blurred and her eyes began to sting, she finally blinked, not able to recall how long she had been standing there, but her legs hinted at an ache. It wasn't the first instance that she'd lost track of time while in a trance. She'd done so on the staircase, a time that felt like so long ago at the end of her previous life. The day Mr. Thompson had abandoned her; the day she reached out to her mother, and her mother walked out on her. So funny how the tables had turned in just a few months, from Lilly needing her mother to her mother acting as though she needed Lilly. And Lilly walking out this time, leaving Kate sitting on the mattress. What did it mean?

Lilly showered and put on a thick black sweater and her long hunter-green skirt, packed three sets of clothes in her backpack along with her bundle of sheet music and journal, and then ate a breakfast of oatmeal, an apple, and a mug of unsatisfying chamomile tea—she would have much preferred Russian Caravan's strong and smoky and purposeful flavor. Yet, still, she was fatigued and only wanted to close her weary eyes.

Run, Lilly! Hurry! And she would fling her eyes open again.

Clouds had reemerged, thick and greyish blue, converting the bright and cheery colors to a sickly, wan hue.

Would Svetlana be awake or would her schedule be altered by yesterday's horrors? It wasn't 8:45 yet, the time she usually left on Saturdays, so Lilly grabbed her backpack, unlocked the stairway door, searched the living room, then went into the bedroom. No Svetlana. Had she had trouble sleeping, too, and decided to go for a walk? No. Lilly would have heard her moving about, heard the door close. She must have left either last night when Lilly had gone back downstairs or while she was in the shower. The bed was made, and there were no dirty clothes anywhere and no Svetlana. It looked as though she had not even gone to bed last night, but just left. The piano still had the sheet music open to what they had played last night.

Feathers in her stomach, Lilly dropped her backpack and sprinted out of the bedroom, but what she saw by the stairway made her stop on a dime and gasp. A man stood there, someone she'd never seen before, wearing jeans and a black leather jacket. Brown hair. Hazel eyes.

"Well, hello there, little girl."

Her tongue was mashed against the roof of her mouth, her neck now showing every vein.

"No need to be frightened," the man said, raising his right hand so that his palm faced her. "I'm just looking for the person renting out this apartment. Would that happen to be your mother?" His voice was light and friendly.

She just stood there, the tension in her neck easing, but she knew that this man meant trouble for Svetlana. He was probably a cop, a detective. Had the cameras at the Metro stop picked up Svetlana killing that man? Even if it had, Svetlana had been protecting someone, so it couldn't be against the law; she couldn't go to jail for killing a killer. It was like her father's job, protecting the country from the bad people. Killing the bad people was okay, and that's what Svetlana had done. She didn't need a uniform to justify that.

"Are you police?"

The man smiled. "Yes."

"Then let me see your badge. And don't you need a search warrant?" Though her legs were weak and wobbly, her long skirt thankfully hid the fact.

"Of course, little girl." He reached in his jacket and pulled out a folded piece of paper with fine black print, too small for Lilly to read from her position several feet away. "Search warrant, signed by Judge Brackett himself." With his other hand, he pulled out his wallet and opened it. An identification card with a blue star next to the photo. "My detective badge, not like a uniformed cop."

He put both items away. "Now, please do Detective Morris a favor and tell him where your mother is because he has a few questions that he has to ask her, and then he'll be on his way."

The man thought that Svetlana was her mother. Under any other circumstances, the thought would have her face beaming with a smile. But having him go downstairs and talk to Kate for a minute would give her time to grab her bag and run, get away from this whole mess and try finding Svetlana to warn her that the police were looking for her. Or maybe she already knew, had to leave in a hurry, and that's why she wasn't here. So, Lilly just told the truth: "My mother is downstairs."

The man's eyebrows raised, his lips turned down, and he nodded once. "Thank you."

When he turned to go downstairs, Lilly noticed a scar on the man's cheek, barely noticeable at this distance and in the poor light, but it was there, black like a shadow.

At the sound of his footsteps turning the corner and going down the final flight of steps, Lilly snatched up her bag and ran out of the apartment, leaving the door wide open. Down the side steps, she saw what she believed to be the detective's footprints in the snow, but she also saw shoeprints pointed in the other direction, some meshed together with the detective's and some alone—Svetlana had left recently because there was no snow covering her prints. Lilly took one step at a time, trying to step in Svetlana's prints as she went, and followed them. The detective's looked like they had come from a Lexus with tinted windows parked several cars down the wet street, but Svetlana's went in the other direction, toward the Metro. Of all places the Metro, where it had all happened yesterday. Lilly couldn't go back there so soon. Maybe ever. But, she had to get away, had to tell Svetlana that someone was looking for her—the police—so she kept going, the weight of her backpack heavy on her right shoulder causing her to slip where the snow was packed in Svetlana's tiny footsteps, but she never lost her balance completely and fell. No, she made it to the end of the street, but then it was pointless. The homeowners here were more responsible and had shoveled the snow, so Lilly didn't know if Svetlana had turned right, left, or went straight for the snow was all melted on the macadam save a few ranges of grey and black slush gathered near the gutters.

Lilly looked in all three directions helplessly, her breath appearing and then disappearing before her eyes. Then she turned around and gazed back down her street. The detective looked like he was jogging toward the Lexus, cell phone pressed to his ear and a smile on his face as he spoke. Then, he glanced in her direction. The man stopped for a moment, smile disappearing as he took the cell phone from his ear, then he rushed to the car. Lilly panicked and ran left toward the Metro, crossed the street, and found herself back at the hedgerow she had hid behind yesterday, burrowing herself in the stranger's yard which had plenty of trees and other shrubbery, thankful that her footprints could not be tracked on the sidewalk. But her pursuer was a detective, so she would have to be careful and plan an escape should he find her.

A few seconds, and the Lexus sped by the hedge, stopping abruptly near the Metro stop. The detective got out of the car and glanced in several directions, then another person got out of the passenger side. He was wearing a hat and coat, but she saw that his face was tanned like the Hispanic kids at her school. Lilly hadn't noticed someone else in the car before. Were there more in the back seats? How much trouble was Svetlana in? Was *she* in? What had Kate told him? And more importantly, what had he told Kate? Lilly quickly regretted giving the detective Kate's whereabouts, but she stayed still, keeping watch on the detectives. They didn't stay long, just scanned the area for a minute or two and then drove off. Where was their back-up and the helicopter? Wasn't that the next step, the step they always showed on those TV cop shows?

It took the steady breeze a few more minutes to penetrate her sweater and attack the line of body heat that had been insulating her, but she willed herself to stay put, chattering teeth and all. The detective could be hiding and watching for her to show herself or Svetlana could return on a Metro line and she could warn her. Lilly would have to bear the cold for now, surrounded by leafless elms and evergreen shrubs.

Chapter 19

When Alexei regained consciousness, he couldn't feel his hands, his feet, and there was not much sensation in his ears or nose. What he did feel was intense pain in his chest. He opened his eyes to dead leaves and frozen soil, the taste of earth in his mouth even though the mask covered most of his face. *Am I having a heart attack?* He couldn't remember how he'd ended up on the ground. Was this his front yard? Backyard? Moving didn't come easy, but he forced his body onto its side, the ache turning into a sting as he was forced to use the muscles in his torso or else die face down in who knows where.

When he saw the laptop on the ground where he had lain, he began to laugh. "Thank God," he said.

And when the image of the laptop sunk in and the previous night flashed in his mind, he said, "Oh fuck."

Panicked and ignoring the soreness, he got to his feet only to fall to his knees from the wave of pain that crashed inside his forehead. "Jesus fucking Christ!" Closing his eyes helped, but he knew that he'd have to persist. Getting the laptop in his hands and noticing that it was broken, the frame section behind the monitor with an indention and a large crack extending in separate directions. The DVD drive was bent, and the side USB ports were mangled. But he couldn't worry about that. As long as the hard drive was intact, he could extract the information later.

He stood more slowly this time, his brain responding with hammers rather than daggers, and pulled the ski mask up so that it looked like a beanie again. Staggering through the park, he made it to the main road where he was able to get a cab because there was no way he would be able to walk the four miles to his house in his condition. A hot shower was all he could think about right now as the feeling slowly came back to his limbs in the warm cab.

Alexei had the cabbie drop him off at the end of his street in case Aletta had recognized him last night and the police were waiting or if Brother happened to be there. Turning the corner of the car-lined street, Alexei moved slowly, deliberately eyeing every car along the way, using the hedges, large trees, and SUVs to camouflage his approach, even on the opposite side of the street from his house. Four houses from home, he stopped cold. Emily's car was parked on the street. Three cars down on his side of the road sat another car with two adults sitting in the front; he couldn't see the make and model, but it had to be Brother and Hawthorne's replacement.

Did Emily have the children inside, too? How would he explain his being gone all night, his filthy clothes and broken laptop? She would think him crazy. Maybe the children would still be in bed, so he could clean himself up before they saw him, if Emily didn't throw him out. The time may have come that he had to confess his true identity, open up to her completely and share his secrets. Hadn't he been a coward to keep her in the dark all this time? Wasn't that the truth of it all? It wasn't that Emily couldn't handle it, that she wouldn't accept it, it was purely and simply cowardice. Alexei gripped the laptop so tight, he could hear the plastic protest. It was time.

Alexei backtracked, crossed the street, then went through his neighbors' backyards so that he could get in his home without being detected by Brother. And it worked. But what awaited him inside surprised him—Emily and Jenny sitting at the kitchen table drinking coffee.

"Alexei, where have you been?" Emily stood, but did not approach him. "You look awful."

"Emily, what are you—"

"Jenny explained what you've been going through. Oh, Alexei, it'll be okay," she said while taking a few steps closer to him and finally standing in front of him, blocking Jenny from his view. "They're always talking budgets in higher ed. They need you there, but even if you get laid off, we will be okay." Emily took his gloved hand and held it.

Alexei could see that she was still playing the ever-supportive wife, a natural role for such a wonderful woman...so trusting that she didn't know that all she was getting from those around her were lies.

He leaned forward and kissed her on the lips. "Are the kids here?"

"I took them to my parents' house."

"You've got yourself quite a wife there, Alexei. If I had a husband that told me to go away for a week—"

"Thank you for clearing things up, Jenny." *You bitch.*

"Come and have some coffee with us," said Emily, mechanically going back to the table.

Emily was not an idiot, but she certainly had blinders on this morning. Or maybe Jenny had said something to make her ignore his condition because she hadn't followed up on asking where he'd been or why he was filthy. Just what had Jenny told her?

"I think I should go up and take a shower first."

"I should probably go," said Jenny, standing up now. "Alexei, your computer."

"Yes, I dropped it and it fell down the stairs."

"Give it to me," she said. "I can take it to a friend of mine who can either fix it or hopefully save the hard drive."

"It's okay, Jenny. I'll handle it."

"So stubborn, never letting me help. How do you put up with him, Emily?" She smiled and let out a quick giggle the way a child might do after flicking a pea at her brother.

Why would she say that right after doing him a favor just yesterday?

"Come on. My friend owes me a favor and can do all the work for free. It's no big deal."

"Jenny—"

"My goodness, Emily, do you have to beg this man to help him with something, too?"

This was all very strange. Jenny, her tone and her smile, even her being here seemed out of place, odd. But surely it was the tranquilizer's after effects because his head still ached and probably would for another few hours until it made its way out of his system completely. Either way, he had to keep possession of the laptop and use someone Donya suggested instead.

"Why don't you want Jenny to help you, Alexei?"

"I'd just like to do it myself."

Jenny's smile went away, her lips mashing together and her nostrils beginning to flare. She'd been holding something back and now it seemed as though she hadn't the power to do so anymore.

"Emily, honey, will you give Jenny and I a moment alone please?"

Emily started to rise, but Jenny spoke: "I think you need to stay right where you are, Emily."

"Alexei—"

"Sit down, Emily," said Jenny. "Give me the fucking computer, Alexei."

He took a step toward Emily as he said, "No."

Jenny reached behind her, saying, "Don't you fucking move," and then produced a small black gun with an even smaller silencer and pointed it at Emily, who gasped but didn't scream.

"Jenny!" he yelled. "What in the fuck are you doing?"

"Put the computer on the table and back away."

It didn't make sense. Alexei's heart rate seemed to double.

"Is it Brother?" he asked.

"This isn't a fucking movie. Put it on the table or I'll shoot your wife."

"Why are…" Emily began, tears pouring down her face.

Jenny fired the gun, and a high-pitched scream stung the air as Emily's body jerked back out of the chair and fell to the floor.

Alexei dropped the laptop but didn't hear it crash on the ground. When he got to Emily, she was breathing asthma-attack hard, but the blood only soaked her right arm sleeve. "It's going to be okay, sweetheart." Alexei pulled her to him, keeping her attention off her arm.

"Take her to the bathroom," came a voice Alexei hadn't heard in ages, but it was softer, seemed to have lost that rocky rigidity that could pierce a person's courage.

He turned his head in the direction Jenny had been, and in her place stood Donya. Saving him again.

"Now," she said.

Broken from his trance, Alexei picked up Emily's trembling body, one arm behind her knees and the other around her back, and Emily held on to his neck with her left arm. She was still breathing erratically, and Alexei knew that he had to calm her so she wouldn't hyperventilate or have a panic attack. When he stood, he saw Jenny's bloody body slumped near Donya's feet, leaning against the wall, hands around her own neck to stop profuse blood flow. The small gun lay on the floor by her knees.

"Where is your first-aid kit?"

"In the bathroom," he said.

"Go."

It was just around the corner, and Alexei, in the calmest voice he could muster, repeated, "You're okay, sweetheart. Everything will be okay."

Emily didn't speak, just held on to her husband as he took her to the bathroom, kicked the lid down on the toilet, and placed her there. He sat next to her on the tub's edge, grasped her left hand, and put his other on her cheek, leaning toward her and resting his lips on her temple. Her breathing began to slow.

"It's all going to be okay, sweetheart," he said again, her body still trembling.

Donya came in a second later. "Where is it?"

"Under the sink."

Donya flung open the doors, pulled out the first-aid kit and a bottle of rubbing alcohol, and stood to Emily's left side.

"Help is here, honey."

"Wha—"

"Shhh, everything's okay."

Alexei pulled Emily's head to him, and she buried it in Alexei's shoulder. He watched as Donya systematically ripped Emily's blouse sleeve to expose the seeping wound and inspected it.

"Good. Not serious. You have nothing to worry about."

Donya ripped open bandages and took out medical tape. "This is going to sting. Put this in her mouth," she said, handing Alexei a rolled-up elastic bandage.

"Bite down on this, honey."

Emily's scream was such that it startled Alexei, but it only lasted a few seconds as Donya applied the bandages.

"It's going to be okay," he told Emily.

She spat out the bandage, and her expression changed to one Alexei had not seen before in his sweet wife. Lips together as if she were sleeping, breathing closer to normal, but her eyes gave off what Alexei took to be distrust or disappointment. An alien stare that burned to the core of his soul amidst a still-trembling body.

"She's going to need hospital," Donya said.

But Alexei did not break eye contact with Emily.

"Lenka!" She slapped him across the face, hard. "Now."

He finally looked at her.

"There are two federal agents in a car out front, so you'll have to find another way."

"Those aren't federal agents. It's Brother—"

"The woman in there is Brother's presence. Those federal agents cannot know what happened in here."

He looked back at Emily and realized that the look she was giving him was not distrust or disappointment. It could only be described as unfamiliarity. Alexei's fear had come to fruition—Emily now saw who he really was. And he was going to lose her because he was a stranger to her. A man with a hidden life who had been playing the role of husband and father to keep his cover intact. That's what that look meant. Betrayal.

Alexei closed his eyes and bowed his head. He heard Emily speak: "Who are you?"

When Donya didn't answer her, he opened his eyes and realized that Emily was speaking to him, her expression sober and frighteningly calm now.

"Your loving husband."

He saw her chin begin to quiver, then she stood and stormed out of the bathroom.

Alexei got to his feet and made for the door when Donya grabbed his shirt and pulled him toward her.

"Let her go for now. Why did you put in the message to the *Globe*?"

"Because they're looking for you."

"I know that, idiot. Why do you think my letters stopped?"

"What the hell are you talking about, stopped? They didn't stop."

Donya was silent for just a couple moments, letting out a deep and annoyed breath.

"How deep are you?" she asked.

This question was a revelation: she had not kept as tight of tabs on him as he'd thought. So how much did she know? Oh God.

"Drowning."

"This is bad, Lenka. You have to get her to the hospital, then you have to tell me what the fuck you're involved with. I just hope it's not what I think it is because that has gotten Boris and Lester killed, and I'm probably exposed now."

This was not how Alexei wanted to reunite with his sister.

"But that's later. Where are your children?"

As Donya asked the question, Emily bellowed out a scream that would draw attention from outside. Surely, she had come across Jenny's dead body.

Alexei ran to Emily, who continued to scream and back away. When he got behind her to take her out of the room, she turned around, tears back on her cheeks now, and let out a different kind of scream, one of fear rather than terror, as she stepped back toward the kitchen now.

"Stay away from me, Alexei."

"Emily, let me—"

"Get away from me," she cried out, barely able to get the words past her tears as she brought her arms in close to her chest, bending her legs, and sinking to the floor—the fetal position.

"Lenka," whispered Donya from behind him.

Pounding at the door. "Hello! Is everything okay in there?"

"Help me! Help me, please!" Emily wailed now before letting her body tilt back against the wall.

Donya made for the door, but it was kicked open before she even made it halfway. Two men entered. Alexei noticed that they had handguns drawn.

"On the floor, now," said the first man, in the process of bringing his gun up to aim at Donya.

But she was too fast and had a pistol drawn and up before the man finished his command, and she fired, hitting him in the forehead—he collapsed. And she fired again, the second man dropping immediately like a marionette whose cords had all been severed at the same time. Blood poured out of their noses, two thick streams making a mess of their shirts and the floor as their bodies wriggled and jerked.

Alexei's ears rang as he felt the first of the cold air rushing in his warm home from the doorway, and he didn't hear Emily's screaming anymore. He glanced back at her and saw that she was unconscious. Thank God. But police would surely be on the way now; Donya's gun didn't have a silencer.

Donya was in Alexei's face a few seconds later, not missing a step. "Where are your children?"

"Gone."

"Then get her to the hospital and go here," she said, pulling out a folded-up piece of notebook paper. "It's a safe house. You can never come back here."

"But—"

"Life here is over, Lenka. I'm sorry. Our past will not let us go."

"I can't accept that. We need to finish here because I can't run anymore."

"Len—"

"I'd rather die, Donya."

She didn't respond to this, and how could she? Alexei walked away, picked up his broken laptop, and handed it to Donya.

"This is what they want. My colleague, Dr. Jin Won Suh – here is all of his research on autism. The reason why I put in the message was because they insisted that I deliver you to them so they can get some information. I had to warn you."

"Wait," she said, taking a deep breath. "It's been you getting all of this information? Lester's intel showed that it was David Delk that Brother was using. I thought they were just using you to get to me, but you're involved in this whole fucking mess. Jesus, Lenka. I thought breaking contact with you would leave you in the clear."

"They said I had to repay Boris—"

"He was repaid a long time ago." She holstered her gun. "You're involved in something much bigger than you know."

"Gathering information—"

"This is much more than a few medical advancements, Lenka. They want to use Suh's techniques on humans. Genetically modify them to build a newer and stronger Russia. And I'm sure you know the darker side."

This *was* bigger than he'd thought. It wasn't weapons information for war, nuclear information for power, but this was information that would change the human race. Armor and advance the world's new sleeping giant.

"Do you?" she asked.

"Yes. I've seen Suh's rats."

"All the more reason you have to leave this place and never come back."

"It's not as easy for me, god dammit! I have a family here...that...that I have to try and keep together. Ten fucking years, Donya. Isn't there anything that you care about enough to fight for? To sacrifice for?" His throat began to tighten. "I'm not as strong as you. I can't do those things," he said, pointing to the dead men in the hallway. "I can't be alone." Alexei had kept it together for this long, but boxed-up emotions were exploding inside him. "I need my family. And I need you. How can you be so fucking detached and keep living?"

Donya's expression didn't shift, she didn't even blink.

"I remember Lukerya and Fyodor every night."

"They're dead, Donya. Emily and Nina and Victor are alive. And I can't leave them or take them away. Don't you have anyone that you care about? Anyone worth..." He couldn't finish because he just didn't know what more he could say, but he did see her gaze shift from him to the floor, which was an odd movement for her.

Silence for several seconds, then, "There is someone." More silence.

"Then we need to fight for our loved ones and stop living in shadows, Donya. I miss my sister," he said, eyes blurring. "I want my children to know their beautiful aunt."

Donya made eye contact again. "Okay, Lenka. Get her to hospital, then go to the safe house. I will meet you there late tomorrow night. By then, I hope to have freed us." Donya threw her arms around her brother and pulled him to her so tightly. "I've missed you, too. And I love you very much, my brother."

Her hair smelled of fresh coconut, and her skin was soft and warm. Alexei put his arms around her tightly, the same way he had so many years ago when he'd seen her last on that chilly day in New York City. Memories were all he had, for every letter she had written him had to be burned, even the fake ones that had come the past few years. No pictures, no phone calls, and no family reunions. He could now at least remember this moment—soft coconut with a hint of gunpowder covered in blood and riddled with screams—the norm in his former life.

"Promise me that you'll be there tomorrow night."

"On my life," she said, then released her arms and backed away. "I am going to kill Brother and anyone he's connected with here in Boston. We will still need to be distant—"

"No! No more. Together, for as long as it lasts. Without family, you might as well be dead."

Donya nodded. "So be it. But I'm called Svetlana in this life."

Alexei smiled. "Momma's name."

"Momma's name," she said. "Now, take your wife, Lenka. Protect her and your children. I will be with you soon. When the smoke has cleared."

And that's what he did. When Alexei got Emily in her car and began driving, the rearview showed shallow smoke beginning to emit from his home. Upon turning the corner, it left his mind until he reached the hospital. Emily had not regained consciousness, but after her wound was tended and stitched, Alexei explained to her that their home had caught on fire. That the children were safe. That they were going to a friend's vacation home in the country. He was sweet to her, keeping his hand on her cheek or running it through her silky hair, keeping his lips close to hers. And she accepted his story, had no bouts of hysteria, and went along with it all, as if Jenny's betrayal, Donya's murdering FBI agents, and even her being shot hadn't actually happened, that it was all a bad dream that she chose to suppress.

After pulling in to her parents' driveway and cutting the ignition, though, Emily said, "You are my husband, and you know everything about me." Her dark eyes glistened in the lamplight emitting from her parents' home. "I thought I knew you. But I don't." She turned her gaze from him, staring at the floorboard while swallowing hard. Then, she looked forward, toward the outside light, making her eyes and skin look younger and more flawless—innocent. "If you ever want to see me or your children again, I must know everything about you." She looked at him. "Right now."

There was silence between them, a silence that seemed to last hours but only spanned about fifteen seconds.

"I don't think you're going to like what you hear," he said.

"I don't have to like it. But I do have to know it."

Alexei was staring at the lamp blazing down on them from above the garage door, the skin on his face beginning to itch. "Before I knew you and before I came to this country, my name was Lenka…"

Chapter 20

26 January 2011. 2:01am. Home of Dr. Jin Won Suh.

Dr. Jin Won Suh and his wife sat next to each other on their front porch steps, a grey trauma blanket wrapped around each of them, reminding Anna of the night she had been shot. Police officers and paramedics give victims those blankets not because it's cold outside but to calm them and make them feel safe like a child clings to a quilt to protect him from what's hiding in the dark. Suh's wife had bandages on the side of her face and her left eye looked swollen. A paramedic was talking to her, but there was something else in her expression, disgust, and she didn't seem to want to face her husband. Anna tried to stay out of Jin's line of sight, knowing that her presence could alarm him since he knew that she was FBI. Dobbs or Hobson could speak to him and act like regular cops when they got there.

"I didn't know the FBI was interested in burglary and assault cases," came a deep voice from behind Anna.

When she turned around, she recognized the tall black man from the park.

"Or are you just following me?" he asked with a smile.

"You're a cop," she said flatly.

"Detective."

"So what do you want with me? The park wasn't a coincidence."

"No, it wasn't," he said. "If you have a couple minutes?"

She followed him to his unmarked cruiser and got in the passenger seat, thankful when he turned the car on and warmth hit her face.

"Your former partner, Jonathan Meeks, was my friend. We helped each other out."

Anna remembered the code word from Meeks' files and blurted out, "You're the Snowball in Snowstorm."

He smiled. "Yeah."

"So talk."

"There was a double homicide yesterday. Two people linked to the case you and Johnnie were working on earlier this year."

"The Hawthorne guy?"

"Yeah. He's American, but we know that he has an affiliation with a Chechen man, but we don't know his name and don't have a photo of him—"

"Then how do you know he's Chechen?"

"We have an audio recording—"

"How would you get an audio recording and not a picture or video?"

"Will you just let me finish?"

"Go ahead," she said, realizing that her getting upset had nothing to do with the detective's revelations, but it had to do with Johnnie doing all of this behind her back with another partner. Why couldn't he have just told her?

"The murders would have stayed under the radar, just another couple homicides, if I hadn't worked with Johnnie on all this and knew some of the players."

"And the other guy?"

"Lester Nords. Finnish. Doesn't try to hide his identity, but his name has come up a few times. Johnnie thought he was back in Europe, but then he shows up dead right here in Boston. We don't know what his role is, only that he has a role."

"Had," she said. "Why didn't you just tell me this at the park?"

Malcolm bit his bottom lip before saying, "A woman walking alone in a dark and dangerous park is a woman who has something serious on her mind. Didn't seem like the right time."

"Well—"

"And then this," he said, pointing toward the Suhs.

"What exactly happened here?"

"According to Mrs. Suh, she came home and was attacked by

an intruder, a man wearing a mask. She fought with him until he knocked her unconscious; that's about all she remembers, but, as you know, the details will probably come back more in a day or two, at least that's what we hope."

"No sexual assault?"

"No. None."

"Where was her husband?"

"That's the part that doesn't make sense. He was there, but he didn't hear anything. And the neighbor says that he remembered seeing Mr. Suh getting home, but then saw a dark Escalade show up not long afterward. Mr. Suh denies having company, and the neighbor didn't see when the vehicle left or see the license plate."

"And burglars tend not to pull right up in their vehicle to rob your house. They're keeping something from us. It couldn't have happened that way."

"So, to the point, two players get killed, then this incident with a researcher at the campus where Johnnie suspected the next wave would hit after you all took down the first group last year."

"I'm glad he told me about all this and let me help."

"He wanted to, but he knew that if he got caught, it could mean his career, and he didn't want to put you in that position." He looked at her, his features softening just a bit, that tense jaw of his slackening. "Good partners always back each other up, no matter the risks."

That was true. She knew that whatever Johnnie would have asked, she would have complied. He had always tried to protect her. Such a good man. Why did good men always have secrets? At least the assholes were open about everything, wore it all on their sleeves. All you had to do was look.

"There are two working close to Jin that we're watching," she said, not wanting the conversation to continue regarding Johnnie. Poor Johnnie. "A woman and a Russian at MIT."

"The Russian's too obvious, and the woman's too clean?"

"How would you know that?"

"Same way you do. And we both know that they're both involved at some level."

"Yeah, we both know that."

"Where were they last night?"

"They're both missing."

"You don't think they're dead, do you?" he asked.

"No. Just a colossal fuck up in management." She let out a deep breath, the windshield fogging in front of her for half a second before the heater made it vanish.

"Well, that's all the information that I have. That's as far as Johnnie and I got. It wasn't like we could work on it every day, and after he was shot, it didn't seem important anymore. Until yesterday." Malcolm put his hands on the steering wheel and gripped it hard, that sound of straining leather like colliding storm clouds. "Someone screamed and caused an avalanche."

"That's one way to put it."

Anna saw Dobbs and Hobson pull in and called them over. After filling them in, she said, "Talk to them and find out what really happened, but don't tell them you're FBI." And when they left, she said to Malcolm, "I want copies of all of your files on this, okay?"

"Yes, ma'am," said Malcolm.

"I know it's against protocol to talk to you about any of this, but I just don't give a shit anymore. Do you understand?"

"Yes, ma'am."

They exchanged cell numbers.

"I'll be in touch," she said, then went back to her car. And when she was inside her car, she yelled, "God fucking damn it! This fucking case."

She started driving down the dark road slowly, her heater breathing out hot air but her skin remaining cold. Fifteen minutes later, she was standing alongside the black Charles River reflecting the city lights but no stars; the city was too bright to see all those stars overhead. It was peaceful out there in that living canvas, each ripple of water distorting the buildings, the lights, a city of malleable substance—nothing permanent. And then down, she saw herself in that gloomy water, an amorphous shell contracting and widening and disappearing in a violent ripple.

"Nothing as it seems," she whispered to the air.

Danielle was awake and alert when Anna arrived.

"Tell me something good," she said as she got in the car.

"I hope no news is good news."

"It's not," said Anna.

"Her car's still here."

"But we're in Boston, Danielle. You don't have to have a car to get around."

"Young and Herrera are at the Volkov house and reported that everything looked normal. The wife is home, but there is no word on Alexei. He might be there, might not."

"I'll be right back," said Anna, then got out of the car and approached Jenny's front door. Her gut told her that the small house was empty. She rang the doorbell once, then again. Then again. No answer. She peered in the front windows—nothing. There was nothing to do now but head back to the car and wait.

Anna knew that she was being reckless, but there didn't seem to be another choice right now. Major things were happening, and they all played some role—Alexei, Jenny, Jin, the two murder victims, the mysterious Chechen, and even Malcolm, and she knew that he hadn't told her everything, at least her instinct told her that. He'd wanted her to think that he was upset over Johnnie's death, but he had really been trying to hide the lie that he'd told her everything. What bit of information had he left out and why? There was nothing to suspect that he was involved because he could have simply stayed away from her and been left in the clear. And he could have easily killed her in the park if she was a threat to him. But Johnnie hadn't mentioned him, not even in the home, just given her his files that had made mention of "Snowball" three or four times. It was clear that Johnnie had told Malcolm about her, though, or else he wouldn't have known to come to her with any information. Unless he had been tracking Johnnie, had stolen his files...that would make him the enemy. But, no! He knew that she hadn't made any connection to Hawthorne or Lester, so why would he turn the heat up on himself, especially in such a complex—

"Agent Stern," said Danielle, approaching her. "Dobbs said that David Delk had been at Jin's house tonight, that it was his Escalade."

"Why would he keep that from police in the first place? It doesn't make sense. Nothing makes sense tonight."

Half a block down the street, a parked car flashed its lights. Anna looked in its direction, then back at Danielle. When the lights flashed again, she approached, having Danielle stay in her car and watch Jenny's place in case she returned. It was DeLaurent.

She got in the passenger seat and said, "You really fucked us up tonight."

"Shut up, Anna." His jawline tightened. "I ordered an immediate forensic autopsy on Agent Meeks, and the pathologist found that he had been injected with potassium chloride, which stopped his heart and ultimately killed him."

No! That couldn't be. Is that what Malcolm hadn't told her? Did he know that Johnnie had been murdered?

"Your rookies are looking over security tapes from the home, but I'm guessing they'll come up short."

Her body was numb and cold. Maybe DeLaurent hadn't fucked everything up. Maybe she was the one that was fucked up. After all, he had been the one trying to rule out foul play, not taking what was handed to him as the truth until checking all possibilities. Murder had not been in Anna's mind, not in Johnnie's condition. He put agents before the case, and she could be nothing but grateful for that. That is what made him a good leader.

"I had a team go to the hospital, which is why I had to pull some of your people off for a few hours."

"Murphy's Law," she said in an almost incomprehensible whisper. Then, louder, "It's all gone to shit."

"I can't let you be part of the investigation, Anna. I'm sorry."

"I get the feeling that I already am."

Anna had every right to be afraid now, to look over her shoulder. If they would go so far to kill Johnnie in a place with video surveillance and people present around the clock, they would have no scruples putting an end to her.

"Does that mean you're pulling me off *this* case?" she asked, pointing to Danielle's car.

"No, but I can't have you involved directly with the murder investigation."

"I don't want to be involved with that." In her mind, she wanted to cry, but her physical body rejected that idea. "Just keep me in the loop with an update every now and then, okay?"

He nodded.

The dark and cloudless sky had lightened, welcoming the approaching dawn.

As she opened the door, DeLaurent said, "I'm sorry, Anna. I know the past twenty-four hours have been absolute hell, but—"

"It's part of the job, right? That's what we sign on for."

When he didn't respond, Anna got out of the car, and DeLaurent drove away.

Anthony Hawthorne. Lester Nords. Jonathan Meeks. Chechen Man. The Ten. Jenny Frautschi. Alexei Volkov. David Delk. Jin Won Suh. Burglar Guy. Meeks' Killer. Snowball. Dead. Dead. Dead. Mystery. Extradited. Missing. Missing. Hmmm. Victimized. Mystery. Mystery. Hmmm. Who killed Hawthorne and Nords? Same person as Meeks? Not the same as Burglar Guy because Burglar Guy is not a killer. She put her notes down.

"Agent Stern," came Herrera's voice through her earpiece.

"Go ahead, Herrera," she said, everyone on the team able to hear the conversation.

"Hearing screams from Volkov residence. We know the wife's inside, potentially innocent victim. What would you like us to do?"

God damn it. "What's your gut telling you?"

"To go in. There's no time for backup."

"Okay, but cover your asses. I'm on my way."

"Yes, ma'am."

She couldn't let this escalate further. Too many dead already.

"We know Jenny's not there, so stay alert here, Danielle. I'll be back when I can. The moment Jenny gets back—"

"I will."

The sun had risen above the horizon now, bright and blinding, but not taking any of the early morning chill out of the air.

Traffic was congested, so Anna turned on her flashing lights and siren to get through the ridiculously crowded sections of the morning rush hour. Six miles to destination.

"Herrera," she said into the microphone.

Nothing.

"Agent Young!"

Nothing.

She continued to speed to Alexei Volkov's home.

Five miles to destination.

"Herrera," she yelled this time.

Nothing.

"God dammit, can anyone hear me through this thing?"

"Crystal," said Danielle.

"Good here," said Dobbs.

Four miles to destination.

"Herrera or Young."

Nothing.

"Dobbs, meet me at the Volkov house immediately. Hobson,

stay there."

She then called in to dispatch two ambulances.

Three miles to destination.

Anna's cell rang—Malcolm.

"Hey, just giving you a head's up. Someone called 9-1-1 and reported hearing gunshots on the same street Volkov lives on—"

"Fuck. I'm on my way there now." She ended the call.

This was turning into the worst-case scenario. Two agents missing. One lead assaulted, another missing, and now one might be dead…one agent murdered. Pressure on her chest and tears forming in her eyes as she weaved through seemingly endless lines of commuters.

Two miles to destination.

"DeLaurent, Herrera and Young aren't responding."

"They just might be in a situation where they can't respond. Update me when you get on scene. I'm heading there now."

One mile to destination.

Volkov's street was the next right turn, and she took it with such speed that the back end of the car slid and almost hit a parked car or maybe it did hit the parked car. Anna's attention was on the house two blocks down.

Smoke.

It came from a few chimneys. It came from exhaust pipes of the cars in front of her and those warming in parking places on either side of the street. It came from her tires after she mashed down on the gas pedal because she saw plumes of it, black and thick, coming from Alexei Volkov's home. Her tires made that nails-on-chalkboard screech in front of Alexei's house.

You have arrived.

Anna glanced toward Herrera's car. Empty. She got out.

The house's windows glowed, all of them. Nothing could be alive inside.

Pedestrians were on the sidewalk, some in suits and others in robes.

"I just called 9-1-1 about the fire," an old woman said.

"Did anyone see anything or anyone?" she yelled.

"Gunshots," one man said.

"I saw someone leave and drive away."

"It was probably kids," the old woman said. "They've had vandals here."

Anna knew that she couldn't go inside and that it wasn't safe to get near the house. Again, it didn't make sense. Who shot a gun? Who set the fire? Who drove away? Where in the fuck were Herrera and Young?

Dobbs arrived, followed by Malcolm Youngblood and two police cruisers, the ambulances, and the sound of fire-engine sirens not too far away.

"Dobbs, come with me. Malcolm, please try to find out what the fuck happened here."

Dobbs silently followed Anna as they went through the neighbor's yard to get into Alexei's backyard, staying away from the house in case of an explosion. And when they reached the backyard, there were two distinct sets of footprints, one set going toward the house and the other away. Those approaching were big and they dragged through the snow, almost looking like two parallel lines going from fence to back door. But the other set were different. They began at the back door and went to the back fence, small and spaced far apart as if the person was running and maintained balance and control. The only other tracks in the snow had clearly come from birds and squirrels.

"I have to follow these as far as I can. Stay here and radio me when DeLaurent arrives."

"You shouldn't go alone with all the shit that's going down, especially if this is an arsonist."

"It's an order, Dobbs." She didn't have time to argue, even though Dobbs had a good point. It was irresponsible to go alone, but her gut told her to do so. She knew that the fire was arson, and she also knew that these prints belonged to the arsonist, but the arsonist was more than just a pyro. Because two of her agents were missing, and they hadn't followed this person. They may not have even seen this person.

Dobbs obeyed.

She climbed over the privacy fence and saw the same prints in the snow on the other side—small crosses in the middle and large blocks around the edges like the average workman's boot. They led to the sidewalk, where the snow had been shoveled. A dead end. But maybe not. There was a slight shift to the left after what seemed a straight line of prints. Anna stood in the middle of the street and faced left. Nothing special, so she began jogging in that direction. At the end of the block, she heard it—the Metro.

"Fuck me," she said, then ran to the commuter rail station.

The train had left by the time she got there, but she looked at the structure and saw them—cameras.

"Malcolm," she said, her cell phone going in and out with static. "Pick me up at Uphams Corner."

"Yes, ma'am."

She knew what Malcolm had not told her now. It was the cameras at the Endicott commuter rail station. He hadn't mentioned them. Had he not retrieved the footage from security? And if not, why?

Anna called DeLaurent and told him that she needed that security video feed along with yesterday's at Endicott "right fucking now because this case can come to an end. I can feel it."

"Slow down, Anna," he said. "We still don't know where Herrera and Young are."

"Sir, I know. I really know. I—"

"There is procedure to—"

"Sir, please. This is happening right now. I might be able to pinpoint the person who set fire to the Volkov place. It will have to be someone involved at a deeper level, and I think I can track the person if I get those video files."

"I'll call it in."

"I'm going to their security office to view them there."

"Authority takes a little longer than that, Anna."

"Will you please trust me?"

"No. You come back here and we'll go by the book."

"These people might be the same ones responsible for Meeks. Please just let me do this."

And that's when it hit her. DeLaurent was responding to her, but she couldn't make out the words. In all the chaos of the predawn morning and then finding out that Johnnie had been murdered, it finally surfaced—she *could* be a target, too. If they knew so much about Johnnie, they had to know about her. Her computer and several files were still at her apartment. Locked up, but these were professionals so locked up didn't matter. And Klein! He was there.

Oh, Christ.

She hung up on DeLaurent and dialed Klein's number.

"Come on. Pick up, for fuck sake." Her hands were shaking. "Klein, answer the phone."

And he did on the third ring: "Hey there, beautiful. I did make the bed and lock—"

"You're not at the apartment?"

"Nope. Just heading toward work right now."

There was urgency in his voice, only slight, but it was there. And Anna knew that it could be that he was at the apartment and that someone might be there with a gun pointed at his head. But why would the person let him answer? These people were not about keeping others alive.

"And everything's okay?"

"Of course it is."

"Promise me."

"What's going on, sweetheart?" he said.

Through the speaker, she could hear a door closing and then brief gusts of wind.

"You just went outside?"

"Had to get a coffee. It's cold and I didn't have time to make any at the apartment."

Anna dropped to her knees then sat on the cold, deserted sidewalk. "That makes me very…" The words caught in her throat. Something good in all of this mess. "…happy," she forced out as tears fell down her cheeks.

She heard Klein give a brief laugh as he said, "Hey, you're just having a bad day. I'm fine. I'm okay. And I'll be here for you when you get off work."

"Okay. Bye," she said.

Anna stood back up and regained her composure, wiping her cheeks dry and taking a few deep, freezing breaths. So there was still something good about today. Something to look forward to.

When Malcolm picked her up and they headed to the transit security office, she let it out: "Why didn't you mention the cameras at Endicott? Did they pick up anything? Did you see who killed those men? Did you see anything?"

"I didn't bring it up because there was nothing to bring up. The analyst saw Lester Nords at the stop, but the cameras don't reach far past the tracks. The intersection cams aren't out that far yet, and the cams that detect gunfire are still waiting on further approval. It's just a spot that we can't see."

"And these bastards are smart enough to know that beforehand."

"There's no cameras on Volkov's street because there's no lights, just Stop signs."

"Then what are you keeping from me?"

"I'm—"

"Don't lie to me."

He hesitated, then said, "Johnnie thought there might be someone inside Boston FBI, but there was never enough to move forward with it."

It couldn't be, but it would make sense if this whole case was designed to give them the surface-level spies and keep hidden those deeper in the framework. It was like arresting drug dealers off the street. It didn't do any good because the kingpins and bank launderers remained hidden and safe. When you started going after bigger fish, the consequences grew. No one had died or had even gotten injured when they arrested the ten last year, so that meant the case had taken a turn because death was popping up all around her. Anna was getting closer to a big fish, for the waters it inhabited were treacherous and murky.

"That's because everyone there is clean, at least as far as this case is concerned. And that's the last I want to hear of that."

"It was you that pried it out of me."

DeLaurent's voice came through her earpiece. "Agent Stern, I'm on scene now. Let me know what you find out from the cameras."

So he had listened to her and given his blessing. "Yes, sir," she replied.

The supervisor at transit security didn't keep them waiting. Anna screened the footage over the past hour of activity at Uphams Corner rail stop. Pedestrian traffic was heavy, but she was looking for someone acting strange beyond being in a rush to get to the stop or impatient because he was late for work. No one stuck out. And it was difficult to see the shoes people wore as she tried to find out who wore work boots that would have made such prints in the snow. But that proved impossible because it was winter and many had on boots that would have that pattern. Such a common pattern.

"I'd like to see Endicott stop's footage from the homicide."

As the supervisor retrieved it, Malcolm said, "I told you there wasn't anything there."

"I'm looking for something else."

The video up, she said to Malcolm, "Show me Lester Nords."

Malcolm fast-forwarded the video until Lester came into view, wearing a trench coat and holding a small messenger bag. He put the bag on the ground and faced away from the tracks, then he seemed to be talking to himself. A few minutes later, he left the station.

"Are you kidding me?" said Anna. "You didn't make some kind of connection here? That person on the bench took his bag. He was talking to her. Malcolm, did you not think it odd that he was just talking to himself?"

"This is the first time I've seen the footage. I told you that our analyst viewed it."

"And what kind of qualifications does a fucking analyst need? A fucking GED? This woman," she said, "who is she?"

"Don't know."

"Can you bring up the Uphams Corner footage again?"

It took Anna fifteen minutes to locate her at Uphams Corner, approaching calmly and dressed casually, easing on to the train while carrying something black under her arm. The woman had blonde hair, rarely allowed the camera to get a clear shot of her, and seemed petite, but her winter clothes could be deceiving. The supervisor took the initiative to retrieve in-train footage to show where the woman got off. It was Endicott.

"I need printouts of these right now, and need you to forward these video files to FBI Boston," she told the supervisor, and he left the room to do so. "You're positive that you don't know who this is?" Anna said to Malcolm.

"Yeah, I've never seen her before."

"I think this is our arsonist. And if not, I have a feeling that she was in Alexei Volkov's house this morning."

"The only thing, and this may be nothing at all, is that Lester used to have an address in that area."

That was it, thought Anna. "Tell me that you remember the address."

"Let's go," said Malcolm.

Anna got the photos on her way out. They were grainy and blurry, all of them, but they were all they had to go on. Dobbs' voice came through her earpiece: "Agent Stern, firefighters have found bodies in the Volkov home."

So not just an arsonist, but a murderer.

Chapter 21

Clouds had moved in, and snow flurries began dancing down in calm, whipping about in breeze, Nature's ballet. Muscles tense and teeth clamped together, Lilly could take the cold no more. Leaving her bag hidden underneath thick shrubbery, she snuck into the neighboring yard through the hedge, its sharp bark scratching at her skirt. Creeping, moving from behind one tree trunk to another, hiding, and creeping again. She was still young enough for adults to think she was just playing hide-and-seek, she thought, and a moment later she realized that it was exactly what she was doing. The safety of home base was really home, at least for now. The seekers—Boston police.

She would go to Svetlana's apartment and grab a blanket before going back outside and waiting again. She couldn't handle being in Kate's presence for she would surely be angry that some cop was searching her house, waking her up or disturbing her from whatever she was doing. Lilly could sneak down the stairs, retrieve her violin, and then leave. Then she'd have no reason to ever return.

Each time she made it to the next tree, Lilly would look around in every direction for that Lexus, for anyone watching her, for Svetlana. It was when she was four houses from home base that she turned around to see Svetlana almost jogging down the sidewalk toward the house carrying a laptop. Chest fluttering, she dashed out from behind a large elm and onto the sidewalk.

"Svetlana, stop!"

"Lilly?" she said, breathlessly, meeting her on the sidewalk. "What are you doing out here in the snow? You'll freeze."

"Somebody's looking for you. Police."

Lilly couldn't read the expression on Svetlana's face. Was that anger? Worry? Nothing at all? Her lips were barely together,

271

cheeks not moving, eyes shifting from Lilly to a diagonal gaze toward the house.

"Do you think they know about—"

"No." Svetlana put her hand on Lilly's cold cheek. "Is the person still there?"

"No," she said. "There were two of them I think, and they were driving a Lexus."

Svetlana leaned closer to her, looking more like she was going to kiss her than anything else.

"Lilly, those were not police. Police do not drive a Lexus."

She pulled her hand away and stood erect, blowing out a cloudy breath.

"Then who are they?" she asked, suddenly worrying about Kate's well-being. Had she directed a madman to Kate's bedroom? Was she okay? The thought sent heat to every part of her body, and her shivers, she realized, were of fear now rather than cold.

Svetlana was silent long enough for Lilly to then say, "Like the man who killed Lester."

"Yes, like the man who killed Lester," Svetlana replied.

"And he wants to kill you?"

Two seconds of silence, then, "I don't know, Lilly."

"He wanted to talk to my mother. She was downstairs, and he went downstairs. I took my packed bag. I left, and then the man came after me when he realized that I had left."

"You're going to be okay, Lilly."

"I know. I know that you'll never let anything bad happen to me."

Svetlana drew her lips in, her chin making the slightest quiver, and she turned to look down the street, then stared at the house for what felt like a long time, and then back at Lilly.

"Is your mother in there now?"

Lilly nodded.

"Wait for me here."

"No. I'm going in with you."

"It would be best for you to stay outside."

"No."

"You don't need to go inside, Lilly."

"I have to get my violin."

"I can get it for you."

"You're not leaving me alone again," she said, surprising herself that she maintained an erect posture, an unbroken tone, and strength to walk back into that house one last time. The strength to see Kate Rebeck, alive or dead.

"Very well." Svetlana started for the house, Lilly in tow. Up the side stairs and into the apartment, Svetlana took a book from the sparse bookshelf, slipped a few pieces of sheet music between the pages, then put them and the laptop in a one-shoulder backpack, then got something from the closet and put it in her pocket.

"Stay behind me," Svetlana said to Lilly as they went downstairs, slipping the pack over her shoulder. She wasted no time and didn't worry about making noise as she almost ran down, glancing quickly into open doors before taking the second flight of steps.

The television was on, a commercial playing, but Lilly didn't look at the screen and the words sounded muffled as her focus was on Kate's bedroom door, which was still closed.

Svetlana knocked on it loudly. "Miss Rebeck!"

No answer.

Svetlana twisted the knob and pushed the door open to the dark room.

"Wait here, and I will get your violin."

Lilly watched Svetlana disappear into the darkness and followed, flipping on the light switch when she entered the room.

Svetlana glanced back at her as if startled, but she didn't say anything.

The room was dirty, clothes all over the floor, glasses on the nightstand, nothing in order except the bed. There was what looked to be a rushed job in making the bed, the comforter top not aligned with the headboard, but cocked a few degrees, the bottom corner hanging off the end and resting on the violin case, half of which was under the bed. And under the comforter, Kate Rebeck. At least Lilly thought it was her.

"Take your violin, Lilly, and let's go," she said, opening Kate's purse and taking out the set of keys and her wallet.

She was right there, her first mother. Right under that comforter. The last thread of an old life. She wanted to see her one more time, to pull back the fabric and know what that man had done. Two steps forward, and Lilly was standing next to the bed now gazing down at the bulge where the pillows were side by side. Leaning forward and reaching for the comforter, Svetlana grabbed her wrist and pulled her back gently, but Lilly didn't feel it because she was numb.

"It's best if you don't."

"Why?"

"Just trust me because I know."

Lilly didn't want to listen to her. She knew that Svetlana was right, but it was an experience that Svetlana must have had back in Russia. Something that shaped who she was, this magnificent and talented woman. If it was some rite of passage that completed the shift into a new life, then so be it.

"I have to, so please don't try and stop me."

Svetlana did not respond, so Lilly turned around and pulled the top of the comforter down, letting it fold over and fall. Underneath, the beige sheet. A gentle tug and it too slipped down to reveal Kate Rebeck's death mask. Eyes open, the left almost bulging while the right was half closed like a lazy eye. Mouth a silent scream, lips covering her teeth save the tips of her bottom front four, her tongue balled up in the back of her mouth as if sealing her throat. Blonde hair strands snaked this way and that across her face, one locking itself in her left eyelash, curling down under her nose. Others frilled under her ears and across her cheeks. There was no blood.

Lilly didn't gasp, but she did stare for nearly two minutes, then took the comforter and covered Kate Rebeck's face again. She did love her mother, but this just wasn't her mother anymore, hadn't been since Kate had let those two army officers inside to tell her the news of her husband's death in Afghanistan. Would it be the same? Would Lilly let herself cry later when she tried to talk about it? If she tried to say, "I miss Mom," in a few weeks, would that choking sensation seize her and pull a tear out of her? Lilly didn't know because she didn't feel that obligation to cry right now like she had when hearing those officers speak the worst news. And it wasn't a sunny and cool November day. No, while this day had begun with the sun shining, it had turned grey and snowy, freezing and dark.

"What do we do now?"

Svetlana put her hand on Lilly's cheek. "We have to burn it down, Lilly. Right now."

Was that necessary? To burn down all remnants of this place, this real brick and mortar, real wood, real home? The home that her father had approved of, that wasn't hollow and artificial like those newer models farther out in those subdivisions. Wouldn't that leave something hollow here, in this neighborhood? Wouldn't that mean that there was no way back to this life? That she had to move forward and never look back? And what about her mother? Was this a proper burial? Cremated in her own home? Yes. The woman seemed to love this place more than her own daughter, spent more time attending to and working for it than caring about Lilly's passion for music. So, yes. It was the right thing to do, even if she didn't completely understand the reasoning.

"Why?" Lilly asked.

"I will explain it to you later. Our time is too limited right now."

"I can't."

"I will do it," said Svetlana, withdrawing her hand, picking up the violin case, and holding it out to her. "Take your violin, go get your bag, and I will come and get you."

"No. I told you, you're not leaving me alone again." Lilly went to her, pushed the violin case aside, and hugged her tightly, burying her face in Svetlana's coat. "You're all I have."

Svetlana knelt slightly and placed the violin case on the floor, but Lilly kept her grip.

"I'm not going to leave you, Lilly," she said, now putting her hand around the back of Lilly's head, the other around her shoulders.

Lilly could hear Svetlana's heartbeat, how it started throbbing just a little faster. Her warmth. The only person she'd ever sought who had accepted her freely rather than out of obligation. Rather than the result of being sought the way Mr. Thompson had come to accept her. To others, like Kevin Kaiser, she remained invisible. And part of her was okay with that right now because she was ready to move on.

"I love you, Svetlana," she said, and that's all she would be able to say right now with an unbroken voice, so she left it at that.

"I love you, too, Lilly." And after a few moments, she said, "It's time."

Lilly let her go and took a few steps back. "I can help," she said. "I wanna help."

"Okay. Bring me the red canister in the cabinet under my sink. And hurry."

Lilly took two steps at a time, and when she opened the cabinet, the red canister sat there alone, the only item. And it was big and heavy like several gallon jugs of milk all meshed into one. She took it with both hands, each step back down an added burden to her already aching arms. She noticed her violin case next to the front door and heard Svetlana in the kitchen. Lilly put the canister on the floor.

"Here you go."

"Stand by the front door. This is going to go up fast."

Lilly watched Svetlana go room to room, splattering the gasoline. Kate's bedroom. The living room. The kitchen. And, finally, the hallway and base of the staircase, making a final trail toward the door as she backed toward Lilly. Then, she threw the canister down the hall and took out a box of matches.

"Get your violin and open the door."

Lilly did.

When Svetlana struck the match, that raspy coughing sound, then the sizzle, Lilly said, "Wait."

Svetlana turned, match in hand, flame beginning to burn down the stem.

"I want to do it. I think I need to do it."

Svetlana blew out the match and handed the box to Lilly.

"Give me your violin."

Lilly did.

Svetlana standing in the doorway, Lilly slid the match across the side of the box, and the flame burst to life. Holding the matchstick with her forefinger and thumb, she let it drop a foot in front of her, and the gasoline ignited like a low, growling thunder. It took only a second for the fiery snake to grow and begin consuming everything. The heat was instant, Lilly's skin feeling like it was burning until she felt Svetlana pull her backward and out of the house. Like jumping into a pool after being in a hot tub, the snow-filled air stung and froze her, consumed her.

"We have to hurry. Come on," Svetlana said, getting Lilly into the passenger seat of Kate's Jeep.

Svetlana then got into the driver's seat, started the Jeep, and started pulling out onto the street when the clear windshield let out a faint thud-like sound, then cracked, looking like one of those stickers soccer moms put on their cars of a baseball going through the window.

It was so sudden that Lilly didn't scream. But another hole appeared in the windshield and then another, tiny shards of glass spraying through the Jeep. She knew now why she wasn't screaming; she was paralyzed with fear.

Svetlana grabbed Lilly's coat and pulled her down. She was saying something to her, but Lilly couldn't hear it. She could only hear ringing, the loud and constant kind that seemed to only come in silence.

Both of them jolted forward as the Jeep had probably hit a parked car. More glass fell, even Lilly's door window shattered now, the cold air streaming in and circulating around them.

It was the cold air that seemed to wake her, that made her senses work again, and Lilly realized that she was screaming. Svetlana was holding her tightly, keeping Lilly's body against hers, protecting her, and Lilly was screaming. They were both going to die right here. On the road. Just like her father had died on the road. The bad people suddenly attack, and there's nothing you can do.

Metal ripping and screeching, but no sound of gunfire, just the bullets hitting the Jeep, mangling the frame and shredding the glass and seat foam, the orange puffs dropping down on them like raindrops, not feathery like snow. And screaming. Lilly's own screaming. Until Svetlana covered Lilly's mouth and said, "It's okay, Lilly. I've got you," did Lilly pull back and be silent, the bullets still hitting the Jeep.

"Get all the way down to the floorboard," Svetlana said, then pulled a pistol from her coat pocket. She was bent over the middle console and had to raise up a bit while moving back so Lilly could get all the way down to the floorboard.

Svetlana reached her hand back and opened her door. It would only open enough to squeeze through because they *had* hit a parked car at an odd angle. She put her feet out first, then tried to slide the rest of her body through as the thudding sounds continued.

Lilly watched as Svetlana had almost gotten out when the left side of Svetlana's forehead began gushing blood and her body fell out of the Jeep.

"Svetlana!" cried Lilly, leaping from the floorboard across the middle console, grabbing the steering wheel to help pull her body across the seats. Svetlana was on the ground with her hand to the side of her head, the blood seeming more vibrant against her pale skin.

"Ugh...dammit," Svetlana said, noticing Lilly now. "Stay down!"

Svetlana had dropped her gun on the snowy asphalt, the drops of blood forming funnel-like holes in the powdery snow, red at the top and black on the bottom. She reached out her hand to Lilly, who took it. The power of the tug felt as though it came from three men, and Lilly was outside the Jeep in one shot.

It hurt to breathe, each freezing intake seeming to instantly ice up her insides, only to break apart and prick and scrape her vulnerable throat like tiny dull razors as she tried to swallow.

"You stay down here," she said as a bullet hit the front tire and the Jeep seemed to shake as the front-right side sank with a sneeze-like cry.

Then, the thuds stopped.

Svetlana picked up her pistol and stood up enough to see past the parked cars, keeping her hand firmly on her forehead, even though the blood still seeped from under her palm.

"They are near the end of the street. The Lexus. There are two of them, but only one with a weapon, it seems."

She knelt back down.

"Are you going to be okay? There's so much blood?" Lilly said, again thinking about Lester.

"It's just a scratch, Lilly. I will be fine."

Lilly could smell smoke now. She instinctively glanced back at her former home, streams of white and black smoke bellowing out the front door, the roof, the chimneys, and the side door to Svetlana's former apartment.

"Agent Stern," said Dobbs, his voice raspier than before. "I think the bodies are Young and Herrera...unless two people stole their badges." There was a pause. "Agent Stern, are you there?"

"I'm here, Dobbs. Keep at it."

"Yes, ma'am."

"We better be fucking close, Malcolm."

"What in the hell... ?" said Malcolm, slowing the car.

Anna saw a car stopped in the intersection a block and a half away, a man standing outside the driver's side door firing some kind of rifle.

"How do you want to approach?"

Anna pulled out her Glock 23 and made sure there was a bullet in the chamber and that the safety was off. She opened the door and got out.

"On foot. Call for backup. I'll take the left side, you the right. We have to help whoever he's firing at."

Malcolm called it in, then got out.

Cars lined the street, giving both of them plenty of cover. Anna could see him firing, but couldn't hear the gunshots. Silencer! That meant he was a pro. That also meant the potential victim was someone important.

Anna got Malcolm's attention and waved him to her side of the street when they were a block away.

When she told Malcolm, he responded, "I bet it's her. I bet he's trying to kill her!"

They stayed bent down as they ran from car to car until they were only three away from the intersection. Anna tried to look at the shooter through the car windows, but they were covered with snow, so she went in between a pickup and a Sentra.

Gun raised, she saw a person in the passenger seat, an Arab or Hispanic. Then, the shooter. It couldn't be.

"I've got him," Malcolm said.

"Don't shoot! Wait."

Staying behind the pickup, keeping her gun aimed strong, hoping she was wrong, that the snowflakes had distorted her perception, she called out, "Klein."

The shooter paused, slowly let the rifle barrel point to the ground, and turned toward her.

It was Klein, her wonderful and sweet Klein.

No.

No!

His facial expression had been stone until he made a disgusting half smile, then gritted his teeth, and raised the rifle to point it at her. She fired once, hitting her lover between the lips, breaking those teeth and sending his body back against the car. The rifle fell. Klein fell to the ground, the passenger in the Lexus having moved to the driver's seat. He sped away.

Malcolm fired two shots, each hitting the driver's side door.

Anna heard three gunshots, then a crash. The stench of burning...wood? Another gunshot. Faint sirens in the distance over the ringing in her ears. She holstered her Glock and then approached Klein's body, not caring who the man in the car was. Malcolm went to her, keeping his gun out.

"Wait," he said. "Someone else has a gun. Those shots weren't mine."

But she didn't seem to hear him or acknowledge his presence until he grabbed her shoulder and spun her around to face him.

"Wait!"

And she did, but she stared at the convulsing body staining the intersection.

Malcolm approached a car near the edge of the intersection and peered down the street. A few moments later, he stood and holstered his pistol.

She took the action to mean that it was all clear and went to Klein, kicking the rifle from his reach, then rolling him over so that his face was toward the dark grey clouds. Her adrenaline was already calming. Anna wanted to take her Glock and finish out her clip in his twitching face so that it would never be seen again. Rot was too slow. She didn't even want his skeleton to resemble a human being, rather just a mixture of bone shards swimming in pools of blood and brain tissue like maggots might do. And then a dam broke in her mind and flooded out those malicious thoughts, replacing them with a single thought.

"Motherfucker," Anna said quietly, kneeling and leaning in close, the gurgling sound in Klein's throat prompting her to turn his head so the blood wouldn't choke him so she could hear the answer to her question: "Who killed Jonathan Meeks?" Turning his head to her again, it was obvious that he would be dead very soon. "You? Did you?"

That smile. That grotesque grin. The bastard was trying to give her that disgusting half smile again but couldn't as that gurgling sound came again, choking the son of a bitch. And she let him. And a few moments later, he died.

"You okay?" said Malcolm.

She was okay. At least for now.

"We got another fire. And there's a body down there."

Anna stood and gazed down at her former lover's body, then broke that gaze and marched down the street as fearless as a Cossack, Malcolm trying to keep up behind her.

"It's the passenger that drove away," she said, when they'd made it to the man.

He was on his back in the middle of the street. His shirt was soaked with blood. A close-range gunshot wound to the middle of his forehead the way a professional assassinates someone.

An icy breeze sent smoke from the burning house toward them, burning their eyes as if sitting around a campfire.

"What do you want to bet that that's Brother?" said Malcolm.

"Even if it is, it doesn't mean that this case is finished."

"No shit. Whoever killed him took the Lexus. That woman."

"Who was living in that house, I'm sure," Anna said, pointing to the inferno.

"Agent Stern," came Dobbs' voice.

"Go ahead."

"We've found another body over here."

"Let me know if you're able to identify it."

"It'll probably take dental records, ma'am."

"Did you put out an APB on that Lexus?" she asked Malcolm.

"Yes."

Searching the Arab's pockets, she found a knuckleduster, derringer, prepay cell phone, and a wallet that had no identification inside, only three hundred dollars, a slip of paper with numbers on it, and lint.

It took four minutes for the fire trucks to arrive and another two for the ambulances and first police cars. In that time, Anna stood beside the Arab's corpse.

Her gut told her that the third body at the Volkov home was Jenny Frautschi, so she pulled Danielle Morgan from surveillance and ordered her to pick her up.

"This doesn't happen for some stolen science research," she said to Malcolm. "I think we're missing a big piece to this case. Do you know what I mean?"

He nodded.

"These kinds of people stay under the radar. They don't stand in the middle of an intersection in broad daylight firing a rifle at someone. For God's sake, they don't even come out." She looked back at Klein's corpse in the intersection, two paramedics doing something to him; she was too far away to see what. "They burrow themselves in deep and blend in unnoticed." She said these words in monotone, as if she was in a trance.

"It was a clean shot," said Malcolm.

He stood on the other side of the Arab's body, hands on his hips.

"I know," she said. Another secret.

If Brother was even one step up the ladder, he would not be exposed like this, not ride in the same car as his assassin. He'd likely not even be in the same city or state where those beneath him were collecting data. The only logical reason was that it had personal significance. That the woman responsible for triple homicide and two counts of arson was wanted by this man, was wanted dead by this man. Why?

"You don't know anything about this woman at all?"

"Never seen her before. Johnnie never mentioned anyone by her description either."

She was getting repetitive, and she knew it. But, sometimes it took going over something again and again to establish some reason behind it all. To find out what the motives were. Spies rarely murdered for information. Their objective was to obtain the information without anyone knowing that it was even taken. Assassins took out high-level targets, those with some form of significance whether political, cultural, or to prevent someone from exposing the organization. But, again, this woman just didn't fit the profile. Even those who were elusive, like Brother, had something on record.

Anna looked more closely at the piece of paper she had taken from the dead man's pocket. Longitude and latitude coordinates.

"This is where we go next. Another agent is on the way."

"Are you sure I should be part of this?"

"You have a choice not to be. But if you do keep moving forward, I'll fill out the paperwork later to add you to the task force."

Anna could see his hesitation, how his torso leaned back slightly and how his eyes shifted from hers to the ground. He was shaken by all this. Maybe it was the first time he'd fired his weapon in the line of duty, that the anxiety of it all was just now catching up to him when knowing that this case had just started to get deep. How deep would it go? And who would survive? And would he have to kill someone?

"It's okay if you want to stay here," Anna said. That line was never an option for her. She had felt anxiety and insecurity, had felt like she was useless and a burden to her fellow agents, but never had she backed down. Maybe that's what Meeks had seen in her and why he believed in her so much.

"I'm going with you."

"Good. Then you should know that Brother had something personal with that woman or else he wouldn't have been here for this. Unless he's much farther down the totem pole than we thought."

"Any idea about the other guy?"

She didn't respond immediately, just enough time to take in a deep breath. "He's responsible for killing Jonathan Meeks."

"So does that mean that this woman is on our side?"

"Two of my agents are dead. She is not on our side."

"Maybe she's being set up. Maybe she was at the Volkov house and made to look as though she killed them all and set the fire. Then they were going to kill her."

"Even if that was so, they wouldn't do it out in the open like this."

"They did to Lester."

Such a jumbled mess. All she knew was that Young and Herrera were dead and that this woman was the only link to it, the only link to everything—Lester, Hawthorne, Alexei, Jenny if Jenny was at Alexei's, and now Klein and Brother. Alexei and Jenny were connected with Jin Won Suh. And now she knew that Klein was connected with Jonathan Meeks. She needed to speak to this woman.

"Can you find out who lives here?" Anna said, pointing to the burning house.

"Rebecks," came a voice.

Anna turned around to see a man in his robe, his gray hair naturally curly, but clumps sticking out this way and that. He had a mug with steam coming from the top. Probably coffee.

And he looked like he hadn't shaved in four days.

Anna approached him as quickly as she could while still keeping her footing in the snow.

"You saw what happened out here?"

"Sure. That Rebeck woman shot that man," he said, nodding in the Arab's direction, "and stole his car. Put her daughter in the back seat, loaded something from the back of that Jeep to the car trunk, then took off. She's probably crazy," he said with a heavy Boston accent, sipping his coffee. "Husband died in the war few months back, so's they tell me."

"Do you know her first name?"

"Ah, yeah. It's…" He stared at the snow-covered sidewalk.

"Katherine," said Malcolm, cell phone to his ear. "So, Katherine Rebeck and her daughter were the ones who took the car?"

"Yeah. Katherine shot the guy. Poor bastard." He sipped from his mug again. "If you ask me, she probably lost it after that husband of hers died."

So, the blonde mystery woman's name was Katherine Rebeck, and she had a husband in the military who died.

"Can you tell me what her daughter looks like?"

"Young. Teenage. Black hair. I think she was a damn recluse if ya ask me."

"Thank you for your help. An officer will want your official statement, of course," said Malcolm.

"I'm off work today."

He was so unaffected by it all, Anna thought. 9/11 had done that to people, especially in the northeast. Made them a little tougher, harder to surprise and frighten.

Malcolm and she went back to the body as Danielle pulled up.

"I heard about Herrera and Young," said Danielle.

"We have to keep moving forward right now, Danielle," said Anna, handing over the slip of paper. "That's our next move and hopefully our last."

"I don't understand."

"Plug those into the GPS and tell me what comes up."

Agent Morgan did so.

"You'll need more than just the three of us to do this."

"I know that, Malcolm, but I have to know what I'm dealing with first before assembling the team to go in."

She called DeLaurent. "Sir—"

"This better be good news. The director's coming in from DC over Meeks, and now two more agents."

"I think it's good news." She filled him in on what had happened and about the piece of paper, leaving out her relationship with Klein and his involvement with Meeks—there was no evidence, just her word, and the case was too close to throw a wrench in now.

"By the book, Anna. This one's too big for any fuck ups."

"It's in the woods, southeast about twenty miles outside the city," called Danielle.

"Any structures?"

"Can't tell. Summer shot."

"Keep me informed, Anna," said DeLaurent.

"Yes, sir." She put her Blackberry in her pocket and said to Danielle, "Call it in to get the ops plan started. We don't have a lot of time."

Part IV

Spiccato

Chapter 22

"I need some time."
"I need some time."
"I need some time."
"I need some time."

Emily's voice kept repeating in his mind as Alexei stared at the driveway light that remained burning as the sun came up. He'd left the car running, and the gas gauge was nearing E. He would go to the safe house early to give Emily her time rather than continuing to sit in the driveway like a stalker and frighten her more. Because that's what he had done last night. She had cried, but not hysterically. She had diverted her gaze from his eyes, but not out of disgust. She was a librarian, he thought, and just finding out that her life had suddenly turned into one of those novels that she was constantly surrounded by, she refused to respond melodramatically or even show much change after wiping away her initial tears. Four simple words, "I need some time," and then she stepped out of the car and went inside her parents' house.

It took nearly two hours to make a petrol stop and get to the safe house, and snow had started falling. It was pointless trying to hide his footprints, so he just plugged on, hoping the snow would cover his trail. And he wasn't cold...funny how it seems warmer when snow falls. Squirrels and birds were non-existent in the leafless trees, and the woods were silent except his footsteps in the damp snow which sounded like biting into popcorn. And there was a smell in the wind as familiar as that popcorn—campfire. Certainly no one would be camping in this weather, but he moved along more slowly, watching for any plume of smoke. He knew that sound traveled farther atop snow, and the last thing he needed was to draw any attention to himself or to be mistaken for game.

He found no sign of a tent, of another person or animal, or the smoke before the cabin came into view. And there it was, white clouds bellowing out the narrow brick chimney jutting up above the wood shingle roof and then disappearing in the snow.

Donya...Svetlana was already there. Alexei doubted he'd get used to calling her that. Did that mean it was already over? That Brother was dead and that they were finally free?

Alexei remained cautious, moving slowly but not trying to hide his approach. And when he was at the front door, no red flags went up except one—Donya would have known that he had arrived. She would have opened the front door. He wasn't naïve enough to believe that she was in the bathroom or just hadn't been keeping watch. That wasn't Donya.

He turned around to go back to his car, but a man was standing several feet from him, a pistol pointing at Alexei's head. At least he thought it was a man; his eyes were focused on the blackness of the barrel and the slight gold hidden far back in the chamber. His stomach churned, and a tingling anxiety in his bowels. *"I need some time."*

"Where is she?"

Alexei knew that the man was referring to Donya, and he wanted to know the same thing. A ripple in his spine like ants fleeing to his brain—the incident at the Suhs had not made him stronger after all. Alexei was the same child he had always been.

"If she were with me, you'd be dead now," he said to the stranger.

Alexei heard the squeak of the wooden door open behind him, the hint of smoky warm air strangely inviting. When he turned to see who had opened the door, the person punched him, sending him to the snow.

"I didn't say that you could turn around," said the man with the gun.

Bloody spittle hung from Alexei's bottom lip like syrup, and he wiped it away.

"I don't have the information," said Alexei, then he spat a red glob into the snow.

"Get on your feet, little Lenka," said the man behind him in Russian.

He didn't move.

"Or have you forgotten your mother tongue already?"

For a moment, the voice from behind sounded like the man's who had helped them escape the USSR—Boris. But Boris had been killed at Domodedovo. *"I need some time."*

He got up and turned around this time, the Russian having already gone inside and out of sight, but the gunman had closed the space between them and had the pistol jammed hard into Alexei's ribs.

"Inside."

It was not as warm as he thought it would be, chilly actually because the fire was a mere two half-burned logs, enough to give the illusion of heat. Alexei sat on the couch, the gunman in a chair to the side.

"I really don't have the information."

"I don't know what you're talking about, so shut the fuck up."

He had black curly hair, deep furrows from nose to chin like parenthesis around his mouth, and a furry unibrow. Jersey accent.

When would Donya arrive, and would she suspect anything since he was expected to be there? The multiple footprints, if they were still there, could be explained as his family. The smoke from the chimney expected. And Alexei hadn't seen another vehicle, but he hadn't thought to look for one either. Would she be walking into a trap or would she know that the plan was fucked?

"I'm glad you were as dumb as we thought you would be," said the Russian, stepping back in to the room with a mug of coffee.

It wasn't Boris. The man was old enough, probably early fifties, but he was toned so had few wrinkles, jaw rigid like a bull and lips wearing the Russian frown.

"Nevertheless, you managed to cause us plenty of problems."

"I don't know what you mean. You're not with Brother?"

"We are." He sat in the chair opposite the gunman. "Where is Donya Morozova? Your fucking sister."

"I don't know where she is."

"But you know where she will be, yes?"

"No."

He sipped his coffee. "I'm not a patient man, Lenka."

The ceramic mug hit and broke against Alexei's forehead before he realized that the Russian had thrown it. Coffee the temperature of lava burned his skin and left eye, and Alexei screamed, holding his hands over his face and falling to the floor, trying to protect himself from further assault.

"Get off the floor, little girl," said the Russian.

He didn't budge, but then felt himself being jerked up and thrown back on the couch. Hands away from his face, he saw the gunman sit back down.

With his left eye closed, he said, "I don't know anything."

"Lenka, you're familiar with your sister's job in KGB before you two...fled, yes?"

He didn't respond.

"I thought so." He sat back in the chair, crossed his legs, and interlocked his fingers. "I was part of her group, so you know what I'll do to you if you don't give me what I want."

"If you were part of that group, you'll do it anyway." His skin still stung, but he was able to open his left eye, though only slightly, the sensation like cold air whirling around his eye as if missing his eyelids, making it water.

"Where is Donya?"

"I don't know where she is."

Not breaking eye contact, the Russian said, "I'm going to start with your fingernails, Lenka. If you're still playing the imbecile, I'll dig that watery eye out of your skull and make you swallow it."

Alexei's throat tightened and he had to pee. He knew that the man was not lying.

"Tie him to the chair," said the Russian.

When the gunman stood, Alexei yelled, "Wait."

"Now he wants to talk."

"She was at my house yester—"

"Where she killed our woman, then burned it down. Yes, I'm aware of that. Tie him—"

"I can bring her to you."

"Anthony, if I have to tell you one more time, I'll tie *you* to the fucking chair," he said to the gunman.

A small drop of blood had crested the tiny tear on Alexei's forehead, and it drew a line down the side of his face. Alexei stood in an attempt to defend himself from the approaching gunman, but the Russian was on him like a wolf, locking his arms back while the gunman punched him in the stomach three times. Alexei couldn't breathe, and when the Russian let him go, he fell to the floor trying to get air back into his lungs. When he looked up, his body allowing the first breath in, the gunman kicked him in the face hard, and he fell on his back, his head hitting the hardwood with a hollow thud. The ceiling shifted this way and that, and he felt nauseous. Alexei closed his eyes and kept them that way, a spinning blackness that he could somehow see. And when he opened them again, he was bound with plastic ties to a cold metal chair.

"Where is Donya?" asked the Russian, now holding a thin metal icepick.

There were three people behind the Russian—the gunman, who was staring at Alexei, and two others at the other end of the room talking, but he couldn't make out what they were saying, and their backs were to him.

"One," the Russian began. "Two. Three," he said in a deeper voice. "Anthony, hold down his right hand."

"I don't—"

"And put this in his mouth."

Alexei closed his mouth tight as the gunman approached with a dirty rag.

"Open up," he said.

This wasn't happening. This wasn't happening. Where was she? She couldn't have set this up. Unless it was a test. How else would they know about this place?

"Open your fucking mouth," he said again, pushing the rag against Alexei's lips, the odor of mildew creeping up his nose.

"Fuck him. Just hold his hand down."

This was happening. When the Russian seized Alexei's right index finger with his icy hands, Alexei pissed himself. And when the Russian gently placed the needle-point tip of the icepick under Alexei's fingernail, Alexei opened his mouth to take in a deep, hopeful breath because the metal made his fingertip tingle slightly, and it felt good. Until the Russian slowly pushed forward, and the tip scraped the underside of his nail and separated it slowly from the nail bed, fluidy sounds as from a butcher-shop meat grinder loud in his ears, louder than his screams. He couldn't bear to look, so his eyes remained fixed on the window. And then a sickening crack as the Russian yanked up on the icepick.

Alexei stopped screaming, replacing it with clenched teeth and a deep, incessant growl. The pain, thank God the sharp pain stayed isolated to his hand.

"That's a nasty wound, Lenka," said the Russian.

And then Alexei was just moaning until he heard a grinding sound, then the constant wind-through-the-tunnel, and he knew what would happened next. The Russian lifted the butane torch, beautiful blue flame, then cauterized Alexei's wound. Gripping the chair arms and jerking violently, his cries sounded feminine, high and sharp, as arrows of pain ripped through his muscles and bone to his head, where his brain seemed to swell and push against his skull. And he kept shrieking even as the torch flame disappeared and the gunman stepped away, the only silence coming when he took in breath.

In the time it took him to calm, about a minute, his vision was blurry with tears, but he could still see the other two men standing at the far end of the room. He thought they were looking at him now. If he could wipe his eyes, he'd know.

The Russian's voice stole his attention: "Now, Lenka, where is Donya?"

He really didn't know, but there was no way for the Russian to believe that. He was old style. KGB style. Donya style, and she wouldn't have believed him either. Would it do any good to tell him that she would eventually show up, later that evening? Would that be a betrayal to Donya? Could he trust that she'd know that there were problems and that she should proceed with caution?

Alexei's silence was both golden and bloody.

"Anthony, hold his right hand in place."

28 January 2011. 10:11am. FBI – Boston Field Office

In the briefing room were both teams, investigative and SWAT. DeLaurent was there, too.

"First, most of you know him already, but this is Detective Malcolm Youngblood with Boston PD. He's part of our task force in this investigation."

Anna hooked in her laptop and turned on the projector. The first picture to fill the Smart Board was a cabin surrounded by tall trees. "We have eyes on the cabin at these coordinates from the senior surveillance team since yesterday afternoon," said Anna to the group. "Agent Morgan has just informed me that the Lexus taken from the shooting yesterday was found in Needham, which is in the direction of this cabin. We haven't moved in yet because we haven't gotten a positive ID on this woman," she said, bringing up a driver's license photo of Katherine Rebeck, blonde hair in a ponytail, no smile.

"Mrs. Rebeck's husband was killed in Afghanistan last year. She's suspected of murder of Hassan Al-Amri, the passenger of this Lexus which was involved with the shooting yesterday. She's also wanted for questioning in the multiple murder case and arson at the Volkov home, arson of her own home, two victims which could be our own, Agents Herrera and Young, and a woman, who we suspect to be Jenny Frautschi, a scientist at MIT. As of now, we don't know what was in her home because the structure collapsed and is still being investigated. This is all stemming from an ongoing espionage investigation, so if she is involved, it may well have stemmed from her husband's death." Anna put up an aerial photo of the cabin. "The structure has two entry points—the front door and the back door. SWAT Team 1 enters the front while Team 2 covers the back on my order. Boston PD will have roadblocks covering a one-mile radius. SST has counted three males inside, but no positive identification. Any unknowns leave, we follow them. Anyone approaches, we let them through, even if it's Rebeck. Take her into custody if she tries to leave. Al-Amri and his accomplice were trying to kill Rebeck, and this cabin looks to be the next place on their list of places she'd be. That's what we're working with. We need to gather as much intel as possible before moving in, find out who these people are."

"And the Volkovs?" asked Agent Dobbs.

"Whereabouts still unknown." She let out a deep breath, then said, "Kate Rebeck was last seen with her fifteen-year-old daughter Lillian Rebeck, so you know the drill with kids."

Anna looked at the room of men, save Danielle, their angry faces and determined gazes both welcomed and worrisome. Everything had to be perfect this time. Director Mueller would be in the office soon with DeLaurent discussing Meeks' murder and possibly more if the lab positively identified Herrera and Young. When the thought passed, she found DeLaurent's eyes on her, hand on his chin and index finger across his lips. He nodded once, slowly, showing that he approved, then he stepped out of the room quietly. He'd be keeping track of the operation from his office.

"One last thing, everyone. We'll be doing this without an eye in the sky due to the President's speech today at Harvard." She closed her laptop, then said, "Let's go."

"Anna, need you a minute," said DeLaurent as she and Danielle passed his office.

"Meet you downstairs," she said to Danielle, then entered the office.

"Records are confirmed."

She just nodded, unflinchingly, then turned and joined her team. Federal agents killed in the line of duty, that was rare. But so were cases like this, and she was in charge of bringing it down. That's what she had to do.

In the SUV, the surveillance team reported a fourth person inside the cabin. And just before they had reached the halfway point, they reported one man leaving the house as one approached. Both Caucasian. Photos were taken and sent to their Blackberries.

"License plate is registered to Alexei Volkov," another voice said in her earpiece.

Anna checked the pictures.

"Okay, team, I've confirmed that the man approaching *is* Alexei Volkov. Now we have five. We need—"

"Oh, Jesus, he's got a gun on him."

"Hold your position and keep the video rolling," said Anna.

What was Alexei doing there? She was right to have kept eyes on him, Russian or not. Where the hell had he been? What was his role in all this?

"Door's opening. Male Caucas—he hit him."

"Who?"

"The man who opened the door struck Volkov…he's speaking

Russian…okay, Volkov's up and they're forcing him inside."

Was he being set up? What was this man's role? She couldn't rule out that Alexei had murdered everyone and burned his own house down, but it didn't make sense because he wasn't there. He'd run off. That gap in surveillance was proving to be the black hole that was swallowing this case.

Lilly followed Svetlana through the snow, walking in her footsteps, to a mound, where Svetlana took the knife she had bought on their way here and knelt. She had also bought them thin white jackets and white snow hats, both of which they were wearing inside out right now. Lilly couldn't see what she was cutting, but after a few snaps, she put the knife away and lifted a cellar-like door, the creak like something from a horror movie. And when it was up, the snow fell away, but the forest floor atop the door didn't move.

"I thought we were going to the cabin," said Lilly.

"Do you remember the tunnel you asked me about?"

Before Svetlana finished her question, Lilly did remember. The secret tunnel—sneak in, sneak out.

"You first. Let's go."

Svetlana helped her down the short ladder, and Lilly saw that the thick branches and pallets and a few stones were actually bolted to the doors, their rusty undersides tight with nuts and washers. Vines had naturally grown over the top, and she now realized what Svetlana had to cut away so that the doors would open. The tunnel was low and damp, the only source of light now shut out after closing the entrance doors. Dirt on all sides except the floor, which was rotting and slippery wood.

Svetlana snapped a glow stick, and the neon-green light helped them keep their footing as they were hunched over and working their way into the blackness.

After ten minutes, Lilly said, "I thought you said that this tunnel wasn't very long."

"It's not," said Svetlana. "You're just cold."

"It's just a little hard to breathe down here."

Svetlana moved quickly, never slipping on the slimy wood, and Lilly had a hard time keeping up, even though she didn't have to carry anything. Svetlana had her gun in her pocket, a knife she'd bought at the hardware store in Needham strapped to her ankle, and the small bag of food and drinks in the hand without the glow stick.

After five more minutes, Svetlana stopped.

"Take this," she said, handing Lilly the glow stick and bag of provisions. "Wait right here."

"But I'm not—"

"I know. You're not going to let us separate," she said. "But you are not to come out of the tunnel until I've checked over the place, that's our agreement."

"But—"

"Lilly," she said, putting her hands on Lilly's cheeks, "I don't know if you can understand everything that's happened lately, but it's not normal. It's not something you should want."

"It made you who you are."

"You don't want you to be like me, hiding all the time because you're being hunted."

A man's scream startled Lilly and she jumped slightly, hitting her head on the clay ceiling.

"What's that?"

"Stay right here. I will be back to get you."

Another scream.

"I don't want you to go. Let's just go back together and leave Boston. Please."

"I have obligations," she said, taking her hands away now. "Do not move from here."

Lilly nodded.

Svetlana turned around, and her image was sucked away by blackness with each step until a light shone down suddenly at the end of the tunnel, and Svetlana disappeared up a short wooden ladder. The light disappeared a moment later as another scream filled the tunnel.

Chapter 23

28 January 2011. 11:47am. Outside the Cabin, North.

"Everyone is in position," said Danielle.

"SSG," said Anna, "make sure the team has eyes for anyone approaching. We have to let this play out and not spook anyone. It might take a while, if Rebeck even decides to show up at all, so stay alert."

"Yes, ma'am," replied the team leader.

"Just waiting on your word now," said Danielle.

Anna nodded, and when she did, she could feel the fatigue in her neck as if her forehead weighed a ton. She hadn't left work or slept in more than thirty hours, but her adrenaline kept her alert. But that alertness was telling her that there was something missing. She had been so careful to map out the terrain, strategically place each member of the teams, and set up the full operation. What could be wrong? Where was the flaw? She had to check the south side; her teams had approached from the north, and they did so single file, the last team member raking over the tracks in an attempt to make the snow appear undisturbed. And the surveillance team had approached from both the east and west side, but their tracks had long since been filled.

It hit her hard. That last case she'd been working on with Jonathan Meeks, the one that had ended his career and led to the end of his life. Aziz. In Providence, it had been a similar situation. Ali Nur Ed-in and Muhammah Shiraz had been sitting ducks while Aziz took an alternative route and escaped. That wouldn't happen again. Not this time.

"Danielle, you stay here. I'm going to check a few things out around the perimeter. Make sure no one makes any moves without my order, and keep me updated on the situation inside." She then told the teams what she was doing.

"You should let me come with you," said Malcolm.

"I need you here."

He nodded.

When Anna was about twenty yards from Danielle, snow still falling steadily, a scream erupted from the cabin, prompting her to look back at Danielle, who was now staring at her. She pointed to her own eyes with index and middle finger, then to the cabin, signaling for Danielle to keep her eyes on the targets. And then she walked until she reached the south side. Moving away from the cabin, it took fifteen minutes and going outside of SSG's perimeter, until she located footprints, one set of them, nearly covered by new snow.

Clouds of breath increasing in frequency and thickness in front of her, she drew her Glock and followed the depressions until they stopped at a snowy mound.

"There's a lot of screaming coming from inside the cabin, Anna," said Danielle. "SSG says it's Alexei Volkov."

"Hold your position right now," she whispered. "We don't know—"

"I know we don't know his status," Danielle interrupted. "But, regardless, do we really stand by while someone is tortured?"

"Hold your position," she ordered.

The Russian had mutilated Alexei's index finger, middle finger, and ring finger on his right hand. Soaked in his own urine, blood, and tears, Alexei Volkov tried to prepare himself for more torment. His only wish now was to pass out.

"Believe it or not, the pinky hurts the most," the Russian said. "So where is Donya?" he asked, lighting a cigarette now and blowing the smoke in Alexei's face.

It didn't stink like regular secondhand smoke, but it was piercing and bitter like fumes from a bleach canister. Alexei's hand didn't throb, but it was a constant pain, like being crushed in a vice but the nerves just firing and firing and firing. Where the hell was she?

He didn't realize it, but he spoke aloud, "Why do you want her?"

His words prompted one of the obscure men at the far end to approach him. When he got a few feet from his face and said, "It's none of your concern," Alexei now knew that it was Brother. Still Brother.

"I don't know why you want her so badly."

"Ivan does what I tell him to do," said Brother. "He's paid a fair price."

Ivan, the Russian, didn't respond, just held the bloody icepick in his hand and smoked his cigarette.

"Your sister, Donya, murdered my family." He leaned in close to him so that Alexei could smell his bad breath. "She put it on video and sent it to my home address. I watched her torture my wife, daughter, and two sons. She asked them each where I was located. They didn't know. So she took an icepick, and I'm sure you know what happened next, again and again. So if you think I have any sympathy for you, you're wrong, Lenka, Alexei, whatever the fuck your damned name is."

"Why did she want you? What made you so desired by the KGB that they'd do such a thing?"

Brother laughed at this. "Nothing. I was just a businessman who probably got too much money. But I broke no laws."

"Until now."

"Until my family was killed." He leaned in even closer now, his stench like a Frenchman. "By your sister." Now, mouth to Alexei's ear, he said, "She took everything from me. So I will take everything from her. Your pain, your agony does nothing but make me feel a little more complete."

"That was so long ago."

"Shut up. Your voice makes me have to piss." As he started walking away, he said to the Russian, "Continue."

"Where is Donya?" asked the Russian. A few silent seconds

later, he added, "Anthony…"

28 January 2011. 12:13pm. Outside the Cabin, South.
"Agent Stern, we have a voice match to the recording given to us by Detective Youngblood. Codename Brother is present, ninety-seven percent."

"Brother's in there?"

"Yes, ma'am."

"Continue to hold your position until I give the word. Is there any sign of Katherine Rebeck?"

"No, ma'am."

She started feeling torn. So Al-Amri wasn't Brother. Brother was still alive and in reach. The problem was evidence. She wanted more than what was happening to Alexei Volkov. Torture was one thing, but espionage was much more. It made the case national, and made countries' relations clearer, at least to the public. And most of all, it helped the FBI gain more prestige in the war on terror.

She kept her gun drawn and took cover behind a thick tree about fifteen yards away, behind the doors in the ground gathering snow and becoming invisible.

Lilly stood under the tunnel door where Svetlana had gone, the glow stick greening the walls where she and Svetlana had stood several minutes ago. The stink of mildew still filled her nostrils, and she wanted to sneeze, but she buried her nose in her coat sleeve to make the tingling go away.

Footsteps above snagged her attention.

"Hurry up, Brother. Don't want to miss this," came a voice in the same accent as Svetlana's, only male.

There were gaps between the wood slats, and she could see the shadow of the walker above. Climbing the short ladder and putting her ear to the underside of the door, Lilly heard the man urinating in the toilet.

From the door, which she remembered being by the sink, she could see the man clearly at a diagonal, and then she saw a hand cover the man's mouth and nose.

"Hello, Brother," she heard Svetlana whisper.

The urinating stopped. Lilly saw Svetlana's other hand gripping the large knife under the man's beltline.

There was strange noise coming from the man she had called Brother, a muffled moan. Eyes as large as apricots. Lilly kept her eyes there.

"Did you really think you would get to me?" Svetlana said.

"Wait," the man said, his voice broken. Svetlana removed her hand. "It's you. Fuck."

"Decades."

"I'm not Brother," he said. "I'm not." He turned his head, and Svetlana leaned slightly as if getting a good look at him.

"Where is he?"

"I don't know."

Svetlana covered his mouth again, yanking his head back. There was a faint sound like the first puncture into a tin can, then a splash. The man moaned loudly, then Svetlana lifted the knife and slit his throat, keeping her other hand over his mouth. His clothes caught most of the blood, then she lay his body on the hardwood.

Another scream from somewhere in the cabin.

When Svetlana had left the bathroom, Lilly pushed up and opened the tunnel door and made sure it rested on the floor quietly rather than letting it slam. Peeking her head up through the floor, she stared at the dead man lying bleeding in front of the toilet. Another bad man dead, and she didn't feel different this time. What did catch her gaze was metal reflecting the overhead lamplight, snug in the man's waist, and she crawled from the tunnel and took it. A revolver, six shots. The bullets looked big, but she didn't know anything more about it. Svetlana had a gun, so now she did, too. And she was satisfied with that, as she stepped back down the ladder and closed the tunnel door behind her, going back to the phosphorescent glow stick several feet into the dark and damp tunnel.

The Russian lowered the butane torch to Alexei's bleeding pinky and let it burn. And while Alexei screamed, he knew that it would happen six more times. That his nostrils would fill with the bitter stink of his own melting skin and boiling blood.

"The thumb is the largest nail," the Russian said, leaning back and turning the torch off.

Alexei's words, "Just kill me," were met with laughter.

"I'm not going to kill you, Lenka. But I am getting bored with your fingers." He threw his cigarette on the floor and let it burn. "Where is Donya?"

"I don't know where she is," he said, his voice a labored whisper.

"Yes you do. You've always known. And Brother tried the easy way when he should have just called me in from the start." The Russian turned around. "Where the fuck is Brother?" he asked the man at the end of the room.

"Taking a piss."

"This is the last time I am going to ask you, Lenka. If you do not tell me what I want to know, I will take this torch and set fire to your genitals. Then, I'm going to leave and drive to your in-laws' home to kill your in-laws, rape your daughter and wife, then bring back your family's heads. Now, where—"

The Russian's head exploded with a loud crack, and Alexei heard two more successive cracks. Alexei couldn't see for the blood in his eyes, but he heard footsteps approaching, the plastic snapping, and Donya's voice: "I'm sorry I wasn't here sooner, brother. Can you walk?"

"Yes," he said, rubbing his face with his left arm, and he felt her pulling him through the cabin.

The sound of water now.

"Here," she said, "get it out of your eyes. Quickly!"

The cold water felt good as he cupped it in his left hand splashed it on his face, then rubbed his eyes. The blood diluted and washed down his face, and he could see again. He could see Brother on the bathroom floor, bloody and dead.

The fingers on his right hand felt like they were being pressed against a sander, the incessant pain hadn't eased, and it had made him more nauseous, but he still refused to look at them. To see the carnage.

Donya yanked the tunnel door up and said, "Hurry down the ladder." Then, a bit louder, "Lilly, we're coming."

"Who is—"

"Go."

Alexei knelt down and let his feet start down the rungs, keeping his left hand firmly on the bathroom floor for support, but his foot slipped and sent him crashing to the bottom of the tunnel.

"I'm okay," he said, but he'd landed on his side, and it hurt, but nothing had broken. Getting to his feet and out of the way, he watched Donya begin down the ladder.

As she took the first step down, there was a crashing sound from somewhere inside the cabin, and she yanked the tunnel door closed and hopped down.

"We have to hurry. Go!"

"What happened?" said a young girl.

"Go, Lilly. Leave the food. Hurry."

And they did hurry, crouched down and slipping on boards, the man and Svetlana followed her, the girl with the green glow stick to the other end of the tunnel.

It made Lilly feel important to be leading them as Svetlana had led earlier. The darkness in front of her, she imagined, was just like performing, just like standing before the world in Svetlana's apartment, just like closing her eyes and being consumed by the music.

"I guess you were right. It's not that far," said Lilly. Funny how the trip there always seems longer than the trip back.

And Svetlana took the lead again, quickly taking her jacket off, turning it right side out, then putting it back on so that it was clean white. She did the same with her hat, then climbed the ladder, peeked out after lifting the door slightly, then pushed it open and climbed out. Alexei was on her heels, working his way up slowly.

Lilly wanted to wait so that Svetlana would not see the pistol she'd taken from the man in the bathroom, which was snug in the waist of her pants.

"Zipper's stuck, but I'm coming," she said. Throwing the glow stick down, Lilly mimicked Svetlana's clothing switch. As she held the pistol in her hand, ready to put it in her jacket pocket, she heard a stranger's voice.

Chapter 24

28 January 2011. 12:19pm. Outside the Cabin, South.

As Anna knelt down on one knee using the tree as cover, she heard a distant gunshot and immediately called through, "Danielle—"

Two more gunshots.

"It's from the cabin," Danielle said.

"SWAT, move in now," she commanded. "Team 2, hold your position until the house is clear." She ordered Danielle to back her up and gave her position. "You need to approach me from the south, gun at the ready. Dobbs, you're my eyes there."

"Yes, ma'am."

After two long minutes of waiting, staring at the mound, Dobbs reported that SWAT had cleared and secured the house and that there were four bodies, which meant one was missing.

Either the person whose footprints she had found was dangerous or Alexei Volkov was far more than he had seemed and that his being a victim was just a setup.

"Team 2, move in with caution. Look for a tunnel entrance."

Snow was dropping in large clumps as fast as rain. Anna's focus remained on the mound, blurred by the snow.

"I should be there in seven minutes," said Danielle.

"Copy."

Keeping her mind clear of distractions, Anna didn't feel the cold wind pick up. She didn't think about time, but it was two minutes after Danielle had given her ETA that the mound shifted slightly, and she rose and hid behind the tree on the back side of the doors.

The creak of rusted metal. Grunting. "Come on," came a female voice. Compacting snow.

Anna slowly peered around the bark, saw two figures walking in the opposite direction. She waited a few seconds, then came out from behind the tree and approached them. The tunnel door had been left open, and she glanced down—empty. A few more steps forward, another glance down—empty.

The two were walking fast, so Anna yelled, "FBI, let me see your hands."

They stopped, hands visible at their sides, and turned and stared at her.

"Kneel down, and put your hands behind your head."

As Anna halved the distance between them, they were obeying, but she kept in mind that one of them had to be armed and was very dangerous. The man was Alexei Volkov. The other was the woman, Katherine Rebeck, she had to be.

Alexei kept one hand down but visible. "I cannot lift this hand. See," he said.

Anna didn't challenge him, seeing the grotesque digits, Alexei's entire hand shaking like a creepy old man's. Danielle would be approaching from behind them soon and would cuff them.

"I've got Alexei Volkov and Katherine Rebeck. Need some backup," she said, keeping her gun trained on Katherine's head

"Almost there," said Danielle.

"Backup's on the way," came a male voice.

"Where's your daughter?" Anna asked Katherine, getting an icy stare from the woman now.

"My daughter?" she said, breaking eye contact with Anna, but only slightly, then she slowly turned her head left and then right, left and then right again.

That Slavic accent. Katherine Rebeck was not Russian! So was this the person responsible for Herrera and Young's deaths. Had that neighbor been wrong? Had this woman kidnapped Lillian Rebeck? Was the neighbor part of it all?

Compacting snow.

Lilly heard a woman shout out that she was with the FBI, but that didn't mean it was true. She wouldn't be fooled twice. The detective that had snuck up on her in Svetlana's apartment had killed Kate, and now someone else was going to try and kill Svetlana, maybe the man's other partner. She looked down at the chrome pistol and stared at her own reflection, gazing deep into her dark eyes. It was time for *her* to save Svetlana.

Lilly took a few steps toward the light where white bundles of snowflakes floated down like ballerinas, but there was no grace when they hit the wood and dirt floor, crumbling and decaying, their clear blood soaking into the earth. And then she was at the ladder and climbing skyward. When her eyes were above ground, she saw Svetlana and the injured man kneeling, and there was a woman pointing a gun at them. Quietly, stealthily, she took a few more rungs upward until she reached the top and planted her feet in growing snow.

"Where's your daughter?" the woman said.

"My daughter?" said Svetlana, looking at Lilly now and shaking her head slowly.

Lilly took a defiant step forward and, with both hands now, raised the gun and pointed it at the woman.

As the woman turned toward her, Lilly said, "Leave us alone or I'll kill you." And she meant it, pulse throbbing in her temple and hands shaky.

"No, Lilly," said Svetlana.

"Lillian," said the woman in an easy tone, lowering her own gun. "I'm not here to hurt you or them. I'm the police, one of the good guys."

It had started getting harder to breathe, as if the cold air she was taking in wasn't making it to her lungs. Why was her skin getting tingly and numb around her neck and cheeks and forehead? It scared her, chin quivering now.

"Just leave us alone," she forced out as she found herself crying, the knot tight in her numbing throat now. "We just want to be left alone so we can live our lives."

"If you put the gun down, Lillian, everything will be okay."

Lilly watched the woman look at her and then back at Svetlana. The tingling had worked its way to her knees, like mites eating away the tendons and cartilage, and it was hard to keep standing.

"Throw your gun down and run away," said Lilly. "You'll never see us again."

"I can't do that, sweetheart." She put her left hand out in front of her, showing Lilly that it was empty. "I'm not here to hurt you. I'm just here to help."

"You can't help us except by leaving us alone." The woman's figure blurred a moment until Lilly blinked hard to force the tears out.

"I know that you don't want to do this. So put down the gun and everything will be okay." The woman took one step toward Lilly.

"You're not going to leave us alone are you?" Lilly asked in broken speech, a violent rush of adrenaline now seizing her chest. She was getting dizzy and wanted to collapse, the gun getting heavier and more difficult to keep steady.

"Do as she says, Lilly," said Svetlana.

She was not going to listen. The tears, the weakness in her joints, jolts of adrenaline, Lilly knew they were all warning signs that life was about to change for the worse if she gave in, if she didn't stand up for what she wanted and for the only one who really cared about her. Whether the woman was really an FBI agent or an enemy posing as one, the outcome would be the same—she would be separated from Svetlana forever and be completely alone in this cold, cold world.

Lilly fired the gun, and it jumped back in her hand with such violence that she lost her grip and screamed as it fell and disappeared into the snow.

A second gunshot, then several more in succession while Lilly's eyes were on the hole in the snow where the gun had fallen. And she was screaming, on her knees now, hands over her ears screaming as gusts of wind sent snow smacking against her face like tiny pebbles of fire. She had to run now. She had to get to her feet and run. But trying to stand, she slipped on some object in the snow and began falling backward. And when her body couldn't stay up, she felt it falling, expecting a cold clumpy sound as she fell into the snow, but she kept falling past ground level, down and down like the bundles of snow she had seen from the darkness in the tunnel.

As the wind picked up and the snowfall shifted from vertical to diagonal, the icy air enhanced the pain in Alexei's hand the way alcohol does when poured on a wound, and it made him wince. He had to cover it and get some relief or else he'd just scream, but he tried to hold out, tried not to move because the girl, Lilly, was pointing a revolver at the FBI agent. She was lucky to still be alive...all of them were.

Even under the circumstances of potentially going to prison or getting killed, of possibly losing his family, of the immediate pain in his hand, Alexei did not know why his sister had brought a teenage girl with her. Who was she? What was her story? And how in the hell had she gotten mixed up in this fucking mess? But his thoughts were interrupted by movement in the forest.

"Don—" he started to say, but then there was a gunshot, yanking his attention back to Lilly and the agent.

The agent had dropped to the ground, and Lilly, no gun in her hand now, was falling to her knees.

A gunshot from the person in the woods, toward Lilly. Before Alexei could react, he saw Donya with a gun in her hand, firing into the woods and then standing and running toward the agent that Lilly had shot.

When Alexei got to his feet, he realized that the agent had only dropped for cover and was now aiming her gun at Donya, who fired once, hitting the agent's gun, making it lurch out of her hand.

The agent stood now, weaponless, and stared at Donya, not even a flicker of fear in her face.

"You better shoot me because I won't stop hunting you. Ever."

"Two of your agents were killed and that man," she pointed to Alexei, "kidnapped and tortured by the man dead in the cabin bathroom. Brother. Your partner is in the woods, but shot in the vest. Leave us alone. We're innocent. I will not spare you in the future."

Donya then began backing away, and Alexei looked to Lilly, but she was gone. Disappeared.

The agent didn't move, only stared at Donya as she backed away quickly to the spot where Lilly had fallen to her knees.

"Lenka," she said. "She's down in the tunnel. Help her."

And he did. She was unconscious from the fall, but he climbed down, without falling this time, Donya keeping her gun trained on the agent, and woke her. And helped her. And a minute later, they were back up in the snow, trudging along to somewhere. When the agent was out of sight, Donya, practically carrying the girl, took the lead and they made it to a van that was perhaps a half mile from the tunnel entrance. It was sitting on what he presumed to be a dirt road, one side level and the other leading to a drop off of several feet to more thick trees and snow. The road itself was covered with snow.

Alexei nearly passed out from exhaustion as he got in the passenger seat. He heaved in deep breath after deep breath, the frigid air burning his throat and lungs. The girl was in back somewhere and Donya in the driver's seat. The van started on the first try, and Donya threw it into Drive and eased on the gas enough to make the vehicle move without getting stuck in the snow.

28 January 2011. 12:31pm. Outside the Cabin, South

When the suspects fled into the woods, Anna retrieved her

weapon, looked back to the place where Danielle had been shot. Her partner was now standing next to a tree hunched over, but she was okay. Thank God she was okay.

"Call in more backup. They're going east," she said, checking her Glock to make sure the woman's bullet hadn't rendered it useless. It had hit the top right of the gun, just above the barrel, so she holstered it and retrieved her backup Glock 27.

Anna ran, following the footprints through thickening snowfall and stronger wind. If it kept up like this, there would be a whiteout. And if backup didn't hurry, the footprints would be gone and they would be slow-going to help her. Minutes of running and she saw something moving about ten yards ahead, the edge of her line of sight before everything was just white. It was a person. Anna didn't slow her pace, and a blue van came into view, the kind plumbers and technicians use—no windows past the front doors. It was Alexei Volkov, and he was getting in the passenger seat.

She shifted, running diagonal to the van, trying to get in front of it as the engine fired and the tires began rolling forward slowly, and then faster. Anna wasn't going to be able to head it off, so she dropped to one knee and fired. She unloaded her Glock 27 at the escaping vehicle, the last bullet hitting the back tire, but the vehicle didn't slow, rather sped up and disappeared quickly behind the white veil.

"Suspects heading south in a blue van. They're on a back road about a mile south of the cabin. Road should intersect 1672 outside the perimeter, so units need to get there asap. I'm following on foot."

It was all she could do right now—call it in and hope for the best. But Anna followed the tire tracks toward 1672 with thoughts beginning to flood her mind. What was that young girl thinking back there? Was Katherine Rebeck Slavic and her file just didn't show it? No. But there had to be some kind of strong connection between them for the girl, Lillian, to point that gun at her. And

Alexei. He *had* been tortured. They *had* saved him. Could it be that this woman and Alexei were on her side? Defending themselves from people like Brother? She knew people were capable of anything when backed into a corner.

Five minutes of walking and she heard a gunshot. Thirty seconds later, an explosion, both from somewhere ahead in that colorless veil.

Chapter 25

Alexei checked his body for gunshot wounds. There were none.

"Are you okay?" he asked Donya.

"Fine. Check on Lilly."

He glanced back at the girl. She was lying flat on the van floor as if sleeping peacefully. There was no sign of blood, but he got up and went back to her. He noticed two red gasoline canisters in the back, an instrument case, and something beige covered in a sheet of plastic. The broken laptop was there, too.

Looking Lilly over, he then said, "I think she had a concussion from that fall, but she's breathing normally. No blood."

"Good. There's a body wrapped in the sheet in the back. Bring it up here."

After what he'd been through over the past hour, this shouldn't have made him wince and grow more anxious, but it did.

"Who is it?"

"The girl's mother," she said.

"Donya."

"I didn't kill her."

"But the girl," he said, thinking about his own daughter and how a situation like this would completely fuck up her mind. And how much more knowing that her dead mother was rolled up in the back would multiply that.

"She doesn't know. I kept it from her."

"But—"

"The police think I'm her, so come on. We don't have much time."

Alexei knew the plan now. It was the same at his house after Donya had killed Jenny and the others. So he dragged the corpse to the front with one hand, and that was all he could do.

Donya stopped the van and said, "Get Lilly, that violin, and the laptop out."

And he did. And several feet from the van, he knelt next to Lilly, who was lying in the snow, and watched his sister take the plastic and sheet off the body, put it in the driver's seat, and then pour gasoline inside the van. She made a gasoline trail, the liquid creating a canyon in the snow, then she threw the canister in the van.

"What are we going to do, Donya? The police know who we are. Emily knows."

She lit a match and dropped it, and the gasoline ignited, creating an instant fireball when it reached the van.

Turning around, she knelt next to them and said, "Survive, Lenka. For as long as we—"

Blood sprayed Alexei and Lilly as Donya lurched forward after letting out a pained sound that lasted only a second. Her shoulder had turned crimson. She tried to stand, but another bullet hit her leg and she fell into the snow.

Alexei didn't move as he saw the man emerge from beyond the flames, a tall black man dressed in white. The gun he was aiming at them had a silencer on it.

Donya rolled onto her back.

"Reach for that gun and I'll fucking kill you," he said, just a few feet from them now. He reached in his pocket and pulled out handcuffs. Throwing them at Donya, "Put them on. Tight."

She did.

The man did the same thing to Alexei before checking their pockets, taking Donya's pistol, and throwing it in the woods.

"Help your sister up. It's time for you to see the real Brother."

He stayed behind them, gun at Alexei's back, as they trudged toward 1672 and a Boston PD cruiser arrived. The uniformed officer got out and approached them.

"Detective Youngblood," came the booming voice behind them, making the uniformed officer stop. "With the FBI task force, taking these two into custody."

"Orders are to keep them here, sir."

The pressure of the gun left Alexei's back, then a loud clinking sound, and the officer dropped to the ground as if his bones had suddenly disappeared.

"I didn't say stop," the man said, the gun to Alexei's back again.

Donya looked back, but not at the man. She must have been checking on the young girl, Lilly. The mysterious young girl whose mother was dead. Who Donya obviously felt deeply for. So much time the two of them had been apart. What had happened between them? Why were they together? How did Donya bring herself to care about anyone outside of family so much that she'd risk her life to protect them.

The man, this Detective Youngblood, slapped Donya's face. She would have fallen had Alexei not been holding her up and helping her walk.

Alexei could see the unmarked cruiser now, parked several feet behind the dead officer's car. Alexei knew more police were on the way. He had to stall.

When they reached the front bumper, Alexei stopped, keeping his eyes forward and holding Donya up, and said, "You forgot the laptop with Suh's information. It's back there by the girl."

"Your boss already gave us that information, dumb ass. Your only purpose was to get her. Brother's going to enjoy finishing you pieces of shit off."

That's why Delk had been there. Jenny must have been working with him.

The sound of metal, keys, and the trunk opened.

"Get in."

Alexei didn't move, and a second later he felt the silencer against the back of his head.

"Get in."

Three steps, then an explosive crack. Alexei dropped to the snow, Donya falling on top of him. When he looked back, he saw part of the detective's body quivering above the snowline. The girl a few feet away, gun still aimed.

"Lilly," said Donya. "Lilly."

Alexei stood and started toward the girl slowly, but before he could reach her, the van exploded, flinging her forward into the snow and slamming him back against the car.

In the van, Lilly could hear the man and Svetlana speaking. She then felt herself being pulled out of the van and placed in the snow, soft like she thought a cloud might be. Such weight on her eyelids, and the flakes falling on her face—she listened to them speak and thought of Grandfather Frost and Snow Maiden. What had Svetlana called them? Ded Moroz. But the other word, she didn't remember, just that it began with S, like Svetlana began with S. They were certainly up there in the clouds, sending blocks of ice through a grater and letting them fall down and chill her already cold cheeks, then melt and slide down her face and into her hair like tears. But then warmth spattered her face, pulling her from those clouds and magic. A mean voice.

When she opened her eyes, all three had their backs to her. Police car approached. A murder. The man in white was a murderer. To her hands and knees, she crawled, then stood. Then loomed over the corpse of the uniformed officer and reached down and took his pistol.

She didn't hesitate this time. Aimed and pulled the trigger. And stood there. Svetlana would be proud. She had saved her this time, really saved her. Lilly would be like Svetlana now. Had matured and become the woman she looked up to.

Like an invisible ocean wave, a boiling force threw her down, but she was back up in just a few seconds. Another gun lost in the shin-deep snow. Lilly was by Svetlana's side, noticing all the blood on Svetlana immediately.

Her throat clenched, and she said, "No," through quivering lips and real tears this time, salty and warm. "Svetlana."

A rare smile on the woman's face now. "I'll be okay, Lilly."

Svetlana raised her arm, and Lilly buried her face in her shoulder.

"You saved us," she said. "Thank you, Lilly."

As Lilly leaned back, still kneeling, the man had approached.

"This is my brother, Lenka," she said, coughing.

"Your brother?"

Svetlana nodded and leaned up slowly, wincing. "Lilly, the police think I am your mother. Her body is—"

"I know. I heard."

"You have to make them believe that it's true." She gazed at Alexei now. "Throw the laptop in the van, then they have nothing on you. You found out about your boss, then they kidnapped you. Tortured you. You two do not know each other." Svetlana stood now, blood still soaking into her white jacket as she turned back to Lilly. "Police burned your house down, so you thought the woman was another criminal."

"How do I know her mother?" asked Alexei.

"You don't. Let them figure it out. She was just there saving you." She put her hand on Lilly's cheek. "I know that I said we would not be separated again, but I will find you, Lilly. This has to blow over, and then I will find you. I promise."

"No. I'm going with you."

"We'll never be free that way, Lilly. Don't you want to be free of it all? And not have to worry anymore? Don't you want to get into Juilliard?"

"I saved you. I should go with you. You can teach me more than Juilliard."

Lilly couldn't see Svetlana's face anymore. She couldn't even hear anything either of them said. Her crying was coming from somewhere deep inside her from a painful place, and it attacked her throat. It made her eyes practically close, and her lips spread across her delicate face so tightly they split just a little in more than one place. And she knew her face was a pitiful mixture of those salty tears and snot and sweat all tinted red by her own blood. But she didn't protest anymore. She just let her go, hoping that the promise would be kept. Feeling the hug, the kiss on her forehead, and hearing the whisper "I love you, Lilly" in her ear.

She heard the cuffs come off, a car drive away, and what felt like a minute later, Alexei hold her until the police arrived. He had gotten her violin case and put it next to her. The police pulled him violently and threw him to the ground, a knee in the back of his neck pushing his face into the deep snow. They didn't care about the pain they were causing him with that horrible hand as he was manacled again. But they left Lilly standing there for just a moment, guns pointed at her. And she saw the woman, the one she'd fired the gun at. The FBI agent. She approached Lilly and cuffed her. And she sat next to her in the back of the car. Silent.

Would Svetlana really come back for her? Would they drive back to her hiding place and get her backpack she'd left hidden with her journals? Would she audition for Juilliard and get in, and then move to New York where she'd become a violinist and live a happy life with a mother that loved her and cared for her? A mother that would help her practice and push her to be better and show up at all of her performances? The one who she'd thank if she ever won an award, saying "I wouldn't be here without her, my dear mother." She hoped so.

Gazing out the window at the trees and snow, at the city when it came into view, she imagined playing for the whole world. For Svetlana.

Chapter 26

29 January 2011. 4:55pm. FBI Boston Field Office
Anna sat in the leather chair in front of SAC DeLaurent's desk as he placed a manila folder down slowly.

"How long has it been since you've slept?"

"Couple days," Anna said.

"Sounds like you need a couple days off," came a voice from behind her.

It was Director Mueller. He walked in with a confident stride and perfect hair, leaned on DeLaurent's table so he could face her. And when he was balanced, he crossed his arms like a parent might do when about to hand out punishment.

Anna didn't know if it was a genuine concern for her well-being or if it was an order. And, quite frankly, she didn't care. She had done the best she could. And the case was on the brink of being closed.

"You haven't been SSA status very long," the director said. "But tell me how you feel your performance has been so far."

This was sounding like she was about to get a demotion and transfer. But she had done her job. She had killed the man that had infiltrated the FBI—Klein, her lover. The bullet from Detective Youngblood's gun matched the bullet in the murdered officer's head. All those involved with this case had either been killed or arrested. Alexei released to his wife. The girl with child protective services. There were no loose ends, except, "Two agents were killed and one injured under my watch." She then stood and met eyes with the director. "You can demote me, transfer me, or dismiss me, but you'll not find another as devoted to this job as you have standing right here."

"I'm not here to demote you, Agent Stern. I'm here to tell you 'job well done'." The director then put out his right hand, and she shook it.

"Thank you."

"Not perfect, but this case, and a very big case at that, is on its way to being closed. Forensic reports will hopefully finish it up." He let go of her hand and turned to DeLaurent. "I'm going back to Washington. I want to know the results the moment they get in."

"Yes, sir," DeLaurent replied, then watched the director leave his office. "This case has stirred up a bee's nest. There's an internal investigation in Boston PD because of Youngblood, and a shitstorm at MIT after David Delk was arrested."

Anna didn't have a response to this. She wanted to get the results from forensics showing that the body at the Volkovs' burned home was indeed Jenny Frautschi and that the woman in the van was Katherine Rebeck. And the next day, when they were confirmed and she had finally gotten some sleep, Anna started a fire in the fireplace at dusk, then turned off all the lights.

From the closet, she took out her mother's journal, then sat on the floor in front of the fire. Staring into the flames, her index finger rubbing the tight leather knot under the name Annabelle that kept bound the secrets of her mother. Would Dad have been proud of her? Would he have said 'job well done' too? Anna knew that it was a case that could never really be closed. There were plenty of others above the real Brother, plenty on his same level, and plenty of underlings all branched out across Boston, across the state and country. At least she had made a dent. Her father had told her that the job was about winning small battles before they could turn into big ones. That if you win a hundred and lose two or three, that was okay. That's a helluva winning percentage.

Anna broke her gaze from the hypnotic flames eating away the logs a few feet in front of her, and, slowly, set the journal on top of those logs. A few moments, and the leather strap had snapped and the cover bent back revealing the first page for just a second before it, too, rose, curled, and turned black, giving

Anna a glimmer of her mother's handwriting, but not long enough to read the words. Only when the journal was ash and smoke did she stand and go to the window to gaze at her city standing tall above the harbor. She was going to be part of it tonight. She was going to go out and celebrate with Danielle Morgan, Louis Dobbs, and Brian Hobson. They would each take a shot of sweet Four Roses bourbon in memory of Patrick Herrera. They would each take a shot of smoky Talisker scotch for Finnegan Young. And in the morning, the four of them would enter the Boston field office and begin working on the next case stacked on the pile.